# SHADOW WARS

# SHADOW WARS

### A NOVEL BY
# CLYDE
# FARNSWORTH

*11/10/04*

*For my dear friend Cal —
All the Althen! Happy
reading —*
*Clyde Far*

**DIF**

DONALD I. FINE BOOKS

Donald I. Fine Books
Published by the Penguin Group
Penguin Putnam Inc., 375 Hudson Street,
New York, New York 10014, U.S.A.
Penguin Books Ltd, 27 Wrights Lane,
London W8 5TZ, England
Penguin Books Australia Ltd, Ringwood,
Victoria, Australia
Penguin Books Canada Ltd, 10 Alcorn Avenue,
Toronto, Ontario, Canada M4V 3B2
Penguin Books (N.Z.) Ltd, 182–190 Wairau Road,
Auckland 10, New Zealand

Penguin Books Ltd, Registered Offices:
Harmondsworth, Middlesex, England

First published by Donald I. Fine Books,
an imprint of Penguin Putnam Inc.

First Printing, February, 1998
10 9 8 7 6 5 4 3 2 1

Library of Congress Cataloging-in-Publication Data

Farnsworth, Clyde H.
Shadow wars / Clyde Farnsworth.
p.      cm.
ISBN 1-55611-518-0
I.   Title.
PS3556.A724S53   1998
813′.54—dc21              97-27698
CIP

Printed in the United States of America
Set in New Caledonia

*To my sister,*
*Suzanne Farnsworth Czech*
*And in memory*
*Of our brother, Franklin Guy Farnsworth*
*And our mother, Marthe Herailh Farnsworth*

# ACKNOWLEDGMENTS

THIS WORK OF the imagination required long hours of struggling with doubts in a black hole. The idea came while working on a story for the *New York Times*, but would probably have never been more than a gleam in the eye without encouragement, and more, from my wife, Elisavietta Ritchie. Half Russian and a Russian speaker, she became the sounding board for the Russian characters. She also edited successive drafts. As a poet, she has never seen a line she doesn't yearn to tighten.

I am indebted to others as well: Miron Pukshansky Lior for comments on the Israeli sections; John Hore for advice on the esoterica of short sales and derivatives; Dean Marquis for brainstorming titles; my son Andrew for some of the Swiss background; my son Alexander for reading and correcting an early draft; my agent Tom Wallace, who was a steady beacon of light in the darker moments, and my editors Don Fine and Tom Burke, who put it all together.

I also want to thank the Virginia Center for the Creative Arts, which gave me a working environment a lot nicer than a black hole.

Between the idea
And the reality
Between the motion
And the act
Falls the Shadow

    —T. S. ELIOT

Money is like muck, not good
unless it be well spread.

    —SIR FRANCIS BACON

They wonder much to hear that gold,
which in itself is so useless, should
everywhere be so esteemed, that even men
for whom it was made, and by whom it has
its value, should yet be thought of
having less value than it.

    —SIR THOMAS MORE

Stability might not be everything, but
without stability, everything is
nothing.

    —KARL SCHILLER

# 1

Satisfied with his position about five miles to the southeast of Ol'khon Island, the lone boatman drew in his oars and watched the whorls and eddies of his most recent strokes merge into the shimmering surface of the inland sea. After rowing for nearly eight hours, he let the boat drift, licking sweat from his lips, feeling the breeze off the taiga brush his face.

Dmitri Leonidovich Sherbatov hunched against the gunwales, a frayed straw hat shielding his eyes from the fiery central Asian sun. From inside a tin pail by his feet, he tore off chunks of *cherniy khleb i vyderzhanniy syr,* black bread and cheese dry in his mouth. Staring in a southwesterly direction toward Irkutsk, he finished the apple juice from a battered thermos.

Dmitri was a fair-skinned European Russian of medium build, in his early fifties, with a thicket of black hair that protruded around the straw of his hat like the profuse July weeds in the tiny backyard gardens of Goryachinsk. The wildness of his hair contrasted with the orderly, almost geometrical lines of his face. His forehead was a massive rectangle. The lower part of his face, from high, wide cheekbones to protruding jaw, was an isosceles triangle, bisected by a rectilinear, sunburned nose.

Yet every few minutes the facial lines collapsed into a limp, rubbery mass. Not even the long hours of hard rowing brought release from the contractions. His right eye shut, and the left side of his jaw opened wide, as if he were playing monster games. Then in seconds the facial geometry was restored. His eyes bore the affliction with serenity. They were the

1

eyes of saints in the icons, suggesting accumulated wisdom, as if the spasms somehow unlocked the world's deeper secrets.

As his face fell into and out of alignment, he let his blistered hands play in the cool, green-blue water. Although it was an old, wooden working boat, these were not the thick, callused hands of a waterman. Neither did they betray work in a factory, kolkhoz, or penal camp. There were no scabs, splayed fingers, or missing parts. The hands were slender, the fingers long and tapered, the nails attentively cut.

He pretended his hands were detached, and let them float freely like pieces of driftwood. The water soothed. He tried to loosen up. He had an urge to immerse his head in the water, but feared that would capsize the boat. Under the weight of rocks in the stern, it was already low in the water, creaking and yawing against the smooth swells. He cupped his hands and splashed water on his face and neck.

From a tin can, among feathery and furry contrivances, he pulled out what looked like a surrealistic butterfly with wispy antennae, fluttering wings, and a succulent midriff, from which extended an innocently rounded but finely sharpened hook. Attaching it to the line beside him, he cast, and expertly playing the rod, he watched his lepidopteran flit on the surface in lifelike motions. He thought he saw several meters below the swift movements of a pair of salmonlike *kharius* with their elevated dorsal fins like upside-down rudders.

The prospects of an early catch would normally have excited such an avid angler. The *kharius* was a plucky fighter, always a challenge to his lures, painstakingly made during breaks at the linear collider, and fashioned from wild duck feathers, fox fur, hair of squirrel and wild pig, bartered from the Buryats. If fishing is a sport, it is also a game, and Dmitri usually excelled at games. He was far and away the best chess player at both Mount Z between Goryachinsk and Ust' Zaza and the Limnological Institute at Listvyanka, the two hubs of scientific activity around Baikal. Yet he much preferred his contests with the fish. He whipped even the Class A chess players. It took more cunning to outsmart the *kharius,* or the equally spirited and tasty *omul,* which he ate in the local style—s *dushkom* or slightly rotten.

But despite his passion for fishing, today Dmitri was less interested in what might be in the water than the sky. Slowly reeling his line in, he scanned the distant hills and looked once again at his Japanese Navigator watch with quartz movement, bought six years ago when he visited the

50-MEV CERN accelerator near Geneva. It was already after the appointed hour of 4:00 P.M.

Dmitri looked around 360 degrees. Nothing in the air. A smudge on the water to the south, probably a tanker or freighter, on the regular run from Irkutsk on the Angara to the rail terminals of the Baikal Amur Mainline at the lake's northern tip.

From least to most important, he enumerated his worries: dryness of his mouth because the apple juice had run out; slivers of food between his teeth because he had no toothpick; gas in his stomach; heat of the late-afternoon sun; a need to urinate; fear that his new friends weren't coming. He dropped to his knees and pissed, more into the boat than outside it.

Although the *kharius* had vanished, a *nerpa* was cavorting a few meters away, apparently curious about this curious boat and even more curious man. The silvery seal dove and then reemerged almost instantaneously on the other side of the boat, bounding into the air like a puppy.

Again he scanned the horizon. The sky was empty, the ship from Irkutsk a little larger. Surely they would come, but in case of emergency, just in case, he'd put in at Ol'khon and return to Goryachinsk tomorrow. Maybe he could arrange a tow with one of the motorized fishing boats. At least he would see Kyril again.

Though primed for his new undertaking, his main regret was abandoning his son. It would be many years before they would reunite. He had been tempted to bring Kyril along, but because of the risks to the nine-year-old and the shock to Tanya, he decided against it.

It had been more than two years since the divorce. Tanya lived with the boy in Irkutsk where she had a low-paying job as an agronomist in the East Siberian Section of the Academy of Sciences. He still sent support money. Kyril had just spent two weeks with Dmitri in Goryachinsk, and was now back in Irkutsk with his mother, preparing to go to pioneer camp near Ulan-Ude.

Until now, Dmitri Leonidovich's life had avoided risk. He had been a privileged Russian, one of the *nomenklatura* freed from the concerns of daily existence by his extraordinary talents as a physicist.

In the global competition with the United States, Moscow used Dmitri, as it did virtuoso musicians, astronauts, sports figures, and premiere ballerinas as testament to the superiority of Soviet ways. His papers on the elusive Z particle, on "fat" electrons and "up" and "down" quarks, published internationally, contributed to the Soviet Union's prestige in high-energy physics. The State Science and Technology Committee always made sure he was among the Concerned Scientists for Peace.

Dmitri had had no particular objections to this arrangement. In those days he cared little about politics. Like Richter, Oistrakh, Gagarin, Karpov, and stars of the Bolshoi, he had all his basic needs taken care of. At the institute, he was left to do what he wanted most: examine relationships in the structure of matter.

The collider had been built to his specifications in an old limestone cave deep inside Mount Z, between Goryachinsk and Ust' Zaza. The government committed resources to widen its research and development base and move more economic, scientific, and industrial activity to Siberia. GKNT, the State Science Committee, convinced the general secretary the collider not only fit in neatly with these objectives but would help sell socialism internationally.

For the tube in which particles were propelled at close to the speed of light, the Ministry of Construction, under the overall direction of the Science Committee, used men from the camps to gouge a three-kilometer tunnel out of the rock. Materials and supplies arrived on a spur line from the new BAM railroad that ran across the northern tip of Baikal to the Pacific. The line cut south, following Baikal's east coast, to a siding near the mountain, bringing power equipment, explosives, twenty-ton magnets, damping rings, special sensors, electron guns, East German computers, and even computers purloined from the West.

Mount Z was completed in the mid-1980s as one of the most advanced centers of its type in the world. Dmitri and his team hurled beams of the high-speed electrons and positrons in opposite directions and recorded the debris from the collisions. From the infinitesimal, he made deductions about the infinitely large. From reconstruction of the collisions, through computer-assisted photographs of the atomic debris, he contemplated the origin of all matter, the beginning and the end of time, the birth and death of the universe.

Were some particles truly elemental, or was matter infinitely complex, an endless regression of parts within parts, quarks within quarks, matryoshka dolls within matryoshka dolls? If the universe was infinitely large, must it not also be infinitely small? He did not have the answers, but was obsessed by the questions.

Not all he did was so theoretical. Over his half-dozen years as director, he had made certain findings about cold fusion, the harnessing of heavy ions for cancer treatment and the transmutation of cheaper elements into gold.

Dmitri discussed his breakthroughs in memos to Moscow, but encountered only apathy. The Science Committee was losing influence to Defense. Bureaucrats were reluctant to encourage new scientific projects. Like bottles in the sea, his memos tossed from one desk to another, and eventually disappeared, except for the copies he made himself, and last night alone in his office destroyed.

After the emergence of a new general secretary, the Defense Ministry became even more powerful. It tried to make his Center for Particle Physics, deep in its mountain and far from the probing eyes of satellites, a center for advanced weapons research. He complained in a memo that quoted Andrei Sakharov.

This time there was a reaction. He found his functions restricted and budget cut back. A KGB major arrived in the town. He feared displacement, internal exile, or worse.


A RUST-BOTTOMED DUCK wheeled over the boat, seemingly lost from its mates, and for a moment looked as if it might alight on his cargo of rocks. How far had it flown today? From Irkutsk, Ulan Bator, Krasnokamensk? Unlike humans below, it could go where it wanted. It needed no exit visas, didn't have to know the regulations.

The bird's droppings splashed on the rocks. Dmitri laughed. An appropriate parting gift. The duck knew that even under the reforms that were being vaguely talked about, conditions would never really improve. Absolutism, pettiness, envy, dumbheadedness were too well entrenched.

The duck flapped east across the water. Dmitri pursued it with his eyes toward the broad bands of stratus clouds that raced across the filmy blue sky. After reaching the shore, perhaps it would fly over Mount Z and the cedar and birch forests of the Barguzin Hills, approach the forced labor camps at Chara, Tynda, Chita, Komsomolsk, Zolatoya Gora. In more recent times, some of the camps had closed. Those still in use were supposed to be less for political prisoners than hardened criminals. The duck would have to exercise caution to stay out of a prisoner's pot.

The bird was good luck. Of that he was certain. Especially since the droppings had landed smack on his rocks. He watched the bird get smaller and smaller—"a speck amid a cloud of dust," he thought, recalling the line from Gogol.

He was less nervous now, relaxed by the breeze, the gentle rolling of the boat, the food in his belly.

The ship was closer. Damn those vessels anyway. Like so much else in the Soviet Union, they were a scandal. A menace. They smelled like vodka factories. They dumped their trash into the sea, polluted with their oil, neglected running lights, overran smaller vessels.

The ships polluted Baikal, but they were not even the worst offenders. The cellulose plant at Baikalsk was another outrage, pumping its wastes daily, hourly, into the lake. And the Selenge had become a virtual sewer, flowing into Baikal with the heavy metals and other industrial wastes of Ulan-Ude.

Yet Baikal was better than some of the lakes. He knew of one outside of Kemerovo so fouled that the local authorities used it as a grave for stray dogs. After a few days even the bones disintegrated. Around Chelyabinsk containers of nuclear waste were dumped into lakes and rivers and were easily visible when waters were low.

Soon enough he would be away from all this. He yawned, leaning against the starboard gunwale. The sun made him drowsy. His head drooped, eyes shut. Now he, like the duck, was high above the region, borne by the winds, diving and soaring, the air whistling in his ears. No more earthly constraints. Merely by pointing his head he could go up or down, right or left.

Far below, the winds were starting to roil the sea. Even from his height he could feel spray on his face. With him was Princess *Angara,* daughter of the jealous and vengeful god *Burkhan,* lord of Baikal. She wore nothing but her golden hair, like a long streamer in the wind, and had a wild, hunted look. In pursuit were *Burkhan* and his three sons— *Verhovik,* ruler of the North; *Gornyashka* of the West, and *Nizovik* of the South.

*Burkhan* shook his fist, heaping frightening oaths upon them, then lifted a mountain-size rock, and flung it. It grew larger and larger, darker and darker . . .

THE HUGE BLACK prow of the tanker towered over him a little to starboard. The noise in his ears was the roar of a thousand freight trains. The steel hull was sliding through the churning tumult, cold, hard, mindless, black.

He made out the name in rust above the clawed anchor: *Marshall*

*Timoshenko.* It was part of the fleet of vessels that worked Baikal in the summer, carrying oil products from Irkutsk to the BAM jetties at Nizhneangarsk 200 miles to the north.

The bow waves engulfed the skiff, which promptly sank.

In the water, spinning in the maelstrom, thrashing wildly, Dmitri was aware of only one thing, that he had to get away from this tornado of white water and death. The tanker's bulging midsection was already bearing down upon him. He fought to pull away, but could not break the force pulling him downward.

Mountains of water engulfed him. He could not see. His lungs were on fire. He was a strong swimmer but now needed more than strength to stay above the lethal foam. First one arm, then the other. He kicked his legs, twisted his body, struggled for air. Finally with his last reserves, his bent legs gave an immense springing movement away from the blackness, away from death's pounding crush.

Again he was under water, sucked into a whirlpool. The propeller beat louder and louder. He shot up, sucked a watery mouthful of air, prayed that he had enough in his lungs to swim away. One, two, three, an infinity. He felt the currents of water stirred by the blades tug him downward again. His chest was aflame. He could stand the pain no longer, and rocketed toward light and air. Should the propeller slash him, so be it.

He rose a little to port of the arcing fantail. He could hear the rhythmic drone of the murderous wash. The sound was receding. He had swallowed too much water, but he could still breathe, still see, hear, smell. Incredibly, he was alive. The black steel superstructure kept moving rapidly away. The sounds continued to subside, and the sea was returning to calm.

Still, his world was whirling. His body ached. His legs and arms felt about to drop off. He still couldn't get enough air into his lungs. He looked up at the departing ship. No sign of life. The captain and crew were probably dead drunk.

As its distance lengthened, the once dark agent of malevolence was toy-sized, cutting a golden swath in the water, its tapered stern bathed in the glow of the slanted sun. Yet while it had almost doomed him, it also symbolized the presence of other human beings. Now he was totally alone.

His world was water—where the continent had split thirty million years ago to form the greatest single deposit of fresh water on earth, a past ocean, a future ocean, a watery grave.

Dog-paddling, he tried to relax and reassess. At least he could now fill his lungs with air. Otherwise, his prospects were not good. Though he could tell from the sun's position where he was, he was too low in the water to see the Ol'khon coast. He must be about six kilometers off-shore. Even if he could find the coast, would he have strength to swim to it?

The water was chill beneath the surface, testament to the long Siberian winter that had been and would be again. Night was approaching. How long would he be visible from the air? They were expecting a boat, not a bobbing head. He had no way of attracting attention. To have survived the *Timoshenko* only to drown because he was too tired to swim. He shuddered at the irony.

His shoes and clothes weighed him down. He tried to remove his shoes. He went under water, laboriously working them off. He kept his shirt on but removed his trousers. He tied knots at the ankles and drew the trouser legs skyward, water pouring out, and let them fill with air. He used his cloth belt to seal the waist. Now he had a horseshoe-shaped life preserver.

What a long journey his shoes must be making to the bottom. Since childhood, numbers had been his passion. He made some calculations: 240 million persons end to end would reach the moon; nine million red Komsomol scarves would stretch across the Soviet Union. He once worked out that the number of different chess games that could be played was of the order of $25 \times 10$ to the 115th power, more than the number of atoms in the known universe. On the charts this part of the lake showed a depth of 2 kilometers. At least an hour of descent. At a half meter a second it would take 66⅔ minutes for his shoes to descend.

Heat from the earth's interior, left over from its creation 4.5 billion years ago, bubbled through vents. Where tectonic plates of the earth's crust were even now pulling away from each other, the rocks were 2500 degrees Fahrenheit, generating convection currents of heated water circulating upward to be cooled. If his shoes rode those currents, it could be many, many more hours before they finally settled.

His body would descend more slowly, checked by the buoyancy of gases in the stomach and intestines. He imagined falling for hours, even days, into the ever-darkening depths, limbs slowly waving, hair radiating like a hydra's tentacles.

Floating aimlessly, hearing only the irregular gasps of his own breathing and the lapping of water around his ears, he wondered whether he might will himself into a creature of the sea. Man's ancestors had wriggled out of the water. Could he not reverse the course and become part of the primitive force of *Burkhan*'s glorious sea?

# 2

THE PERCUSSIVE SOUND of rotors grew louder. But not until spray began slapping his face did the realization shoot through his numb brain that they had found him. He looked up. The helicopter was about 100 feet overhead, hovering like a tenacious pterodactyl. Across its tail, he made out the letters GLAVOKHOTA.

He was in a localized hurricane, struggling to keep his mouth above the brachiating spume. The belly hatch opened. Out dropped a harness at the end of a line. Dmitri paddled hard to reach the harness. He swallowed more water as he slipped into it, leaving the now waterlogged horseshoe of his trousers behind. He signaled thumbs-up. The pilot trimmed blade pitch, and the idling Soloviev turboshaft engine emitted a new sound of surging power.

Dmitri was snatched from the water and miraculously lifted into a new world of flight, borne away like the wind, the wild duck, like *Burkhan* himself. As if loath to allow his escape, the sea with its thousands of clutching, groping tentacles tried to draw him back. But he was well out of reach. His hair blew wildly. Folds of his shirt slapped his skin. His insides butterflied the way they used to when he rode the giant wheel at Gorky Park and counted the boats in the Moscow River.

As the chopper climbed and accelerated, the blue-green world of Baikal opened up dazzling new perspectives. To the west were the marble cliffs of Ol'khon and beyond the wooden houses of the fishing settlement of Khuzhir. He could even make out the Buddhist holy site at the gnarled promontory of Shaman Rock.

Dots in Khuzhir harbor on the island's far side were probably fishing boats. To the north he spied the spars and booms above the deck of the *Marshall Timoshenko.* Three silvery teals beat a path across the sky above the hovering rotors.

Dmitri was weaving just below the hatch. Strong arms drew him into the belly of the aircraft. Rubbery all over, he slithered out of his harness and like a landed fish flopped and jiggled across the slippery steel floor. Despite the hard surface, he felt as if he were still in the sea. He made no effort to stand. His legs would never support him.

"*Shalom,* Dmitri Leonidovich," shouted the man who helped him, kneeling next to the cable-wound cylinder of the winch anchored to the floor. "I am Lev."

He was a giant, pug-nosed, with hands like chopping boards, arms like loaves of peasants' bread, a wide mouth and great cauliflower ears. Lev was the mechanic, engineer, navigator, steward. He was a trained killer, a former Spetznaz commando who fought hand to hand around Jalalkot in eastern Afghanistan. Wearing a peasant's cap, silver-rimmed sunglasses, and a large lapis lazuli ring on his right pinky, he grinned broadly, gave a thumbs-up signal to the cockpit, and secured the hatch.

Mordecai was behind the controls, wiry, tense, dark-haired, with long bony fingers and a cicatrix from that same war. His hands were deftly playing the two control sticks.

Mordecai had mastered helicopters over the Hindu Kush, taking to them as Oistrakh to the violin. He flew Cosmos and Hind MI 24 gunships and Gagarin rescue choppers, making them hop, skip, jump, pirouette, practically turn somersaults. He flew in any weather, penetrated all sectors, fearing nothing, dodging cliffs in driving snow, dropping into remote and hostile valleys for bold rescues. He had been shot up but never down. Hundreds of soldiers, including Lev, owed their lives to Mordecai.

The deck of the MI-6 Skyhook was slick with oil stains and water that dripped from Dmitri's shirt. After the blinding brilliance of the sun on the water, the compartment was dark. Spears of light pierced the cabin portholes, illuminating the spaghetti of pipes, tubes, and wires along walls and ceiling. Dmitri shared the deck with a cargo of fifty-liter steel drums filled with Jet-A high-grade kerosene.

The Skyhook lifted to clear the hills of the eastern littoral and begin its 2,500-kilometer journey to the sea. At Goryachinsk they had walked him through the route and the routine. Soon they would be over Mount Z, flying northeast until they picked up the Baikal Amur Magistral, their path east to the Sea of Okhotsk.

The Glavokhota helicopter belonged to the Soviet hunting society that counted one million members. It managed 200 million acres of hunting grounds, 134 *zapovedniki* or game preserves, six giant *zakazniki* or national parks, and 27 breeding farms, including farms for breeding pheasants and waterfowl. In addition to serving the *nomenklatura* of privileged Russians, Glavokhota earned substantial sums of hard currency by offering tours to wealthy foreigners. For such clients as the Deutsche Bank, Mannesmann, Fiat, Occidental Petroleum, and Pepsi-Cola, it arranged hunting trips for Manchurian deer and bear. It used surplus army helicopters, including, for larger tours, the Skyhook, a cargo helicopter, maintained at a remote corner of the Irkutsk airport.

Mordecai and Lev had worked for Glavokhota since their discharge. As they had already taken any number of European and American groups on hard-currency-earning expeditions, they had easy access to the helicopter. They created documents for a fictitious party of German bankers who were to be picked up at the Karl Marx sports stadium near the Intourist hotel and taken into the taiga for two days. In obtaining the extra fuel, they greased palms with Mossad $50 bills.

Lev threw two blankets at the physicist, along with a dry shirt, trousers, and leather jacket, and opened a bottle of Cha Cha Georgian brandy.

"Drink," he said.

Dmitri did as he was told. Fire bolted through veins, arteries, and capillaries to the polar tips of his being, restoring feeling to his numb arms and legs. He shivered, took another swig, got out of his wet shirt and pants.

Wrapped in both blankets, he watched Lev pull a large can of Red Star caviar from a basket and open it with a blade of his pocket knife, spooning some of the caviar with the blade to taste it. The basket also contained thick black bread, chunks of sausage, a tin of caviar, more Georgian brandy, and packs of Marlboros and Balkan Sobranies. Lev tore off a piece of bread and handed both the bread and the can of caviar to the physicist.

"Eat," he said.

Dmitri tipped a little of the rich, black, glutinous caviar onto his bread. The eggs were smooth and oily on his tongue, and as he chewed, they popped and tingled almost erotically. In a few minutes, he gulped down more caviar than in his previous lifetime. He belched. Lev laughed, showing black specks of sturgeon egg on the steel caps of his teeth.

"Sleep," said the giant. "Dream of circling for the hora." He laughed, then disappeared inside the cockpit.

Still shaky, Dmitri teetered toward the hard bench by a porthole. The excitement of the ride overpowered any desire to sleep. Breathing deeply, feeling better, though his limbs and chest still ached from the ordeal in the water, he peered out at forest and sky. The sun, like some giant sea anemone, was throwing lush feelers of pink and orange into the western sky. Below a profusion of wildflowers and berries splashed reds, pinks, and violets on endless pines, birches, and spruce.

They were on a northeast course following the Muya River. Wooden huts in tiny logging settlements broke the natural line of trees. On a few primitive dirt roads battered trucks looked as if they had been through two world wars. Animal skins hung near smoky fires. Piles of wood were everywhere. Then each settlement was suddenly engulfed by the ocean of dappled green.

From his aerie, Dmitri meditated on the splendor and majesty of the land. Thanks to the brandy, the blankets, and the probing sunlight, warmth had returned to his body, and he was feeling almost giddy, as if a weight had been removed. He couldn't figure it out. His whole body seemed to be waiting for something that didn't quite happen.

Suddenly, he knew. He touched his face, pinched it, patted it, pulled it, squeezed it. No more contractions. No more tic. He shut his eyes and tried to remain absolutely still, holding his breath, fearing any movement, even an untoward thought, would bring it back.

It didn't return. He couldn't believe it. He tried a new tactic, flexing all his facial muscles, slapping his right cheek. Why pretend? He would force it. If it was destined to return, he wanted to know now. Still not even a twitch. Nothing.

He sat for fifteen minutes, a half hour, his face in his hands, primed for its return. Surely it would spring back to life like a fly warmed by the sun. He ran over in his head the total number of spasms. Perhaps five million already. Every two to three minutes of his time awake. Maybe during his sleep, too, but that didn't count. At least 500 times a day, 15,000 a month, 180,000 a year.

The tic had plagued him since he could remember. Schoolmates twisted their faces grotesquely when he approached, while others giggled. Their taunting drove him to a frenzy.

"I can't help it," he would scream.

He flailed at them, and they bloodied his nose, so that blood ran down his star-shaped Lenin badge awarded for good behavior and stained the navy blue jacket of his uniform. "Why do you hurt me—I have done nothing to you," he would cry.

In time, his anger turned into contempt and then pity; he realized they were reacting from ignorance and stupidity. Yet he withdrew from contact with other students and retreated into his own silences.

It had been little consolation that while he was seething against his classmates, he was recognized as the most brilliant student who ever matriculated at Moscow School No. 479. He had extraordinary gifts of memory and rational thought that made his studies absurdly easy. Thanks to his *babushka*—grandmother—who had preserved her library, he devoured Russian fairy tales and then Pushkin, Gogol, Tolstoy, and Dostoevsky, and lived in their richly peopled silent worlds, which he found easier to deal with than the school playground.

Of all the characters in his fictional encounters, he most loved Prince Lvof Nikolayevich Myshkin, Dostoyevsky's dreamy-eyed, saintly epileptic in *The Idiot,* the Seraph of Sarof, who spoke to birds, enjoyed a strong power over wolves, and suffered an immeasurable pride and passion for truth.

While moved by literature, he was fascinated by numbers. He fantasized about them. He loved their objectivity, their purity. They were clues to the mysteries of the natural world. Words were clumsy, imprecise, ambiguous. They could injure, distort, prevaricate. Numbers never hurt and never lied. Often he ignored words and conceptualized in the language of mathematics. While his classmates were still doing their multiplication tables, he had reduced the natural world to the dependent and independent variables of differential and integral calculus.

His mother, Irina Leonidova Sherbatova, having already seen him do simple addition, asked him at age three whether he knew the total of seven times eight. They were living with her mother, Ludmilla Davidovna Perlova, off Tsvetnoy Boulevard in central Moscow. Irina excitedly reported his response.

"He said, 'seven times eight means seven plus seven, double that and double that again, makes fifty-six'. That is remarkable."

His *babushka* wore a knowing smile. She had earlier told her daughter the tic was the mark of God. *"Chto budet, to budet,"* she said. "What will be will be."

A year later his mother asked him to add up all the numbers from one to 100. He saw immediately that the answer was 50 times 101 and gave the correct answer of 5,050. Failing the ability to reason conceptually, most children, and indeed most adults, physically tried to add up all the numbers.

His teachers helped build a protective wall between him and the other students. They told his mother and *babushka* that his intellectual level was that of genius. Because he was so gifted, they helped to find specialists in nervous disorders, neurologists who treated the *nomenklatura,* even members of the Central Committee. But the doctors could do nothing about the tic except offer advice about washing his face in warm water and taking aspirin to relax the muscles.

FLYING IN A CLOUDLESS, crystalline sky, the Skyhook found the BAM. The electrified line, Stalin's biggest construction project, lay about 500 miles north of the Trans-Siberian Railway built by Czar Nicholas II. The sinuous ribbon of BAM track, below filaments of overhead electric wire running from steel pylons, stretched endlessly along a route of five mountain ranges, seventeen rivers, 3,000 bridges, and four tunnels to the Sea of Okhotsk.

Dmitri made out distraught herds of reindeer jumping the tracks, feeling the frightening drumming of the twin rotors. Settlements were fewer. Stations were bare, roofless, inhospitable wooden platforms, like ghostly barges on the great sea of trees. Old freight cars stood vigil on lonely sidings. He had yet to see a single train.

The sun began to set. As the last flecks of light fled the cabin, he curled into a fetal position on the hard wooden bench, and, despite the roar of the rotors, slept for almost three hours. Again he dreamt he was flying, this time above the golden domes of the churches of Novodevichy. Then the setting changed. He was still airborne, but in an enclosed place, head and shoulders painfully hitting walls and ceiling, like a trapped bird. The walls and ceiling were of solid gold, like rooms of the Hermitage. Here was all the gold anyone could ever desire. But he searched vainly for doors and windows.

He awoke stiff and aching. The tic hadn't returned. He looked around the dark cabin. He could see dull dial lights from the cockpit and the backs of two figures at the controls. Attracted by the luminescence, he went forward.

As the craft swayed in the night currents, he pitched between fuel drums and metal struts. He steadied himself at the door frame of the cockpit. Having emerged from the darkness, he beheld through the glass dome of the cockpit a night sky of three-dimensional splendor. In the southeast quadrant, creeping above the line of distant mountains, a rising moon illumined meringue-capped summits below the foam of the Milky Way.

Mordecai was in the pilot's seat to the right. Before him were the control sticks for pitch and rotation of the twin rotors, a panel of myriad gauges, switches and small, colored lights signaling the aircraft's state of health.

Turning his face slightly to the rear, the pilot greeted the silent presence. "Welcome aboard Flight number one to Jerusalem. On your right, to the south, in the Chita oblast, the foothills of Skalistyy Golets, 3,000 meters. We hope you relax and enjoy the flight, and we thank you for choosing Mossad Airlines."

His head was small, bony, with a pointed nose, a scar along the left cheek, and dark hair. There was something almost ferretlike about the determined way the head was thrust forward, suggesting nothing could ever deter this man from his objective.

Lev, who was sitting in the copilot's seat, held a folder of charts on his lap. A radio headset covered his ears. He was jotting some things down in a notebook. "GOES-4 tells us weather conditions ideal. It should be a smooth ride."

They were flying below radar-detection levels a few hundred feet over the treetops, hoping not to attract attention of the MIG-23s and 29s at the air force base at Takhtamygda, a few miles north of the Ussuri near the top of the hump of Manchuria.

Mordecai switched on two spotlights, cradled fore and aft on the Skyhook, cut forward speed and gently rocked the elevation stick. Descending rotors generated localized hurricanes that whiplashed the trees. Shadows flitted on the ground like battalions of Lilliputian soldiers. In the distance, Dmitri thought he saw a herd of reindeers.

Mordecai veered north of the rail line, maneuvering the Skyhook toward a rock-strewn bluff the size of a basketball court. One house-size boulder stood sentinel at the point where the bluff fell into slopes of larches, spruce, and fir.

As they touched the ground, Mordecai activated the rear doors of the Skyhook and then shut off the engines. Cold air rushed through the cabin. The five-bladed main rotor and four-bladed tail rotor wound themselves down until the only sounds were the high-pitched susurrus of the woodland crickets and the whine of attack mosquitoes.

In the light of the moon and the side and rear lights of the aircraft, they cleared rocks from a path on which they rolled out the heavy fifty-liter drums from the Skyhook's loading bay to a spot just beside the fuel tank. Lev dropped one end of a length of hose into the drum and sucked the other to set up a suction flow from drum to tank. Using a second tube, they drained two drums at a time. But the refueling was still a laborious process.

After more than an hour on the ground, they heard a crackling of branches from the slope behind the big boulder. They froze, expecting to see a bear or other large animal emerge. They heard the clicking of hooves.

Into the clearing a band of men rode on the backs of reindeer, tattered mukluks scraping the ground, long-barreled rifles tucked under their arms. They were Yakutsk herdsmen, dressed in odd-colored tunics and reindeer skins. They were small people, more like little boys, until you looked at their furrowed, cracked, age-wizened faces. Seven of them rode into the clearing and slowly circled the helicopter. Hooves kicked up small stones. Antlers swayed menacingly. No one spoke.

After eyeing Lev, Mordecai walked purposefully toward the man who seemed to be the chief. Like the others, he had slit eyes, a pancake nose, and high cheeks that looked and probably felt like sandpaper. A rawhide lasso circled his waist. He peered curiously at Mordecai behind a profusion of antlers.

"Halt," Mordecai shouted in Russian. "Your presence here is not authorized." He had to back off suddenly when the reindeer lowered its head and lunged for his groin.

The Yakut laughed. The others, who were clustering around Mordecai, also laughed, their mouths showing an assortment of rotting or missing teeth. The weapons were all pointed in the vicinity of Mordecai's chest.

"You are interfering with an official mission," Mordecai protested. "I command you to leave immediately."

The leader tried to catch Mordecai in the loop of his lasso. Mordecai sidestepped. The Yakut found this very funny. He yanked the cord back, but instead of trying again, he pointed to Mordecai's feet.

"Your boots," he demanded in broken Russian.

One of the other reindeermen moved closer to Mordecai from the rear and encouraged his beast to give Mordecai a not too gentle shove. The antlers knocked him to the ground. The Yakuts were now beside themselves with laughter.

Mordecai tried to raise himself. This time the lasso found its mark and drew tightly around his upper body, throwing him off balance.

"Your boots," the Yakut chief said, "and your jacket."

The raiders were having so much fun they ignored Lev. They did not see the nose of the semiautomatic .22 pistol surreptitiously sliding from Lev's belt under his flight jacket. Within a split second, he had emptied a full clip at the tight cluster of men and beasts.

Mordecai, loosening the lasso, found his own pistol and shot from the ground. Raked by a cross fire, riders fell, arms flaying the air, rifles discharging wildly. Hit themselves, the reindeer panicked, bucking, kicking, dumping their charges, and bolted into the forest.

The seven bodies lay scattered like bundles of rags across the clearing. Dmitri, weak-kneed, was staring at the bodies.

Mordecai came up to the physicist. "Don't waste your pity. Those bastards would have stripped us, buggered us, then murdered us."

Dmitri said nothing.

"Back to work," Lev said, returning to the oil drums. Mordecai and Dmitri followed. The refueling process continued. Dmitri tried to make himself useful, but felt more in the way. He couldn't get his mind off the dead Yakuts.

One of the bodies was on its side, eyes still open, away from the others, following Dmitri's every step. Blood was trickling from the lower corner of its mouth.

Dmitri couldn't escape those eyes. No matter where he went, what he did, they pursued him, as if casting an evil spell. Even as a scientist, he had a healthy respect for the occult.

Finally, he could stand it no longer. He had to shut those eyes. He drew away from the drums, approached the body. The eyes, reflecting floodlights from the Skyhook, were flickering blue flames. Dmitri leaned over and firmly shut the lids, skimming the grainy, whiskered face, still warm and sticky with blood.

The lids wouldn't stay shut. Sound hissed from the yawning mouth. In an incredible spasm of life, the herder's left arm sprang out like the peen of a steel trap. Clenched in the herder's fist was a dagger arcing toward Dmitri's back.

The physicist twisted away. The knife grazed his jacket and sank into spongy tundra. Eyes of hatred clamped on Dmitri, then suddenly on Lev, who appeared from nowhere. Yanking the knife from the Yakut's grip, Lev slit his throat.

"Don't stray from the aircraft," he told Dmitri. Lev walked to each of the bodies and aimed a single executioner's shot at the head.

They went back to refueling. No one spoke. The routine was now familiar. During the process, Mordecai ran into the cabin for paint, brushes, and a stencil. He painted out the identifying name GLAVOKHOTA on the nose of the helicopter and inscribed SAKHALINNEFTGAZPROM, Sakhalin Oil & Gas.

The last two drums were being emptied when the three men froze. From below the ridge they heard the thumping and crackling of what sounded like a new group of visitors.

"Into the aircraft!" Lev ordered, recapping the fuel tank. "Fast."

Mordecai was already in the cockpit, switching on the engines. Unleashed into the night air was the percussive bark and roar of 2,000 horsepower. The long, drooping rotor blades started turning and then stiffening with centrifugal force as their revolutions increased. Even before Lev had secured the rear doors, Mordecai adjusted the pitch of the blades for lift, and the huge 60,000-pound aircraft, improbably, began to rise.

The clearing was now bathed in illumination from the twin spotlights. Dmitri hunkered over the porthole in the cabin. The corpses seemed to come alive as their loose-fitting tunics and trousers flapped in the whirlwind. The debris of empty cans and hoses flew against the rocks and trees.

Shadows glided on the lower ridge leading up to the plateau. Dmitri could make out a half dozen more reindeermen with slung rifles following a trail toward the clearing. Their faces were turned upward toward the airborne monster. One took a bead while still on his mount. Others fired from steadier positions on the ground.

Mordecai cut the lights, banked to the east, and gave the Skyhook maximum forward thrust into the shimmering night.

# 3

ON A LATE November morning, Rachel Ravid boarded a blue-and-white Volvo bus in Dimona, a little oasis community of whitewashed stone houses and concrete apartments in the Negev. She peremptorily greeted her fellow passengers and sat by herself in the rear, burying herself in *Ha'aretz,* a copy of *Yediot Aharonot* under her arm. Like most Israelis, she was an avid consumer of newspapers and worried about what new disasters the Arabs had managed.

Rachel fervently hoped for peace. Peace would not only save lives but help the country realize its great economic potential. Having concluded free trade agreements with the United States and the European community, Israel was the natural gateway for exporters to both areas.

But who would invest in a place that had been a war zone for four decades? she wondered. Taxes and inflation were crushing. The bureaucracy was too big, the settlers' movement too strong, the police too aggressive. She was not opposed to giving up land for peace. If it was good enough for Golda Meir, why not for today's leaders? To anyone who would listen, she quoted the philosopher Martin Buber in his letter to Mahatma Gandhi:

> We love this land and believe in its future, and seeing that such love and such faith are surely present also on the other side, a union in the common service of the land must be within the range of the possible.

Rachel's face was long and narrow with luminous eyes and a strong, determined chin. Her thin arms seemed to fit awkwardly, as if there were no convenient place to put them, but she held her head high, almost regally. She was simply dressed now in white cotton blouse and slacks with no makeup. Her hair was wavy, collar-length and black, pinned in back in a chignon.

A physicist, Rachel had studied at Ramat Aviv University in Tel Aviv and Brandeis, where her father, Yosef Ravid, a deputy chief of Mossad and admirer of the United States, had sent her to college. Later after military service in Israel, she did graduate work in physics at Imperial College of London. She had a series of mostly unsatisfactory love affairs, never married, and was childless. Tired of wandering, she returned to Israel in her midthirties and got herself a coveted position on the physics staff of the Negev Nuclear Research Center of Israel's Atomic Energy Authority, also known as Kirya-le-Mehekar Gariny, or simply KMG.

The bus speeded north on the 25 toward Beersheba. After only ten minutes, it turned right into a compound of strange, reinforced-concrete, blockhouselike structures totally out of place, as if dropped from another planet, on this wind-sculpted desert. At a checkpoint next to an electrified fence and barbed wire several hundred yards in from the main road, a soldier waved the bus into the sprawling research complex, certainly one of the most secure places in the world.

Radar scanners on hilltop observation posts picked up the slightest movements anywhere near the fencing. Helicopters and infantry patrols kept the place under constant surveillance. Missile batteries had orders to down any aircraft wandering into the air space, even accidentally.

Built with France's help in the 1950s and designated as just a bigger textile mill, KMG was far more than a research center. Over the years it has become Israel's nuclear bomb factory. After being photographed by an American U2 spy plane in 1960, Israel acknowledged the nuclear center, but insisted its purpose was purely peaceful research. Not many believed the story, especially after 200 pounds of enriched uranium, enough for thirty nuclear bombs, were hijacked in the Mediterranean in 1968. Western intelligence sources concluded the hijacker was Mossad.

All pretense was brushed aside in 1974 when visiting science writers asked President Ephraim Katzir whether he was worried by reports that Israel had atomic capability.

"Why should that worry us? Let the world worry."

By the mid-1980s, an investigative team of the *London Sunday Times* reported, Israel had an annual production of forty kilograms of plutonium, enough for ten bombs, and had built up an arsenal of more than

200 bombs. Arabs knew they couldn't make war successfully against this Middle East superpower. So they started making peace.

Rachel worked the 7:30 A.M. to 4:30 P.M. shift in Machon 2, a six-level concrete bunker where plutonium, lithium 6, tritium, and deuterium were converted into the components of bombs. It was one of ten machons, or production units, within the compound.

A technician in the control center on Level Two, she chiefly oversaw a process of chemically stripping uranium fuel rods of their aluminum coating and immersing them in heated nitric acid to dissolve the uranium and obtain plutonium. Later the plutonium was dried, converted into a powder, and baked.

She had security pass number 8346–7, a further pass number 444 for entry to Machon 2, and a locker (No. 8) for changing from her street clothes into a white lab smock. After a morning in Unit 37 of Machon 2 making a 1.16-gram "cake" of plutonium, she broke for lunch at 11:30, walking outside in the blistering heat to the main dining room of the compound, a couple of hundred yards from Machon 2.

Today she ate her tuna fish salad by herself, still catching up with the newspapers. But then beyond a table of canasta players she noticed a group of about a half-dozen people listening to a newly arrived Russian physicist discuss conditions in Russia. Tiring of the news of the same Arab provocations in a political situation that never seemed to improve, she decided to pull up a chair and join the group. She was the only woman.

Most around the table spoke in English, which the Russian knew better than Hebrew. Sometimes there were lapses into Russian, which she knew vaguely from her mother's mother who came from Odessa. Later she took a Russian course at Brandeis.

The new arrival was Dmitri Sherbatov. Like others who had emigrated recently, he looked a little lost in his new surroundings. She knew from her father that Sherbatov was someone very special, some kind of genius, whom Mossad had just extracted from Russia. It was rumored he would be put in charge of an important new project. People around the table were curious about him, sympathetic, deferential. He was a celebrity.

He was talking about conditions for science in Russia:

"How can you have science in a country where people are still altering the facts to fit the politics. Lysenkoism is an old disease, but it is still rampant."

"But surely Russia has great scientists," Rachel argued. "What about Sakharov?" She hadn't been intending to speak.

"Russia has great scientists," Sherbatov said with exaggerated emphasis, "despite the system, not because of it . . ." People around the table shook their heads in agreement. ". . . Sakharov gave Russia the hydrogen bomb and Tokomak. Russia gave him internal exile at Gorky."

There were more nods.

Sherbatov stared at the Formica table with a reflective air. "Years ago," he said, waving his hand expansively, "I studied under Sakharov at the Lebedev Institute in Moscow. Andrei Dmitriyevich had already designed a trigger for igniting hydrogen. He built the bomb because he felt that balancing the power of the United States was the best way to assure peace."

Someone brought him more coffee. Sherbatov put four brimming spoonfuls of sugar into the cup.

"I was still a teenager," he went on, "the youngest of a team working with him on the vacuum chamber that became the Tokomak reactor for controlled fusion reactions. It could heat plasma to as high as 100 million degrees, seven times greater than the interior of the sun."

Sherbatov was seemingly lost in this awesome statistic. He suddenly looked up at the assembled faces, his eyes widening, seeming to grow moist.

"I remember Andrei Dmitriyevich's words: 'We should not minimize our sacred endeavors in this world, where, like faint glimmers in the dark, we have emerged for a moment into material existence from the nothingness of the dark unconsciousness. Man has a sacred endeavor to deepen and widen knowledge. There is a wonderful, divine progression of knowledge, provided by the collective of man, which provides the only possible way to make sense of the universe and roll back the darkness.'

"I cited these words once in a memo. The authorities were not pleased."

Rachel liked the man's passion, felt caught up in it, something like being swept along at a peace demonstration.

He stopped talking. There was a moment of silence. Rachel broke into it. "But don't you feel you can . . . perhaps know too much?"

"No," he said without hesitation.

"How about knowledge of your own death?" she asked, "or death of the human race, the end of the universe?"

Sherbatov sipped his coffee, staring at her curiously. "You are talking about prescience, not knowledge. The seer, not the scientist."

"Well, knowledge also helps us predict the future and reduce the element of mystery." Her chin was out, and her head was high with a fractious tilt. "Look at weather forecasting. Our knowledge helps us predict the storm. Astronomers predict an asteroid's collision. With no limits to knowledge, won't we eventually know the future? Then the suspense and tensions will be gone. It will be like seeing a movie a second time. Life will be a big bore. Why bother with it at all?"

She said it with a straight face, unsure whether he was serious or testing her. "Then you want curbs on knowledge?" He seemed bewildered.

"I do think we can know too much."

"Well, the reality is there is no way we can curb knowledge. They have tried in the past, but the lantern's light always finds its way from under the bushel."

"Well, I don't want answers to everything, such as knowledge of how and when I will die."

Someone interrupted to ask Sherbatov in Russian how he got out of the USSR.

"I did not apply for an exit visa. Once they know you want to leave you lose everything. Vladimir Kislik was a physicist from Kiev, fired from the Institute of Physics of the Ukrainian Academy of Sciences after he applied to emigrate. He took menial jobs, but lost these as well. He was arrested for vagrancy. Foreign scientists who visited his home were assaulted on the street by the KGB. He was jailed on charges of hooliganism. He was sent to a psychiatric hospital, locked in a ward with dangerous psychotics . . ."

"They did not make it easy for us," the questioner said. He was gray-haired under his plaid kipa and wore a neatly trimmed goatee like Lenin. He had emigrated some years ago from Russia. Rachel knew him as a technician in Machon 1, which housed the reactor itself.

"May I tell you about friendship in the Soviet Union?" The man turned to Rachel and the others. He tugged at his beard, face deadpan. "Friendship means Armenians take Russians by the hand, Russians take Ukrainians by the hand, Ukrainians take Uzbeks by the hand, and they all go and beat up the Jews."

Around the table people nodded in agreement. Another in a scraggly salt-and-pepper beard whom Rachel did not know began another story:

"Three inmates in the same prison cell started talking about why they had been jailed. The first said his crime was beating up an old Jew named Khaimovich. The second said he had defended an old Jew named Khaimovich in a fight. The third said his crime was being Khaimovich."

"*Ma la'asot*—whatcha gonna do," someone said.

Sherbatov drank more coffee. "My half-brother and his wife had to wait fifteen years before coming here, and were beaten up several times. Misha, a violinist, lost his job with the Odessa Symphony. Ekaterina was a pediatrician. She lost her job with the Odessa Health Institute. But they were luckier than most. Misha gave violin lessons. She earned money from private house calls."

"So how did you get here?" the goateed man asked again.

"The means were irregular," Sherbatov said. "I am sorry. I was told not to comment on anything related to my leaving."

"Many Jews are assimilated," another man said.

"Not so many," Sherbatov said. "How can Jews ever be absorbed in a country that stamps Jew on your internal passport?"

Nods in agreement.

"I managed for many years," he continued, "but only because people did not know me as a Jew. My father was not a Jew."

People were now starting to leave to go back to their jobs. Rachel stayed. Sherbatov was obviously very smart, and she liked very smart men. But there was something more. She tried to put her finger on it. Altitude. That was it. In his presence she felt as if she were standing on a high precipice above the earth. Most of the men she had met never left the ground.

"How did you learn to speak English the way you do?"

"Believe it or not"—he smiled—"from my *babushka*. She was raised by an English governess. That was before the Revolution, obviously. I spent much time with her. When no one was around we spoke English together. It was our little secret. She also knew French, German, and enough Italian to understand operas."

"I love *babushkas*. Tell me about her."

"She had eyes like melting chocolate, but she was also crafty and cautious. You had to be to live under those conditions. She survived two world wars and the death of two husbands. Even in the food lines, where she stood more than three hours a day, winter or summer, rain or shine, wearing a simple black dress and cloth coat, she knew that one questioned nothing, confided in no one. Six decades in the Soviet Union had taught her how to keep eyes straight ahead, see nothing, and notice everything."

"It must have been terrible," Rachel said.

"As a war widow, she had only a small pension, but together with my mother's salary, it allowed them to have a two-room apartment on the fifth floor near the Pushkinskoye Metro. She slept in a corner of the living room, partitioned off with the extra sheet on a clothesline. My mother and I shared the bedroom, which we curtained with a table-cloth."

He seemed to warm to the subject as the memories returned. "*Ba-bushka* took full charge of me. We went on numerous excursions, to Gorky park, where in the winter we laughed at the men in brief bathing suits jogging in the snow, laughed at the clowns at the Moscow State Circus. We walked in Novodevichy. *Babushka* knew the way inside the walls of the Novodevichy cemetery where her favorite writers, Gogol and Chekhov, were buried, along with the composer Aleksandr Scriabin. I remember the bust of Gogol looked sorrowful, as though saddened by all the events since his death in 1852. Some steps away was the final resting place of Nadezhda Alleluyeva, Stalin's wife. But on summer evenings, when the sun set the golden domes of the churches on fire, the place evoked the magic spell of our fairy tales, of witches, wood sprites, and sorcerous birds."

"You sound already nostalgic for Russia."

"They say the wood smoke is always sweeter in the homeland." He allowed a smile.

"Eugene Onegin," she remembered. "Were your parents physicists, too?"

"My father was a professor of engineering at the Polytechnical Insti-tute. He died when I was three in a crash of a Tupelov 144 flying to a conference in Krasnoyarsk."

"I'm sorry."

"I hardly knew him. . . . My mother was an economist with the Vneshekonombank, the foreign trade bank. She was a nonpracticing Jew, usually taken for Tartar. I saw her briefly at bedtime but throughout my childhood it was *babushka* who looked after me."

She smiled, encouraging him to talk more, which he seemed eager to do. "My father was not Jewish, so I am only half-Jewish. My mother divorced my brother Misha's father, who was Jewish, to marry mine. My brother told me of the terrible wrongs being inflicted on the Jewish people by the state. He was influential in my coming here . . ."

"I expect it will be good for Israel."

"I hope so."

"People say you are a genius."

He laughed. "I am a scientist, a mathematician of sorts. I have always been fascinated by numbers."

"I find numbers fascinating, too."

"Did you ever consider similarities between numbers and people?"

"Not exactly."

"There is an infinite supply of numbers," he explained. "And potentially an infinite supply of people, at least until procreation stops."

She nodded, eyes fastened on him . . . fascinated by him.

"When I was a child, I found myself thinking that each number has a different character. I wondered why some numbers can only be divided evenly by themselves and the number one."

"The prime numbers."

"I called them the commissars. One, two, and three are commissars, while four is not. Between one and ten there are five commissars; between ninety-one and 100 only one, ninety-seven. What accounts for the long stretches without commissars? Are there only so many commissars? How many commissars differ by only two, such as eleven and thirteen?"

The dining room was now practically empty. Two official-looking men were walking toward the table. Sherbatov got up.

"I have to leave you now," he said abruptly. "I must work. They don't want me talking too much . . . I have enjoyed this."

"I hope we will meet again," she said. *"Lehitraot*—bye."

# 4

AT FIRST, NO one knew what Ilya Rostov did for a living, or why he chose to visit Goryachinsk. Walking down the streets, he looked like a flagellant in one of the religious orders. He seemed to be flailing himself, but he was really swatting mosquitoes. No one told him about the local Evenk repellent made from mint from the marshes, pennyroyal and other local herbs. No one offered him a jar of *Vietnamskiy* balm. People preferred to keep their distance.

He was not a hunter or a fisherman. People guessed he must have business at Mount Z. As the days of his stay turned into weeks, he showed special interest in the center. Some days he would drive out in his black Zhiguli, park at the gate and watch people enter and leave, jotting things down in a black notebook. Then he would visit with Igor Borisov, the local party official.

Those who provided food and services for him said he was demanding and arrogant, and always seemed to have plenty of rubles. They compensated by overcharging.

Rostov was portly with sweat-shiny flesh and plump arms and legs. His head was enormous and bald. He went without a hat. Perhaps he could not find one large enough to cover it. Just wait and he will have sunstroke, someone said.

Below eyebrows that ran together in a perpetual scowl were passionless eyes, calculating, like an undertaker's measuring those he meets for the coffin they would eventually need.

He wore crepe-soled shoes that gave him a bouncy, pigeon-toed walk.

His clothes, though finely made for Soviet clothes, seemed too small, making him bulge like a sausage. Despite the heat, he always wore a jacket.

Rostov had taken a four-room cottage at No. 2 Second Plan Avenue just behind that of the center's director, Dr. Dmitri Sherbatov, on Pëtr Ilich Tchaikovsky Avenue. Their backyard gardens were contiguous, and neighbors noticed Rostov sitting for hours beside his gooseberries, staring at Director Sherbatov's house across the patches of tomatoes, melons, cucumbers, string beans, and purple basil.

Dr. Sherbatov's curtains stayed drawn, so Rostov could not see inside. The only entrance to the director's house was through a side door. Rostov always placed himself in such a position that he could see all who entered and left. He had been in his garden when two dark-haired young men, strangers, one very big, the other sharp-faced and bony, called on the director.

Although Sherbatov and Rostov were neighbors, it was as if a Chinese wall separated them. Dr. Sherbatov was always preoccupied, and never even acknowledged Rostov's presence. Still, he could not have been unaware of him. Rostov, for his part, never initiated a conversation with the physicist.

Rostov retained a young Evenk woman as a housekeeper. Sometimes she stayed the night. He apparently made it worth her while because she went on a shopping spree at the market, buying herself a new pair of shoes, a new pocketbook, soap, which had suddenly become scarce and expensive, and fragrant Indian tea.

No one had ever seen Rostov agitated or excited about anything more than mosquitoes until the day of the accident.

It was a Sunday, and director Sherbatov did what he loved to do every summer Sunday, rent Oleg Roussovsky's old wooden skiff, take his rod and reel and box of lures, and go fishing.

Rostov spent Sunday morning walking along the small beachfront of the village, watching Sherbatov row out to sea. The boat became smaller and smaller. Rostov grew bored, went home, lunched on herring and cucumber prepared with sour cream and onions by his housekeeper, and napped. When he woke up, he went to the garden but could not tell if Sherbatov had returned. He walked to the beach and asked people if they had seen Dr. Sherbatov row back. No one had.

It had been a quiet day, except for some helicopter activity. But helicopters often flew in the area. Sometimes they were military, or police, but mostly they were from Glovokhota, taking western bankers and industrialists from Irkutsk to hunting preserves in the Barguzin hills.

That night Dr. Sherbatov still had not returned, and people observed that Rostov forced entry into the professor's house. He seemed to spend a long time there, then took over one of the few telephones in the village, belonging to Borisov, and spoke for a long time to Moscow.

The lights stayed on all night in the Rostov and Sherbatov cottages. Early in the morning, Rostov was again by the water. He looked tired and he was chain-smoking Pamirs. Maybe someone told him smoke was one form of mosquito protection.

Now several helicopters circled overhead. One landed in the village square. Rostov went aboard and flew across the lake toward Ol'Khon island. In the afternoon he returned. A police motorboat arrived as well from the river police detachment at Ust'. They had found oars that Oleg Roussovsky said were from his boat. Also recovered from the water was Sherbatov's straw hat.

The villagers agreed it had probably been a freak accident. There had been no storms. The weather was perfect—blue skies, bright sun, light breezes. But the director must have been out in the tanker lane. Collisions were frequent, often went unreported.

Roussovsky asked who would give him money for a new boat. No one knew.

Rostov could not get the Sheymov affair out of his head. A few years back his colleague the First Chief Directorate Viktor Ivanovich Sheymov had vanished in Moscow, along with his wife and child. There were little clues that made it look as if they had been kidnapped and murdered. But the bodies were never found. He recalled the shock and recriminations at Dzerzhinsky Square when the directorate learned from a mole in the CIA that the family was living somewhere in New England with new identities.

There would be problems if he declared Sherbatov dead only to have him turn up again later, like Sheymov. He could lose his promotion. He could kiss his new apartment near the Mayakovsky Metro good-bye. He could be demoted and reassigned to Irkutsk.

His orders had been to keep Sherbatov under surveillance. He had done so faithfully. No one had warned him that Sherbatov might flee.

Luckily, he still had a copy of the cable he had sent three weeks ago after the two dark-haired young men visited the physicist. They had been traced to Glavokhota. Both were Jews and had done their military service in Afghanistan.

On the beach, he barked out orders to the platoon of security people. He wanted those two men brought in now. He shouted their names. "Mordecai Simler, Lev Geldman." Men in uniform saluted and squeezed back into blue-and-white Volgas, flasher lights revolving.

In a glass-domed police helicopter, Rostov was flown to Mount Z. Even with his VIP arrival and KGB identification, it took him a few minutes to gain access. Impatiently he waited at the security post at the entrance to the compound for the guide who had to accompany all visitors, even personages from Moscow.

They literally walked into the mountain. Huge portals opened into a spacious well-lit chamber dominated by a large picture of Lenin and a wall clock that read 11:03. Behind a second security post that handed out special visitors' passes was a bank of elevators. Rostov and his guide, a pale, diminutive European Russian with a slight limp, made what seemed an interminably long descent to a platform resembling a Moscow metro station.

Personnel walked purposefully, holding clipboards and wearing white coats like doctors. Instead of the intermittent rumble of trains, there was the constant whine of scores of twenty-ton magnets, which his guide said were strung out along the three kilometers of circular track that stretched out from either end of the platform.

Through the center of each magnet passed reinforced steel pipe. Inside the pipe, racing at almost the speed of light, were negatively charged electrons and positively charged positrons, which could be made to slam together in a near-perfect vacuum at combined energies approaching 100-GeV or 100 billion volts.

The guide was a technician whose additional duties included memorizing a long speech for the big turnips from Moscow who visited from time to time. The guide had begun his speech as soon as he introduced himself to Rostov:

"This is the most advanced high-energy physics center in the world, Comrade. The nearest European equivalent is CERN under the Jura Mountains in Switzerland. The Americans have smaller centers at Stanford University in the state of California and the Fermi National Accelerator Laboratory near Chicago. They are considering a Supercollider in Texas, but it costs so much it may never get built.

"Our mission is to widen the lead of the USSR in science and technology by answering the basic questions of what the fundamental elements of matter are and what the forces are that hold the elements together. These are steps in a scientific journey begun by Kepler and Newton . . ."

The guide never stopped talking. These were new areas for Rostov, scientific inquiry, advanced physics, the exploration of the natural world, and he tried to pay attention. It could help in understanding Sherbatov.

"In its wisdom," the guide went on, "our party leadership knows our work here will lead to major advantages in high-technology research for the advance of socialism. Our efforts will benefit medicine, improve medical diagnosis, aid in the development of laser techniques for the treatment of cancer, give our state industry better electric power generation, transform our ability to refrigerate efficiently and safely, even pave the way for magnetic levitation railroads. . . ."

What struck Rostov most was the influence of GKNT, the state science and technology committee, in obtaining this enormous state investment, billions of rubles, not quite the space program, but impressive nonetheless. It was testament to the clout of Kirillin, Marchuk, and Tolstikh, the leading officials on the science committee. Of course, Defense was now winning the intragovernmental spending battles. Even so, to secure this type of project—he had to tip his hat to those men. It gave him new respect for the science establishment.

"We are investigating the ultimate in nature," the guide continued, "a very heavy particle known as Z, one of only four known forces of nature. It conveys the weak nuclear force between neighboring nuclear particles, and is a source of radioactivity. A so-called strong force binds the nucleus to an atom. The other two forces are electromagnetism, which holds atoms together and lords over light, and familiar gravity.

"Z particles enjoy only the briefest flicker of life, less time, if you can imagine, than it takes for light to traverse a single atom. The particles are created after the annihilation of the electrons and positrons. Our special equipment, including high-speed supercomputers, measures the characteristics of Z. We have already observed that Z breaks down into neutrinos . . ."

"Enough!" Rostov shouted. It was numbing. "Remember," he told the guide sharply, "I am here to conduct urgent business of the state." He brought out his black notebook. "Is Glazunov the physicist closest to director Sherbatov?"

"Yes, they work in the control center," the guide said tremulously.

"Take me to him."

Nervously and silently, the guide led Rostov to what looked like an aircraft control tower, entered by climbing a flight of circular steps from the main platform.

"Up there," he said, pointing. As Rostov started climbing, the guide disappeared.

The glass-enclosed center consisted of several workstations and an inner office built atop a large cylindrical slab of steel. Inside, crisscrossed by layers of wires and cables on the ceiling, were several cubicles, fitted with East German computers and a great display of sparkling gauges, dials, and meters.

Glazunov, hair white as his jacket, was alone in the section working on rows of numbers on the screen of his Kamstar 386 from Dresden. He did not look up as Rostov approached. Rostov hovered over Glazunov's chair.

"Dmitri Sherbatov has disappeared in a boating accident."

"Yes, I have heard." Glazunov had seen the visitor around Goryachinsk and like everyone knew he was KGB. He peered at his computer screen as if preoccupied. There was silence.

"Is that all you have to say?"

"I do not mind the director's business."

"Maybe you have regrets. Maybe you have theories."

"I am sorry he has disappeared. I have no theories."

Oh, for the old days, thought Rostov, when people like Glazunov could be taught to be a little more forthcoming.

"Have you worked with him long?"

"No."

Again silence.

"It would be in your interest to give somewhat fuller responses." Rostov tried to give the words an undertone of menace.

Glazunov removed his glasses. His eyes were a bright blue-green, slightly crossed, making it impossible to tell whether he was looking at you. He had a hook nose and outsize floppy ears.

"No offense. I really have little to say. I only joined the center in January. I had never worked with him before, though I had met him some years before when I was still at the Semenov Institute of Chemical Physics of the Academy of Sciences. Vitali Goldanskii, the director, introduced us."

"What did you think of him?"

"He was a nice man."

"Meaning?"

"Not the sort that hurts people."

"You say 'was.' Do you think he drowned?"

"All I can say is that Dmitri Leonidovich loved to fish. It was his main amusement. He went out every Sunday. He was a strong swimmer. Knew the waters of Baikal."

"Then you doubt that he drowned."

"I do not doubt that he did, or that he did not. Perhaps it was an accident. One of those tankers from Irkutsk. They are heedless of smaller craft. Boats are swamped. People drown."

Rostov pointed to the inner office. "Is that where he worked?"

"Yes."

The compact workspace was partitioned by panels of opaque plastic, offering little privacy. A tall man could have peered over them. Rostov walked in and rummaged through the desk. There were odd scientific papers, a book on fly-fishing, eagle and duck feathers, strands of fishing line, an old tackle, erasers, pencils, a ballpoint, paper clips. Glazunov was standing by.

"Who is the boy?" Rostov picked up the photo of a boy in a sailor suit.

"His son. I think his name is Kyril."

Rostov already knew about Kyril and about Sherbatov's divorced wife Tanya who lived in Irkutsk.

Something caught his attention. A piece of paper had fallen into the crevice between desk and wall. The paper looked like it had been taped to the wall and had slipped to the floor. He picked it up excitedly. Pasted on yellowed paper was a single unattributed paragraph cut out of similarly yellowed newspaper.

The science of alchemy I like very well. I like it not only for the profits it brings in melting metals, in decocting, preparing, extracting, and distilling herbs, roots; I like it also for the sake of the allegory and secret signification.

"What does this mean?"

Glazunov read it and handed it back. "I do not know."

"Was it hanging on the wall?"

"I did not notice. This was Dmitri Leonidovich's private office. I almost never entered."

"Do physicists normally ruminate about the art of alchemy?"

"Not me, but I cannot speak for others."

Rostov put the paper in his pocket, again looked around, at Glazunov stooped like an old fox in the entrance, at the keyboards, buttons, dials, and gauges inside the workspace.

"What did Sherbatov actually do here, besides study fly-fishing?"

"Dmitri Leonidovich was the director, and he took personal charge of the particle detector. The steel cylinder that you see below is filled with sensors that surround the beam path of the colliding particles. He did all the analytical work, and prepared the final report of each experiment for the high-energy physics section of the Academy of Sciences."

"Did you detect any unusual behavior in recent weeks?"

"Not especially. There is something unusual in all human behavior. That is what makes us individuals."

"You know what I mean." Rostov's voice rose. "This is a matter of urgent state security."

Glazunov stiffened, but remained calm.

"Dmitri Leonidovich was incommunicative. He kept to himself. He lived by himself. I knew him only as a professional colleague. We never socialized. But . . . yes, he was an unusual man. For someone like him, it is hard to know what is unusual behavior. He had a nervous tic, and that put many people off. It did not help his marriage, I am told. But he had one of the most original minds in our scientific community. He studied with Sakharov at the Lebedev Physics Institute, helped Marchuk at the Dubna plasma physics laboratory, worked with Basov and Prokhorov on the laser. He was a conceptual genius. But he never confided in me."

Rostov persisted. "I am interested in what you observed, whether he seemed nervous, jumpy, out of sorts in any way in the past few weeks, as if he expected some big change to take place in his life?"

"I noticed no such thing. He came to work every day, and did his job. If anything, he was even more assiduous. He worked so hard that sometimes he forgot to sleep. I have left here in the evening and come back in the morning to find him still over his desk. He seemed totally oblivious of time."

"But was he frustrated, disappointed, upset about anything? Surely, not everything went the way he wanted it to."

"I did not notice." Glazunov did not meet Rostov's stare. His eyes locked on silvery cables strung across the ceiling.

Rostov sensed the old man knew a lot more than he was saying. Information would have to be teased out, like the coarse fibers peasant women endlessly separate from raw wool. He walked over to a table on which there was a half-filled bottle of Bonshomi mineral water and some glasses. He poured two glasses and gave one to Glazunov.

"Do you enjoy life here, Vadim Alexandrov?"

"Yes." Glazunov blanched. He was uneasy with the familiar address by a man from the KGB.

"And your quarters, are they satisfactory?"

"Yes."

Rostov already knew that Glazunov lived with his wife and her ancient mother in two small rooms of a bungalow on the edge of Goryachinsk and owned a broken-down Fiat. Because most of the time his car did not work, he took the bus that plied the fifteen-kilometer route to the center every hour.

"You wouldn't mind bigger quarters, would you?"

"There is an acute shortage of living space," Glazunov said, drinking some water. "These were the best quarters I could get at short notice."

"And yet the big cottage of Dmitri Leonidovich is vacant."

"So it is."

"It need not be empty any longer." Rostov, smiling, paused to let the words sink in. Glazunov's eyes widened, but he remained silent.

"Today, in fact, you and your wife and your mother-in-law could move in. You could borrow my Zhiguli to help you move, and keep it for as long as you like."

The physicist again looked away. What a difference bigger quarters would make. Mashenka would be happier. Life here was difficult for her. Her mother, Elena Federovna, who was ailing, could have a separate room. And they would have a car that didn't belong on a junk heap. They could drive to Irkutsk.

How far could he trust this man? This was the same KGB that many years ago, in the middle of the night, arrested his father. That had been a terrifying experience. He was only four, but he could still remember the soft cries of his mother that went on for days. He thought it was the end of the world. His father had made a joke about Stalin. Someone had reported him, he never found out who his accuser was, and never returned from Kolyma.

Young Glazunov learned from his father's experience. Never did he crack a joke or even mention politics as he advanced through school and the science establishment. Though hardly noticed, he was always alert to what was going on around him.

"I can do things for you if you do things for me," Rostov said smoothly.

Glazunov said nothing. It was still his move, but he needed more time to think. He did know some things. In parleying them, he would be betraying nothing. Sherbatov was either in the next world, or far away in this one.

"Time for vodka," Rostov said with a broad smile. He had pulled out a hip flask and was pouring some into Glazunov's empty mineral water glass and into his own. "Then we talk."

Glazunov drank. He was not a heavy drinker, but he liked good vodka, and this was very good export vodka, probably Stolichnaya. He savored the liquid, thinking about his move. The vodka helped him think.

"Dmitri Leonidovich did not tell me much, but I do know he was recently made very unhappy by Moscow's refusal to approve his experiments in transmutation . . ."

"Transmutation?" Rostov looked puzzled.

"We can bombard elements with electrons and give them new properties. Dmitri Leonidovich was fascinated by our capacity to convert base metals into gold."

"Is transmutation alchemy?"

Glazunov nodded.

"So there was some significance after all to the quotation he hung up on the wall. Your memory is better now." The KGB man laughed. "I will not press charges on the withholding of relevant material from the state."

"Some things have come back."

"And what else has come back?" It was easier than Rostov had anticipated, and more rewarding.

"All Dmitri Leonidovich needed was a cheap source of energy, and he believed he had that through some experiments he was conducting. He never confided in me, but I think it had something to do with controlled nuclear fusion."

"Fusion? You mean nuclear explosions?"

"Something like that. You get energy when you split atoms. But even more energy is released when atoms are forced together despite their mutually repellent positive electric charges. The bombardment of elements to give them new properties requires enormous amounts of energy. We are lucky we have that energy here through hydropower. But it is still costly, the dams, turbines, power transmission lines that give us the electricity to accelerate our particles. Imagine if there were unlimited energy at practically no cost. One could produce gold forever, and soon there would be more gold manufactured than has ever been mined."

"That is possible?" Rostov was incredulous.

"Sherbatov believed so."

"Then he should become a Hero of the Soviet Union?"

"Yes, you would think Moscow would be very happy. Even before any of this happened, his work with Basov and Prokhorov had made him a candidate for a seat on the Academy of Sciences. Yet the idea drew little support. Mining industries were threatened. Here is Russia with more gold than other countries. If mined gold becomes obsolete, Russia loses its advantage and the industry its reason for being. And the military saw nothing in it for them. They are interested in bombardment of cities, not particles. They want the center to redirect its research toward superweapons . . ." He paused, holding the choicest piece of information for last.

Rostov was at the edge of his seat, trying to grapple with the flood of unfamiliar data. "Go on, go on!"

". . . And there were rumors that Sherbatov was a Jew."

"Really?" exclaimed Rostov.

"It is said that is the real reason why his operational functions were restricted."

"Restricted?"

"Yes. He was about to be made redundant."

Rostov was amazed. The story was far better than he'd dared hope. But why hadn't his people alerted him? It made him angry that he had to learn all this from a venal scientist. Or was he just being led on? Was this man making it all up?

"How do you know all this?" Rostov asked sharply.

"From references in the files."

"Files?" Rostov was beside himself.

"Yes. Dmitri Leonidovich kept files. He obtained copies of some ministerial memos, probably from Jews in the ministries. He made copies of his own memos. He wanted a record."

"Where are the papers?"

"They should be in his desk."

Rostov rushed back into Sherbatov's office and rummaged through his desk again. He came up with nothing. "Find them for me," he ordered.

Glazunov pulled the desk drawer out all the way. It had a false bottom, which he removed expertly. The compartment was empty.

"Odd," said Glazunov. "He kept all his documents here."

"I want those papers."

"Maybe Dr. Sherbatov took them home."

"I went through his cottage from top to bottom last night."

"He could have destroyed them."

"I want those papers." There was new menace in Rostov's voice.

"I have told you what I know."

"Not enough."

"I do not know what happened to those papers."

Rostov stared at Glazunov. There was a heavy silence. Rostov suddenly laughed. His belly shook and he popped a button. "Of course, you are right, dear friend. How could you possibly know."

Glazunov looked warily at his interrogator. He was in over his depth.

"Come, have another drink," Rostov said, passing the flask.

Glazunov drank. Why not. He prayed Rostov would honor his part of the bargain. He uncoiled slightly and lowered his voice.

"I hesitate to admit this, but maybe you will not think the worse of me if I tell you that I secretly copied his files . . ."

Rostov rubbed his hands together.

". . . It was because of shared interests," said Glazunov, "and also because I suspected things were coming to a head. I wanted to be able to assist. So I kept a duplicate record. Every Sunday, while the director was fishing, I came in and copied longhand anything new that had been added during the week."

"Where is it all?"

"Right here."

The KGB man was ecstatic.

"We could make you a Hero of the Soviet Union."

Glazunov smiled nervously. He pulled from under a false bottom in his own drawer a sheaf of papers, bound by a rubber band. "I hope you can read my writing. Every word is exactly as it appeared in the original."

Glazunov returned to the Kamstar. He hoped soon to be able to tell Mashenka about their new cottage and automobile.

# 5

## DOCUMENT 1

8 June 1989
To: Guri Ivanovich Marchuk, full member of the Central Committee and president of the Academy of Sciences.
From: Dmitri Leonidovich Sherbatov, director, Particle Research Center, Goryachinsk, Buryat Autonomous Soviet Socialist Republic.

1. For centuries man has tried his hand at the art of Hermes. Alchemists sought to turn mercury into gold, but had neither sufficient tools nor adequate knowledge of the composition of matter. The twentieth century has given us both the tools and the knowledge. The theory of relativity changed our views of space and time. The quantum theory transformed our understanding of the behavior of matter and energy. Together, they made exploration of the atom possible, opening up the vast world of electrically charged particles that bind the atom.

2. Particle accelerators now duplicate the high-energy conditions under which matter was created. At Goryachinsk, thanks to generosity of the state, protons from the nuclei of hydrogen atoms are accelerated too close to the speed of light and then crashed into an aluminum rod or opposing stream of atoms. In the collision, the speeding protons and target atoms are destroyed, after being transformed for the briefest of instants into pure energy. The way the particles fly apart and come together tells us about the composition of matter.

3. I directed experiments to break down atoms of bismuth and lead. I chose these two elements because they happen to have almost the same

number of atoms as gold. I was curious to see whether by restructuring the atoms of bismuth and lead I could achieve what had eluded thousands of alchemists before me. I used two relativistic heavy ions, Argon 40 and Neon 20, stripped of their atomic electrons, leaving the bare nucleus. Then I began accelerating them to energies close to their rest mass so that they were traveling at up to 95 percent of the speed of light. I aimed the projectiles at target foils of bismuth and lead.

4. Out of bismuth I produced isotopes of gold, including the stable one that has precisely the same chemical properties as newly mined gold. Several times I repeated the experiment and found the same distribution of gold isotopes.

5. Production of gold in this way requires large amounts of energy to power the magnets that speed particles in the accelerator. Thus it does not become cost effective without a supply of low-cost energy. I believe I have solved this problem. I am at the threshold of building devices that will reproduce in the laboratory the processes that power the stars.

6. Nuclear fusion can be carried out in a relatively simple palladium electrode. I chose palladium because it absorbs large quantities of hydrogen gas. A current passes between the palladium electrode and a platinum anode in an insulated tube full of heavy water, containing deuterium, the heavy isotope of hydrogen. The palladium electrode in the center of the cell absorbs a large volume of deuterium. Under the influence of the electric current, the deuterium nuclei are squeezed so tightly that some of them fuse together to form helium, despite their mutually repellent positive electric charges. I observed gamma rays and neutrons, a sign that some fusion was occurring. Although energy was released, it did not promise to become important until I used a mixture of deuterium and tritium.

7. I believe I will be able to confine a hot plasma of deuterium and tritium within a reactor vessel and achieve a self-sustained or ignited fusion. This would become a cheap power source for the projectiles aimed at target bismuth. Gold would become available in unlimited quantities at a fraction of the world market price.

8. I communicate directly in hopes that you, having knowledge of my abilities of the workings of our most excellent government, will be able to solicit the kind of support that will advance these discoveries for the benefit of our motherland.

**DOCUMENT 2**
31 August 1989
To: Political Bureau of the Supreme Council
From: Vladimir Kuznetzov, Minister of Mines

1. Potentially available gold "economically" minable in the USSR is between four and five billion ounces, compared with three billion ounces of total gold mined so far on earth since the beginning of time. Unmined gold reserves in South Africa are one to 1.5 billion ounces.

2. The expansion of gold has been a goal of every Five-Year Plan since 1928. Geologists have discovered six new gold fields that are suitable for commercial exploitation in the Soviet Far East. Large deposits were found in the lower reaches of the Amur river and in Lantar on the coast of the Sea of Okhotsk. Gold is even being extracted from ocean sands. New areas that are promising for this kind of activity are the Sea of Japan, the Sea of Okhotsk, the Arctic Ocean, the Tatarski Gulf.

3. A large reserve of labor in the penal camps facilitates cheap production while furthering the objective of redemption through work. Most mines now being exploited are near labor camps and the Trans-Siberian Railroad. Some mines operate in the Arctic regions. Shipments are made by boat, which can sail only a few months each year. The new Baikal-Amur Mainline opens new territories to gold mining that will further stimulate the development of Siberia.

4. Gold sales in the West are a major source of wealth for the USSR. In the late 1970s, global investors bought gold as a refuge against the weak dollar. Market prices exceeded $800 an ounce, and the USSR earned $6.3 billion a year in hard currency from sales of bullion chiefly in Zurich. Although world market prices have declined in more recent years, earnings are still in the area of $3 billion a year.

5. The discovery of a cheap source of bullion would eventually wipe out the value of the minable gold resources of the USSR and eliminate a strategic asset in the economic competition with the capitalist powers. It, therefore, cannot be in the interests of the state or its people.

6. It is ludicrous to posit that cold fusion can be achieved through the use of palladium electrodes. Two Americans, Stanley Pons and Martin Fleishmann from the University of Utah, were laughed out of the scientific establishment after making such claims and failing to support them.

7. I strongly recommend that not only no action be taken on Director Sherbatov's proposal, but that he be removed from direction of the high-

energy center at Goryachinsk because his ideas for the use of the center are at such variance with the goals of our motherland.

## DOCUMENT 3

21 October 1989

To: Guri Ivanovich Marchuk, full member of the Central Committee and member of the Academy of Sciences

From: Marshall Nikolai V. Ogarkov, chief of the General Staff, Moscow

1. The state has a five-billion rubles investment in the Center for Particle Research at Goryachinsk, where work is in a narrow and specialized sector of the physical sciences that has yielded little for the cause of the defense of our motherland.

2. The center's existence inside a mountain has obvious attractions for national defense. It is an ideal location for useful work in the field of advanced weapons research.

3. These ideas have been discussed on an informal basis with the General Secretary and other members of the Politburo. We have been encouraged to make a formal proposal.

4. This is to inform you that such a proposal will be forthcoming and gives you time to prepare the personnel for the eventual reorientation of the center.

## DOCUMENT 4

12 December 1989

To: Dmitri L. Sherbatov, director Center of Particle Physics, Goryachinsk

Dear Dmitri:

I have the unhappy task of conveying to you that your scientific proposals are not acceptable to the state and that the Defense Ministry is preparing to take over the center and convert it into a research establishment for advanced weaponry. Though I personally do not agree with this course of action, I am an old man, and there is little I can do to alter it. I have enjoyed our long association, and know that you will succeed in any new endeavors.

Marchuk

**DOCUMENT 5**
5 January 1990
To: Guri Ivanovich Marchuk, Academy of Sciences, Moscow
From: Dmitri Sherbatov, Center of Particle Physics, Goryachinsk

Dear Guri:

I was, of course, deeply saddened by your letter. We have achieved much in the six years that the center has been operational. The mass and other properties of the Z particle, which is the carrier of the weak force of subatomic physics, have been determined to unprecedented precision. Even more important, this early work has determined with high probability that the universe is, in fact, made up of not more than the three known families of elementary particles (each with two kinds of leptons and two kinds of quarks).

I was prepared to further our very important work in this area, perhaps defining more precisely the basic building blocks of matter. I was also prepared to create new sources of wealth and energy for the motherland.

Our particles in this center are instruments of peace, not war. In light of our accomplishments, it is not appropriate that the center be used for military research, and I would very much hope that this proposal be resisted. Did not Andrei Sakharov say: "We must make good the demands of reason and create a life worthy of ourselves."

Sherbatov

**DOCUMENT 6**
3 February 1990
To: Dmitri L. Sherbatov, Center of Particle Physics, Goryachinsk

Dear Dmitri:

I have passed your letter on to members of the Central Committee, but I am not optimistic that any minds will be changed.

Marchuk

**DOCUMENT 7**
21 March 1990
To: Minister of Mines Vladimir Kuznetzov
From: Director of State Security Vladimir Kryuchkov

We have reliable information that Dmitri L. Sherbatov, Director of the Center of Particle Physics, Mount Z, Goryachinsk, Buryat Autonomous Soviet Socialist Republic, is a Jew. His mother is a Jew. He has a half-brother, Mikhail Abramovich Shifrin, a Jewish violinist, who has applied for an exit permit to Israel.

### DOCUMENT 8

7 April 1990
To: Dmitri Sherbatov, Center of Particle Physics, Goryachinsk
From: Vladimir Kuznetzov, Minister of Mines

1. The highest authorities of the Supreme Council of the USSR have determined that the bombardment of bismuth to achieve isotopic gold is an activity that is contrary to the interests of the people.

2. You are hereby ordered under Directive X/15/KYC to terminate all operations related to high-energy transmutation of Au, Bi, Pb, or any other element, and destroy all records of such operations.

### DOCUMENT 9

Excerpt from the journal of Dmitri Leonidovich Sherbatov.
15 April 1990 Goryachinsk

Another sad day for the Soviet Union. We harm ourselves when, for whatever reasons, we try to hold back scientific advances. My personal reverses follow a pattern. I think of Sergei Nitkin, whom we all knew at the Dubna plasma laboratory. He designed a chamber to trace atomic particles through the bubbles they make in liquid hydrogen. Construction was started on our bubble chamber years before any were built in the West. But ours was never completed. Liquid hydrogen was said to be too dangerous. Yet it was a false problem, thought up by the little minds of petty clerks. Never did it faze the Americans. Two of their physicists later won Nobel prizes for discovering and designing our bubble chamber.

We all remember the Synchrophasatron. It was the prize accelerator at Dubna with a potential for making first-class discoveries. But our planners were only interested in the accelerator, not the discoveries. They forgot that the accelerator is only a tool for doing physics. To our horror, we discovered that the walls surrounding the machine confined it so closely that there was no room to move in the experimental apparatus essential to carrying out measurements.

Although we spend a greater percentage of our resources on particle physics than the United States, no high-energy accelerator in the USSR, until Goryachinsk, has ever accomplished an important experiment. We have a strong tradition of physics education in this country, but it is the Glasers, Alvarezes, Richters, and Rubbias of the West who carry off Nobel prizes.

I hesitate to write such things down, but this is the truth. Are they already readying for me the old man's apartment in Gorky?

## DOCUMENT 10
16 April 1990
To: Vladimir Kuznetzov, Minister of Mines
From: Dmitri A. Sherbatov, director, Center of Particle Physics, Goryachinsk

As a loyal Soviet citizen, I am in compliance with directive X/15/KYC.

# 6

On the helicopter to Irkutsk, Rostov sat behind the pilot. Sherbatov's straw hat lay on his lap, along with Glazunov's file. He fingered the hat, tawny, battered, softened by its long soak. He lifted it, sniffed it, tried it on. Even without hair, his head was too big.

In forty-five minutes he was walking from the helipad into the three-story cement-block building on Karl Marx Street that housed the main police headquarters in Irkutsk. Everyone was deferential.

One of the officers immediately reported on the results of the inquiry at Glavokhota. A large party of wealthy German bankers yesterday had commissioned one of the Skyhook helicopters and extra fuel and food, and had embarked on an expedition that would yield much hard currency for the state. Armand Hammer, the American industrialist who was a great friend of the Soviet Union, had taken out a similar party just the week before.

Rostov asked whether anyone had seen the bankers. The officer said he was sure someone had.

"Where did they stay?" Rostov asked.

The agent did not know.

"Find out," Rostov roared. "Bring me back answers."

The officer could find no one at Glavokhota, or in Irkutsk, who had seen the bankers. Every hotel was checked. They apparently did not stay in a hotel. Yet they left $10,000 in cash to finance a hunting trip for three days. They also paid a lot of money for extra drums of fuel.

"The arrangements," said the agent, "were made by a Glavokhota helicopter pilot named Mordecai Simler."

"He is one of the men I want."

"But he is with the group on the hunt."

"There is no hunt," Rostov said.

He gave orders to arrest Boris Shturmak, the general manager of the Irkutsk office of Glavokhota. Whether guilty or not, he would have some explaining to do. That organization needed to be taught a lesson. Its western connections had made it too bloody independent, and its people were assuming airs.

At the same time he ordered the arrest of Glazunov for withholding information from the state and copying classified state files.

A printer ticked out all incoming police messages. Rostov examined the overnight file. Only two reports attracted his interest. One related to a railroad work party at one of the camps near Anamzhak.

"A helicopter bearing markings of the Sakhalin Oil and Gas Company hovered over the tracks near a squad of prisoners. It unloaded several cases on the tracks. Men in the helicopter seemed to be waving and smiling. Then they flew off. Members of the work party opened the cases, which were found to contain cans of the finest beluga caviar and bottles of imported Pommery champagne. Several of the bottles were wrapped in old clothes. All of the provisions had been consigned to Glavokhota in Irkutsk. Guards confiscated most of the cases."

The second described the interception of a radio message from a non-Soviet vessel on the Sea of Okhotsk: just a two-word message, "Zolotaya Gora." The security agency radio monitors were puzzled, and passed it on to the KGB station at Vladivostok.

"Dmitri Leonidovich," he muttered to himself, smiling at the English witticism he had picked up some years ago, "You are too clever by half."

Rostov folded the messages in his pocket.

He entered a black Chaika with darkened windows and was chauffeured past older red birch houses decorated with open work carvings to a nondescript newer cement and cinder-block apartment house at 104 Yuri Gagarin Boulevard.

Still carrying the straw hat, he entered a dark hallway smelling of slightly rotten cabbage, walked up a flight of well-grooved stone steps, and knocked on the door of flat #4. No answer. Inside Rostov could hear arpeggios on a violin. He paused, waited for a break in the music, then knocked harder. The door opened on its safety chain, and peering through the crack were the frightened eyes of a tow-headed boy about ten years old.

"You must be Kyril."

The eyes stared. The boy said nothing.

"Is your mother at home?" Rostov tried to soften the normal gruffness of his voice.

"No, she is not here." Kyril was about to shut the door.

"You see what I am carrying? It belonged to your father."

The boy glanced at the hat in Rostov's hands. There seemed to be a hint of recognition, but he said nothing.

"Your mother will want to see me. May I come in and wait?"

"My mother told me never to let strangers in."

"But I am not a stranger. I am a friend of your father."

"You are not from Goryachinsk."

"Neither is your father. We were friends in Moscow. I have something important to tell your mother about your father."

"Did he lend you his hat?"

"Yes. It protects from the hot sun."

The boy hesitantly lifted the safety chain.

Rostov entered what seemed to be a two-room flat composed of a bedroom and living room that angled off into a tiny kitchen area. Small rectangles of old Oriental rugs lay on the scuffed wooden floor. The walls were dark, covered with a kind of mottled paper that tried to look like marble. On one wall hung a cheap oil painting of a forest scene. Displayed on a bureau were decorative plates and framed photographs. A daybed in the living room was covered with a paisley-wool blanket. Rostov laid Sherbatov's hat on the daybed.

Kyril stood with his violin securely held under his right arm, the bow loosely held and swinging.

"*Babushka* said never put a hat on a bed. Bad luck," Kyril said, removing the hat with his free hand and placing it on the mantel next to a blue vase of freshly cut flowers. He sat stiffly on a wooden chair.

Rostov laughed. "Continue to practice. I love the violin."

The boy didn't move. He stared at the scroll of his violin.

Rostov walked over to the bureau and studied the photos. "I assume these are all friends and relations." Kyril was still silent. Rostov made out Sherbatov and an attractive woman who may have been Kyril's mother, but could not identify any others. A man in one picture was next to

Sherbatov and holding a violin. Possibly the stepbrother Mikhail Abramovich Shifrin?

The boy, still holding the bow, quietly strummed his violin like a guitar.

Beyond the door to the second room was a music stand.

Rostov took a seat on the daybed. Kyril continued strumming.

"I could hear you playing in the hallway. It sounds like you have played for a long time."

"Since I was four." The boy looked down on the violin, but every few seconds cast surreptitious glances up at Rostov.

"Will you play something for me?"

"I don't know anything."

"Please."

The boy shook his head.

"What are you studying now?"

"Airs by Dancla."

"Play me Airs by Dancla."

"I don't know them by heart."

"Play me what you know."

The boy stood and put the violin to his chin, gave the strings a perfunctory tuning, and played all of the Airs of Dancla from memory with perfect intonation.

Rostov applauded. "Bravo, Kyril. That was wonderful. I can see that you have much talent."

The boy looked pleased.

"May I see your violin?"

"You must be careful."

"Yes, I know. I will be very careful."

The boy gingerly handed it over.

"It looks like a very good one."

"It is very old."

Rostov looked at it admiringly, peering inside one of the F-holes below the fingerboard to see whether the maker had left his mark. He read: FECIT CREMONA 1731 CARLO BERGONZI.

"Did your father get it for you?"

"No."

"How did you get it then?"

"My uncle."

"Your uncle must be very rich to be able to give you such a valuable violin."

"He could not bring it with him."

"Where did he go? Far away?" Rostov returned the violin.

The boy did not answer. He began wiping the resin dust from the strings and the bright, shimmering wood around the bridge. He seemed uncomfortable and suddenly retreated to the other room, positioning himself in front of the music stand. Shortly after a burst of arpeggios, a key turned in the front door.


AT THE SIGHT of Rostov she started. Tanya was a European Russian. She wore a light cotton dress and red kerchief over her hair, and carried a battered, cheap-looking plastic briefcase.

Rostov rose from the daybed and extended his hand in greeting. "Your son let me in. He has been a perfect host."

"Who are you?" She glared at him, ignoring the hand.

"I need to talk to you. It has to do with your former husband."

"Who are you?" she repeated in a louder voice.

"State security." He pulled out a red KGB identification card bearing his name, his photo in a major's uniform, and ID number 04036.

"That is your Chaika in front?"

He nodded.

She now looked more frightened than angry. She tossed her briefcase on a faded damask chair opposite the daybed. "I am only an overworked, poor single mother."

"It has nothing to do with you," he said smoothly. "Please sit down."

"Please, don't tell me to sit down in my own home," she said, still trying to collect herself.

She rushed to Kyril. He had the violin again tucked under his arm and was standing in the doorway to the second room watching the scene. She hugged the boy, then disengaging, addressed him sharply.

"I told you never to let anyone in the apartment."

"But the man said he knew Papa." The boy was about to cry.

Rostov intervened. "Kyril is right, Comrade Sherbatova. I told him I knew his father and I needed to speak to you."

Her eyes stayed glued on the boy. "Darling, no matter what they say, from now on you must not answer the door. Whoever it is can wait outside until Mama returns." She let the words sink in. Then she patted his head. "Now go back into the room and continue practicing. Close the door. Mama loves you."

She removed her kerchief letting a waterfall of wheat-colored hair tumble over her shoulders and ample bosom. Beads of sweat glistened on her brow.

Better than in the photo, Rostov thought: sultry eyes, a wide mouth, flushed cheeks and, yes, well-turned legs.

She collected herself. From her pocketbook, she withdrew something that looked like a thick Popsicle stick. It opened into a lavender fan, and she began fanning herself.

"Now what about my former husband?" she asked.

"I am sorry to have surprised you." Rostov's voice was as appeasing as he could make it. He offered her a Pamir. She hesitated, as if the choice were one of the major decisions in her life, and then accepted. "Why not?" she murmured. He lit it with a western Zippo lighter. Both were still standing.

"May I at least sit down?" he said.

She nodded, recovering her composure. "You will appreciate I don't like people entering my home unannounced."

"I certainly agree. One cannot be too careful these days. So much hooliganism. Still, you must make certain allowances for state security." He resumed his place on the daybed.

She dislodged her briefcase and sat in the chair opposite. Her eyes suddenly fell on the straw hat on the mantel. She looked perplexed. "Is that yours?" she asked.

Rostov cleared his throat, searching for an appropriate funereal timbre in his voice.

"I knew Dmitri Leonidovich in Goryachinsk. For the last twenty-four hours we have been searching for him. It seems that he has disappeared after rowing a small boat out into the far reaches of the lake." He pointed to the hat on the mantel. "That hat was fished out of the water. The oars of his boat were also still floating. No signs of anything else."

"Oh, dear. That is not good news."

"I am sorry."

"We were divorced. I stopped loving him but I still felt—feel—some regard for him—at least concern—he is the father of my son." Her face looked worried. "He sent support."

Rostov gazed at her, said nothing.

"You haven't told Kyril yet, I hope."

Rostov shook his head.

"Good. I will tell him."

She picked up the hat, weighed it, looked inside, fingered irregularities in the sun-bleached straw.

"Yes, this must be his hat." Her face was pensive, but showed little emotion. "There are not many like it around here. I gave it to him soon after we were married. It belonged to Chinese peasants. My father brought it back from a trip to Hunan."

"Your father?"

"He was in the diplomatic service."

"Really? What was his name? Perhaps I knew him."

"Piotr Petrov. He died some years ago. My mother lives on a small pension in Moscow."

"Oh." Rostov made a notation in his black book. "Did you travel with your father?"

"Never outside socialist countries. We lived once in Bulgaria."

"And you gave the hat to your husband to protect him from the sun when he went out fishing?"

"Exactly. He loved to fish. I think he preferred fish to humans. He had an affinity with the cold-blooded."

He studied her as she leaned against the mantel still fingering the hat. Her flushed cheeks gave her an added allure. She looked a lot better than his Evenk housekeeper. "I gather then you were not that fond of fishing yourself."

"Fishing bores me. As a bride, I used to accompany Dmitri, but it was not to my liking. Too windy, too wet, too cold, or too hot. Nothing to do for hours but hold a pole out over the water and wait. Wait for a poor fish to swallow a hook. The fish is miserable. You are miserable. I had better things to do with my time. But Kyril and his father have fished together many times. Kyril even cut short an outing with the Young Pioneers two weeks ago to be with his father."

She asked Rostov to give her a few minutes to try to explain the situation to the boy, who had resumed arpeggio and scale practice in the other room.

Rostov reexamined the photos on the bureau. When she returned, he asked her how the boy took the news.

She seemed perplexed. "I don't think he understood it. Or it didn't sink in. He didn't seem upset. No reaction at all. He was more interested in what Boris Yefimovich, his violin teacher, will say during tomorrow's lesson."

"You would think he would express some feelings about his father," Rostov said.

"Maybe it takes a while for the news to sink in. I said only he had not been found after a day on the lake."

"He and his father were close?"

"Yes."

"Strange," Rostov said, smiling enigmatically. "And the man who gave Kyril the violin. Tell me about him."

"You must have had a good chat." She resumed her position on the chair. Kyril was practicing again. "He was Dmitri's older half-brother. Thirteen years older. For much of their lives they lost contact. Then in more recent years they started seeing each other more frequently. I met Misha only a few times when he came out to visit Dmitri and give violin lessons to Kyril. . . ."

"He was that free to travel?" Rostov interrupted.

"Free? He was not tied down to an orchestra."

"Financially?" Rostov persisted.

"Perhaps."

"What were his dealings with the Jewish community?"

"Perhaps some sort of leader," Tanya conceded. "Misha mentioned he made speeches to synagogues, bar mitzvahs, poor relatives' clubs. He was especially popular because he also played his violin before the same groups."

"He had support from international groups?"

Tanya shrugged. "I am not interested in those matters."

Rostov rose to look at the photos again. There was Misha, a tentative smile on a fleshy face, looking down at his shoes. Next to him was Dmitri, unsmiling, stiff, topped by a mop of black hair. The fat man and the thin man.

"Where is Misha now?"

"Israel. His exit papers came through a few months back."

"Did you ever hear of Mordecai Simler and Lev Geldman?"

"No. I personally don't know many Jews."

Rostov turned his attention to one of the older photos, a girl with blond hair, no more than five or six years old. She was seated on a swing, wearing a pleated dress and shiny shoes, and her eyes were staring at something in the distance.

"Who is that?" he asked.

"Their mother, Irina Leonidovna Sherbatova, as a little girl. She died two years ago, just before Dmitri and I separated. Cancer. She was a mathematical economist in the ministry of industrial manpower. She married Shifrin, the father of Misha, then divorced him for Sherbatov, the father of Dmitri."

"Many divorces."

"That is the way it is today in Russia."

"So it is." His voice trailing, he turned from the photos to the forest painting on the wall: towering birches, birds circling overhead, mountains in the distance. He stared at the painting, saying nothing. In the next room, the violin soared into the higher registers with a series of pizzicatos and double stops.

Tanya finally broke the silence.

"I was outside the circle. They did not trust me very much. I think that was one of the problems of our marriage."

He crushed his cigarette in an ashtray.

"Did Dmitri have many friends?"

"No. He did not make friends easily. I was the gregarious one. For a long time even before we split, we lived separate lives. Our only common interest was Kyril."

"Why did you marry him?"

"Oh, why does one do many things? I was young, still a student at Moscow University. He taught me calculus. Although he was already doing advanced nuclear research, they made him teach one class a week at the university. He hated standing up before a class, and soon got out of it because his other work was too important. I think I was the only student who didn't laugh at his tic. He invited me for tea and told me how much science meant to him and what it could do for the world. I found his intellectual passions physically exciting."

"But it must not have been easy to live with the tic. I know it's not contagious, but didn't you fear you would wake up one day and get it, too."

"I still feel some guilt. The tic is hard to look at, impossible to ignore. I thought I could make it go away. I almost did. I made him relax. But later he would again become tense. He refused to accept things the way they are. He said Russia had to change. Nothing ever worked and nothing ever fit. *Nye dyestvuyet. Nye gaditsa.* He liked Siberia because things were newer out here. There was a chance to start again."

"But you do not like Siberia."

"Life is too primitive for me. It is hard. In winter, my feet are always cold and damp, no matter how high and thick my boots. But the work, though not very remunerative, is good."

"You are at the Irkutsk Economic Institute?"

"As usual, you are well informed." She smiled a little nervously. "I have been there ever since Dmitri and I came out here to live about ten years ago. I am in the group of microeconomic studies. We prepare mathematical models on the impact of economic or industrial developments—natural gas in Yakutia, the Angara network of power stations, the Neryungri coal deposits, the BAM."

"It is unusual that you and Dmitri's mother, Irina Leonidovna, were in the same line of work."

"Yes, Dmitri used to say he had two mothers and could understand what neither of them did. I had worked for his mother in Moscow. Dmitri helped me get the job."

"I am sure your work is very interesting."

"Not nearly as interesting as yours, Comrade Rostov." Her eyes seemed cool, yet deep and inviting. She continued fanning herself. "I miss Moscow, Comrade Rostov. I grew up there, my mother lives there. They have promised that I shall return. . . ."

The violin had stopped for a moment, then resumed.

"You may call me Ilya." He watched the slow rise and fall of her breasts inside the floral patterns of her light cotton dress.

She tightened her legs modestly and returned a smile he interpreted as not unfriendly.

He made no sign of leaving. It seemed as if she did not mind his staying. He was not much to look at, but he was from Moscow and certainly had the power to do things for her.

"But I am being rude." She rose quickly. "Let me make you some tea."

"Tea would be very nice."

In the service, the best assignments always were those that mixed business and pleasure. Although he was now tiring of Kyril's violin playing, of the same notes tirelessly played over and over again, he was intrigued by the woman. The daughter of a diplomat, she was definitely not one of the unwashed locals, but almost a part of his extended family. He was anxious to find out more about her, both as a key to physicist Sherbatov, now with increasing certainty defector Sherbatov, and for herself.

He was conscious of his bald pate and pushed hair from the side of his head to cover it. He pulled in his belly, suddenly conscious of buttons popped and not resewn.

He followed her into the kitchen. As she was rinsing the teapot, he placed a hand on her hand.

"*V dukhi*?" he asked. "Are you in a good enough mood?"

"For what?" she asked with a startled expression.

"For going out."

"Out where?"

She stared at his hand, which was still covering hers on the sink. "Are you arresting me?"

"Perm thirty-nine or the Baikal Hotel dining room." He released her hand. "Someday Kyril will be a great violinist, but for the moment I prefer you without accompaniment, except perhaps for a bottle of Napareuli. We have much to discuss."

"How do you know I don't already have something to do tonight?"

"You prefer the camps then." He exited the kitchen and retrieved Dmitri's hat.

She wasn't sure whether it was a joke. "Do I at least have time to change my clothes? I must prepare dinner for Kyril."

"Be ready in an hour."

# 7

During the late-afternoon meeting in the White House East Sitting Room adjoining the Oval Office, President Halleck sipped a Smirnoff martini straight up. "Maybe Marx was right," he cracked, flexing arms that had just been lifting weights in the White House fitness center, "and it's time to tile the world's lavatories with gold."

The inner circle of aides dutifully smiled. The President looked askance on those who didn't appreciate his pleasantries. Despite the summery disposition he presented to outsiders, they knew another side to the man: egocentric, mean, vindictive.

The President sat in a brocade wing-back next to the Theodore Roosevelt cherrywood coffee table. His term started just after the collapse of the Soviet Union, and he badly wanted to run again. The half-empty martini glass and a refill pitcher lay on a silver tray. At the table's other flank was an empty wing-back for the absent Vice-President. There were any number of variations to a joke that the Vice-President did nothing.

The Secretary of State occupied all of a Victorian sofa whose designer had forgotten about the needs of the human back. Other senior officials perched on straight-back Sheraton chairs, or the cane-back swivel chairs that were the latest addition of the White House curator to accentuate the nineteenth-century motif demanded by Rose, the President's wife. She studied decorative arts at Northwestern, where they had met. Everyone in the room except the President wore a dark suit and tie. The President was in a sporty argyle sweater and tieless shirt.

Outside the windows, the lawn beyond the fountain of Presidents'

Park, a lush mid-September green, sloped gently toward the Ellipse and the Reflecting Pond. The marble obelisk to the founder of the nation gleamed in the background, a linchpin in the axle of the universe.

Orville Halleck, or just plain Hal, as he urged people to call him since early childhood, was a bear of a man, with a large chunky face, dyed (Just For Men gel) black hair, facile smile, wily black eyes, and a mellifluous baritone. Despite workouts, by sixty-one he'd added about twenty pounds since his days at Northwestern as the country's most effective linebacker and 1954 Heisman Trophy winner. He toyed briefly with going into pro-football, but chose law school instead.

His parents were immigrants from Moravia. Through a cousin in Chicago, his dad had landed a job in the Department of Parks and Recreation. Quickly learning the political ropes, friendly old Joe Halleck rose in the Kelly-Nash and later Daley political machines. Joe distributed Thanksgiving turkeys, remembered birthdays, sent flowers to funerals, and slapped dollar bills in people's hands outside the ward polling station on voting days. Consistently, the vote came in over 95 percent Democratic. To Joe, it should have been 100 percent. He never found the sons of bitches who took the money and voted Republican.

The old man saw what the political arts could do for the good life and instilled an appreciation in his son, whom he named after one of the Wright brothers. He told his cronies, "I want the kid to fly."

Young Hal gave up labor-law practice to run for Congress, beat the older incumbent in a primary, handily won the election, and now was going into his third decade in Washington, and, he hoped, his second presidential term. In his early days as a member of the House of Representatives he had been a firebrand populist, demanding easier money, fair trade with Japan, more environmental cleanup, universal health care, a higher minimum wage, plant closing notification, antiscab legislation, and more occupational safety.

He had presidential ambitions, but McGovern had demonstrated the futility of running from the left, Goldwater from the right. So in the Senate, Hal Halleck courted business, and slowly positioned himself in the great flaccid center of American politics. He discovered fiscal responsibility, deregulation, elimination of waste, fraud and corruption. He talked about government as the Problem, not the Solution. He curbed earlier demands for environmental cleanup, restrained his bashing of Japan. He was silent on increasing the minimum wage, expressed concern about overall labor costs, noting if they rose too steeply they could hurt employment.

He bridged the ideological poles by promising to end class warfare and create a new coalition of business, labor, and government—what he called "Tripartism." Urging Cooperation Not Confrontation, he promised economic growth, job creation, infrastructure renewal, and unflagging efforts to "put America back on the front burner."

Now about to start a reelection campaign, he worried about a Fed chairman whose keenness to fight inflation threatened to keep interest rates too high and choke growth. He also fretted about slowdowns in Europe and Japan that could hurt the U.S. recovery, and about sudden oil price increases as in the 1970s that had crushed both the Nixon and Carter presidencies. He told his advisers, "I want no economic surprises."

PROFESSOR HILLSDALE P. LANDOVER JR., director of the Stanford Linear Accelerator Center (SLAC), figured his presence at this meeting must have something to do with Chernobyl and the recent article in *Positronics,* the nuclear industry trade journal. The call came only yesterday from Harry G. Spitz, the President's chief of staff, and a former chief counsel on the House Science and Technology Subcommittee. The professor, who was on advisory committees to the Department of Energy, had testified on four occasions before Spitz's panel, and the two men had struck up a casual friendship. Spitz admired Landover's ability to explain esoterica so that even the representatives of Congress could understand.

Spitz wanted him at a White House meeting pronto, but refused on the phone to say why. All he disclosed was that the President needed his advice and counsel on an urgent matter of national security and that people would meet him at the airport.

Though a frequent visitor to the halls of Congress, Landover had never yet been asked to the White House. It was an invitation one didn't refuse, like an offer to sit at the right hand of God. He canceled all engagements in Palo Alto, including his weekly evening of duplicate bridge with Kate, and grabbing his overnight bag, flew to National Airport.

Two men in dark suits met him at the Delta gate. One, very tall, with aristocratic bearing, who introduced himself as Greg Oberling, seemed the friendlier. The other, Cyrus Richards, looked like Savonarola and was missing his right index finger. They were vague about where they worked.

On the drive into Washington, his guides only made small talk, and there were long silences. The physicist speculated that Spitz or one of his people had seen the *Positronics* interview. The write-up had turned out well. The reporter, a pleasant chap named Andreas Vogl, living in Zurich, asked him whether a Chernobyl-like disaster could happen in the West. Landover replied No, and the resulting article quoted him accurately.

". . . The Soviet reactor used water for cooling and absorbing some of the neutrons. But the reactor had a tendency to overheat, turning water into steam. Less water absorbed fewer neutrons, leaving more to fuel the chain reaction, making the reactor unstable, and, in the blowout of 1986, uncontrollable. Three Mile Island was completely different. When a valve failed to close, radioactive fission products escaped, causing excessive heat, but no chain reaction, and no deaths . . ."

He felt less inhibited with Vogl than with his graduate students who might try to flaunt their brilliance by challenging him. The reporter seemed only interested in eliciting information. The questions helped clarify his own thinking.

Landover, who received laudatory calls after publication from people he hardly knew, enjoyed the ego trip. But he also felt as if he were making a contribution to the world by breaking barriers. The gap was widening between the scientist and layman. Scientists could hardly talk to nonscientists, or even to scientists outside their fields. Research chemists barely comprehended nuclear physicists. Landover felt like an emissary shuttling between worlds in a C.P. Snow novel.

Landover was a rangy, slightly stoop-shouldered man with a wide face and high cheekbones. Edgy brows arched over squinty Clint Eastwood eyes. An unruly shock of slightly graying brown hair and a certain prowess on the tennis court made him look younger than his forty-eight years.

His parents met at the University of Oregon, and he was born in the university town of Eugene. His mother later taught math at the local high school. His father parlayed a love of internal combustion engines into a prosperous chain of auto garages, and along the way invented a better hydraulic rod for lifting trunks and hoods. Landover, always interested in how things worked, learned to take a car engine apart and put it together again before he was twelve.

A good student, he went to the best schools: Lawrenceville Academy, Princeton, then MIT, where he earned his doctorate in physics. He joined the Los Alamos National Laboratory as part of a team working on wake-field acceleration, in which one batch of particles was dragged along by the electromagnetic wake of a preceding batch, as a car is pulled along behind a moving truck. It was the key to bringing down the size and cost of new ultrapowerful accelerators. He had been at Stanford for the past thirteen years, and some colleagues thought him in line for a Nobel prize for his work on a new quark.

The black White House Chrysler, lead foot on the accelerator, tore up the George Washington Memorial Parkway, across the Arlington Memorial Bridge, around the Tidal Basin, and past the OAS and DAR buildings and the majestic lions of the Corcoran Gallery. It stopped momentarily at the 17th Street gate, then swept into the cocoon of the South Lawn. As the car pulled into the Rose Garden driveway, Landover couldn't resist.

"Was it *Positronics?*" he asked eagerly.

"What?" Oberling looked mystified.

Richards grunted something incomprehensible. The two men leapt out. "Just follow us," Richards said.

They were in the backyard of a gracious Georgian mansion, all white and cream colored, in sylvan splendor. Well-tended rose garden. Shrubs of rhododendrons, box hedges, and hydrangea. Cardinals flitted between the branches of the two magnificent tulip magnolias. Immaculate lawn. But he knew you didn't stroll on the lawn because sensors would relentlessly ping the security screens. On the roof, he'd read somewhere, were SAMs.

The driveway extended to a canopied walkway to the back door to the house. Men in dark suits, all seemingly hard of hearing, scurried along paths and porticoes. Traffic noise was muffled. His guides ushered him upstairs to the East Sitting Room just as the President made his crack about Marx and gold lavatories.

The remark puzzled Landover. He was hardly a gold expert. If the issue wasn't Chernobyl and nuclear safety, why then was he here? One thing he thought he remembered from Princeton was that it was Lenin, not Marx, who wanted golden bathrooms after victory of the Communist revolution. Should he correct the President? He forgot Trivial Pursuits as Spitz made the introductions.

The President shook the professor's hand heartily, motioned him to take an empty chair near the window. Landover was dressed as an academic. His seersucker, shiny, wrinkled and boxy, his too-wide tie, askew, scuffed Oxfords, brown instead of de rigueur black, stood out amid the assembled Armanis, Guccis, and Puccis of the cabinet officers.

There were no chairs for Oberling and Richards, who stood inconspicuously in back. Richards still looked sour. Landover wondered what was eating him.

A stiff black man in a tuxedo asked Landover if he wanted a drink.

Why the hell not? Everyone else seemed to have one. "Scotch on the rocks," he said forcefully.

"A preference of Scotch, sir?"

"Chivas."

As soon as the man left, the President bore right in. He handed Landover an EYES ONLY piece of paper.

"Read this, Professor, and tell us what you think."

Landover perched near the windows under a portrait of Woodrow Wilson. He wished he had his drink. He crossed his legs, then noting not one other hairy calf, immediately uncrossed them.

As Landover perused the sheet, people suddenly stopped talking. It was like a fermata, the President holding the silence as a conductor might to signal a new symphonic motif. Landover felt people staring at him.

Whoever wrote this knew little about physics, Landover discovered, but the basic message was clear. He put the paper down, met the eyes of the President, who had resumed his seat and taken another sip from his drink.

"We've known for a long time you can make gold by bombarding bismuth, or even lead. The problem is to do it in a way that's commercially feasible. You'd need tremendous amounts of energy."

He shot a gaze around the room, suddenly very self-conscious. This was no graduate seminar. Anything said here could have enormous consequences.

"A few years back," Landover continued, "some physicists at the Lawrence Berkeley Laboratory fooled around with transmutation reactions in their BEVELAC accelerator. I remember Dave Morrisey from Berkeley saying that in all their work, and they bombarded a lot of projectiles, they produced gold that was worth less than one billionth of a cent."

The President had resumed his seat. He leaned an elbow into the arm of his wing-back, smiling a sunny smile. "Do you think the Israelis could have made a breakthrough, Professor?"

"I don't know, Mr. President."

"We'd like you to find out. Undertake some sleuthing for us. Go to

Israel and get us the straight story. We have to know for certain whether
this thing is real or not."

"Mr. President, can't you just call up the prime minister? From what I
read, you talk to leaders all the time . . ."

"We got this through irregular channels, Professor. I can't call him up
and tell him we've been spying on him. Their nose is still out of joint for
what we did to Pollard a few years back. Remember, Pollard gave them
our secrets, and we gave him the business. Stiff prison sentence. Solitary.
He's still there, and they don't like it. . . ."

The President, stretching, looked down at the bald eagle in the golden
carpet, then slowly around the room. ". . . No, I can't deal with the
sensitivities of an enraged Israeli prime minister, not in an election year."

The stiff man finally returned with Landover's drink on a silver tray. It
smelled like Chivas, tasted like Chivas. Landover gulped a large mouthful. Another fermata.

Rising again, the President approached Landover. Ignoring everyone
else in the room, he intimately tossed an arm over his guest's shoulders
and walked him to the great bay window. It was an always effective
technique picked up from Lyndon Johnson.

"It's a great country out there, Professor, and I have a great responsibility. I can't take any chances with America's economic security. . . ."

Landover could feel the heat from the man's arm. The animal energy.
The President went on, speaking slowly: "We've got a stash of gold at
Fort Knox and other places. Other countries have their hoards. If it's all
suddenly worthless, if gold is a glut on the market, that could be a shock
to the economic system, bigger than all the oil price increases in the
1970s. Force majeure. . . ."

A small man in a tight-collared, monogrammed shirt stiffened at the
use of the legal term. The two men standing in back winced.

". . . It's an economic surprise we don't need," the President went
on, ignoring the barely perceptible reactions. "If they actually can produce cheap gold, we would need contingency plans, something to neu-
tralize the effects, boost the money supply, whatever. We need the
intelligence, Professor. I don't want to scare people. But neither do I
want the Halleck administration to usher in a world depression. . . ."

The President again drew close to his guest, smiling tentatively. His
Beefeater's breath was rancid. "We've booked you a plane tonight."

Landover felt even more uncomfortable. He'd planned an overnight
trip to Washington, not an extravaganza in the Middle East.

"It's pretty tense over there, I understand, Mr. President," he blurted out, "people being killed in the streets, bombings, buses blown up. . . ."

"All exaggerated, Professor. The *Washington Post* and *New York Times* and TV do a good job in the hype department. It's safer in Israel than Chicago . . ." He smiled.

"I run fourteen hundred people at the SLAC, and we're kind of busy right now. . . ." It sounded ridiculous in front of the President of the United States.

The President's eyes locked on his.

"Of course, sir, I would be happy to do what I can."

Which was all the President needed. His eyes diverted, twinkling merrily. "That's marvelous, Professor. Just what we were hoping. Consider it a little sabbatical to the Holy Land. A government-paid holiday . . ." The President winked. "Full expenses. Anything you need. Back in a couple of days, a week at most."

The President looked at the Vice-President's empty chair. "You've got a deputy director back there, don't you, Professor?"

Landover nodded.

"So get him to do a little work for a change."

The room broke out in reflexive laughter.

# 8

THE PRESIDENT SEEMED well pleased. He glanced at Spitz, sitting on one of the Sheraton chairs. ". . . Now that Professor Landover is on our team, I think we can all breathe more easily."

The chief of staff, round-faced with rimless glasses, looked like a cat in a bowl of cream. His chief rival in the administration, Admiral Carlos P. Jackman, the CIA director, twitched in his Sheraton, glowering at Richards and Oberling in the corner.

The Spitz-Jackman rivalry was the talk of Washington. That the two could have joined the administration was something of a miracle, showing the magnitude of its political reach. Though both men were longtime supporters of Hal Halleck, they had little else in common. Spitz, a lawyer from Detroit whose job on the Hill came through Democratic labor connections, was the tie to the old Hal of House days and sought to pull the administration to the left; Admiral Jackman, conservative, navy, patriotic, with close links to business, represented the Hal of the Senate, tugging from the right.

The admiral was proud, fastidious, Annapolis, a veteran of Naval Intelligence during Vietnam, later E Ring of Pentagon, and a Georgian. Though he liked to call himself "just a little country boy," he was a political operator who loved to pull strings behind the scenes, which advanced both his military and postmilitary careers. He came into the administration from a San Diego conglomerate, Paradigm Systems Inc. But his relationship with the President started while still at the Pentagon, when he outspokenly supported then Senator Halleck's bill to cut nuclear submarines in the navy.

That stand had little to do with conviction. It did not make him popular at General Dynamics, whose Electric Boat division made all the nuclear submarines. But other companies praised his courage to speak out, including Paradigm, whose founder, Walter Goddard, had been his Annapolis classmate. Most important, he came into alliance with a rising politician, who might with a little string pulling reach the White House.

Admiral Jackman wanted more than to push Pentagon paperweights, more than to sell Paradigm systems. In the autumn of his career, he was bored. He knew the presidency was beyond his own personal reach, but figured he could ride on a coattail, get a command, and at least have something interesting to do before packing it all in.

Despite different backgrounds, the admiral and Halleck hit it off. Each knew what the other wanted. No competition between them, no confusion. Halleck wanted the presidency, and the admiral helped him to it by drawing him to the political center and pulling strings in the business community. The admiral wanted CIA, where he could play games and pull strings to his heart's content.

Though Admiral Jackman enjoyed a close personal relationship with the President, today that relationship was strained. Richards, the CIA deputy director for operations, and Oberling, the national intelligence officer for warning, rivals for the top job once Jackman retired, had been too damned dismissive about the piece of raw, unevaluated intelligence received from Tel Aviv. Failing to comprehend the President's consuming passion for economics, they hadn't even moved to have the intelligence properly evaluated. The agency had no fallback position; it hadn't covered its backside.

Spitz's recruitment of Landover and the President's enthusiastic acceptance of him for a mission the agency itself should have thought of were accusatory fingers at CIA shortcomings for all to see.

Neither was the admiral happy with the President's flaunting of the term Force Majeure. For years in utmost secrecy the director of Central Intelligence operated at his complete discretion an assassination unit known as Force Majeure. Presidents were aware of it, but for deniability kept their distance. Halleck's use of the term, even in a different context, seemed to signal pique with the agency. This President never said or did anything accidentally.

Those in the loop called it FMB or simply the "accident bureau." Its victims leaned too far from high places, collided with buses, suffered sudden heart attacks, met unexplained brake failures on highways, or were prey to muggings, holdups, carjackings and other acts of random violence. FMB had terminated Allende, Lumumba, Count Bernadotte, Dag Hammarskjöld. It botched Castro and Saddam Hussein. So far. Generally, it targeted obscure people, who made hardly a ripple in the press: Soviet double agents, obscure aides to Qaddafi, Saddam's cousin from Tikrit.

The admiral cleared his throat. He was wearing a dark Armani herringbone and a tight-collared monogrammed shirt. He puffed out his chest self-importantly, which made him look like a cormorant with a collar around his neck trying impossibly to swallow the fish.

"We're going to find out what's going on over there, Mr. President." From his diminutive stature bellowed an incongruous voice: big, resonant, hard as the teak trim of the sailboats he sailed in the Chesapeake.

"Our man Shepherd in Tel Aviv smoked this thing out. He's on call and is ready to steer the professor to the source . . ." He tugged at gold cuff links on the sleeves of his monogrammed shirt. ". . . My own gut feeling is don't count our gold out just yet. I go back far enough to remember people saying that atomic energy would make electricity too cheap to meter. Well, I just got my electricity bill. And it metered a lot . . ." He paused for laughter that didn't materialize, anxiously cleared his throat.

". . . Science has promised other things that never arrived. Cold fusion is hot confusion. High-temperature superconductivity was supposed to deliver the 500-mile-per-hour train. But we're still waiting at the station. . . ."

"We have to be ready for any contingency, Carlos, you know that." The President swished his little finger in his martini and licked it with relish. "Where was the CIA when oil prices were hiked in the seventies? That's what really did Nixon in."

"Of course, Mr. President." The admiral seethed. Richards and Oberling had gotten him into this mess. They had better get him out.

The chairman of the Federal Reserve Board, Dr. John Gray, in one of the cane-backed chairs, swiveled around to face the President. "Gold is a valuable tool for us at the Fed in helping manage the dollar. The dollar price of gold is the market's perception of the future value of the dollar, in other words, whether inflation will make big inroads in that value. I'd hate to see us lose that tool."

Dr. Gray, a long-necked, unsmiling man of the old school, in his midsixties, spoke phlegmatically. His leonine head was crowned with a mat of white hair. He was wearing thick horn-rimmed glasses and a golden watch chain that dangled from the vest of his navy blue suit. Because of his agency's independence, he was not a member of the administration or a regular at White House meetings. But he attended the most important ones. His job was a series of delicate balancing acts. To fight inflation, he had to keep interest rates high enough to restrain money supply growth, yet guard against making money so tight as to arrest economic growth. When the economy was in an upswing he usually boosted interest rates.

"Gray takes the punch bowl away," people joked, "just when the party starts to get good." What they didn't joke about was Gray's enormous influence over the economy.

He had been appointed by the previous administration, and his term didn't expire for another two years. So the Halleckites were stuck with him. Yet he tried to be accommodating. He had gone some months now without hiking Fed Funds. The word was that despite his age, he wanted his term renewed. He would do anything to stay on the right hand of God.

Dr. Gray adjusted his glasses, grimacing slightly. As he spoke, he folded his hands into his vest pockets as if subtly calling attention to the Phi Beta Kappa key on the golden chain.

"We and other central banks now use information embodied in the gold price to influence open market operations," he intoned. "A falling gold price suggests deflation. So we inject bank reserves. If gold is rising, that suggests inflation and we withdraw reserves.

"Ironically, this news of synthetic gold comes just as the BIS is helping us run scenarios that give gold an even bigger monetary role. Many would like to see restoration of the pre-1971 gold exchange standard, under which countries could exchange excess dollars for gold at a fixed price. The system worked well until it was overwhelmed by inflation from the Vietnamese War. In my view, the gold exchange system gives us greater economic stability. But it restricts political freedom to manage the economy."

The President stifled a yawn. "Thank you, Dr. Gray, for explaining things so clearly."

Robert Quincy Green, the national security adviser, a former Marine general, with cold blue eyes and a compact frame honed by daily hour-long jogs along the Potomac embankment, was getting edgy with all this heavy-duty economics. He shifted his weight on the sofa and began speaking slowly, eyes on the President, index finger-waving as if he were lecturing at the War College:

"I think we must look at reasons behind the leak. If they can make artificial gold and haven't told us about it officially, then the leak means deep divisions over there—major policy choices that must be hard for them. Someone wants to bring us into the debate, presumably hoping we'll influence his side of the argument.

"Assume they do have this process. It's as if they've suddenly won the lottery after being on welfare for years. But then there are big questions of how to spend the money, especially when no one is supposed to know they've got it. Does it go to the military? Build new homes and infrastructure for Russian immigrants? Buy new capital investment for industry? Repay loans to us? End up in the pockets of the elite?"

"I would tell them to put it into West Bank and Gaza Strip redevelopment," the secretary of state interjected. Robertson Cato was florid-faced with puffy features, designer suspenders, and a rep tie. He stretched his arms across the back of the sofa almost touching General Green. "Peace is the economic growth."

The President made a few notes on a yellow legal pad. He liked it when his people batted things around. He was the judge arbitrating between battling attorneys.

"Maybe they need some help." The words came across the room from another of the leather-backed chairs. The chairman of the Council of Economic Advisers, Donald Makins, was square-faced, tanned from recent windsurfing off Virgin Gorda, athletic-looking. He pulled on one of the sleeves of his leather-patched tweed jacket as he spoke.

"Remember, if they have all this new gold, they've got to be awfully careful about selling it. The gold market is small, not much more than ten to twenty million dollars of transactions in a normal day. It can't absorb large quantities from Israel, or anywhere else, without prices falling dramatically. And Israel has no gold mines. So market people might start asking questions. They, or at least a faction over there, could want us to help them market the gold."

Treasury Secretary Richard Aschenberg, sitting near the President, spoke for the first time. His crutches lay on the floor from a recent back operation. He was tall with a long, skeletal face and pointed jaw. As he spoke he rubbed his hands together nervously. He had come with index cards that lay idle on his lap. He gave the admiral a challenging stare.

"If it's not authentic, why should they be wasting our time, even unofficially? No, I have more respect for them than that. I think something big has happened, and I'm afraid it presents some major economic problems. Let me cite a few numbers . . ." He picked up one of the cards. ". . . World holdings of gold are about two billion ounces, more than half in the central banks. So when gold went from $35 to over $850 an ounce there was tremendous wealth creation. You might say the world was richer by $1.5 trillion. As for the U.S., we've got more gold in our reserves than any other government, at market prices nearly $100 billion. Individual U.S. citizens hold another 3,000 tons of gold, more even than the Swiss, worth $60 billion. Even though explicit linkage with the dollar has long been severed, and we officially value gold at only a nominal $42 an ounce, our gold holdings still implicitly back the dollar.

"A nation's wealth is many things, the education of its people, productivity, powerful computer chips, the technology of the information revolution. Vive le Microsoft libre . . ." Appreciative chuckles broke the monologue. ". . . But you can't do anything without some form of payment, and you need something that people trust, that has a value beyond the nation state, beyond currencies or even baskets of currencies like the SDR.

"With the benefit of hindsight, we can agree that we have followed pretty strange gold policies. In the late 1960s, Nixon and Connally were fighting General de Gaulle over the price of gold. De Gaulle wanted it to rise to challenge the dollar. We tried to hold the $35 price, and then when we couldn't control the markets, we tried to show we couldn't care less whether we had any gold or not. The Carter people actually sold off some of the stuff, but Mike Blumenthal soon realized it was a mistake. Our gold added luster to the dollar. No one since has even whispered the idea again.

"France, Italy, Switzerland, and Holland hold large gold reserves. Gold in the reserve stock of Germany and Japan is rising. The European Union pegs its Euro to gold. Japan, Taiwan, Malaysia, and Indonesia are all accumulating. The Russians want to make their ruble partially convertible into gold. So should gold prices suddenly plummet, as they most certainly will once markets get wind of this Israeli development, I am afraid that in the place of wealth creation we will have wealth destruction, a lack of liquidity, a good old-fashioned financial panic. Without countermeasures, it could mean an economic tidal wave."

The silence was broken only by the trickle of the Beefeater's dividend the President was pouring from his martini pitcher into his glass. He looked up at his assembled advisers and said, slowly punching out each word:

"No tidal wave on my watch."

No one spoke. Landover thought of King Canute.

Suddenly, the President's mood changed. He was beaming. He said he was reminded of a story. He begged the indulgence of the secretary of the treasury and the chairman of the Council of Economic Advisers because it was a story about economists. They smiled politely.

"A surgeon, engineer, and economist died," the President related, "and were ascending into heaven. But Saint Peter said he had only one spot left, which would go to the man with the oldest profession. 'That's me,' said the surgeon. 'I took care of Adam's rib.' 'But I helped God create order out of chaos,' said the engineer. 'But,' said the economist, 'who created the chaos?' "

Everyone laughed. The President stood up, an appreciative grin on his face, to signal the meeting was over. He had to dress for a dinner for the newest President of Italy, he said apologetically. The ormolu clock with gold leaf on the mantel said 6:34.

The President stared at the clock without moving, as if it reminded him of something. Everyone remained silent and in place.

"Time plays funny tricks on us, doesn't it?" the President mused. "Once there wasn't enough gold in the world, and the metal was a perfect store of value. Now maybe we can make as much of it as we want. Someone once said there are two tragedies in life. One is not to have your wishes granted, and the other is to have them granted."

The President left the room. The meeting was over in less than an hour.

Although Landover was struck by the frankness and informality, he came away let down. Halleck was outwardly charming, but the inside peek at the powerful was disquieting. He had expected an august deliberative group. The reality was that most were just ad hocing it. Everything was loose and boozy. People said anything they wanted. What assurance was there that all the facts had been ascertained, or that the President had not been influenced as much by his martinis as by rational discourse?

Better, Landover thought, not to know the imperfections of the process. Someone—was it Bismarck?—once said it was a mistake to know how either one's laws or sausages are made.

As people were leaving, Admiral Jackman pulled Landover aside. "Our man will meet you at Lod. He's one of the best." The admiral added conspiratorially, "I still think there's nothing to it. I expect you'll be back by the weekend."

Jackman drew away from Landover when he saw Spitz approach.

Spitz was all smiles. "Thanks for taking this on, Professor. You're a real credit to your country."

"You're welcome," said Landover. He didn't know what else to say. He still couldn't believe he'd agreed to do this.

Spitz walked him back to the chauffeured Chrysler sitting in the shade of one of the tulip magnolia trees by the Rose Garden. As they reached the car, Spitz turned to face the professor.

"The President also told me to tell you he is requesting $10 million more for SLAC."

"What?" Landover couldn't believe it.

Spitz repeated.

Landover stood with hands in his pocket, looking down at the manicured grass. Perhaps it was worth it. Over how many years had he struggled with private donors for far lesser amounts. This time he didn't even have to make a sales pitch.

Spitz looked pleased. "Another thing. You'll need money for yourself, Professor, for expenses. Remember, this is Uncle Sam's treat."

"How about another ten million dollars?"

Spitz, laughing, handed him a brown envelope. Landover opened it.

"Count it," Spitz said, presenting a yellow sheet on a clipboard and a ballpoint, "and then just sign here."

Landover counted fifty $100 bills, signed, and stuffed the envelope in his inside jacket pocket.

"Anything you need, get. Account for it when you return." The chauffeur was waiting, but Spitz opened the door of the Chrysler. Landover, like a visiting emir, got into the backseat for the four-block ride to the Hay Adams.

"Oh, I almost forgot," Spitz said, handing him another envelope through the window. "Your tickets. Ten thirty-five p.m. from Dulles. The car will pick you up at the hotel at nine."

Across the west lawn in the recesses of the Old Executive Building, lights were starting to go on. Dark suits with wired ears were still flitting about under the eaves of the west wing.

The car slipped out of the inner sanctum and joined the glutinous rush-hour traffic flows in the outside world.

"Where's a Banana Republic?" Landover asked the driver.

"Georgetown. M and Wisconsin."

"Do you mind taking me there and waiting?"

"Be my guest."

The car made a left on Pennsylvania, and despite the traffic they were in front of the store in ten minutes. It wasn't crowded. He bought a soft, lightweight skin-colored money belt, top of the line, guaranteed to merge with natural bulges, and paid for it with one of the $100 bills.

At the Hay Adams, in a bright third-floor room that looked out over Lafayette Park and the White House lawn, he stuffed the forty-nine bills into the belt and the change in his pocket. He'd get used to wearing it.

He phoned Kate. Predictably, she was not home. He left a message on the answering machine, saying he would have to be away a few more days, government business, and she should find another partner for bridge. He knew she would have no trouble finding one. That was one of the things that troubled him.

# 9

"THE AMERICAN COLONY HOTEL was built in 1840 as a mansion for a Turkish pasha and his four wives. Fifty years later a group of Americans acquired it as a hostel for pilgrims. . . ."

Ripping along the superhighway from Ben Gurion International Airport into the Judean hills, the U.S. Embassy driver was a mine of information about the hotel. He had introduced so many American visitors to it over the years he regarded himself as its unofficial historian.

His name was Mickey Cohen ("just like the gangster," he proudly declared), and he set about describing the time the hotel had been picked as the site of a meeting between Palestinian leaders and senior State Department officials from Washington. Mickey, an embassy driver for nearly ten years, had been one of the chauffeurs for the American party.

"The conference tables were set up in the courtyard, with glasses of water, freshly sharpened pencils and new pads of note paper at each place setting. There were cold meats, salads, and pitchers of orange juice on beds of ice. The Americans were standing by expectantly. And you know what"—Mickey paused for effect—"an hour later, they were still standing by. They had been stood up. The Palestinians never showed."

Mickey made a hissing sound through his teeth. "They're not only thieves and murderers, but they don't keep appointments."

Landover could see the eyes inspecting him in the rearview mirror. He slid back in his seat and said nothing. He was curious about politics in the

Middle East, but more than anything else now he wanted to sleep. What a mistake to have acknowledged this was his first time in Israel.

Landover was still holding the note from James C. Shepherd, the CIA man in Israel. Mickey had delivered it at the airport. The note was written in longhand on U.S. Embassy stationery.

"Welcome to the Holy Land, Professor. I suggest we defer our business until you're unjetlagged. Get a little sleep. I'll call your room around nine p.m., and we can meet and talk then about the program for tomorrow."

Now 4:03 P.M., local time. Landover had left Dulles fifteen hours ago with a stopover at Frankfurt. Although he had maybe an hour or two of fitful slumber before the morning sun fired the Hebrides, he still felt like one of the zombies in the *Night of the Living Dead.* It was thoughtful of Shepherd to leave him alone for a few hours. If only Mickey would shut up.

Landover had met the chauffeur just the way they had said he would. Mickey was standing a few feet from the portal marked Customs and Immigration. The trouble was at least a dozen other Mickeys were dressed almost exactly the same—in aviator glasses, open-collared shirts, flight jackets, and light slacks, each with a small sign identifying a VIP passenger to be met. Landover had to read several placards before finding his name.

Once they made contact, Mickey, a compact, muscular, ruddy-faced man with jet black hair, snatched the professor's Hartmann bag and bolted for the doors to the sidewalk, deftly sidestepping his clones as well as importunate *sherut* drivers, squads of khaki-clad security men and women cradling Uzis, and a diverse cluster of civilians in kaffiyehs and skullcaps milling around the busy airport lounge.

Landover, carrying his thin attaché case, had trouble keeping up and was relieved when he finally saw the black embassy Impala and Mickey already stowing the luggage in the trunk. Though it was illegally parked, a policeman looked on indifferently. It was clear that it was an official American Embassy car on official business. They pulled off in a screech of horsepower, leaving at least one ply of the radials at the curb.

Landover stretched his legs across the full width of the backseat and folded his arms over his chest. He had hung his blue-corded seersucker jacket over the back of the front passenger seat. His necktie was still tucked into a jacket pocket, where he'd stowed it during the ride from Frankfurt.

He thought briefly of his seat mate on the plane who was making her first trip to Israel. She had been a teacher at the Francis Parker school in Chicago, she told him, and her mother survived the Holocaust. She had asked him for his window seat as they made their approach to Ben Gurion, and when land came into view, her nose pressed to the window, she suddenly started crying. He leaned over to ask whether anything was wrong, and she replied, "You wouldn't understand. You're not a Jew."

Through the maze of roads around the airport, the Impala unerringly homed in on the superhighway to Jerusalem.

"I could drive this route blind," Mickey said.

With a high state of military as well as business activity, the late-afternoon traffic was heavy, but fast-moving. Some cars looked like mini-tanks with steel grilles covering windshields and windows to protect against Palestinian rocks. Trucks of all sizes were hauling everything from watermelons to irrigation pumps.

The Impala overtook an army jeep and an eighteen-wheel articulated-container truck, then was overtaken by a stretch Mercedes *sherut* doing the Indianapolis 500 to Jerusalem. Two military jets suddenly appeared out of nowhere zooming north toward Golan. A single helicopter swooped low over the road, disappeared beyond hills to the east.

The car was slicing through a plain of coppery rocks and irrigated fields of avocados, melons, asparagus, roses, carnations, orange trees, wheat, and corn. He thought of the thousands of tiny dots of color of Georges Seurat. Along the side roads were packing houses and warehouses, trucks at loading bays, preparing El Al deliveries of produce and flowers to major cities in Europe and the United States.

"From biblical times," Mickey was saying, "the land has been amazingly fertile. Moses led an advance party into Canaan. It returned with figs, pomegranates, and a single bunch of grapes so large that two men were needed to carry it back to camp. That's the national symbol today, two men, like those in the Bible, carrying a huge bunch of grapes hanging from a pole."

Landover recalled an old musical called *Milk and Honey* about Israel's early years, where everyone sang stirring songs, worked for the kibbutz, danced horas, and made love.

The countryside reminded him of southern California—the same pink rock outcroppings and desert hues, the same dense network of irrigation, same asparagus fields and orange groves. But the people couldn't be more different. Nothing laid back about the Israelis. They drove faster, honked more frequently, gesticulated more furiously.

California never fought a war. At the edge of the world's largest ocean, it was far removed from the eternal conflicts at the crossroads of three continents. Over three millenniums, Californians didn't have to fend off Assyrians, Babylonians, Persians, Greeks, Romans, Byzantines, Mamelukes, Ottomans, Muslims, Egyptians, Jordanians, and Syrians.

Landover had only a casual interest in foreign affairs, satisfied by the Sunday *New York Times* and an occasional copy of *Time, The Economist,* and *Positronics.* His politics were slightly to the left of center. "We're both bleeding heart liberals," Kate sometimes explained to acquaintances.

He enjoyed what he liked to think were simple pleasures, riding his bicycle to SLAC's 50 GeV collider, coffee breaks with colleagues, jousting with graduate students, eating out weekly with Kate, bridge at the faculty club, an occasional concert, tinkering with his 1948 Studebaker or some other old car his father passed on.

Mickey honked as he pulled out to pass a mostly empty Egged airport bus. A slower car ahead was also trying to overtake the bus, and Mickey was tailgating. Landover wished the driver would stop talking—at least while performing such maneuvers.

Recently at a gathering of physicists in Budapest, a taxi at close to the speed of sound was taking him to his hotel on the island of St. Marguerite when a pheasant dashed into the road. While discussing the beauties of Budapest, the driver, in midsentence, swerved across lanes to try to run the bird over for the Sunday stew, missing it by only a barbule of its fluttering feathers. Luckily no oncoming cars. Landover associated Budapest not only with that wild ride but the pickpocketing of his passport and wallet and his inability to get rid of stomach cramps. He hoped to avoid similar disasters in Israel. He barely felt his money belt. He was already getting used to it.

Yet even with the problems he associated with foreign travel, he was not unhappy about getting away again. Life in Palo Alto had been losing its luster. Funding shortages meant layoffs, always painful to implement, and overseeing a lot of second-tier science: studying plasma behavior in the elmo bumpy, particle research in radiation streams that had been examined countless times before. That *$10 million* would help.

The real problem was Kate, his second wife. His first wife, Carole, had died of cancer, and he went quickly, too quickly, into the second mar-

riage. Kate and he had too little in common. She took not the slightest
interest in high-energy physics. Her life as a writer of software and now a
senior corporate strategist for a small but successful software engineering
company was diverging more and more from his. He wasn't sure, but he
thought she was having an affair with one of the executives in her office.
She seemed to be taking a lot more business trips, and always seemed to
be unreachable in the afternoon. Often when he picked up a call at
home, the caller hung up. He and Kate were finding that the only activity
they consistently shared was duplicate bridge and an occasional round of
sloppy tennis.

The route was clear, and the Impala was back in the right lane.
Mickey, a little breathless now, was presenting still more forgettable data.
Landover couldn't tune out.

". . . Not that many pilgrims at the hotel these days. But you will see
a lot of politicians, mostly from Labor. Likud people don't like the hotel
that much. They see too much Arab influence. Actually, it's run by the
Swiss . . ."

He was passing the same Mercedes *sherut* that had overtaken him
earlier, but didn't stop talking. Landover dared not look at the speedometer.

"You find a lot of writers and journalists there, people like John Le
Carré, Leon Uris, Saul Bellow, and people from the American networks
and the *New York Times* and *Washington Post.*

"John Le Carré lived there," Mickey droned on, "while writing *Little
Drummer Girl.* That book pissed a lot of people off. He gets full cooperation from Israelis, but gives a blow job to the Palestinians. . . ."

They were starting to climb now. The driver pointed out a single file of
soldiers, walking along an olive grove toward a village against a hill to the
north. The soldiers were avoiding a road strewn with rocks. A red, green,
white, and black Palestinian flag flew from a pole on what looked like a
mosque in the distance. A helicopter thumped overhead.

"The highway cuts through part of the West Bank," Mickey said, "and
up there is a Palestinian village. Janiyeh. They raise the Palestinian flag.
The patrols make them take it down. They write graffiti. The patrols
make them whitewash it away. The patrols leave, the flags go up, the
spray cans come out again."

"It all seems pointless," Landover said.

"Not at all. You Americans just don't understand. If we show weakness,
they'll walk all over us."

"I thought you were American."

Mickey gave a horse laugh. "Since when does the embassy use American chauffeurs? Not since a long time. No, I'm one hundred percent Israeli. I was born here—Sabra. Fruit of the cactus. Hard and prickly on the outside, tender and sweet on the inside."

He chuckled, adjusting his glasses. He was going a little slower now, even let a gray Subaru pass him. "But I've got an uncle in Flatbush. He says he was born in Jerusalem but the Romans invaded Judea and pushed his cradle all the way to Poland. I lived with him in Brooklyn, but I prefer it here."

"So you must have been in the army, too."

"Naturally. Everyone serves here. I'm still in the reserves, subject to call up for a month, at least once a year. I could be out there." He gestured toward the file of soldiers.

"So you don't like Palestinians . . ."

"I never thought I'd feel that way about other human beings, but how can you like someone who's always trying to kill you. You're standing at a street corner, and they cut you up. They stuff dynamite and nails in a canister and hide it on a bus . . ." He became more animated. ". . . It's mainly the kids, what they call the *shebab,* most in their teens, though some are no older than ten. They bait us. They throw stones, use sling shots, hide behind walls, knowing we can only aim rubber bullets at their legs. Stones can kill . . ."

He made a fist with his right hand and pounded the steering wheel. ". . . You try to defend yourself. But they take advantage of us: non-lethal bullets; warning shots first; nothing within seventy-five yards; aim for the legs; no women or children under age thirteen. So you measure off the paces, ask ages as the rocks are flying? Give me a break."

Landover said nothing. He was about ten years older than Mickey, and war was totally outside his personal experience. He had stayed out of Vietnam by earning a doctorate in physics at MIT. He had always felt some wars were good like World War II, you were fighting fascism, fanatic nationalism, and the Holocaust; some wars were bad, politicians' wars like Vietnam, where you were destabilizing a country and destroying a people who had nothing to do with you and were better left alone.

Although thousands acted as he did during Vietnam, he occasionally felt some guilt. Not too many had parents as well-to-do as his who could afford to keep him in graduate school forever. Thousands of others, academically less inclined or financially less well off, had no choice, or had been forced to run off to Canada or Sweden. It was fairer in Israel. No exemptions for anyone.

"In my regular tour," the chauffeur continued, "I was with Arik Sharon in Beirut. There was a real soldier. I'd go with him anywhere. We knocked the shit out of the PLO, bought peace for northern Galilee, forced Arafat out of Beirut. They lost. We won. Simple and clear cut. We won because they're not soldiers. They're terrorists. They fight women and children. They lick assholes. I hope Arafat has AIDS, or a good case of clap."

He again slammed the steering wheel. "They said they would turn Beirut into Stalingrad. That's the biggest joke of the century. We took the city in a week, and they bugged out, all of them. To Tunis, one thousand miles away. Too far for us to chase. I spit on them."

The Impala was making such good time that it had almost cleared the Ayalon Valley, where Joshua commanded the moon to stand still. Rocky, terraced tumescences rose toward a 2,500-foot chalk and limestone ridge, source of the river Jordan. They passed a place called Abu Ghosh. Mickey slowed, smiling broadly. "There's a truck stop near here. I wish I had time to show you. Owner is an Elvis fan, has what he claims is the biggest statue of Elvis in the world. Elvis in Judea. People come from all over to get their picture taken beside it, and buy Elvis tapes and key chains and miniature statues. . . ."

Just past the Latrun monastery, which claimed the lives of 1,000 Israeli soldiers during the War of Independence in 1948, the road forked to the left to Ramallah. Then it narrowed and climbed. Mickey pointed to a graveyard of trucks and tanks, bleached by the sun, further mute reminders of the war that led to the birth of this nation.

Landover looked out the rear window. The dipping sun shot slivers of flame over the filmy strip of highway and the green, beige, and lemony expanses that stretched across the Judea lowlands. A magnificent sight. Yet could it possibly be worth all the blood spilled over the centuries? Landover had no doubt competing religious interests would see to it that the killing continued, at least until God had the sense to move his Holy Land some place else, like Davenport, Iowa, or Perth, Australia.

Ahead, above resplendent, terraced hills, stood Jerusalem. They slowed as they wound up a series of hairpin curves that fed into a complex of arteries at the outskirts of the city. A dusty flower bed spelled something in Hebrew script.

"*Yerushalayim,*" Mickey said. "Believe it or not, it means 'city of peace.' "

Apartment blocks, many unfinished, sprouted like wild mushrooms from the golden-hued hillsides. At the crest of two hills, two symbols of commercial America: the Holiday Inn and the Sheraton. More people were visible now, mostly shawled women and children walking on roads lined with date palms and orange trees. A traffic light changed. Trucks and buses crunched lower gears and went into dead slow. Motor scooters and bicycles darted dauntlessly between stationary vehicles. There was a honking of horns and a gritting of teeth.

They crept on toward a big boulevard. Shops and markets displayed embroidered goods, pottery, and silverware. Cafes and movie houses were busy. Sharing the sidewalks were Hasidic Jews in skullcaps, side curls, and long dark coats, and Arabs in their snowy white *galabias,* checkered kaffiyehs or Bedouin headdresses. Yet most wore simple western clothes, the men in tieless shirts, cotton slacks, embroidered kipas, the women in long-sleeved print dresses, or jump suits, jeans and tank tops. A few were obvious tourists with cameras. Some men and women in khaki were shouldering Galils and Uzis.

Mickey honked in a futile attempt to get the traffic moving faster. At the City Hall, the Impala turned left on Suleiman Road, approaching the old city. Here, in front of the forty-foot honey-colored stone walls built by Suleiman the Magnificent in the sixteenth century, were rows of tourist buses with signs above the windshield reading B'nai Br'ith Rockville, Long Island, Young Hebrew Association Bridgeport, Connecticut, Mitsubishi Tourist Enterprises.

Across from Damascus Gate, a woman was selling white and yellow daisies from baskets beside the rusty metal shutters of the abandoned British Bank of the Middle East.

"Inside Suleiman's walls there," Mickey continued, increasingly eloquent, "you'll see traces of the city's Israelite, Hasmonean, Herodian, Roman, Byzantine, Mameluke, Arab, and Turkish past. Here was where David and Solomon once held sway, where a flagellated Jesus Christ had borne his cross to the crucifixion, where Mohammed leaped into the sky for his nightly meetings with God."

They turned left on Nablus Road, and the traffic became lighter. Mickey sent evil glances toward the *shebab,* the teenage Arab boys walking along the road wearing stonewashed jeans, track suits, and cheap cloth jackets.

A muezzin was calling the faithful to prayer from the minaret of the neighboring mosque as the Impala finally drew into a gracious old world courtyard of orange trees and white tables and chairs around a soft pink-and-white sandstone building. A boy, one of several loitering at the entrance, followed the car up the driveway.

As Landover stepped out of the car, holding his seersucker jacket and attaché case, the boy, wearing an oversized white shirt, cutoff jeans, and tennis shoes, calmly approached, smirking. He was short and wiry, couldn't have been more than seventeen. It was unclear what he wanted, probably a handout, or to carry the luggage in. Mickey was opening the trunk.

Landover saw the silvery blade of the knife before the boy lunged. Huge, like a saber, pulled out from underneath the flowing white shirt. Mickey apparently saw it, too, and leveled a lightning karate kick that struck the kid on the chest, throwing him off balance.

Landover, shielding himself with his attaché case and jacket, cowered next to the open car door. He removed his jacket from the passenger seat and wrapped it around his left arm. He'd once seen that done in a film. Someone yelled out something in Arabic, momentarily distracting Mickey. Landover watched in horror as the kid, nimbly recovering from the kick, sprang toward the driver. Almost faster than the eye could see, he plunged his knife somewhere into Mickey's gut and pulled it out with a wrenching twist.

Sneering, the boy took a step toward Landover. Feinting with his left, his right hand slashed toward Landover's throat. The briefcase took the cut. As the boy yanked the blade back, Landover tried to kick him. The boy easily sidestepped, his black eyes dancing wildly. He arced the blade again, this time catching a piece of the jacket. Some people were hurrying from the hotel. The boy seemed to weigh another strike, thought better of it, and dashed back into the street. He was amazingly swift. No one chased. All the boys had vanished.

The whole incident couldn't have lasted more than thirty seconds.

Mickey lay crumpled on the driveway, his hands over his belly, his blood trickling on the pavement. Several tourists were now awkwardly standing around. A porter ran back inside the lobby announcing he would call an ambulance and the police.

Landover bent over the driver. Mickey's eyes were glassy and he was trying to say something. "Those bastards," he finally muttered weakly, blood welling in his twisted mouth.

Landover was afraid of doing the wrong thing but at least knew the driver shouldn't be moved until the ambulance arrived. He wished he knew more about EMT. "Is there a doctor here?" he asked the people hanging around. No one answered. He loosened Mickey's clothing except around the wound, which was in the right abdomen pulsing blood through the shirt. He knew enough to staunch the bleeding. He tore off his own shirt, tied it around Mickey's waist, sat there in his underwear and prayed. The feisty little Sabra driver with all his ignorable tourist factoids and proud Flatbush accent had saved Landover's life, perhaps at the expense of his own. Landover propped his jacket as a cushion under Mickey's head.

Landover rubbed Mickey's forehead, held his hands. More people from the hotel were standing around.

The wait seemed interminable. With each elapsed second more precious life seemed to be seeping into the tarmac. Landover wanted to scream. Finally sirens from the direction of Jaffa Road. When the paramedic team arrived from Hadassah Hospital a few minutes later, he was still holding Mickey's hands.

After recounting the incident to police and giving a description of the assailant, Landover, pale and shaken, stumbled shirtless into the hotel lobby. The porter, who looked Arabic, trailed with the bag on a cart.

An effusively sympathetic male reception clerk greeted him. "What a terrible experience for you," the clerk said. "And on the grounds of the hotel. It's unusual. I can't remember such a thing ever happening before."

*Why in hell didn't you help?* Landover felt like answering.

The clerk asked for his shirt size.

"Fifteen five."

"You will have a new shirt immediately, sir."

Landover didn't mention the slashes in his jacket and briefcase. Perhaps later. At least he had a second suit.

His was an airy room off the courtyard with a gleaming tile floor, gold-and-blue ceiling, billowy marquisette curtains, checkered feenjon, a mother-of-pearl cocktail table, copper trays, and a tall, three-way floor lamp. But the only thing of interest to Landover was the queen-size bed. Thinking of the poor Sabra, he lay down on the bed. He wanted desperately to shower, but for the moment just had to sleep.

# 10

FOUR HOURS LATER at 10:15 P.M., Landover, in the same position on the bed, groggily picked up the ringing phone. It was Shepherd. He'd be waiting in the Cellar Bar in a half hour, wearing a Scotch plaid jacket and grass-green trousers, drinking a Heineken and reading the *International Herald Tribune.*

Landover wished the man had waited till morning to make the contact. But he agreed to be there. He jumped into the shower and felt the restorative powers of hot water. He wondered how Mickey was. He decided not to wear a jacket. May as well be comfortable.

The bar, in a grotto of vaulted rooms and low couches below the hotel lobby, had few patrons. Lights were appropriately low, the music soft Lenny Kravitz. The air smelled of Za'atar, or hyssop.

Two men sat on stools talking quietly. The bartender in a white jacket was playing chess with a cigar-smoking customer hunched over the board, a folded copy of *Al Fajr,* the Arab weekly, near a tiny cup of coffee.

Two men, with closely cropped black hair, who could have been midlevel Israeli bureaucrats, were sipping brandies and playing backgammon on an inlaid copper coffee table near the steps. On a divan before a similar table in the main room was a man who was obviously Shepherd. He was the only customer with a Scotch-plaid jacket. They made eye contact immediately. Shepherd, a big, heavyset man with a bushy mustache, smiled an easygoing, tourist smile, and lifted the newspaper so that Landover could get a look at it.

As Landover approached, the CIA man extended a hand the size of a baseball mitt. Landover could see nicotine stains on his thick fingers. The grip was flaccid, rubbery, damp.

"I hear you had a little accident, old sport," Shepherd said, resuming his seat on the divan.

The lighthearted, off-hand comment annoyed Landover. He sat down on a low stool opposite Shepherd. "How's the driver?"

Shepherd lit another cigarette from a pack of Marlboros on the table, using a blood-red Bic lighter tube he had been rolling in his hands like worry beads.

"He died," the CIA man said flatly, averting Landover's gaze. "Internal bleeding. On the way to the hospital."

Landover felt a thump in his chest. He stared blankly at multicolored orbs on a batik on the wall behind Shepherd. "Mickey Cohen saved my life."

"We're at war in this country, old sport. The kid probably thought you were some high muck-a-muck. They all want to be *shahids,* to get to heaven faster and earn money for their families. . . ."

"Did Mickey Cohen have a family?"

"I don't know. He was in the embassy motor pool. Not my department." Shepherd shrugged, offered Landover a cigarette.

"I don't smoke."

"Mind if I do?"

"Go ahead." Landover really did mind but hardly wanted to make an issue of it.

Shepherd fished out a card and presented it. In formal script was written: JAMES C. SHEPHERD, COUNSELOR UNITED STATES EMBASSY, TEL AVIV.

Landover studied it, found one of his own cards. "Mine gives a phone number," he said lightly.

Shepherd retrieved his card and wrote on the back a Tel Aviv number—03–623–627. "You can always reach me there, or leave a message. I call in regularly."

"Covert people leave phone numbers?"

"You can't be covert in this country. They're too good. They already know everything there is to know about me, down to when I take a shit in the morning." Sniggering, he went on: "I knew Langley must have gone bananas when they got my message, but what was I to do? I'd gotten a rare piece of intelligence. I had to run with it. That's my job. We're here to beg, borrow, steal, even buy information, and, well, no way I could sit on this."

He spoke in a raspy, phlegmy voice. He seemed in his late forties, about the same age as Landover, though taller and burlier, with sandy hair, hazy, shifty eyes, and a big toothy mouth. Shepherd finished the last of his beer, and some of the foam crested on the mustache, which shaded his jaw.

From nowhere hovered a waiter in white shirt and black bow tie. Landover decided to join Shepherd in a Heineken and Shepherd ordered another for himself. Landover ordered a sandwich as well. He was starving.

One of the backgammon players, a short man with a crew cut and a wide dark jacket, got up to leave, and Shepherd's eyes followed him up the stairs.

"Shin Bet. He knows me," Shepherd said. "He's going to phone. They hadn't yet linked you to me. Now they'll be running a full-scale check. I hope you have no Palestinian connections—the Faisal al-Husseini Holy Land Foundation of Palo Alto, things like that. . . ."

Wondering if the man could be serious, Landover shook his head. "I know no Husseinis."

"Better for you." Shepherd leaned forward. "The terrorists are getting a lot of financial and logistical support from fellow travelers in America."

Shepherd dragged at his cigarette and blew smoke over the table. Landover tried not to breathe.

"There's a lot of paranoia here," Shepherd said. "The Masada Complex and all that shit. They see themselves surrounded by a sea of Arabs, terrorists under every rock, behind every tree. Fatah, Hamas, Hezbollah, PFLP, Children of God, Children of Allah—you name it. The Arabs don't help by their random violence."

Shepherd was still toying with the lighter. "I gather this is your maiden voyage to Israel."

Landover nodded.

"Remember, this country comes with a lot of baggage."

Landover glanced discreetly at the other Shin Bet man, safari jacket, pointed ears, nose over the backgammon board. He couldn't help wondering why, if they really were security men, he had been paraded so deliberately in front of them. "Shouldn't we get out of here? Go some place a little more private to talk?"

"As I said, you can't hide things from these people. Better not to try.

From your background, they'll think you're just another nuke snooper, which is just fine. They love it when people speculate about their bomb. It scares the bejeezus out of the Arabs."

"So you've got a pretty close relationship with them?"

"They don't like me much, but they tolerate me. We have a modus vivendi. They know if they can spy on us, we can spy on them. Strict reciprocity. And they'd rather have me, whom they know, than somebody else, a stranger whose habits they'd have to learn again, meaning more work for them, which may be one reason why I'm here so long. Our people like to oblige the Israelis."

"I assume we give them some intelligence."

"We share what we think they'll learn anyway. We used to share a lot more. Once we even had a slot for them in Langley. Now they have to spy on us. Remember the Pollard case?"

"Yes, the President mentioned it to me at the White House. He said the Israelis were very unhappy about it."

"You'd better believe it. They're livid. Pollard a navy intelligence analyst, who loved Israel, did what he had to do. He gave Israel information about weapons of mass destruction targeted against Jews, including Iraqi chemical weapons manufacturing plants the Reagan people didn't want to admit existed. He was helping Israel defend itself. We branded him traitor. Here he's a hero. . . ."

Shepherd took another swig of beer and wiped his mouth and mustache with a wet paper napkin. Landover tried to look into his eyes but saw nothing but cloud cover.

". . . We know they spy, just as they know we spy. Yet we put their spy in the slammer. I don't think we'd be very happy—I know I wouldn't be very happy—if they put our spy in the slammer."

He stroked his mustache.

"Most Israelis didn't know what the fuss was about. They have a cartoon in the *Jerusalem Post* called Dry Bones. At the time of the Pollard case, one character in the strip asked: 'Did we really do it? And if we did do it, what exactly did we do? And why did we do it? If we did it? And if we did do it, what will they do? I tell you this spy scandal is a case for Solomon.' "

Landover lowered his voice, hoping to get the conversation back on track. "So now with this gold situation, maybe we have another case for Solomon . . ."

The waiter arrived, bringing the two beers and for Landover an egg salad on pumpernickel with a pickle. Landover took a sip of what was still largely foam, and felt an immediate zing as the tingling hops stirred tiny fires in his belly.

Shepherd looked down at the smoldering cigarette in the ashtray and crushed it. The barman turned up Kravitz's "Tunnel Vision" on the tape deck.

"I know that from a scientific viewpoint, it must seem bizarre, incredible . . ."

"That's why I'm here."

Leaning across the table, Shepherd whispered, "Do you know the worst thing that can happen in this business?"

Landover shook his head, wondering what on earth this could have to do with the gold. Still, he had no choice but to listen, hoping the man would finally come to the point.

"Not death, not torture," Shepherd went on, "not even being passed over for a promotion. It's being ignored. Finding that no one is even looking at what you've laid your life on the line to get, that your messages are unread, the seals are still unbroken in files marked SECRET. You risk your life for a picayune pension, and in the end find your country doesn't give a shit."

"So you made all this up to gain attention?"

Anger flashed in Shepherd's eyes. "I don't make things up." He took a drink, wiping his mouth with the back of his hand. "This is already happening anyway. They're making pure twenty-four-carat gold, at KMG, Kirya-le-Mehekar Gariny, the atomic center, outside Dimona."

"I saw that in your report, but I need data on costs, methods, process. I want to talk to some people, find out exactly how they made this breakthrough, if they did?"

"You can talk to the source directly tomorrow."

"How about access to the Russian, physicist to physicist?"

"Can't do anything without going through Ravid."

"Ravid?"

"The source. Yosef Ravid, old Mossad. We've dealt with him for years. Interesting guy. Looks like he dropped in from the planet Vulcan. Round, bald head. Explores caves around the Dead Sea, loves archaeology. Health nut. Swims every day of the year in the Mediterranean. Patriot, Kibbutznik, Givat Brenner. Knows where the bodies are buried. Goes back with the P.M. to Palmach, rose in military intelligence, eventually deputy director of Mossad. Now retired. Curator of a Mossad museum in north Tel Aviv, still active. Wife liberated by Soviet army from Auschwitz, died of cancer a few years ago."

"That's a pretty comprehensive ID."

"It's my job."

"So what exactly did he tell you?"

"They're producing hundreds of ounces of gold at Kirya-le-Mehekar and even selling the stuff. But it's a big secret. If people know, gold prices collapse and no one profits."

"So why does he tell us?" Landover was folding and unfolding a pack of American Colony matches.

"He wants to do us a favor, joint management of the project, that kind of thing. In 1983, Israel signed a political-military agreement with us, in 1985 a free trade agreement. He wants Israel even more involved, like maybe the fifty-first state. He says Israel's lifeline is American Jewry.

"Do the prime minister and cabinet know he's talked to you?"

"I didn't ask him, but I suspect he's acting on his own. He wants us involved in this gold caper. Maybe others don't."

"So we would be watching the Israelis doing it, maybe even doing it ourselves under Israeli license?"

"Why not?" Shepherd was now folding and refolding the cellophane from the Marlboro pack. The crew-cut backgammon player reappeared at the bottom of the stairs and was returning to his table. "It's easier than Iran-Contra. Help for our friends without congressional meddling. More effective foreign policy . . ."

"How would we keep it secret?"

"Not many people have to know. The President, key members of the cabinet, top people in the CIA, top-ranking government scientists. I know Washington's a sieve. But senior officials, high-level bureaucrats, don't talk. They hate the press. Who would have known about Iran-Contra without the leak to *Al Shiraa?* But as I say, I'm not sure the people who control this operation in Israel have made the decision to share."

A waiter was hovering. Shepherd ordered more Heinekens for both of them. Landover's throat was sore from all the secondhand smoke. He should leave. Yet it was difficult to disengage, as if trapped in a bad dream.

Shepherd started talking at length about his marriage to a French woman in Beirut, Nicole. The marriage had been a rocky one. Long periods of separation, then divorce. Nicole had taken up with a series of men with a lot more money. "I went wild when she left me. To try to forget her, I joined every sex club I could find. I must have fucked every woman in Paris. I'm glad to be rid of her now. She was a whore. Basically all women are whores, don't you think?"

Landover didn't answer. It wasn't the kind of question to respect with an answer.

Shepherd took the cellophane he'd been playing with and dropped it onto the ashtray, lit it, and watched it flame up. "Puff." He chortled to himself.

Landover sipped his beer, staring at the man, unable to fathom him, unable to bring himself to leave.

Wound up now, Shepherd revealed more of his past.

". . . I was an Arabist once, graduate work at the American University of Beirut. I wanted to write books about the Arab world, like Saint John Philby . . ." He gave it the English pronunciation Sin-jin. ". . . You've heard of Kim Philby, the Russian double agent. Sin-Jin was his father, one of the great Arab explorers, mapped the Empty Quarter of the Saudi Arabian interior, converted to Islam, changed his name to Hajj Abdullah and lived his final years with a young Saudi harem-girl in a mountain village, fucking himself into oblivion. Ideal way to go. . . ."

Shepherd was distracted by an attractive dark-haired woman in a tight, black pullover who walked slowly into the room, smiled at him, and seemed also to know the men at the bar whom she joined.

"I've fucked that woman," Shepherd said under his breath. "She gives good head." He added, "I can arrange something for you. No better way to learn about a country . . ."

Shepherd was fueled now not only by beer but a couple of stiff shots of Chivas. Landover downed one shot himself on top of two beers. He had been encouraged to drink well above his limits. Suddenly he realized he was learning more about Shepherd than he either needed or wanted.

He rose shakily, slipped the twisted pack of American Colony matches into his pocket. "I'm turning into a pumpkin." His head was spinning from booze and secondhand smoke.

Shepherd curled his hands around the Chivas glass, gently rocking the liquid. His eyes followed Landover's unsteady retreat from the grotto. "Good night, old sport," he murmured, and smiled.

*        *        *

OPENING THE DOOR to his room, Landover turned on the wall switch that illumined the ceiling light and a tall brass floor lamp with an avocado-shaped shade that stood in a far corner. He shut the door, noticed an open window and went to close it.

The boy leaped out of the bathroom, apparently determined to conclude the business he'd started in the afternoon.

Landover saw the reflection of the silvery blade in the window and turned to see the youth bouncing on his feet by the door preparing for the lethal spring. Dammit, Landover thought. Why did he have to drink so much? Gasping, he fell to the floor to use his feet against the boy. His stomach clenched, but instead of fright at the intrusion he felt unadulterated rage. Ironically, the alcohol was also working to his benefit giving him the courage to do things he might never have done if fully sober.

He rolled behind a wooden desk chair, held it out as a temporary shield. The boy approached gingerly, grabbed a chair leg. Landover pushed with enough force to knock the boy off his stride. Still on the floor, he tried a kick at the boy's right shin but missed and rolled into the center of the room. The knife swung, but its arc fell short, thanks to Landover's evasive maneuvers.

Yet no real defenses this time. No attaché case. No Mickey. He wasn't even wearing a jacket. He shouted for help, but it was futile. Inevitably the knife would have to find its mark.

The boy was wearing the same white shirt as this afternoon. He also wore a thin gold necklace. Landover didn't remember that from the afternoon. The boy's hair, the color of mud, was tousled by the ceiling fan. Always rocking on his feet, the boy said nothing, eyes fixed on his prey.

"What do you want?" Landover roared. He was still rolling away from the boy, toward the corner with the floor lamp. "I have a watch I can give you."

He needed some kind of dialogue, diversion. He unbuckled the watch and tossed it at the boy. The boy caught it. Landover was now by the lamp. He would not be that easy a mark for this little son of a bitch, whoever he was.

As the boy for a split second looked more closely at the watch, Landover jumped up, gripping the lamp stand just below the white shade. Mindless of where the boy stood with the knife, Landover suddenly spun around the room, swinging the stand like an Olympic hammer. The room darkened as the plug and wire cracked whiplike against the walls.

The boy sprang with the knife. Landover, dizzily rotating, sidestepped the blade and caught the boy in the midriff with the heavy base. The boy groaned, doubled over, then, half straightening, made one more lunge, but it was slower, more easily avoided.

The momentum of the rotation increased. The base of the lamp hit the boy's reeling body again. One more spin and the lamp crushed the boy's skull.

Landover collapsed, and threw up.

# 11

LANDOVER EXPLAINED TO the police that the boy was apparently trying to rob him. He didn't mention that it was the same boy who attacked him earlier and killed Mickey. He was too tired to go over that episode again, and no one asked. What did it matter anyway? The boy was dead. Nothing more could be learned now. He carried no ID. It would take days, if ever, to identify him, by which time Landover would be out of the damn country.

"This was a long-planned trip to the Holy Land," Landover said, playing the aggrieved tourist. "My wife is joining me."

The supervisory inspector was sympathetic, expressed his deepest regrets, and said he hoped the visit would continue. "Our tourists usually get better treatment," the policeman said, trying to sound cheerful. "Statistically, you know it's safer visiting Jerusalem than Chicago."

Landover smiled wearily. He'd heard that before and almost said, Stuff it. After the interview, the physicist signed a statement. A police photographer worked from different angles, and a paramedic team then put the body into a black bag, zipped it shut, and tagged it for the morgue.

Everything was done with practiced smoothness, so quickly and quietly that most guests in the hotel didn't even know about the incident. The inspector said he might have further questions in the morning and left. An effusively apologetic night manager personally helped Landover gather his things and carry his bags to a new room in another wing.

Before shutting the door, Landover made sure the windows in the new room were locked and inspected the bathroom. After a quick shower, he slept until the phone woke him at eight. The voice was unfamiliar, deep and resonant, the English slightly accented.

"Professor Landover?"

"Yes."

"This is Yosef Ravid. Do you know who I am?"

"Yes, I do."

"Very good," the voice said.

"I was hoping to see you," Landover said.

"I am sending my car for you, a gray Taunus, which will be at your hotel at ten a.m. Pack your bags and check out. It is unthinkable for them to have put you in Arab East Jerusalem. My chauffeur's name is Rafe. He will be waiting at the entrance."

Landover was about to ask when he could see the Russian physicist, but the line went dead.

A few minutes later the phone rang again. It was Shepherd. They arranged to have a continental breakfast in the garden.

Instead of the sporty outfit of last night, Shepherd now looked more like the old comic book hero Smilin' Jack with a battered leather jacket, denim shirt, gray trousers and silver-framed sunglasses. Landover wore his roughed-up seersucker trousers, a new white shirt that the hotel promised and delivered, open at the collar, Israeli-style, no jacket and no sunglasses. They were in a pleasant courtyard under the shade of lemon trees.

"Good show last night," the CIA man said ebulliently.

"I don't feel too good about it," Landover grunted.

A waiter had already brought hot coffee, warm croissants, and iced orange juice.

"My police friends say you whomped him with the base of a floor lamp. Pretty dramatic. You're becoming a Shin Bet legend, old sport, the man who won't die."

Landover glowered at him. "That's not funny."

"No offense. Just a tip of the hat to whoever it was who taught you the arts of self-defense." Shepherd quaffed his orange juice and sipped some coffee.

"Luck," Landover said. "After all that alcohol, I hadn't the foggiest notion what I was doing. Just natural instincts."

"You must have done something right."

"It was the same kid who came after me in the driveway."

"They all look the same to me." Shepherd gave a short laugh. "How can you be so sure?"

"I'm sure."

"Did you tell the police that?"

"No. I didn't want complications. They could start wondering why someone is singling this tourist out. I'm wondering myself."

Shepherd lit up what he said was his first of the day and inhaled deeply. "Don't turn paranoid on me. Too many paranoids already in this country."

"Sorry, but it feels like someone doesn't want me to do what I came over to do, which doesn't make sense, does it, because who would know what I came over to do, and what does it have to do with any wild-eyed Arab kid?"

"The kid simply knew you were important, figured it was open season on VIPs and that he could get some points from the local Hamas chief if he carved you up a little. Nothing personal. You were in the wrong place at the wrong time."

Landover wasn't sure he agreed, said nothing.

"It's the way the game is played here, old sport. It's a war zone. Gotta keep your head down, stay out of the line of fire." He flicked his ashes on the freshly watered grass.

"Thanks for the advice," the physicist said flatly.

"Now to the business at hand, Professor." He lowered his voice as if the lemon trees had ears. "I want to set up something with Ravid."

"He's already called."

"Oh?" Shepherd looked genuinely surprised.

"His chauffeur will be here in a few minutes to take me to see him. I thought you arranged it."

"I didn't realize he even knew you were in town."

"Omniscient Mossad."

"Omniscient Ravid. He's retired, but still knows everything."

Landover looked up through feathery lemon tree branches at the hot leaden sky. "All I know is that the sooner I find out something, the better. I'm getting my fill of this place."

"And you're here for eighteen hours. Wait till it's five years."

"No thanks."

Shepherd rose. "I've some things to do. I'll follow you down in my own car. To make sure nothing else happens to you."

"If you feel it's necessary."

"You're my responsibility, old sport."

TEL AVIV, HOME of half the population of Israel, combines the hustle and rawness of New York with the smells and sounds of the Mediterranean. It's a cosmopolitan city with throngs of people, kids with ice cream cones and balloons, and hundreds of shops, international restaurants, cafes, and open-air markets.

On the drive down from Jerusalem, Rafe, unlike Mickey, said hardly a word. He was wearing a sports shirt and black leather jacket. Landover carried his suit jacket, felt for his passport and other papers in the breast pocket. The gray Taunus, tailed by Shepherd's red Fiat 126, wound through poorer neighborhoods with a distinctly eastern feel. People were boisterous, and the loud, singsongy Arab-sounding music ubiquitous.

In small eateries, spits of garlic-smothered meat revolved around low flames next to counters piled with tabbouleh salad. Religious figures revered by North African Jews looked down from walls. Cheap variety stores proliferated, their shelves full of footwear, housewares, video and music cassettes.

Buildings were of chipped plaster and peeling chipboard, concrete eroded by sea-salt, smog-stained stucco and wood. Some of the streets with squat houses and empty lots looked like an open mouth with missing teeth. Yet only a few blocks away rose luxurious glass and steel high-rise flats in quiet neighborhoods, some with stunning sea views that had the sheen of Manhattan's Upper East Side.

They passed Dizengoff Square, Tel Aviv's Times Square, with its steak-and-pita, shwarma and hamburger stands, and unending traffic flows. As the little motorcade wound its way north, the city became less dense and after several miles they entered an industrial area near a soccer stadium and power station. Rafe stopped in front of an odd-looking star-shaped structure made of sandstone blocks. A sign in front read: CENTER FOR SPECIAL STUDIES IN THE MEMORY OF THE FALLEN OF ISRAEL'S INTELLIGENCE COMMUNITY.

A series of alcoves extended from the core of the building, and beyond was a glass amphitheater. Although it was open to the public, the place seemed deserted.

Shepherd, who had pulled up just behind the Taunus, told Rafe he'd take Landover to Ravid. Rafe, a short, wiry man who looked to be in his late fifties, said he had specific orders from the boss to personally deliver the professor.

The three entered the building together and were immediately confronted by a labyrinth of walled pathways, some of which twisted and turned back on each other, leading nowhere. Landover picked up a leaflet that read:

> "The maze represents the unending search, the shifting directions, the infinity of choices that are the earmarks of the intelligence art."

Led by Rafe, they walked swiftly through the maze and into the alcoves representing periods of Israel's intelligence operations. Exhibits represented Mossad's celebrated exploits over the past four decades: Eichmann's capture in Argentina; the rescue of Jewish hostages at Entebbe; theft of Mirage blueprints in Geneva so that Israel could build a better air force; the picking off of PLO terrorists trying to seize the Greek cruise ship *City of Poros* to take hostages; the assassination of the PLO's number two, Abu Jihad, in his home in Tunis.

Engraved on the walls were the names of all of Israel's fallen agents, except, as Rafe explained, slowing the brisk pace, those whose disclosure would still pose dangers. Shepherd, twirling his sunglasses, drew them toward an exhibit on Eli Cohen and stopped. "My favorite."

Rafe stopped, too. He seemed interested in what Shepherd would say.

"In the early 1960s," Shepherd said, "this guy was planted in Syria. They gave him a Syrian name and the identity of an émigré who had made a fortune in Argentina. He threw fancy parties, gave expensive gifts, and penetrated the Syrian government and army, ingratiating himself so that he almost became defense minister. Imagine, Syria's defense minister a Mossad agent. But he was caught with new Soviet-made signal-homing equipment while making a transmission."

Rafe added: "They hanged him in the public square in Damascus in 1963. We would have traded ten thousand Syrians for Eli Cohen. They wouldn't trade. They wanted an example."

The three resumed their walk and now it was Rafe who slowed the pace before another exhibit.

"One of the world's great forgers, Shalom Dani," Rafe said. "An artist. Could have made millions as a counterfeiter, or just selling his own drawings to a gallery. Instead, he used his brushes, pens, and needles to make passports and identity cards for Mossad agents all over the world.

Dani's passports got the Mossad team into Argentina to capture Eichmann."

"Weren't you one of those agents?" Shepherd asked.

Rafe smiled faintly. "No comment."

"But there were failures, too, big ones," Shepherd said, staring at Rafe. "Failure to predict the Yom Kippur War. Lousy intelligence on Lebanon. No understanding of the Shiites, and what you learned about Hezbollah came from us. No help to us in locating our hostages in Lebanon. But, in general"—his eyes were still on Rafe—"you still make fewer mistakes than others. Our record should be as good."

Rafe stared at the exhibit, didn't respond.

"We have our heroes and martyrs, too," Shepherd went on. "Richard Welch, murdered in Athens. William Buckley, tortured and murdered in Lebanon. Kurt Frederick Muse, tortured in Panama. What does our country do? Zip. Zilch. Nada. No museums. Hardly a working wage."

Rafe let that pass and led them to the office of the director, near the lecture hall. No one was in the anteroom and the door to the office was open. A man was visible inside working behind a desk. He rose, extended his hand to Landover. "Yosef Ravid."

Ravid seemed surprised to see Shepherd, and greeted him coolly. Rafe stood silently in the background.

Ravid, standing stiffly, was a foot shorter than Landover, broad-chested, well-preserved, with little flab. He looked in his midsixties but must have been older if he'd fought in Palmach. His heavy-lidded blue eyes were set in deep sockets in a head that looked too big for his body. The top of his head was bald and shiny. Gray hair rambled along the sides like tumbleweed, covering most of his ears. He was wearing khaki trousers and an open-collared short-sleeved shirt.

On the wall behind him hung the blue-and-white flag of Israel, a topographical map and an autographed picture of David Ben Gurion. On the desk a red carnation poked assertively from a vase between a DEC computer and a gold-framed photograph of a young woman in a military uniform.

Rocking on his feet, Ravid told Shepherd, his voice cold and remote, "I must remind you, I did not request, nor was I consulted about, your guest's mission. . . ."

Shepherd, taken aback, was about to answer, but Ravid cut him off.

"This is a very delicate matter. If you want my assistance, I need to be informed before, not after, the fact. There is no way that I can do anything for your man. Sir . . ."

He faced Landover: "We want to make you a friend of Israel. We want you to visit our tourist sites and see at close hand our struggle for existence in this sea of hostility around us. My recommendation, however, is that you come back another time, when your visit can be better prepared."

"But I thought you wanted to see me . . ." Landover protested.

"I wanted to see you to tell you to tell the White House that it's proved impossible to make the contact. Sorry. You must go and go quickly. An El Al flight departs for Frankfurt at two p.m. We will make arrangements for you to be on it."

Shepherd was stroking the tuft of his mustache, his eyes trying to penetrate Ravid.

"Would somebody please tell me what the hell is happening?" Landover asked.

"Simple," Ravid said. "We are putting the genie back into the bottle."

# 12

"I DON'T LIKE TO go back empty-handed," Landover was saying, but knew that without Ravid's cooperation he had little choice.

Shepherd, apologetic that it didn't work out, agreed. The CIA man had no plausible explanation for Ravid's change of heart.

To Landover, returning home now, though a rather undignified way to end this bizarre adventure, was perhaps for the best, after all. He was out of his element here. There were too many things about this place he didn't understand. He couldn't get out of his mind that someone tried to kill him. Knife-wielding Arab kids now lurked in every shadow.

Shepherd offered to drive Landover to the airport, but Rafe, on instructions from his boss, insisted that Landover go with him in the Taunus. Shepherd knew enough not to argue with a Mossad chauffeur and prepared again to follow in his Fiat.

Rafe drove unusually slowly through the Tel Aviv traffic and talked quietly in Hebrew into the car phone. Again he had little to say to his passenger. But he did pass back to Landover the English-language *Jerusalem Post*. A copy of *Maariv* remained on the front passenger seat. Just about everything on the front page of the *Post* related to the Arab-Israeli conflict.

According to one story, Israeli troops disguised as Arabs shot one Palestinian dead in a beachfront refugee camp, igniting protests in which thirteen Arabs were wounded. The unit entered the camp at dusk and shot masked youths who were painting slogans on a wall, touching off the protests. Dozens of army vehicles rushed reinforcements to the camp. At a hospital in Gaza city, men and women wailed and beat their heads against the wall at the sight of their wounded relatives.

Another article described the discovery of the bodies of two Palestinians near the West Bank town of Deir Ghazala. They had been kidnapped by masked Palestinians from the West Bank village of Kabatiya and were shot in the head and chest, apparently suspected of being Israeli informants.

Betrayal, retribution, trickery, endless war—all themes of the Old Testament. So little had changed in 3,000 years.

His eyes fell on another piece about a wooded recreation area known as Canada Park on the West Bank hills leading to Jerusalem, just off the Tel Aviv–Jerusalem highway. The new park had been three Palestinian villages, Yalu, Beit Nuba, and Amwas, bulldozed to give the Israelis better defenses around Jerusalem. Amwas had been known as Emmaus, on the road to which Jesus appeared to His disciples.

Canadian organizations had provided the money for the park. A Canadian human rights worker berated his countrymen for supporting the project, called it a crime against humanity, as well as the Palestinian people. But an official of the Canadian Jewish National Fund retorted that everything in the Middle East had been layered upon ruins of past cultures.

A soldier who participated in the bulldozing commented: "The villagers clenched their teeth as they watched the bulldozers mow down trees. The fields were turned to desolation before our eyes, and the children who dragged themselves along the road that day will be the Fedayeen of nineteen years hence."

Yes, Landover thought, a good place to be leaving.


WHEN SHEPHERD'S FIAT drew up at the departure building behind the Taunus, he saw a man take Landover's bags from the trunk and move swiftly into the busy terminal. Landover pursued his bags. Rafe remained in the Taunus, phone pressed to his ear.

Shepherd leaped from his Fiat to follow Landover. Shouting, he tried to catch up. But the man with the bags was walking so fast that Landover himself was having trouble keeping up. First the man, then Landover went through a door from the main hall. It resembled doors inside many terminal buildings leading into a VIP lounge. The door shut automatically. Seconds later Shepherd reached the door, opened it, and walked inside.

It was no VIP lounge, but instead a small, unoccupied, windowless room with a desk and a telephone and a single chair and a single, unshaded ceiling lightbulb. Perhaps used by airport security police.

Landover and his guide had already exited through the only other door. But when Shepherd crossed the room to reach it, the smooth, round metal knob wouldn't turn. He knocked, pounded. No response. He retraced his steps, trying to get out through the other door. That knob wouldn't turn.


A RABBI MOVED UP to Landover as he followed his bags. The voice behind the side curls and beard was Ravid's.

"Let's take a leak."

"Jesus, I didn't recognize you, Mr. Ravid," Landover said. "I didn't know you were a rabbi."

"We'll talk in the men's room," Ravid whispered.

The physicist was nonplussed. What on earth did Ravid want? Was he some pervert? Ravid could see the confusion.

"Dammit. Do you still want to go to Dimona?"

"Sure . . ."

"Then follow me, and for God's sake act naturally."

Landover reluctantly trailed Ravid, who was carrying a thick black case, into the nearest lavatory.

They stood over adjacent urinals.

Ravid again whispered. "Don't ask questions. Take my case and go into one of the cubicles. Inside the case you'll find a black suit, white shirt, black hat, and false beard and curls with stickum. Put them all on. Put your own clothes in the case. Then wait for me outside. I'll be back in ten minutes. Don't talk to anyone."

"Why the intrigue?"

"No questions. Don't make problems, Professor, please. Just do as I say and we'll be out of here."

Landover reluctantly picked up the case.

"One other thing," Ravid said as they were washing their hands. "I need to borrow your passport."

"Why?" Landover asked hotly.

"Just do as I say. Your life may be still in danger."

Landover, now wearing his suit jacket, slipped him the passport from his inside breast pocket and Ravid left, walking hurriedly. In the cramped cubicle, the physicist managed to change into the strange clothes, but had trouble sticking on the scratchy beard and silly curls. Finally he emerged to see at the El Al ticket counter Ravid giving what looked like a U.S. passport to the man with the bags. The man checked them and walked toward the metal detection arch in security clearance en route to the international departure lounge. Ravid went to a pay phone.

SHEPHERD HAD TRIED the phone. It was dead. He banged on the heavy steel doors. Of course, no one could hear. He was incarcerated. Goddam those motherfuckers playing their little games. And his car was sitting out there. Towed away by now, to God knows where.

He paced the cell-like confines for what seemed to be hours cursing his stupidity. Despite the clamminess, he was doing back exercises on the tile floor when the dead phone rang.

"Sorry about the inconvenience, Jim." It was Ravid.

"This is outrageous." Shepherd wiped sweat from his face.

"No other way, Jim. No harm meant. Now hear me out."

"Where the hell are you? I thought we left you in your office."

"I'm in the area."

"What have you done with Professor Landover?"

"He's on El Al Flight 101 to Frankfurt and Washington, and the plane has just been cleared for takeoff."

"Why the hell didn't you let me see him off?"

"I didn't want to attract a lot of attention. Frankly, Jim, you're too visible, too well known. Alarm bells ring when you're around. Quiet and easy was the way it had to be. I just wanted the professor to slip away. No excitement. Just another American going home after a tour of the Holy Land."

"I . . ."

"Jim, sorry, but we must drop this whole business. It was a big mistake." Ravid gave a tiny, dismissive clearing of his throat, then spoke rapidly, giving Shepherd no chance to speak.

"There's no Dimona gold. It's all the ravings of an old man who still sees conspiracies everywhere. Forget that we ever spoke. Wipe it from your memory."

"But we've got the President, the Cabinet, the CIA on a high state of alert. . . ."

"Disalert them. Tell them that I was having delusions. People in Washington have delusions all the time. They'll understand. I managed to convince Professor Landover it was all made up. He's going to tell them it was a big misunderstanding. I hope you will now make a similar report to Langley. These things happen. People make mistakes. They will forgive and forget."

"And how in hell do I get out of here?"

"You may go anytime. Take a little vacation, a few days in Eilat would do you some good." Ravid hung up.

Shepherd tried the door and this time it opened. Outside in the main terminal he rushed through the crowds toward the exit. The car was still there, not even ticketed, behind the Taunus. Rafe, in the driver's seat reading *Maariv*, waved, a butterfly of a smile on his lips. Shepherd gave him the finger.

# 13

Shortly after Shepherd's Fiat pulled away, Landover, in his Hasidic garb, accompanied by the bearded Ravid, returned to the Taunus, and Rafe, after stowing the bags in the trunk, sped off with his two passengers.

"Will you *please* explain?" Landover said.

"Later," Ravid said.

"How do I know I'm not being kidnapped?"

"Ho, ho," Ravid chortled. "Be patient, please."

They drove into central Tel Aviv, stopping in the rear of a printing establishment on Yehuda Hamaccabi.

"We get out here," Ravid said.

A little man with furtive eyes and a limp opened a door in back of the building, and they walked into a small photo studio. Rafe stayed with the car in an alley.

Ravid greeted the man, but didn't introduce Landover.

"We're getting new ID pictures taken, then we wait for a few minutes," Ravid said. "Save your questions for later, please."

Back in the car, Ravid this time sat in the front passenger seat as Rafe drove to Dizengoff Street. Rafe stopped at a curb, got out of the car and calmly walked away, leaving the engine idling. Ravid immediately slid into the driver's seat and pulled away.

They took the main highway south to the Negev and soon picked up signs for Beersheba. Ravid was anxiously looking in the rearview mirror.

After some minutes on a smooth, clear road, he seemed to relax. They had now left Tel Aviv behind.

"Sorry," said Ravid, smiling through his beard, "but it was the only way."

"You mean the only way was for me to lose my passport and my bags," Landover shot back angrily. "What the hell am I supposed to do now?"

"It all comes back or is replaceable. So don't worry. We've just saved what isn't replaceable—your life."

Landover was incredulous and exasperated. "How about some answers?"

"For starters, gold really *is* in production."

"That's hard to believe—"

"Suspend judgment, Professor, until we get there."

"The process?"

"I'm not a scientist." Ravid shrugged. "I don't want to mislead you. You'll get answers soon enough."

"Can I at least take off this damned beard and curls?"

"No, please . . ." Ravid shot a swift look at his passenger in the rearview mirror. "They become you. And we must think of appearances. Besides, you must realize that's how we're getting into the compound. Why do you think we got the new ID?"

"I don't know what your plans are," Landover said. "You haven't told me a thing."

"For Dimona purposes you've become Rabbi Levi Yitzhak Gershenson, a physicist from the Institute for Science and Halakha, and I'm one of your assistants."

"What the hell is Halakha?"

"The vast complex of old Jewish religious law. The—*our*—institute reconciles Halakha to the world of modern technology. KMG is Israel's greatest high-tech laboratory. We're going inside the compound as scholars searching for new technology that can be applied to the observance of Jewish law."

Landover had to lean forward over the passenger seat to hear above the hum of the air conditioner. He looked mystified.

"It's just a cover," Ravid said with a flourish. He seemed to be enjoying himself.

Landover was speechless.

"You know about our Sabbath, don't you?"

The physicist nodded. "A little."

"You know then that devout Jews abstain from many common activities from an hour after sundown Friday to sundown Saturday. We apply technology to help them reconcile goals of being both religiously uncompromising and thoroughly modern. For example, Sabbath timers can be plugged into appliances and set before the onset of the Sabbath to turn lights on and off or kettles to heat water. Our institute is always looking for new technology to adapt. It's reasonable to check out KMG for ideas. And because it's reasonable, we get an entry pass that puts us inside for a few hours. Arrangements are made. Don't worry, I'll do the talking."

Landover stroked his false beard. The hat's crown brushed against the car ceiling. Where would all this hugger-mugger lead? He felt foolish and insecure pretending to be someone he was not.

Ravid looked again in the rearview mirror. "You're just fine," he said dryly.

The road was straight as a knife blade. Traffic was light. They occasionally passed clusters of Bedouin tents and scrawny camels, some pulling two-wheeled carts.

"I went to Shepherd," Ravid explained, "hoping he could ring some bells in Washington. I guess I was hoping your country would help keep us honest. Because there's a lot of monkey business in our operation, which I don't like and is bad for Israel. So you're sent as fact finder, which is fine. I'm delighted. But instead of getting our side to open up, your visit has caused things to get even tighter. They know you're here, and don't like it. It seems obvious they want to get rid of you. Somehow you've raised the alarm. I had to go through these charades to convince them you'd left. Empty-handed."

"My mission was supposed to be a secret."

"Secrets leak."

"You knew I was attacked?"

"Of course. Twice."

"I thought the whole thing was premeditated. Shepherd disagreed."

"You were right. You would have been a lot safer and happier at one of our nice big seaside hotels in Tel Aviv."

"At least I saw the Holy City."

"Yes, you made a pilgrimage of sorts." Ravid leaned back in his seat, holding the steering wheel lightly, again eyeing his passenger. "I don't have all the answers, Professor. Just bear with me. I'll tell you what I know."

"I would be eternally grateful."

"Israel is a very divided country. The left wants to make peace with the Palestinians and is willing to give back some or all of Gaza and the West Bank, hoping radical Palestinians then will call off terrorist attacks inside Israel. The right wants to settle the former Arab lands and expand Israel even beyond its current frontiers.

"Some on the left warn that occupation of the territories will turn Israel into an agent of repression. They use a terrible term, 'Judeo-Nazis,' to describe what Israelis may become. Can you imagine, Israelis calling other Israelis Nazis? Those on the right say the Arabs will never make peace and that concessions will only strengthen the radicals and weaken Israel. They accuse the left of selling out. People on both sides are tense and angry. So wide is the gulf that some warn of civil war."

"That would be terrible," Landover said.

"Yes, it would. It took your country one hundred years to recover from civil war. We don't have a hundred years."

Ravid took a deep breath and continued:

"The Dimona gold operation, which is supposed to benefit the nation as a whole, has been taken over by a small group of right-wing individuals. They're using money obtained from selling the gold to strengthen the settlers' movement, fight those seeking rapprochement with the Palestinians, and, yes, stash some of it in their own secret bank accounts."

Landover stared at Ravid's round, smooth pate, a shade of ocher that almost matched the Negev sands. He didn't interrupt.

"When I found out about this," Ravid went on, "I went to the prime minister. I've known him for years. We have had our political differences, but I had thought he was a friend of mine. When I told him I had gathered disturbing information about events at Dimona, he threatened to have me arrested for breaching state security. I have never seen him so furious. When I spoke of our years together building this country, he calmed down, looked at me coldly and said, 'Just stay out of this for your own good.' I asked him whether he knew national resources were being diverted to private hands. He said I was retired, had no official standing, and he had no obligation to explain anything to me. He suddenly asked me whether I liked my job at the center. I asked if that were another threat. Staring at me, lips tight, he rose abruptly. It was the signal the meeting was over.

"I was shattered. When I left his office, I decided I had to take extraordinary measures. I could not leak to the press. It would be too easily traceable, and, frankly, I do like my job at the center, which has given me time to write memoirs. Besides, this is far too sensitive for any newspaper, a matter of state security, and we still have censorship. The only alternative, I felt, was to get the United States involved. For lack of a better course, I went to Shepherd. Somehow I believed if your President, through the CIA, learned about this, our government would have to enter a partnership, which would mean more oversight, making it harder for anyone here to take a rake-off."

"You have a great deal of faith in the Administration."

"I have faith in your country, Professor."

"For a hard-nosed Mossad man, you sound pretty idealistic."

"As far as the U.S. is concerned, yes. I make no apologies. The U.S. is the hope of the world, certainly the hope of Israel. We would be nowhere without you and American Jewry."

Though this fit with what Shepherd had said, it still sounded odd hearing a foreigner actually praise the United States.

"I hope we don't disappoint you," Landover said.

They were going fast now on an almost deserted road. Landover had no idea how far it was to Dimona but he knew Israel was a very small country, and he had many more questions to ask before they got there.

"You spoke about a small group of right-wing individuals."

"Yes. This is the most disturbing part." Ravid now seemed revved up and anxious to talk. "The key figure is Rafe Ben Giton, a former general brought into the government as minister of energy and natural resources. Dimona falls within his portfolio. And that's the root of the problem. I have been in intelligence for forty years and never yet seen so brazen a transfer of wealth from the state to private individuals. That's what I wanted to tell the prime minister, but he didn't want to listen. He's known Ben Giton for years, and needs him in his coalition. Otherwise, the government collapses. Power at any price."

"Doesn't sound too savory."

"I have known Ben Giton for years as well," Ravid continued. "So many of us go back in time." He paused to tune the radio more precisely.

"*Magic Flute?*" Landover asked.

"*Così Fan Tutti. . . .* We were in Palmach. We smuggled arms and Jewish immigrants into Palestine. We blew up a British prison ship in Haifa, spent time together in a jail in Cyprus. After the British quit Palestine, Ben Giton rose in the Israeli army and became a brilliant soldier, courageous, sometimes foolhardy, afraid of nothing, a hero in both the sixty-seven war and seventy-three wars.

"But he had weaknesses. He knew no moderation and could never compromise, which got him into trouble and forced his early retirement. He wanted to bomb not only Cairo, but Baghdad and Damascus. He was fired by a kind of religious zeal. He believed in a crusade. Israel would dominate the entire Middle East as the Kingdom of Jerusalem had done hundreds of years ago under the crusader Geoffroy de Bouillon.

"He also had a fondness for money. He's a multimillionaire. He has a *moshav* in the Negev. I've never seen it, never been invited, but I understand it's presidential—a landing strip for planes, helicopter pad, security. Some of his wealth comes from a company he formed—*Milhemet Mitzva,* he calls it—which sells arms to the third world.

"He also became the key figure in SIBAT, a civilian agency close to the defense ministry, that manages the military export drive. SIBAT is the Hebrew acronym for *Siyua Bitchoni,* Security Assistance. Egypt and Syria caught us by surprise in the Yom Kippur War so we decided we had to be better armed and prepared for any next time. Exports were the key. The domestic Israeli military market isn't big enough to finance defense R & D and keep production lines open. To remain healthy the industry needs foreign sales.

"In the past fifteen years Israel's arms exports have grown tremendously, to more than $1.5 billion a year. You name it, SIBAT sells it. Uzis. Galils. Terminal guidance kits for general-purpose bombs, bugs for telephone, telex and computer monitoring, high-tech riot control vehicles with colored tear gas jets, Kfir fighters, Arava transport aircraft. It's been active in Latin America, especially Colombia and Panama. But there are scores of clients, from Shanghai to Papua, New Guinea.

"SIBAT employs hundreds of agents and middlemen, all former military or intelligence people, redundant at forty but forced to retire with no alternative job training and a pension check of barely $1,000 a month. The 'formers' have become very influential and form the core of Ben Giton's power base. They have even attempted to dictate Israeli foreign policy. It was SIBAT's efforts to sell missiles and other advanced weaponry to Iran that helped bring on the Iran-Contra mess."

"Amazing," Landover said. "I had no idea." His eyes were still on Ravid's oversized dome, which swung back and forth like a round gold pendulum as he spoke.

"Under Ben Giton, personal profits and national interests are blurred beyond recognition. This was the danger with Iran-Contra and is the big problem at Dimona. The general thinks this gold belongs to him and can be used both for personal gain and his warped view of the national interest."

"You say gold is being made at Dimona and smuggled out by this one powerful individual."

"Yes."

"What does he do with it?"

"Sells it, of course. There's a market for gold. You must know that, Professor. Investors, speculators, people in industry pay hundreds of dollars an ounce for the stuff."

"Can gold be sold that easily?"

"Apparently. Dimona's a cash cow. With the proceeds, Ben Giton takes care of his people. Remember, you've got one hundred thousand reserve officers in this country, and some eight hundred licensed military consultancies. Not all of them prosper. SIBAT helps them. And, in return, they further his political ambitions. *Eretz* Israel. Maybe the country stays democratic, maybe it doesn't."

"Sounds like pretty hardball politics."

"Hardball is right. Also conspiracy. Israel needs to grow, yes, but how can it when it's constantly at war? The right wing doesn't understand, and that's very dangerous. I favor people like Martin Buber, Yitzhak Epstein, Moshe Smilanski and Reb Binyomin, the great Zionists who all felt we had to offer the Arabs a fair and just coexistence. Otherwise, we're going to be at war forever."

AT THE FIRST checkpoint the sign read in both Hebrew and English AUTHORIZED PERSONNEL ONLY. The guard, a short, dark-haired soldier with his Uzi hanging loosely from his shoulders, began questioning them both in Hebrew. Ravid told the guard that his fellow rabbi had lost his voice from chanting too much. The guard made a little respectful bow before inspecting their papers.

"It is good to see the Halakha Institute taking an interest in what we do here," the guard said in Hebrew. "We get some South African visitors. You are the first I've met from Halakha."

Ravid gave a divinely encompassing wave of the hand. "This is a new policy. We are here to study how new technology may help in the observance of our religion."

The guard returned their papers and wished them well.

At the second checkpoint, two miles farther into the desert, Ravid parked the Taunus. Though it was late afternoon, the September desert was a furnace.

"The sun can fry your brains," one of the guards said, trying to be friendly. After conversing with Ravid, he beckoned them inside the cramped, air-conditioned guardhouse and told them to wait while he made a phone call.

They sat on a hard wooden bench near the door. A miniature TV set was turned on, but its sound was drowned out by three thundering F-16s that within minutes would reach the border of Jordan, then wheel south toward Egypt and Saudi Arabia in unending vigilance against surprise attack. From windows in the guardhouse, Landover could see some buildings rising from a hollow in the desert, including one with a large silver dome and another that looked like some kind of warehouse with an elevator tower on the roof.

The guard finally gave them numbered passes that they had to sign for and wear visibly at all times.

Within a few minutes a sole Cherokee jeep was bounding toward them on a two-lane macadam strip from the hollow. The driver wore army fatigues and a peaked cap. As the vehicle drew closer, the driver jammed on the brakes, skidding to a halt. Ravid was already outside. Landover followed.

Landover was surprised to see thick jet black hair stuffed under the cap and the hints of a woman's body against the baggy clothes. He also noticed two tiny silver ball earrings. Jumping out of the jeep, the driver approached the two rabbis.

"It is very good to see you learned gentlemen here," she said loudly enough for the guard to hear. "Halakha has much to learn and little time."

She bowed to each. *"Naim meod,* pleased to meet you."

Ravid climbed into the seat next to her, Landover in back. Landover was dying of the heat in his black suit. The woman said a few words in Hebrew to the guard and they were off.


"I TRUST THE DRIVE was good." She spoke in Americanized English. The earrings catching the sun seemed to be her only concession to femininity. The wind was whipping strands of hair across her forehead under the cap.

When they were well under way, Ravid said to Landover, "Professor, I'd like you to meet my daughter, Rachel."

She tilted her face toward Landover and gave him a tight, formal smile.

Daughter. Ah so . . . More pieces of the puzzle were finally falling into place, Landover thought.

She drove them into what seemed to be the main complex. Ravid sat in the front and Landover sprawled in the rear. Two desert hawks had caught the hot air currents and were lazily riding them in long glides overhead.

She drove fast, ignoring speed bumps. The Cherokee was bucking like a bronco. But the moving air dried some of Landover's perspiration, cooling him some. They took a sharp turn, and a sun-baked parking lot came into view, fringed by palm and fig trees and by cactus plants with multihued flowers. Volvo buses were lined up in rows, numbers on their windshields, awaiting the shift change. To the west were low concrete buildings that seemed to lack windows or doors.

"The building with the silver dome is Machon One and contains a 150 megawatt nuclear reactor," Rachel said. "My office is on level three of Machon Two. That's the warehouselike building with an elevator tower on the roof, about two hundred yards west of the parking lot. East of the lot are support buildings, a school, library, and canteen."

"A world within a world," Landover said, aware of the cliché, and inexplicably self-conscious before this articulate, self-assured woman.

# 14

RACHEL LED THEM along a gravel path between palm trees toward the canteen. The air felt only slightly cooler. A few people scurried between the buildings. Inside the air-conditioned cafeteria, walls were off-white and bare. Tables were topped with Formica. The austerity and banality were offset by the aromas of fresh coffee and baking bread. A wall clock said 5:31.

Rachel pulled off her cap, spilling a mass of black curls over her shoulders. Landover was about to remove his hat but Ravid caught his arm. "We keep our hats on eating."

The place was not busy. Men and women alike in shorts or jeans clustered around several of the tables. Some men wore beards and skullcaps. People talked quietly, or read newspapers. Several men were kibitzing a chess game. One section of the canteen was closed off and a man with red hair who seemed tall for an Israeli was wiping tables and mopping the floor.

Although Landover felt self-conscious in his disguise and slouched to make himself less conspicuous, no one seemed to take any notice of any of the new arrivals. He followed Ravid and Rachel through the line. They selected cans of chilled orange juice and straws. Ravid and Landover also took coffee.

Rachel explained her job in the control center of Machon Two as a technician in plutonium production. Ravid added that his daughter had been trained in physics and chemistry at Ramat Aviv, Brandeis, and Imperial College, London.

Landover could only guess what Ramat Aviv was.

"We were fortunate to get her back," said her father, who behind his artificial beard wore an exultant grin.

Rachel cut her job description short. "Your people know what goes on here. Don't worry, that's not why we brought you down."

Her dark eyes seemed anxious. She pulled her shoulder-length hair behind her neck to let air circulate. Landover noticed how small her ears were. The lines of her face were distinct and delicate. She had a long, narrow-ridged nose, strong chin, and determined mouth. Her high cheekbones, tanned and smooth, gave her a slightly Asian look, like women of Modigliani. Like those women, she seemed to have equal measures of confidence and vulnerability. From a few strands of gray in her black hair, Landover guessed she was in her early forties. A bit of sparkle flashed in her eyes when she turned to Landover.

"Why should we talk to you anyway? You're not one of us."

"How do you know that?" He thought of the teacher next to him on the plane.

"Not with your name."

"Lots of people Anglicize their names."

"Not with your looks."

"What am I supposed to look like?"

"You know what I mean. You're as WASP as they come."

"Some of my best friends are Jews."

"Ho ho." She winced. She suddenly turned serious, looking around conspiratorially, clutching her can of orange juice defensively and muffling her voice to almost a whisper.

"It's very irregular. Not just your presence, but the whole situation. This thing is extraordinarily closely held. We know they're making gold. The process comes from one of the new Russians. His name is Dmitri Sherbatov. Some kind of genius, and we're lucky to have him, but I'm not sure how lucky *he* is. They keep him tethered, practically in quarantine, in case some KGB types track him down."

She spoke rapidly, wiping her forehead with the back of her hand. He noticed she wore no rings and still bit her fingernails and that her teeth were small, gray-white, and a little uneven.

Her face brightened. It was like the sun peering through a cloud bank. She shook her shirt collar to let some of the cooler air around her skin. Landover could see the suggestion of a nipple. She reached for her father's hand.

"He took a big chance in telling your government about this, but that's because he's a brave man, and loves his country." She began caressing her father's arm.

"She's the brave one." Gray chest hairs weaved against Ravid's open-collared white shirt. He took her hand and sandwiched it between his two. "She's the whistle-blower. We'd know nothing about these irregularities if it weren't for her. I'm a proud father."

She looked at Landover oddly. "You don't believe any of this about the gold, do you?"

"I'm skeptical."

"Well, it's true. And as my father says, there are irregularities."

She glanced nervously around and again muffled her voice.

"They have quietly built an acceleration ring, underground, extending around Machon Three, all under the guidance of the Russian. From what snooping I've been able to do, I understand they are bombarding target foils of bismuth with relativistic heavy ions, Argon forty and Neon twenty, knocking off four protons from the nucleus of bismuth to create isotopes of gold."

Landover looked unimpressed. "There's nothing unusual about bombarding elements to change their structure," he said. "It's done often at SLAC, Fermi, Brookhaven, CERN. If it's just that, it's not very much."

"You Americans are just so clever, aren't you? You just know everything, don't you? So much money, so much power."

"Rachel," her father admonished.

"All I meant," Landover said, "was that you need some kind of device that can deliver the power not only to blast open the atoms but to do so repeatedly because the amounts of gold that you get from nuclear transmutation are microscopic. You would have to produce meaningful quantities to justify the capital input."

"Professor Landover, *that's* what our Russian has done."

The red-haired man with the mop aimed a glance at them. He was working a new section, a little closer to their table.

"Just listen for a moment," Rachel told Landover. She spoke slowly, with an exaggerated effort to be calm and polite. "They have an unlimited source of energy. Some place in Siberia, this Russian, whom I met briefly before they put him under wraps, found the secret of controlled nuclear fusion."

Fusion. Was it possible? Could this Russian have really harnessed the energy of the sun, a feat that had eluded the best minds in physics for the past century? Or was this all some con game? Landover stared at the tabletop. He thought it wiser to say nothing.

She went on:

"So he was spirited out and brought here. That's fine. It's good for us. Maybe we'll all get rich. But funny things are happening that lead us"— she looked again at her father—"to wonder about the distribution of this wealth. My father got the idea of involving your government to try to keep things honest."

Ravid smiled. "I tried to explain all that in the car."

"Yes, that part I understood," Landover said. "Tell me more about process."

"It's all very tightly held, but my understanding is, after making some assumptions, that they are using dozens of sealed steel cylinders containing palladium rods, platinum wires, and heavy water electrolytes. The electric current passing between the palladium and platinum electrodes breaks the heavy water molecules apart into oxygen and deuterium atoms. The crystalline structure of the palladium becomes supersaturated with deuterium ions. The ions are so densely packed that they begin to fuse, and large amounts of heat are released. This is converted to the power for the acceleration ring. . . ."

"It's what Fleishmann and Pons were doing," he interrupted, "and what the whole physics establishment derided. They couldn't back up their claims." He felt as if he were back at Stanford putting down a particularly rambunctious student.

"Sherbatov had been doing the same thing in Russia, and was far ahead," she argued excitedly. "The key is apparently the use of the gas, combined with the temperature change."

Landover was shaking his head in disbelief.

"You're telling me they have actually done this," he said. "What verification do we have? Neutron emission counts? Tritium production? What about the nuclear ashes, the gamma rays?"

"They have special shields to contain radiation from the gamma rays," she said calmly. "I can't answer all your questions, but I've heard the heat released converts to more than one thousand kilowatts per cubic centimeter of palladium."

"Deuterium nuclei are positively charged and repel each other," he said. "To fuse they would need unimaginable amounts of energy."

"I know it's hard for you to believe."

"I'm just trying to understand," he said irritably.

"You're indisposed to believe, and I know why. It undercuts the millions of dollars of grants your establishment people get at Princeton's plasma laboratory, the Lawrence Livermore laboratory, and, yes, Stanford's SLAC. You use huge amounts of magnetic force and trillions of watts of laser light, and want to hear of nothing as simple as palladium rods."

"I'm sorry you seem to have such a chip on your shoulder."

"I'm sorry you have such blinders on."

"Children, children!" Ravid chided.

The redhead shoved his bucket closer.

"I'm just incredulous," Landover said more calmly, "because the laws of physics apply everywhere in the universe except, apparently, in cold fusion experiments."

"I'm incredulous at your incredulity." She looked at him angrily. "What I'm telling you represents my best knowledge of what is happening. I haven't seen the fusion cells but have talked to people who work there. I've had to piece together about the palladium and the mysterious electric charges. The operation is highly compartmentalized. No one except the Russian, and perhaps a few others at the top, knows the full picture. But I can guess what's happening. I would assume you can, too."

"I can tell you," Landover said, "that if your Sherbatov has indeed found the secret of controlled fusion through chemical means and the Israelis are capitalizing on it to make and sell gold before the world learns of it, they start with one major advantage—no one will believe it."

"Very funny."

"Not so funny if you know the history of phony claims. Are you aware that in the 1920s two German physicists, Fritz Paneth and Kurt Peters, announced achievement of low-temperature fusion but had to make a retraction after acknowledging procedural errors. In 1951 Juan Peron said a German-trained physicist in Argentina named Ronald Richter had produced the controlled liberation of atomic energy from cheap local materials. The project was later discredited and Richter arrested. In 1956 an American physicist, Luis Alvarez, claimed he had fused deuterium atoms, but the process was too slow to provide useful energy. In 1958 Sir John Cockcroft of Britain came up with Zero Energy Thermonuclear Assembly, hyped in the British press as the ZETA Machine and the Mighty Zeta. But Mighty Zeta produced zilch. Then in 1989 we got Pons and Fleishmann from the University of Utah. They were chemists. Their technical paper was sketchy and soon that claim was discredited as well."

"Are you finished?"

Landover said nothing.

"I can throw history back at you," she said hotly. "How many times in the past have learned experts been wrong. Before the railroads, didn't experts warn the public that human beings would suffocate at speeds over thirty miles an hour. A few years later distinguished scientists explained why heavier-than-air flight was impossible. Even after the Wright Brothers flight, it was argued that planes would never carry passengers or achieve speeds faster than a locomotive."

"Yes, but remember, I've got to report something definitive to the President of the United States. I need more than hypotheses."

"Remember Arthur Clarke's first law?"

"No."

" 'When a scientist states that something is possible, he is almost certainly right. When he says that something is impossible, he is very probably wrong.' "

"I'm not saying it's impossible. I'm saying I don't have enough information to report back to the President."

"Do you think these people are going to lay it all out for you on a silver platter?" She looked at her father. "I don't think it was a good idea to bring him down here."

"I didn't ask to come," Landover said indignantly.

"Please, please," Ravid said. He had been looking more and more uncomfortable as the exchange went on. He turned to his daughter. "Tell the professor about Klein."

"Okay, I'll tell Klein's story. If that doesn't convince you," she stared hostilely at Landover, "then I guess nothing will, and we might as well say good-bye."

The lady has fire, Landover thought. "I'm sorry if I'm a skeptic, but I do have to exercise some judgment—"

"Well, see what your judgment says about this."

Rachel sipped some more orange juice from the can to assuage her anger. The redhead was slowly wiping a table about ten feet away.

Rachel noticed him for the first time. "Do you want us to move?" she asked huffily in Hebrew.

"No, it's all right," the redhead replied. "I will work around."

Rachel turned to her two guests. "Let's move anyway. They have to clean up for the dinner crowd." They picked up their trays and moved to where they had more privacy.

Rachel leaned over the newly cleaned Formica top and spoke in barely over a whisper. "Did you note speed bumps as you entered the complex?"

"Yes." Landover feigned interest. For Ravid's sake he decided to be polite.

"One day a Peugeot on the way out broke its suspension and practically collapsed at one of the bumps. The driver, a man named Yair Ben Giton, a former general and very important person in this country, used his car telephone, and within five minutes a second car, a Mercedes, arrived. It backed up against the rear of the Peugeot, and a remarkable thing happened. The Peugeot driver and two men in the Mercedes started taking things out of the trunk of the Peugeot and stowing them in the trunk of the Mercedes.

"A guard checked out the scene. He was Corporal Klein, a friend of mine. Later Corporal Klein told me what happened. The driver of the Peugeot saw him approach and angrily waved him away. One of the loaders pointed an Uzi at his chest. He told Klein that he would be shot if he didn't get back to his guardhouse and mind his own business.

"Klein was amazed that something like this could happen. But he knew the power of the man in the Peugeot. He retreated. Unfortunately for him, he had seen what they were doing. They were transferring what had seemed like loaves of bread. The loaves looked heavy and were covered in burlap. One of the covers slipped and Klein said what he saw was a bar of gold.

"A little later the day of the incident I ran into Klein in the canteen. He was on his break. We had been friends. No—nothing romantic," Rachel added hastily. "He was interested in studying physics after military service and asked me to help him write his applications for universities, and decide which schools were best. I was happy to oblige. He was curious about how I liked the work here. A nice boy, bright, and I was fond of him. His parents were West Bank settlers in Efrat just outside of Jerusalem, but he was not particularly right wing himself."

She spoke slowly. Her lips quivered, and her eyes seemed to water. Landover, no longer simulating interest, bent forward more to hear better.

"When I saw him in the canteen that afternoon, he was very pale. I thought he must be ill or that his mother died and asked him what was wrong. At first he didn't even want to talk to me. But when I persisted he described everything. I thought he was going to cry. He said that even though he was a soldier, never had anyone—not even an Arab—pointed a gun at him before, and that he never believed one Israeli would do such a thing to another. He was a student, not a warrior. His barracks were in Dimona. That night he never reached them. Two days later, he was found behind a sand dune in the desert with his throat cut. They blamed it on Hamas.

"Don't say anything," she told Landover, then went on, her voice stronger. "I had been curious about the construction work around Machon Three. The lorries and cranes and extra workers stayed around here for months. No one I knew could quite understand what they were doing. And one doesn't overtly pry here. We are compartmentalized for good reason. They worked only at night, but the equipment remained during the day. Still, I didn't give it all that much thought until after what happened to Klein. And I brought my father into the picture."

Ravid put in: "I also made inquiries and found that Ben Giton had taken a special interest in Sherbatov and wouldn't let anyone near him. Sherbatov is driven here every morning from a safehouse somewhere in Beersheba and returned in the evening."

"He's taken straight to a delivery bay," Rachel added. "Like a container shipment. No outsider and few insiders have even seen him since the first day he arrived here. I imagine he's not too happy about that, but I never had a word with him, except on that first day."

Rachel looked at her watch. It was a few minutes after six.

"We must go."

They left the canteen and walked back to the jeep.

The wind had come up and the heat was less oppressive, though black coats and beards were as hot and scratchy as ever.

General activity was picking up. The shift was changing. Day workers were pouring out of the buildings to return home to Dimona, Arad, Neve Zohar, and Beersheba. Several kitchen workers, including the redhead, all wearing kipas, headed for a dirt-colored van.

"I don't know how you feel now," said Rachel. "And don't try to tell me, please. Just stick around for the ride."

The jeep peeled away from the crowds toward the north end of the parking area where it slowed in a deserted area following a small service road hugging an electrified fence. Ravid again sat in the front seat next to his daughter.

Through the swaying palms, the silver dome of Machon 1 looked like something out of *Star Trek*. Rachel at the wheel turned south away from the deserted area. The dome was now on their right as they took the service road south toward two other structures. They drove past more workers hurrying toward the buses in the parking area.

"Keep your eyes open," said Rachel. "We couldn't *deliver* Sherbatov, but maybe at least you'll see him."

Presently they approached the drive-in delivery bay at Machon 3, a hulking two-story structure like most of the others. Several trucks and a white Peugeot with a siren on the roof were parked in the driveway. Just outside the driveway, Rachel stopped the jeep and Ravid got out in full rabbi's regalia to tinker under the hood. Three men came out of a sliding steel side door and along the oil-stained concrete apron toward the white Peugeot.

"He's the one in the center," she said. "But don't stare."

Landover saw a tall, gaunt, tanned man wearing a white open-collared shirt and khaki shorts. His dark hair was blowing in the desert wind. Landover was too far away to see the eyes, but the face was angular, geometrical.

Ravid got back into the jeep, and Rachel raced the engine to try to underscore for anyone watching that it had been giving trouble that now seemed to have cleared.

The Peugeot backed out of the driveway and entered the service road, honking as it passed the jeep. Sherbatov was in the right corner of the backseat and turned his head out the window. For a brief moment there was eye contact between the two physicists—and for Landover, a sense of recognition.

He remembered that face from years ago when Sherbatov had been the junior member of a Soviet team at CERN. It was summer in Geneva. Landover himself had been a graduate student from Princeton at CERN between semesters. They had not worked on the same team but had seen each other at some of the parties, and in line with the prevailing spirit of detente they nodded to each other when passing in the halls. Landover had been struck by the young man's facial tic. There always seemed to be another Russian with him, perhaps his interpreter, though from the titles he carried under his arm, Sherbatov seemed to be able to read English well enough. A couple of times they had their trays at opposite ends of the same crowded table in the cafeteria, and it seemed as if whenever his countryman approached, Sherbatov's face twisted even more.

If Landover had recognized Sherbatov, perhaps Sherbatov had recognized him. No, he couldn't have. Not in this outfit.

"I met him years ago," Landover said. "He had a pronounced tic."

"No tic is apparent now," Rachel said.

They entered the outbound traffic. Buses, trucks, and a few cars were lined up in front of the speed bumps. Just beyond the speed bumps, the Peugeot turned on its siren.

Rachel stopped the Cherokee by Ravid's car. Her face tense, she shook hands formally with Landover. "Don't say anything. Do what you have to." She turned abruptly to her father and hugged him. "Daddy," she said. "Have a good trip back. I love you."

# 15

THIRTEEN HUNDRED FEET below sea level, four times lower than Death Valley, Sodom is literally the closest place to hell on earth. The town of ancient carnal depravity seems never to have recovered from its destruction by a Tertiary-era volcano. As if the tortured land were still burning slowly, the air smells of sulphur. Clumps of white brine cling like succubi to the dried shrubs. Gypsum and bitumen crystals hang in twisted shapes from the limbs of petrified trees.

"The way back to Tel Aviv is a bit longer through Sodom than Beersheba," Ravid said, "but no reason to hurry. No flights before tomorrow to Frankfurt and Washington."

The old warrior was going all out to be hospitable. Fiercely proud of his country, he wanted to impress Landover with its industrial vitality and geological diversity.

The road serpented between the chemical factories hugging the shores of the Dead Sea and the canyons and wadis of the sere, unforgiving Judean wilderness. Ravid drove cautiously, in the wake of an eighteen-wheel Koor Industries truck. At the first gas station they filled up and used the rest room for a quick change back into their regular clothes.

A mud-colored van that followed them out of the KMG complex pulled in for gas behind them, and a passenger, wearing a skullcap, bought a six-pack of Coke.

Landover welcomed the extra time with Ravid. He still had questions about SIBAT, Ben Giton, and the gold process. He had not realized how much of an expert in Israeli affairs he would have to become to complete his report to the President. He tried to draw Ravid out more on SIBAT.

"Military sales abroad are important for us," Ravid explained. "We earn foreign exchange, project ourselves in the world, increase our influence. But what's good for the nation may be overshadowed by what's good for individual entrepreneurs. Conflicts of interest . . ."

Landover's eyes were on great pillars of salt on the briny shores. Beyond were dredgers, like king crabs, scooping up a gelatinous muck of chlorides, bromides, and sulfides.

"Ever heard of Yaakov Nimrodi?" Ravid asked.

"Running back for the San Francisco Giants?"

Ravid smiled. "Not exactly. Nimrodi is an early entrepreneur in the arms business. A friend of Ollie North. Through North, he drew the U.S. into a plot to sell arms to Iran for the release of hostages. Iran-Contra. You've of course heard of that."

Landover nodded.

"Mike Harari, another SIBAT entrepreneur, branched out to become the security adviser and personal friend of Manuel Noriega. He led us into closer ties with Panama, just before your country decided to invade Panama and arrest Noriega. Mike was lucky he didn't get arrested himself.

"In Colombia, we ended up, inadvertently, for a while allied with the drug cartel. Can you imagine? The farmers we were training in paramilitary operations in the Colombian hills turned out to be enforcers for the drug barons. The man in charge was a retired lieutenant colonel named Yair Klein. He owned a business called *Hod Hahanit*—Spearhead . . ."

Ravid came upon some clear road and accelerated.

". . . Some two thousand Israeli military instructors have worked in Africa over the last three decades. Pilots in Congo Brazzaville, paratroopers in Uganda, ordnance specialists in Zaire. Initially, we sent them out to help win contracts for our military suppliers. But we know not all African governments are stable. Many are fighting civil wars. The Congolese want our expertise, but so do the antigovernment forces. Both pay well. Result: Israelis may be fighting Israelis in a distant land.

"In all these operations, we're being driven by what I consider a sort of new buccaneer class. God knows where they'll take us. But I do know they'll make us look like a land of mercenaries instead of the genuine, vital democracy we are. Now with Ben Giton, it's not the same thing. It's worse. Talk about conflict of interest. He uses this Sherbatov fellow, one

of our new national treasures, to finance the right, support more settlements in the occupied territories, fight the peace we should be making
with the Palestinians—and make even more money for himself. . . ."

It was a heavier load of dirty linen than Landover had bargained for.
He couldn't even spell the names, and knew he could never get it all into
his memo to the President. Shepherd must be reporting all of this anyway in cables to Langley. He was far more anxious to record before he
forgot as much as he understood of the bombardment of bismuth and the
new cold fusion energy. As Ravid spoke he made notes and schematic
diagrams in a small pocket notebook. He had overcome his initial skepticism. Something big was happening at Dimona.

"Through gas and temperature changes," he wrote in a precise hand,
"the crystalline structure of the palladium becomes supersaturated with
deuterium ions. Ions are densely packed and apparently begin to fuse,
releasing large amounts of energy . . ." The irony of it, he thought.
Fleishmann and Pons may have been right after all, just a few years too
late, beaten by a Russian.

Ravid had now driven them into a more pleasant region of laboriously
nurtured roadside greenery, tamarisk, acacia, and eucalyptus. They
passed signs advertising the charms of air-conditioned luxury hotels with
names like the Moriah Dead Sea, the Moriah Gardens, and the Galei
Zohar. The road widened.

"Someday when you have more time," Ravid said, "you may want to
come back here. Cleopatra was among our early tourists." He chuckled.
"She liked the mineral baths. The waters were, still are, good for all kinds
of ailments: spine, joint, muscle, bone, skin. Spend a few days here and
they'll make you a new man. Rachel came here last month to take the
waters. I still have her letter telling me how great it was—highest mineral
content of any waters in the world."

They had a four- or five-hour drive back up to Ben Gurion Airport.
Since they did not have to be there until morning, Ravid suggested they
have dinner at one of the luxury hotels.

"During our War of Independence—we rebelled against the British
just the way you did in 1776—we smuggled arms and people across the
Dead Sea from Jordan. There's a cave, close to here, near an old gypsum
mine, where we used to hide from British patrols. We could stretch our
legs before dinner if you'd like."

"Sure."

"If we're lucky we'll see Mount Nebo over in Jordan, where Moses first saw the Promised Land." There was exhilaration in the old warrior's voice, a twinkle in his eyes.

They passed a road sign for the Neve Zohar Camping Site and Restaurant. Ravid made a swift turn to the left across the opposing traffic lane, and leaving the traffic noise behind, they found themselves bumping along a wide, rutted wadi that seemed to wind around the mountainside. They drove uphill a couple of kilometers. The car track ended at a rockslide.

As they exited the car, Ravid pointed to an overgrown bush with several trunks, dark green leaves and thorns.

"Spina Christi," he said. "More plentiful two thousand years ago. Many believe this was used for the Crown of Thorns."

The professor touched the plant, pricking his finger.

"We must hurry to catch the last daylight," Ravid said. "Our cave is about a half-kilometer climb from here." He set off around a bend.

The mud-colored van, which had hung back while always keeping the Taunus in sight, made the turnoff as well and followed the wadi. The van drew up near the empty Taunus. One man emerged. He was short, wiry, with black, brilliantined hair and sunglasses. He wore a skullcap, jeans, jogging shoes, a loose white T-shirt over his belt. Inside his belt next to a pager was a Fabrique Nationale 9mm automatic pistol bought recently in Gaza for $239. He spoke briefly with his companions, then nimbly began climbing, hugging lengthening shadows. From the rear of the van, the redhead, also in skullcap, assisted by two others, assembled transmission equipment for a satellite-assisted telephone call.

FOR A MAN in his late sixties, Ravid was in good shape. Despite his diminutive size, he took the lead in rapid, easy strides, showing himself surprisingly athletic. Landover followed, hopping across stones, dessicated roots, and pebbled gullies, wishing he had on a pair of sneakers instead of cordovans.

He found himself increasingly drawn to the old man. Ravid had strong likes and dislikes, but surely that was a trait to be cherished in an era of so many politically correct fence-sitters.

As they gained altitude, the oxygen-rich air seemed fresher and a little cooler. They passed rosebushes, jacarandas, even baobab trees, yet also kept running into the detritus of picnickers, newspaper readers, cigarette smokers, and even lovemakers: a discarded condom stretched across one stone like an outsized flat white worm.

A few meters ahead, Ravid halted, pointing to a dull gray bug that was burrowing away in the ground. "When you see one of those, you know there's water around," he said. "It's an isopod, a crustacean, one of the most populous and popular creatures of the desert. Fourteen legs and always thirsty. They seek water for themselves and in so doing point it out to everyone else."

"Like a dowsing rod?" Landover said.

"Exactly." Ravid laughed. "I have a research scientist friend at Sede Boqer who has studied them. He says they're unusual in another sense— they're actually nice to each other. They're monogamous and spend most of their time underground caring for their offspring. Although males fight each other for mates, it's not a savage contest. The winner is the one who is able to turn his opponent upside down. Then the winner helps the loser back up. The loser retreats, hurt only by sore feelings and maybe a sore back."

Landover looked at the animal, who was unperturbed by their presence, just doing what was in his or her nature. How did you tell the sex of isopods anyway?

Ascending for about twenty minutes more, they reached their first objective, a reddish-brown bluff from which they obtained a splendid view of the Dead Sea. The waters looked smooth; the color of lead. Beyond were brooding shapes that could have been low clouds or the mountains of Moab. Ravid pointed to where Mount Nebo should be.

Now three hawks were gliding on the air currents. One suddenly plummeted behind the hill, as if spotting prey.

"Let's just look inside," Ravid suggested. Landover reluctantly agreed. Again the young Haganah warrior, Ravid sprinted toward the sandstone about 200 feet away as if a British patrol were tailing him.

"It's dry and cool inside, like Qumran, where they found the Dead Sea Scrolls," he said when Landover caught up. "Here no scrolls, only bat shit."

Ravid seemed overjoyed to be with someone willing to explore his cave. "The last time I came up here was about a year ago. Rachel and my late wife Hannah found it creepy. But I love it."

The entrance, a dark hole in a slab of sandstone, was large enough for a man to crawl into. Ravid took out a small pocket flashlight attached to his car keys and shined it inside. "To make sure it's safe."

"What do you mean?" Landover asked apprehensively.

Ravid grinned. "Friendly isopods live out here, along with spiders, snakes, scorpions, wolves, and striped hyenas."

Ravid bent down and scuttled through. Landover followed into the colder air. The pencil beam picked out a well-worn stone path. After a few yards Ravid doused the light. They stood upright now in a broad empty chamber with a chimneylike aperture through which filtered spikes of light.

"Any creatures obviously heard us coming. There's a secret way out, a winding tunnel at the end of a long corridor that begins on the other side of the chamber." Ravid pointed vaguely to the right beyond gleaming stalactites and a twisting labyrinth of shining salt walls.

"It leads to the trail, but lower down. You can imagine it was useful to know about during the war." Ravid strolled toward the center of the chamber. "This was one of our warehouses and way stations. From Jordan we could infiltrate at night. We stored food and ammunition and sometimes hid out."

Landover felt a rush of air near his head, heard the whir of wings. Overhead dark shapes swooped in extended arcs.

"Just a few bats," Ravid said. "Harmless. They can even be friendly. During the war we spent many nights together. They accepted us, practically ate out of our hands. Because of the bats, our rabbi refused to pray in here. He said his prayer was so powerful any bird overhead would burst into flames."

Ravid, caught up in the romanticized distillation of a distant war, smiled remotely, then whistled something that sounded like the "Marche Militaire."

"In those days in the cities, British spies were all around. So we introduced ourselves by whistling bars of music. That Schubert was one of our pieces—"

Two shots exploded.

"On the ground. Arms out," shouted a voice in guttural English. A figure moved in the shadows near the cave entrance.

"What?" Ravid grunted.

A third shot. The sound of each report bounced against the walls in a cascade of percussive decrescendos.

"Down, *now!*"

Ravid and Landover dropped. Landover came down hard on his elbow. Blood pounded in his head, his stomach was tight. Ravid sprawled in front of him. There was a crackle of static that sounded like a pager.

"Palestinian bastards," Ravid said under his breath.

Another shot whistled overhead. Grit stung their faces. The bats were fluttering wildly.

They heard the man speak Arabic into his pager.

"Run for it," Ravid whispered to Landover. "Now."

Ravid rolled on his back, yanked a snub-nosed automatic from under his right arm. He arched his shoulders and shot at the voice in the darkness, then went into a crouching sprint toward the cave's secret rear exit.

From the shadows came answering fire. Bullets cracked and whined in ricochet. Landover froze, hugging the cave floor. Right now remaining perfectly still seemed the key to survival.

He spotted something just a few feet away. Cheek pressed to the cold stone floor, he stared at the glinting metal. Slowly it took the shape of car keys and a flashlight attached to a silver chain. They must have fallen out of Ravid's pocket. If he could only reach the keys without attracting new gunfire, maybe he could survive this.

His fingers moved, as if detached from his body, began inching across the stone, continued until they reached the smooth casing of the flashlight. The hand closed over the jagged edges of the keys.

He looked toward the cave entrance. It was growing darker by the second. He could see neither Ravid nor the Arab. He started crawling, all the time expecting bullets to tear into him. Nothing happened. He maintained his momentum until he paused a few feet from the beginning of the tunnel Ravid had pointed out, must have already ducked through.

He kept his head so low he nearly bumped into a shapeless clump of cotton twill and broadcloth, damp, still warm. Blood had pooled on the stone. Despite the dimness, what light came through reflected on those once marvelously penetrating laser eyes, now flat, marbled, gazing with infinite emptiness upon the cave ceiling. The back of that big domed scalp was cracked open. Landover gently closed the eyes.

More bullets ricocheted. The sound of Armageddon. No time for mourning.

Ravid's right fist still clutched his automatic. Landover freed it. Cold, small, smooth, and heavy. Landover had never before even held a gun.

Hunched behind Ravid's body, he aimed where he thought the shots were coming from. Sweat trickled down his forehead. His hand shook.

He tried to steady it while slowly squeezing the trigger. The pistol fired before he was ready, jolting him. He quickly supported his right hand with his left, fired again, and again, and again. Now that the trigger was responding to the slightest pressure of his finger, he was surprised at the rush it gave him. Suddenly he understood how a punk with a gun could feel invincible. Well, against an invisible Arab terrorist, he could maybe even the odds.

But how the hell many bullets were in a clip? He stopped firing. The echoes faded into a thunderous silence.

He searched Ravid, pocketed an address book and wallet. He knew he couldn't linger, had to abandon Ravid's body. Swiftly, quietly, the pistol pointed into the receding gray-blackness of the cavern, on all fours he backed into the exit tunnel.

# 16

For what seemed like days, Landover crawled backward. Gradually more light appeared. The tunnel turned sharply. Over his shoulder he saw a small opening to the trail that he and Ravid had followed up the hill. There was no further sound from inside the cavern, but he was suddenly aware of rapid footfalls and the static of a pager outside. The newcomers must be associates of the man in the cave.

Even in shadow he couldn't stay where he was without a risk of being seen. He crawled deeper into the tunnel with his gun pointed at the opening. His hands were scratched, his elbows and kneecaps badly bruised.

Two men walked by, both wearing yarmulkes. One with reddish hair wore a Los Angeles Dodgers baseball jacket, the other a white T-shirt. A camera dangled from the redhead's neck. The redhead looked familiar, but Landover couldn't quite place him.

American Jewish tourists? But why the pager? How could Jews be in league with the man in the cave? They took no notice of the aperture and continued up the hill.

Landover inched toward the outer edge of the tunnel, glanced right and left, and exited. Comforted some by the jingling of the keys in his pocket, he loped down the hill back toward the Taunus.

A van stood within twenty feet of Ravid's car. Landover needed the car, but worried about a guard. He considered making a wide arc and returning to the highway on foot. He'd go to the police, lead them to Ravid's body. But he'd have to identify himself and answer questions about who he was and why he was here. They'd make inquiries, find his name among those who had left Ben-Gurion Airport this morning. All sorts of red flags would go up. He'd be arrested for spying, maybe a hostage until Pollard's release. The mission would be blown. He owed it to Ravid not to blow the mission. No question about that. And to his daughter Rachel . . .

He took advantage of the thin cover of yuccalike scrub growth to approach the vehicles. About thirty feet from the van the cover disappeared and he began a belly-crawl. He again heard the static of a pager. Someone speaking what sounded like Arabic. Perhaps to the men on the hill? Had they found Ravid's body? Could the terrorist in the cave have been hit by the return fire? What the hell was going on? The radio in the van was suddenly turned up and he heard the whine of an Arabic song.

The earth was hard. Even with the jacket, rocks cut into his arms and legs as he clawed forward. Absurdly, he thought if he ever survived this he would ask the President of the United States for a new suit. Maybe a couple. Lucky night was falling fast. At the rear of the van he squeezed underneath the chassis and inched to just below the engine mount.

He could still take an engine apart in his sleep. How often had he and his dad worked on the old Studebaker. Oil and grease had a good smell. Dad called it "honest dirt." At Princeton he weighed the parallels between an old car engine and the universe. Some bolts were as tiny and remote as dwarf stars. Piston rings were black holes. God was the universal voltage regulator.

Landover felt around the parts coated with oil, grease, transmission fluid, and layers of sticky sand. He found the distributor, reached up and around for clamps that held the cap. Loosening them, he strained to disengage the cap. He couldn't budge it. With engine heat that could rise to 500 degrees F., the parts had practically welded together.

Don't panic. Pop music now from the radio upstairs. One more huge effort. The cap gave.

He slid out of half of his jacket to tear off a piece of cloth from the arm of the hotel shirt, and rubbed the rag around the crankshaft, carburetor, distributor and oil tank. Enough leaking fluids to make the cloth damp and flammable. He stuffed the rag between a rubber coil and the carburetor, searched his pockets for paper and found an old Kleenex and the itemized American Colony bill along with the American Colony bar matches. He crinkled the papers, tore strips from them to stuff between the coils, then he lit his paper and cloth fuse.

He belly-crawled back to the Taunus, made it to the door of the passenger seat, from the van the farthest and least visible door. In his right hand were the keys, in his left the automatic.

He reached up awkwardly to stick the key in the lock and turn it, holding his breath at the clicks. He opened the door slowly. The metallic sounds merged into the stridulations of the locusts, the distant howl of a jackal, and the van's radio.

He slithered from ground to car floor, bumping both head and shoulders against the base of the dashboard and gear shift. The sky still wasn't dark enough to prevent exposure against the chalky white rocks and sand. He could only pray at this moment no one in the van was paying attention to the Taunus.

He peered over the windowsill. All was quiet. Keeping his head low, he scrunched into the driver's seat and put the key into the ignition.

Finally, wisps of smoke wafted from the underside of the van, then more smoke. In a few minutes he heard a stirring and dropped lower on the seat. A man also with a yarmulke got out, peered underneath the van.

Landover could have shot the man in the back. Except he couldn't. Instead, he started up the Taunus's engine and it turned over right away. He jolted down the wadi in reverse. The man wasn't sure what to make of it, then pulled out a weapon. Landover floored the pedal, ducking below the dashboard, still holding the wheel. He looked out the rear window, hoping to avoid the bigger rocks.

The Taunus was bucking but still moving on roughly the right course. Landover could hear shots. When he peered through the windshield, the man was harder to see, then out of view.

Landover U-turned and assessed damage. No flats. Engine still running. Maybe a few chassis dents, bullet holes. He proceeded down the wadi in forward.

He imagined them trying to start the van. It would take them a while to figure out what was wrong.

He saw a string of vehicle lights ahead and switched on his headlights. At the edge of the main road he had to wait for a slow-moving phosphates truck to pass before pulling into the traffic stream.

He stuffed the automatic in his pocket, and at a FINA station on the road to Dimona called Rachel from a pay phone. The number was in Ravid's book.

"I must see you immediately."

She heard the seriousness in his voice and asked no questions, gave him precise directions to her place: cross the railroad tracks, turn off at a tree-lined esplanade near a Tunisian restaurant, La Maison du Takouit. He jotted down the address, 318 Kadesh, in the town of Dimona. He hesitated, then decided it was better to tell her now. What was the point of holding back . . . ?

"Your father . . . he wanted to show me a cave he knew above Zohar Springs. Some people followed us . . . One of them attacked us in the cave. We made a break for it toward a secret exit your father knew and . . . your father didn't make it."

There was a long silence. He heard her gasping for air.

"I do not believe it." Her voice was strange and distant.

"I am truly sorry." The terrible inadequacy of words. What else to say. Facts. At least give her facts. "Rachel, he was dead when I got to him. I retrieved his notebook, his wallet and keys. And I . . . I managed to escape."

"You were lucky." Her voice was flat, without timbre, like the thud of a falling rock.

"They wore yarmulkes," he continued, "but what I heard sounded more Arabic than Hebrew."

"Have you called the police?"

"No, only you. I just got away, in your father's car."

Momentary silence at the other end, as if she were trying to absorb it. "All right, hurry." And she hung up.

He parked in front of the small, single-story bungalow on Kadesh, among the few finished and inhabited structures on a street that was obviously a busy construction site during the day. Now many idle steam shovels stood next to ghostly skeletons of unfinished houses and apartment blocks. Street lights weren't working yet. He looked at his watch: 7:50.

She opened the door and let him into the sitting room of the air-conditioned house. She seemed hardly to recognize him. He saw her face change from obvious grief to shock.

"Go clean up," she said and pointed to the bathroom. "I can get you another shirt."

He fished out of his seersucker jacket pockets Ravid's wallet, address book, and automatic, and handed them to her along with the keys. As he left her she was studying each article.

The house was compact. A rear entrance led through a utility room into the tiny kitchen. The bedroom door was open. On the floral-patterned spread were assorted photos of her father and a half-empty box of Kleenex. Next to the bedroom was the bathroom. He shut the bathroom door, dropped his clothes and money belt on the floor, and showered.

Reemerging he wished he could burn his clothes. He restrapped the money belt and had to put the soiled pieces right back on, including the shirt without a sleeve. At least he could give himself a shave. He saw an old Bic razor and used soap to lather. When he reopened the bathroom door, he found a floral sport shirt on the knob. He immediately replaced the torn hotel shirt with the new one, which was a tight fit, and put on his jacket.

Rachel was in the kitchen brewing coffee in the Turkish manner, a brass pot over the gas flame. She stood silently watching the foam bubble up, lifted the pot from the fire until it subsided, then let it boil up again twice more. Ravid's wallet was on the table along with his driver's license, keys, automatic, flashlight, and address book, all laid out neatly.

"I hope the shirt isn't too small," Rachel said. "It belonged to my father."

"It's fine. Thanks."

Her eyes were swollen and bloodshot. A dark maroon, almost black kerchief wrapped her coal black hair. She was wearing jeans, loose sandals, and what looked like a man's white shirt tied around her waist over a T-shirt. The white matched the pallor of her cheeks. Her eyes were light green, the color of the sea. She still had on her ball earrings. A large stone, like malachite, hung from a chain around her neck. Noting Landover's eyes on it, she shook her head and sighed. "I shouldn't wear jewelry at a time like this . . . but my father gave these to my mother a week after they met and he gave them to me after she died." She seemed to be asking forgiveness for something.

Landover stood awkwardly, not knowing what to say.

She pulled the kerchief back on her hair. "Take the jacket off if you like."

"No, that's all right. The air-conditioning is comfortable."

As she poured coffee he went over what happened in greater detail. He described his getaway and how he had disabled the van.

"They probably figured it out pretty quickly," he said. "Disconnecting the carburetor cap is one of the oldest tricks in the book."

A phone rang. She rushed to a desk in the sitting room to pick it up.

She seemed to listen a long time before saying a few words in Hebrew and hanging up. She returned to the kitchen.

"That was Lon Gavril. I called him after you phoned. He's with the National Police Criminal Investigation Division. He knows the cave well. He organized a helicopter SWAT team to fly there. He just reported they found no van, and no trace of my father."

"They could have hidden him. Must be lots of caves in the area."

"Gavril's coming over to talk to you."

"I won't be able to tell him more than I've already told you," Landover said. Maybe it was impossible not to get involved in an Israeli police investigation, but he'd better get in touch with someone from the embassy. He still had Shepherd's number.

"Gavril is a friend, an old Palmach colleague of my father. He has questions. It's only natural. His men are still looking."

Landover stared at the bare wood floor, said nothing.

She picked up her coffee cup. "I need to sit down."

He followed her from the kitchen into the larger room, and sat on an upholstered chair. On all the walls were bracketed bookshelves and stunning gravures depicting the British army. He read the tiny script: Balaklava, Khartoum, Kashmir . . .

"My father loved those pictures," she said. "But when Mother died he moved to a smaller apartment and gave them to me."

Landover studied one of the pictures more closely: a British officer carrying a wounded Gurkha from the battlefield at Khartoum, the officer impervious to enemy gunners, his face a model of courage and determination. The battlefield was littered with bodies, but there was no sense of blood or pain, only the heroism of a British officer risking his life to save a fallen comrade. Landover wished he had been able to do that for Ravid. In those pictures war was heroism, romance, goodness. A far cry from the real thing. But the pictures were stirring, good to look at. Landover bent to examine the signature.

"The artist is R. Caton Woodville," Rachel said, "and I don't know anything about him. Dad bought the pictures in London years ago for fifty dollars. Another set is in the British Museum."

"Your father told me he fought the British."

"He hated what they were doing in Palestine, but applauded their fight against Hitler. And overall he admired the Empire, called it one of the great civilizing forces of the world."

She wiped her forehead with a tissue. Her lips seemed to tremble. She rose suddenly, as if she just couldn't sit still. "Do you want something to eat? I think you have not had anything but orange juice all day."

Before he had a chance to respond she disappeared in the kitchen and he heard the refrigerator and cupboard doors open and shut. Indeed, he hadn't eaten since breakfast.

He perused her bookshelves: assorted books on gardening, chess, and physical sciences and such other works as *The Second Sex* by Simone de Beauvoir, *The Female Eunuch* by Germaine Greer, *Outrageous Acts and Everyday Rebellions* by Gloria Steinem, and *The Edible Woman* by Margaret Atwood.

"May I use your phone?" he shouted into the kitchen.

"Help yourself."

He still had the business card on which Shepherd had written his coordinates. He dialed the Tel Aviv number. The recording machine said Shepherd was not available but gave another number for emergency use. Now a woman answered. Landover identified himself and said he needed to talk to Jim Shepherd.

"Oh, yes, Professor. Are you in Washington already?" she asked casually, as if she were expecting the call. Before he could answer she said: "Eilat. You can reach him at 07–597–9555." He thanked her and hung up.

Landover called the number. The operator of the Coral Sea Hotel answered. Shepherd was out. Landover left Rachel's phone number and said it was urgent.

Almost as soon as he put the phone down it rang. Must be Shepherd collecting his message, he thought. As Rachel was still in the kitchen, he picked it up.

"Hello."

"Who are you?" a coarse, unpleasant voice demanded in English with a middle-European accent.

"Who wants to know?" Landover was caught off guard for the twenty-seventh time in twenty-seven hours.

"Don't play your fucking games with me. Who are you?"

Rachel had sprinted to his side, and with relief he handed her the receiver.

She spoke in Hebrew. Again she seemed to be listening for a long time. This time, though, her lips stiffened and her eyes narrowed into tiny red scabs. He could almost see blood draining from her cheeks.

Rankled, she said several words, then hung up.

She walked back into the kitchen. Landover followed her, but thought it best to say nothing. He fingered Ravid's flashlight.

"That was the head of security at Dimona," she finally said. "A man named Bloom. He wants me arrested."

"Are you serious?"

"He had heard about our visit to Machon Three. Said it was outrageous that I encouraged a breach of security by those pretending to be *haredim*. He'd found that part out when he phoned the Halakah Institute protesting your unannounced visit. He's disciplined the border guard who accepted your papers. He wants me behind bars."

"Jesus Christ."

"He knew I'd been nosing around. He's close to Ben Giton and is worried about the secret getting out. He asked who it was I let into my house. When I wouldn't tell him he called me a whore. I told him my father had just been murdered by Arabs, and he—can you imagine—he called me a liar and said I had no shame and hung up. Gavril must have talked to him and told him he couldn't find a body."

"What are you going to do?"

"Feed you," she said. "To hell with that cretin."

She found a hand-embroidered damask tablecloth—"my mother's," she told him—and set her dining-room table. She laid out dark bread and a plate of sardines and tomatoes, then offered him wine. He studied the label: a Carmel sauvignon blanc.

"Are you going to have some?" he asked.

"I don't feel like any," she answered dully.

He could have used a glass but remembering his hangover from last night, he also declined.

She brought out some mineral water. "Gavril will be here in a moment. He'll take care of things . . ." Her voice trailed off, but she lifted her head, chin thrust forward. Her unpainted lips formed a brief tight smile. Then she noticed Ravid's things on the table in the kitchen, and suddenly she could no longer control herself and began sobbing. She looked so vulnerable. She reached for Landover's hands, and as if she could no longer bear the weight, she leaned her head on his shoulder.

"I'm sorry," she said, withdrawing a moment later. She stared blankly at the sardines. "Here my father is dead, my father who gave so much to this country, and now this country, his country, my country, wants to arrest his daughter."

"You should eat something yourself." He laid a piece of sardine on a chunk of dark bread and handed it to her.

She shook her head.

"We'll talk to Gavril," she repeated. "He'll fix everything. He saw me grow up."

"Still, you must eat," he urged.

"You must have children."

"No," he answered rather abruptly. "Why?"

She smiled at him. "You sound like a Jewish mother."

He smiled.

They heard steps just outside the rear door.

"Can that be Gavril so soon?" she asked, puzzled, moving to the utility room. Landover looked out the front window. Too late he saw the mud-colored van.

Two men with guns drawn and long silencers affixed to the barrels stormed into the kitchen through the unlocked door, both dressed in sports shirts, jeans, sneakers, and yarmulkes.

"On the floor," a third yelled, bursting in the front door. He was taller, the same familiar person Landover had seen on the trail, with the Los Angeles Dodgers baseball jacket and reddish hair under a plaid kipa. He carried a coil of rope. The others searched Landover and Rachel.

Landover tried to fight them, but they jumped him, forced him to the floor, tied him up as if he were a steer in a rodeo. The redhead put a hand on his crotch and squeezed hard. Landover yelled in pain.

"You squeal like a critter." The redhead spoke American English with a western accent.

He tried to tie Rachel's arms but she spun around and whacked him with her elbows. One of the other men grabbed her elbows and squeezed them together behind her, then, despite her struggles, the redhead fingered the stone hanging from her neck. "Nice Eilat stone, eh? I'll keep it for you." He removed the necklace and lifted her T-shirt. She wasn't wearing a bra. He pulled on the nipples of her small firm breasts as she kept on struggling and trying to kick, but then one of them started tying her legs.

The redhead relieved Landover of his watch, the same watch Landover had tossed to the boy during the knife attack and later recovered. He opened Landover's wallet, saw his driver's license and Stanford ID card.

"Oh, Professor Hillsdale P. Landover, Junior, Faculty at Stanford. I am so happy to meet you. I thought you must be someone important. I trust you've had a good visit to our lovely Israel. We hope to make your trip even more enjoyable. We will have some pleasant talks about things like fusion."

The redhead punched him in the stomach and Landover keeled over.

"You're supposed to say how delighted you are to meet me."

As Landover spit out blood, he took a kick in the sternum.

The redhead was now looking at his notebook. "Bismuth and isotopes gold . . . yes, we are going to have some lovely talks."

The redhead was momentarily diverted. One of the other men came from the kitchen with Ravid's gun, address book, and wallet.

"Ah, very interesting," said the redhead.

"Bastards," Rachel managed to get out. "Who are you, anyway?"

"We'll have plenty of time to get to know one another better," said the redhead as he withdrew a roll of masking tape from his pocket and slapped a generous amount first over Rachel's mouth, then over Landover's.

"That's for talking foul," he said. "My stepmother used to wash my mouth with soap until I got too big for her."

He left them for a moment for a quick tour of the house. Stopping at the table he ate some of the bread and sardines and after wiping his hands on the damask tablecloth went into the bedroom. He returned to his prisoners carrying the sheets, blanket, and coverlet.

"Anything for your comfort, my dears," he said.

# 17

IT WAS AN afternoon late in the decade of the 1980s, and the men from the Al Qaqaa State Establishment of the Ministry of Industry and Military Industrialization (MIMI) were gathered on the top floor of the air-conditioned thirteen-story Rafidain Bank building on Rashid Street. Sun-baked Baghdad—a jumble of minarets and turquoise-domed mosques, shabby boxlike steel and glass buildings and mud-walled homes, all sprouting TV antennas—stretched as far as the eye could see toward the flood plains of Abu Ghurayb.

At the markets and bazaars, men in white turbans and baggy pants and women in shapeless black dresses and chadors explored racks of tomatoes and chickpeas, old clothes, and Samsung VCRs. Other somewhat more westernized crowds strolled past the teahouses on Jumhouriya Street and Midan Square and the restaurants on Abou Nawas Street offering freshly caught masgouf. Trucks, pushcarts, big and little cars, even London-style double-decker buses inched along the boulevards and narrower streets and across dozens of bridges over the muddy Tigris.

Yet despite the feverish intensity of commerce, much about the city was martial and monumental: the presence of soldiers everywhere, and weaponry from Kalashnikovs to antiaircraft batteries; the ubiquitous sculptures of two muscular arms holding swords in the air; the Martyr's Monument to the war dead with its huge lit dome and acres of gardens.

Saddam's palace was barely visible behind a grove of date palms along the Tigris. Barbed wire barricades kept people out. Photographing the palace was punishable by death, as was any speech against the Father-

Leader. Even ownership of a typewriter without special police permission was a crime.

Saddam knew the fragility of life at the top. Doubles impersonated him at all public gatherings. He used his secret police ruthlessly, executed anyone suspected of plotting against him, including members of his own family. "He who is closest to me is farthest from me when he does wrong," he liked to say.

Like Stalin and Mao he loved statues and pictures of himself to try to show how much he was loved. High above the streets, like an apparition from heaven, were thirty-foot portraits of him, in jaunty commando beret, bushy mustache, and designer sunglasses. He encouraged manifestations of the people's love, and they obliged. "Oh Saddam," chanted masses of Iraqis in Babylonian garb, prostrating themselves at his televised birthday celebration, "your candles are the torches of all the Arabs."

The MIMI meeting was to begin at six p.m., but was late getting started because Kamel had not yet arrived. Hussein Kamel al-Majid headed MIMI and as both Saddam's cousin and son-in-law was probably the second most powerful man in the country.

It could have been any board meeting. Notepads and freshly sharpened pencils waited at each place around the big rectangular mahogany table. There were bowls of fruit, glasses of ice water, silver cups of sweet Arabic coffee fragrant with cardamom. White-pantalooned waiters silently glided around filling glasses and cups, emptying ashtrays, removing orange peels, almond shells, date and persimmon pits, and the skeletons of grapes.

The men spoke quietly together or just looked out the windows at a flaming sun slowly extinguishing itself over the western desert. As light dimmed over the gridlocked traffic, shouting street hawkers, wailing muezzin, thieves, beggars, and bazaari, the city soon began to glow and sparkle from the illumination of thousands of electric lights.

About a dozen men were standing around. Most were in their forties and fifties, bright, western-educated, handpicked by Kamel. Like Kamel they doted on exotic technology and esoteric ideas. They were the brain trust, men with specialized knowledge of 156-meter space guns, Abed and Tamuz-1 rockets, induction furnaces for melting titanium and other exotic metals.

They were responsible for the sulphuric acid plant at Qaim, munitions and chemical sites at Taji, Baiji, and Iskandariyah. They worked on the binary nerve agents tabun and sarin, which smelled of apple and pear and which could be packaged in artillery, rockets, and bombs, and on the plutonium and krypton switches that trigger nuclear explosions.

A fleet of black Mercedes idled downstairs to take the men to homes with big walled gardens, or to their ministries, business offices, or to the big military research complexes in Karabala south of the capital or Samarra to the northwest. These were individuals who lived well and enjoyed unusual freedom and privileges. They returned undivided loyalty.

They were there to make Saddam—descendant of the prophet, deliverer from heaven, successor to Nebuchadnezzar—the dominant political and military figure in the Middle East. On horseback, Saddam looked down from the wall. He was dressed in flowing robes and waving a scimitar, leading the Arabs in the seventh-century battle of Qadisiyya to victory over an imperial Persian army.

Saddam often attended. He listened and asked questions. A special chair with a red velvet cushion waited next to Kamel's.

The monthly meetings had a chairman and an agenda. Participants scribbled on their pads, and quoted from reports and other documents extracted from buffed leather attaché cases with combination locks. Exchanges could be spirited, but what differences the men had were only on technical points. Never was there any question about the broader implications of their work, or about actual results, as when their *tabun* and *sarin* killed tens of thousands of Kurds.

Someday, they said repeatedly, the time would come to strike even at the number one enemy, Israel. Had not Saddam himself predicted that Israel would be "scorched"? The men around this table devised plans to weaken and crush the abominable enemy. It was their holy duty, as it had been the holy duty of their forbears over millenniums.

For as every Iraqi schoolboy was taught, the treachery of the Jews helped the Persians in 539 B.C. defeat Nebuchadnezzar and destroy his capital of Babylon and the magnificent hanging gardens that were among the Seven Wonders of the Ancient World.

Now Saddam was rebuilding Nebuchadnezzar's capital south of Baghdad. Saddam had been photographed in a replica of his hero's war chariot. Someday he, too, would lead an army from Ishtar Gate across the salt plains of central Iraq and the mountains of Jordan to push Israel into the sea.

\* \* \*

KAMEL ARRIVED AND, half expecting also to see Saddam, everyone rose. But Saddam did not appear. Perhaps later. Perhaps not at all. He was unpredictable.

Kamel brought the meeting to order. He was a thin, ascetic-looking man with a puffy face, high cheekbones, and a blow-dried mustache almost identical to his father-in-law's. He didn't smile or apologize for being late.

He recognized a dark-haired man halfway down the table. Wallid Ossa Ahmad took the floor. Wallid had been trained as an atomic physicist and now was a businessman with scientific contacts all over the world. He directed global buying of the technology needed to complete Iraq's nuclear weapons project.

He described progress at al-Tuwaitha or its gas centrifuge systems, which separate fissionable uranium 235 from its stable isotope, uranium 238 to obtain the material for weapons production. Al-Tuwaitha was a nuclear center to the southeast.

"Western industry is hungry for our business," said Wallid, "and western governments are accommodating . . ." He spoke in English for the benefit of Peter Middleton, the ex-CIA man who was paying a special visit. Everyone knew and liked Peter. ". . . Export control regulations are no serious hindrance. Our purchasing agents do especially well with German and American companies. . . ."

Wallid provided details of the plutonium processing program at al-Tuwaitha. "Soon we will have a bomb," he said. "As our great father-leader has put it, having a nuclear weapon is our patriotic duty as a great state . . ."

"Here, here," someone, possibly Peter, said in English. Desultory applause.

"None of this would be possible," Wallid went on, "without our very good friends in Atlanta who are helping us write the checks. Our friend Peter, who has worked closely with Chris Drogoul of BNL and has even managed to get some of its loans guaranteed by the U.S. government, must take a bow."

Everyone knew that at least $2 billion of the $5 billion of Iraqi loans granted by the Atlanta branch of Italy's Banca Nazionale del Lavoro went into Iraq's nuclear and other weapons program.

Peter, wearing a sand-colored linen suit and green bow tie for the occasion, lifted his small frame from the chair and acknowledged the applause by wrapping his hands together and waving them over his shoulders like a victorious prize fighter.

Next to stand was Salam Abdul Rezak, educated in Kings College in London, member of Annabel's and the Travelers Club, fancier of Turnbull & Asser shirts. He was an ordnance specialist and the contact man for Gerald Bull of the Space Research Corporation in Brussels. It was the first meeting of the group since Bull's body had been discovered by the unopened front door of his luxury apartment in the posh Uccle district of Brussels. Bull had been shot five times in the head.

Rezak hoped it would be fitting to say a few words in memory of the beloved Canadian gunsmith. Kamel assured him it would.

Rezak cleared his throat. "When I first saw Gerald I was reminded of a professor I knew at Oxford who sometimes forgot to button his shirt. Gerald, too, sometimes forgot to button his shirt, or even tie his shoelaces. But what an engineer that man was. What a mind. What grasp of the world of ballistic engineering. He was too brilliant for the everyday world, too brilliant for the small minds of North America.

"The High Altitude Research Project, which Gerald developed in the 1960s, still holds the record for the greatest firing range ever attained by any gun—112 miles. He invented the 155mm G5 field howitzer and its motorized counterpart, the G6, and sold them to South Africa, which acclaimed them for what they achieved in Angola. Instead of the credit he deserved as a great inventor he was treated as a criminal for selling guns to South Africa. The Americans put him in prison for five months.

"It was our supreme leader who recognized Gerald's true worth and provided the financial support that after his release allowed him to turn his attention once again to his great love, the Big Gun. The completed weapon was to be 130 feet long with a barrel diameter of thirty-nine inches—four to five times the size of any weapon in existence. Gerald had a dream, and in Karabala we are making that dream come true."

A burst of applause.

Rezak offered some fresh details on the successful test of the forty-eight-ton Victory Rocket, which was powered by a series of connected motors from the Scud-B missiles of the Soviet Union.

"On this, too," said Rezak, "Gerald's help was invaluable."

Rezak picked up a glass of mineral water. "Dear Gerald," he said in English, "we are going to miss you."

Kamel, sipping a cup of highly sweetened Turkish coffee, nodded approvingly, then recognized Arif Suheil.

Arif rose. He was a large, smiling man with a gigantic head, bulbous nose, leathery cheeks, and claw marks on his arm and hand from the falcons that he flew in the early mornings. He loved the hunt, and had broken any number of sparrow hawks to the hood. He flew his birds, including a prized female shaker, twenty-two inches from shoulder to tail, with perfect plumage and coloring, large breast, sharp eyes, at hourbara bustards, pigeons, magpies, and small game animals in the plains outside of Mosul. While some of his fellow falconers hunted from the rear of their white Cadillac convertibles, Arif was of sterner stuff, preferring his powerful Arabian stallions.

Arif had close links with the Department of Political and Social Investigations of the Foreign Ministry, the principal repository in the Iraqi government of intelligence on Israel. P & S men liked to boast that they knew more about Israel than the Israelis. Their sources of information were formidable.

"It was a political execution," Arif said. A practiced rage hardened his voice. "The Jews grabbed our land in the 1940s, took more land in the 1960s, helped Iran against us, repeatedly blocked our efforts to become a nuclear power, sent F-16s 650 miles across the desert to bomb Osirik—and now they actually boast that they have killed dear Gerald."

"Boast?" Kamel asked. It was a common assumption that Mossad had done the job, but no one had claimed credit.

Arif twirled on his right index finger a diamond-encrusted ruby ring that he had inherited from his father, Haj Amin al-Husaini, the former Mufti of Jerusalem. "Yes, dear friend, boast. Brussels police say Gerald had $22,000 in his pockets when he was shot just as he was trying to enter his apartment. Mossad didn't even try to make it look like a robbery. The killing was expressly designed to attract our notice."

"Interesting," said Kamel. He looked at Peter. "And what do your friends tell you?"

Peter rose again and made a slight bow to Kamel, Arif and the other luminaries around the table.

"Arif is right, dear Kamel. The agency thinks there was a connection with the hanging of Farzad Bazoft, the Mossad freelancer . . ." Peter stood erect in his elevator shoes and drew on a Rothman. ". . . We know he spied on Gerald. Mossad had Gerald in its sights for a long time. The only question was timing. It needed some justification. The execution of Bazoft gave Mossad the justification. An eye for an eye . . ."

A sudden air of excitement and nervousness. Servants stood like statues afraid to breathe. Peter stopped speaking. The men at the table jumped up. Security guards with Kalashnikovs in camouflage suits took positions in corners of the room.

Saddam Hussein, wearing a freshly starched military uniform, walked in and took his seat with the red plush cushion next to Kamel. Following him were his half-brother Barzan, home briefly from Iraq's United Nations delegation in Geneva. His other half-brother, Sabawi, who headed Mukhabarat, the security arm of the Baath Party, was already at the table. A servant placed a special red telephone next to Saddam. Another servant presented a box of Cuban cigars. Saddam chose one. The servant expertly clipped the end and put it in Saddam's mouth. Another servant lighted it. The servants then retreated to the far corners of the room.

Saddam looked around at the familiar faces, smiled, urged everyone to sit down, and asked that the meeting just continue as if he weren't there.

"Just consider me a fly on the wall," Saddam said, blowing out a stream of smoke. Silence. People didn't know how to react. No one wanted to take the chance of reacting wrongly. Then Saddam smiled. Everyone smiled and then laughed. Saddam, a fly? It was a funny joke. Saddam held his hand up to indicate he had something else to say, and the laughter stopped as suddenly as it had started.

"As I came in, someone, I think it was you, Peter, was talking about the Israelis believing in an eye for an eye. Let me remind you that we originated that concept. It was our code of law. They stole it from us. . . ."

Everyone nodded in agreement. Peter rose again, his eyes fixed on Saddam, his widow's peak like a piece of hard black epoxy, his voice like oleo.

"My President, that was exactly my point. There is little doubt Mossad executed Gerald Bull—and even boasted about it. I have a plan for fully avenging him, exacting an eye for an eye."

"Let us hear it," Saddam said.

"Yes." Several of the others joined in. "Let us hear it."

Saddam waved his hands for quiet and spoke again. "Peter, I am still grateful to you for your suggestions about BNL. Let us hope your new ideas will be as fruitful."

"Thank you, Mr. President. It is indeed a great honor to be able to make this proposal in your presence. Just bear with me a little second as I prepare . . ."

Peter reached down on the floor for his briefcase, lifted it to the table, opened it, and searched inside. The security guards' weapons all suddenly pointed in his direction. He quickly lifted a manila envelope for everyone to see. He smiled. The guns dipped, the guards relaxed, and he closed the case. The envelope was filled with pictures of a young man in Washington. He passed the photos to Saddam.

"Mr. President. This proposal entails a minimum commitment of resources, but it could trigger a chain of events allowing the tortured body of Gerald Bull to rest in peace. . . ."

Saddam signaled and a servant immediately ran over to open a bottle of mineral water and pour the water into a glass. Saddam sipped, then looked disinterestedly at the photographs.

"That young man," Peter said, "is a secret weapon. As deadly as, perhaps more deadly than, any of Gerald Bull's guns. He is nineteen. His mother is Palestinian. You see that he is big and strong with a shock of red hair, which he gets apparently from his late natural father, who was an American. But he has the Arabic lines of his mother, and while he is an Arab, could easily pass for an American Jew. He talks like an American, and hasn't forgotten his Arabic or Hebrew. He is highly intelligent. He hates Israel with a passion, and, if I may be so bold, Mr. President, he greatly admires you. . . ."

"And why does he hate Israel so much?" Saddam asked.

"The boy was born and raised in the Gaza camp of Jabaliya," Peter replied. "His father, an American evangelical preacher, returned to the States before the birth. His mother enrolled the boy in Fatah and married one of the Fatah leaders. Although the boy had some features of his natural father, he grew up with a passionate hatred of him, of freemasons, the Christian church in America, and Jews in Israel.

"The father later gave money to the mother and asked that the boy be allowed to spend some time with him in America. The mother agreed. This young Hiram, who is now working for me, says he wants to do something important for his people. But he needs direction and an objective. He is, as our departed friend Gerald might have said, a loose cannon . . ." Saddam smiled. Others noticed and smiled, too, at clever Peter's pun.

". . . But, dear Mr. President and friends, when I found him and heard his amazing story I said to myself that he could be made into a consummate cannon, as deadly as anything Gerald made, striking terror in the enemy camp. . . ."

Peter bent down again to pick something else out of his briefcase. This time he pulled out a softcover book in English, *The Manchurian Candidate* by Richard Condon.

"Mr. President, have you ever read this book?"

Saddam shook his head.

"May I present it to you? I think you will find the story fascinating and relevant. It is about a deep-cover agent sent by the Communists into the United States early in the Cold War. If art imitates life, sometimes life imitates art. Hiram can be the Saddam Hussein Candidate. Let him be sent to school for two more years, possibly in Washington, to obtain credentials as a nuclear technician or engineer. Then let him be trained here by your very skilled people in the use of new hand weapons, manufacture of bombs, handling of communications—everything that would make him resourceful and deadly once we commit him in the field.

"Then through Mukhabarat, we get him documents of Jewishness. We make him into a technically trained American Jew from Durango, Colorado, returning to Israel. They will love him, believe me. An Israeli cowboy. Usually, all they get are wild rabbis from Brooklyn. He applies for a job at the Dimona nuclear center. It is not pleasant working in the desert. He will be persistent, and he will get a job, if only on the custodial staff. If it takes a year or two, he will wait. He will work in a kibbutz like a good Israeli. He may have to join the army. That's all right. We have time. He is a long-term investment. Gerald Bull couldn't build his supergun in a day.

"But finally we get a man on the inside of Dimona. Think of the possibilities. We get Israeli secrets that will help our nuclear program. When we have sucked them dry of secrets, you may want him to blow the place to high heaven. An eye for Osirik. An eye for Gerald Bull. All is possible . . ."

He paused. Saddam looked pleased. "Because of his knowledge of Hebrew," Peter continued, "because of his American background, he will never be suspected. He is a dagger at the heart of the enemy."

"I like your idea, Peter," Saddam said. "You must introduce me to the young man."

THE MEN OF the Al Qaqaa State Establishment were again gathered for their monthly meeting in the Rafidain Bank building above busy Rashid Street. Although many analysts from the United Nations and from agencies in Washington and European capitals had warned that the destruction of Iraq during the three-month Gulf war in 1991 would push the country back to a preindustrial stage of development, much of the damage had already been repaired, and Baghdad, although suffering from severe inflation, had returned to a bustling commercial center.

The men could look out the windows at giant yellow cranes dotting the skyline, at a new roof on the Saddam Hussein Conference Center, rebuilding of the baked yellow brick Defense Ministry, and heavy traffic on the newly repaired bridges across the Tigris. Of the 134 bridges knocked out in the entire country by Allied bombs and missiles, 134 were mended and functioning. Telephones were working again, and a limited international service had been restored.

Since the outbreak of the war in January 1991, Peter Middleton had not attended the meetings. He stayed in touch by phone or fax. His fees continued to be paid into the Bank Leu from a pool of secret funds that Saddam Hussein still had available, mostly in Swiss banks. During his years of power, Saddam had placed $15 billion outside Iraq, of which probably no more than a third was frozen.

The men looked more worn and shaken than they had before the war. Each had his war experiences to recount. Wallid had lost a son in the Revolutionary Guard, fighting the Americans on plains near Basra. A sister of Arif lost her leg, crushed by the falling beam of her house near Karabala during a bombing raid at the nearby military research complex. Others had similar sacrifices but they stayed loyal to Saddam, and he rewarded them with continued privileges. Though gasoline was scarce for the population, their black Mercedes were still waiting with their chauffeurs.

Recent meetings had dealt with ways to evade United Nations investigators who were trying to dismantle the war machine that MIMI had painstakingly created over the past decade. Today's meeting focused on Hiram Abif, already on line six months.

He had been put in the hands of both Mukhabarat, Saddam's security arm, and Arif's Political and Social Investigations department. The two agencies worked out a program in which he trained as a nuclear engineer and then took an Israeli identity as a right-wing zealot. He lived in Dimona for a year doing odd jobs before applying to KMG. As turnover was high because of the desert working conditions, he was immediately taken on the custodial staff. The channel worked so smoothly that three other young men from the Gaza camps were similarly planted.

Saddam was present and seated in his customary red-cushioned chair next to Kamel.

Arif, the intelligence chief, was polishing the huge ruby on his ring by rubbing it against the twill weave of his well-preserved $900 Brooks Brothers suit jacket.

"Hiram is in touch with Salam Yacoub in Amman. He has some intriguing information about an ultrasecret project at Dimona. He has an American and Israeli physicist in custody who know something about the project. He found a notebook with references to the bombardment of bismuth to achieve isotopic gold."

Saddam turned to Walid, the atomic physicist. "What does this mean?"

Walid was prepared for the question. "Isotopic gold is the same form of gold with the same atomic number but a slightly different atomic weight. Bismuth is an element close to gold in the atomic tables. It seems like they may be trying to convert bismuth into synthetic gold."

"Can one do this?"

"One can make microscopic amounts of gold by bombarding bismuth in an accelerator, but it is not a commercial proposition. The costs are astronomical."

"Israelis must think differently. Otherwise, why would they be studying it?"

"You are right, Saddam. It is worth investigating."

"More than investigating. I want action." Saddam looked at Kamel. "Tell Salam to tell Hiram we are giving him full-scale support. Dispatch our people immediately to the Jordan-Israeli border to work with our Bedouin friends around Zofar in the Arava Valley. They cross all the time. They will get our two friends across, perhaps wrapped in rugs and thrown over the backs of camels. Or donkeys. Saddam wants them delivered here. This must be a major effort. If the Israelis have a way of making synthetic gold, Saddam must have it, too."

# 18

Rᴇᴠ. Cʟᴀʏ Rɪᴄʜᴀʀᴅsᴏɴ encountered Fatima Darwish in 1970 on a trip to the Holy Land sponsored by the Masonic History Company of Chicago. She taught in the middle school, in Nablus, the largest town of the West Bank. The school stood on a hill where all the buildings looked like chalky soap bubbles.

Reverend Richardson was a biblical scholar, minister in the Church of Jesus Christ, and a member of the Mystic Order of Veiled Prophets of the Enchanted Realm. He was a Christian who understood Arab ways and sympathized with the Palestinian cause. In America he had often spoken out against Israeli oppression in the West Bank and Gaza Strip, comparing Israelis and their treatment of Palestinians with Nazis and their treatment of Jews.

The elders of Nablus liked the burly scholar with fiery red hair and respected him as a learned and courageous man of God who was willing to defy the powerful Jewish lobby in America. They invited him to lecture on the Roman Empire, and on the founder of Nablus, the Emperor Titus, who ruled during the first century A.D. The students, so sensitized to every twist and turn of the Palestinian struggle against Israeli imperialism, should learn more about earlier western imperialism—from a western scholar. They wished more people like him could raise the consciousness of Americans about Israel's heinous crimes. He stayed for a term, living at the home of the mayor.

The mayor encouraged Fatima to be his guide and make his stay a pleasant one. She had studied at Bir Zeit University and was now living at

154

home with her mother and grandmother who ran a small dry goods store. Fatima's father had been killed by a ricocheted bullet during the '67 War. Her mother, devastated by the loss, never remarried and spent her life constantly sorting sheets and towels, cozies and aprons on the counters. Local women, in *higabs* and long, shapeless dresses, came more to talk than buy things, and spoke of their hatred of Jews.

Fatima's years at Bir Zeit, a chrysalis of Palestinian nationalism, had made her as passionate as anyone about the evils of the oppressor. But she gradually grew tired of the subject, just as she grew tired of being sequestered and chaperoned. She was a restless young woman, better educated than most in the town, interested in life beyond Nablus, especially interested in life in America. Although she had seldom gone beyond her garden gate without her mother, grandmother, or another woman, more and more she came to enjoy her moments of escape with the American scholar, who was the same age as her father.

She could not understand everything that Clay said, but she had never before met anyone so unusual, so different from the coarse *shebab* of the town. Clay's hair was like the sunset; his voice had the resonance of the surf. He even walked with a swagger, more like John Wayne and Gary Cooper than the priests in the Catholic mission. When she was with him, she felt excitement, joy, fulfilment, radiance.

One day Clay invited her for a drive in his rented Dodge station wagon. The early spring air was chilly. Cloud shadows danced on hills dotted with acacias, lemon trees, and grazing sheep.

He talked about Mohammed and his beloved daughter Fatima, her namesake, about Jesus and Mary Magdalene, and about Abraham, the patriarch of both Islam and Christianity. But Fatima was more interested in his stories about the big skies of the American west, the herds of cattle stretching farther than the eye could see, the ranch house that he had built with the earnings of his gold mine. Alone at night, she dreamt of Durango, Colorado.

They stopped by the vineyards at the Latrun monastery. She had never had wine before. He did not encourage her, but she felt both curious and reckless. After they had consumed a bottle of the local Tokai, the chill left them both. He asked her to call him Clay.

Night was approaching, and they could see the rise of a gibbous moon over the valley of Ajalon. The great scholar swept her into his arms. "Help me to Paradise," he muttered huskily. "They that dwell in the land of the shadow of death, upon them hath the light shined. . . ."

She gave herself to the tone and rhythm of his voice, the heaving of his chest, the lunging of his passion.

Although they were increasingly seen together, the mayor and other men of the council always greeted her warmly and seemed to encourage the friendship. But some of the younger men, including a toothy one with a long sallow face who had been an earlier suitor, made lewd comments as she passed. These ended immediately after she complained to the mayor.

Clay invited Fatima on day trips around the yellow-gray stone walls of Jerusalem and to the sites of ancient buildings described in Chronicles, Kings, Ezra, Ezekiel, and Nehemiah. He talked to her of cubits and plumb lines, the rebuilding of the walls of the city, the building of the second temple two generations after its destruction by the Babylonians. "I want to show you God," he said, "as the sovereign, grand architect of the universe."

Sometimes they drove off to secluded spots where the wind blew gently through olive groves. He locked the van, drew the blinds, and made love to her. He was, she began to realize, both her lover and the father she had lost.

Her mother and grandmother shouted that she was a fool—and much worse. The encouragement of the elders, they said, was shameful. She should not be seen alone with a man. And he was not only twice her age but from a different continent.

She didn't care what her mother and grandmother thought. They didn't understand.

One day she realized from what her married friends had told her, friends who at sixteen were already mothers, that she must be pregnant.

Once he knew, surely he would take her in his arms as usual, tell her how much he loved her, and bring her back with him to America to have their son; she knew it would be a son, and that they would live together happily ever after in the glorious mountains of Colorado.

Just before he was due to leave the Holy Land, she delicately broke the news. He said nothing, but she felt a sudden chill in the air, as if the season had changed and winter was already upon them. The radiance was gone. His face turned to ice, and when he spoke, his voice was like a knife blade scraping glass.

"Terminate the pregnancy," he said. "I will pay for it."

"I don't want to," she cried. "I want to have our baby!"

He looked away. He did not touch her or try to comfort her. He made her feel cheap. Was she of such little value? She repeated through spasms of sobbing she did not want an abortion. She had no idea about these procedures and didn't want to know.

He rose. He said he had to get ready for the flight to America—and to his wife. Never before had he mentioned a wife.

"Do you have children, too?" She stammered.

"No."

Before leaving for America, he awkwardly tried to shake her hand. She turned abruptly away and wiped her tears, but her sobs continued convulsively. She could not say it with her voice, but she did with her lips:

"I hope you are ravaged by the fires of hell."

Her mother and grandmother, whose worst fears had now been confirmed, also told her to terminate the pregnancy. Her grandmother tried to make her drink a foul-tasting potion. She refused. They said if she did not abort the baby, she would no longer be welcome at their house, or in the village. She knew the school would dismiss her.

As soon as she could no longer hide her swelling belly, she took her suitcase and left Nablus. Someone had spoken of babies being delivered without much ado in Nuseirat, Bureji, Rafa, Jabaliya, and other camps in Gaza. She took the bus to Jabaliya because she liked the sound of the name. She told people there she was a widow, that her husband had fallen, as had her father, a victim of the abominable Israelis. No one asked questions, even at the clinic. People were too busy preparing for war.

She gave birth to a healthy baby boy. He did not look Arab, especially with that fuzz of red hair, which as he grew into boyhood she kept clipped as closely as possible. In time the other boys in the refugee camp teased him about it, but he was taller than his peers and eager to fight. Later she enrolled the boy and herself in Fatah and married one of the Fatah leaders. Although the boy looked like his natural father, he grew up with a passionate hatred of him, of freemasons, the Christian church in America, and Jews.

Ten years later Clay returned to Nablus. Making discreet inquiries, he found her whereabouts from a teacher at her former school who knew her secret but remained friendly. He drove to Jabaliya. She refused to see him, but her husband did.

Through the husband, Clay offered her $100,000, but on two conditions: that Fatima allow the boy, who was being called Abdularim, the name of her father, to be renamed Hiram Abif, after the great Master of workmen who is celebrated in the Third Degree of Freemasonry. Second, that she would allow the boy to come to the States when he was twelve years old to complete his schooling. He could visit her during holidays and in the summer.

Fatima did not want to accept the money, but her husband, who had never been at ease with his stepson, insisted. If she was such a fool not to want the money, he said, Fatah did.

In Jabaliya, the black-eyed, pale-skinned, red-haired boy remained Abdularim. In the big ranch house outside of Durango where he went to live with Clay and his wife Sarah, he did not mind being called Hiram. He liked the idea of two names, two distinct personalities. It gave him a sense of mystery and power.

Hirim soon forgot his preconceived hatred of America. He loved McDonald's, Ice-T, Mr. T., television wrestling, and horror videos. Although Clay's wife would not have let them in the house, when his elders were at church suppers, he rented all six parts of *Halloween,* three parts of *Texas Chain Saw Massacre,* four parts of *Friday the 13th.*

While Clay seemed to like having him around, they rarely talked. Hiram's only duty was to spend Sunday morning in church with his stepmother and listen to his father. Hiram wasn't interested in ancient history, but paid attention when the sermons touched on events in the Middle East, as they invariably did. Hiram loved it when his father tore into Israel.

Hiram's passion was guns and Clay indulged him. It was one of their few areas of common interest. Proud father bought his son a 9.6 pound AK-47 with pistol grip, telescoping stock, and a bayonet mount. Hiram used it to hunt deer. The bayonet came in handy for skinning the deer, which he liked to do while the animals were still alive.

Clay added a Colt AR-15 and Ruger Mini-14 to Hiram's collection and finally a Makarov machine pistol, which the boy wanted because it was similar to the weapon used in the Neve Shalom Synagogue massacre in Istanbul.

Clay never punished the boy. When Sarah tried, she was scolded by her husband. Once she threatened to wash his mouth out with soap for "talking dirty," but her general strategy was to avoid him. She was sickly much of the time and stayed in her room. Hiram almost forgot she existed.

At the regional high school in Durango, Hiram worked just hard enough to get by. The subjects weren't difficult, but they bored him.

Though athletic, he had no desire to try any of the organized sports. He played soccer in the refugee camp at Jabaliya, but soccer was not one of the sports of the school.

Girls avoided "the guy with weird red hair." The few Hispanic girls whispered about his "evil eye."

Hiram made friends with only one of the boys at the school. This was a quiet, detached fellow who didn't seem to like girls much, either. The two boys spent a lot of time with each other. Then a tragedy occurred. On a hunt together, the friend accidentally shot and killed himself while cleaning his weapon. Police put it down as one of those accidents that are always happening in hunting season.

Clay had a friend, another Mason, who ran an animal research center in Durango. In his later high school years Hiram worked part-time at the center. He enjoyed the experiments with the mice, rats, guinea pigs, and gerbils. He also learned about digitoxin, a cheap drug extracted from the leaves of the foxglove plant, used in animal research. Administered orally, the drug strengthens weak heart muscles and corrects an irregular heart beat. It was easy to mix the drug in animal food. An overdose causes the heart to race, and in large quantities the heart has a seizure.

After dinner one evening soon after Hiram's high school graduation, Clay had a sudden and unexpected heart attack and died on the way to the hospital. People said the great evangelical minister had been working too hard—all that travel—poor man never took any time to relax.

When it came time to parcel out his estate, the lawyers learned that the old gold mine was largely depleted and the minister had borrowed heavily. Provisions were made for sickly Sarah, but Hiram was left virtually penniless.

Hiram wrote to his mother with the news and when Fatima received the letter, she muttered, "Allahu Akbar" (God is great), but noted errors in his Arabic. "Time to come home," she wrote back.


PETER MIDDLETON RARELY stopped for hitchhikers and wasn't sure why he did that day on the empty mountain road in Colorado. It might have been the young man's shock of red hair blowing like a tumbleweed against the aspen forest, the flash of an earring in his left ear, the red scarf draped rakishly around his neck, or the cockiness of his entire demeanor that almost dared Peter to pull over.

Peter Middleton was a short, dapper, baby-faced man with a widow's peak of dyed black hair. He always wore thick-heeled shoes and held himself erect, even in the car, to take advantage of every inch God gave him. He fancied bow ties, which he thought made him look taller, and silk shirts. He loved the sensual almost human feel of silk: the next best thing to a pair of tight buns. He put creams on his round, sunny face to soften it and delay wrinkles. His mom had called it the prettiest face in the world.

Peter was now retired after twenty years at the CIA, including long experience in the Middle East. He liked to imagine himself in the mold of T. E. Lawrence: solitary, contemplative, romantic, intellectual, closet gay. He even learned how to ride a motorcycle, though he had no intention of killing himself.

After making eye contact with the hitchhiker, Peter put his foot on the brake of the Buick Centurion. But he carried a little insurance just in case things didn't work out—a Ruger .38-caliber semiautomatic in a shoulder holster.

The last incident in Georgetown a couple of years ago had cost him $500 in cash and a nasty roughing up. They'd kicked the bejesus out of him and left him whimpering in an alley, his pockets turned inside out, his face bleeding, four teeth chipped. He'd had them recapped at $600 apiece.

Luckily, he'd been in mufti. While cruising, he always assumed a fictitious identity.

He loved to pretend he was someone else. He had a whole closet of personalities: accountant, journalist, even dentist, after memorizing a tooth chart and preparing some stories about root canals, and now recaps. In his younger days he occasionally cross-dressed, painting his pouty lips blood red and giving himself bazooka bazooms. But that was too much work, and too much risk. Now he just painted his hair.

On that unfortunate night in Georgetown, he had impersonated a professor of Middle Eastern studies from the University of Indiana named Peter Jones. It drew snickers when he told people to call him Indiana Jones, and he had a ball pretending he was from Bloomington.

Now in Colorado, Peter was just completing a skiing vacation and after a stop to see his mother in her retirement community and leaving off the rental car, he was flying back to Washington, where he operated a consulting firm on P Street in Georgetown called International Opportunities Unlimited (IOU). The firm was prospering on contacts he'd developed as the CIA liaison with Iraq in the mid-1980s. Through much of the war, he gave the grateful Iraqis the data from satellite reconnaissance photographs that assisted their bombing of Iran's oil terminals. He had been received personally by both Saddam Hussein and the second most powerful man in the country, Hussein Kamel al-Majd.

IOU worked closely with Kamel and earned several million dollars a year, helping Iraq secure sophisticated American military technology, including components for atomic weaponry. Kamel's people paid their fees directly into Peter's secret numbered account, XTY 86549, at the Bank Leu on the Zurich Bahnhofstrasse. It was all business.

Although Peter was apprehensive about any hitchhiker, he felt like having someone to talk to. His tape deck had broken down, and he hated country and western, all he could get on the radio. Why did the DJs never play Maria Callas?

The Centurion rolled to a stop a few hundred feet up road of the boy, and in the rearview mirror Peter watched him run. With long, quick strides, the boy was there in seconds. All hair, rusty, dangling and frizzy, brows hanging over black eyes like storm clouds. Flashing earlobe. Flared nostrils. A T-shirt advertising Hard Rock Cafe, leather jacket and tight jeans. He tossed his black suitcase in the backseat of the Centurion.

With this hitchhiker, Peter would be a journalist. That was one of his favorite guises, allowing him to ask lots of questions. The *New York Times*? Why not? Few people challenged journalists.

"Howdy. My name's Pete."

The boy hesitated. ". . . Hiram Abif," he muttered.

Beyond that, he said little at first. He sat on the edge of the passenger seat, ignoring the seat belt.

A wild animal sniffing new terrain, Peter thought. His big frame gave off a raw energy. Peter felt a sense of menace, as if the young stud were weighing something stupid. Peter kept his left hand close to his chest. If the boy made an offensive move, he'd kill him there and then. Despite the tension, Peter actually enjoyed the situation.

He did like living on the edge. Although cruising could be dangerous, there was nothing like it for erotic stimulation. The thrill of the unknown, the delight of speculating about the delicacies on the next bar stool stirred wild fantasies. Anticipation was almost better than consummation.

"I'm a cowboy," the boy finally said, "headed for Denver."

"Well, and I'm a newspaperman. *New York Times.* I'll drive you to Denver. Gotta see my mother. She's getting on."

They were going about fifty mph along a winding mountain road. "I'd just as soon get out now," the boy said.

Peter looked surprised. He started slowing. "Do exactly as you choose," he said coldly. He kept his right hand ready for any trouble. "Do you mind if I ask you why?"

"My father said that's a paper controlled by Jews and it always slants the news in favor of Israel."

"I have nothing to do with the foreign side," Peter said, annoyed and a little defensive. He was now enormously curious about the boy. "I must say it's unusual finding someone who cares about such things out here."

"I know how the people suffer under Israel's oppression . . . I was born in Palestine."

"Really? What in the world are you doing out here?" Peter had slowed but not yet stopped.

"Living with my dad. My mother lives in Gaza." The boy reached in back for his suitcase.

Peter turned to the boy, smiling. "You won't believe this, but I've been to the Middle East and I share your views one hundred ten percent. I think we have a lot to talk about. You still want to get out?"

A single car passed them, and a slow-moving truck was approaching from the other direction. The boy seemed to be considering something. Peter's right hand drew closer to his holster. The boy shrugged. "Okay, let's go."

As Peter pulled away, the boy asked: "How long have you worked for the *New York Times*?"

"I just write travel articles for them. I actually have a small business in Washington."

"Do you agree that the *Times* slants the news against the Arabs?"

"I agree that the *Times* and the Jewish-controlled media are responsible for the woeful lack of understanding of the Palestinian cause in the United States."

"That's exactly what my father said."

The boy settled back in his seat, almost seemed to relax.

Peter discovered Hiram had been raised in one of the Gaza camps, spoke Arabic and Hebrew, had just buried his father after a heart attack and was hitchhiking to New York on his way to Gaza to see his mother. "I want to help Palestinians," Hiram said.

Having considered killing the boy, Peter now was tempted to seduce him. But as they talked, a brilliant thought struck him. If his clients in

Baghdad were willing to bankroll Gerald Bull's supergun, they might just go for another kind of secret weapon. By a stroke of fortune, this amazing boy straddling two cultures had fallen in his lap. It was like a win in the lottery. With a professional interest in Hiram rising, Peter kept his hands on the wheel. He had learned over the years it was never a good idea to mix pleasure and business.

Peter talked about his own love of the Middle East, his frequent trips to Cairo, Jiddah, Damascus, and Baghdad. He did not mention the CIA. Hiram had become much more friendly. His eyes lit up at the mention of Iraq and Saddam Hussein.

Peter considered himself a pretty good judge of young people. This one seemed to have the brains and the experience for what Peter had in mind.

"What sports did you play at school?"

"Why?"

"Just curious."

"I never liked sports."

"Did your dad ever take you hunting?"

"Yeah."

"Ever fire a gun yourself?"

For the next seventy-five miles, it seemed, they discussed makes of hunting rifles and went on to pistols and assault weapons. Hiram told him about the Makarov.

In Denver, Peter bought Hiram a steak dinner, gave him his business card, a genuine one showing his affiliation with International Opportunities Unlimited, and asked if Hiram would be interested in working for IOU in Washington.

"You're pulling my leg?"

"Not at all. You have some assets that would be useful in my business. And I think I could help you in your goal of helping Palestinians."

"What's your business?"

"I act as an adviser to certain clients. I counsel them on problems they may have and help them deal with the United States government. My clients find my services useful. It is a successful business."

Hiram brushed his hair back. His eyes were excited but he said nothing.

"You could start—we need someone right away—doing general office work. Entry level five hundred dollars, soon work up to a thousand a week. That should pay for lots of tickets to Gaza."

"But I've never done office work."

"You could learn."

"I don't even type."

"Not to worry. I have a secretary to do the typing."

"Then what do I do?"

"You learn to manage."

"Manage what?"

Peter smiled. "I take on associates now and then for specific assignments."

The waiter brought Hiram a banana split, and a demitasse for Peter.

"How do I help Palestinians?" Hiram asked.

"Working for me helps them." Peter smiled patiently. "But I do have something more specific in mind. It would be interesting and challenging and involve an assignment in the Middle East, and you could make some real money."

"Doing what?"

Peter hesitated, then, no longer worried he might be moving too fast, said, lowering his voice, although given the Muzak he really didn't need to, "Perhaps as a kind of undercover agent."

"Are you serious?"

"Very." Peter did not smile now.

Hiram did. "I wouldn't mind that. I'd like to know more."

"Not at this time. I think it'll work, but I need to get clearance from the client."

"In the Middle East?"

"Yes, in the Middle East."

"Like Saddam Hussein?"

Peter laughed. "Yes, like Saddam Hussein."

The boy effervesced. "I can't believe it."

They shook hands across the table.

Peter held the hand a little longer than he should have. He controlled himself, reached into his wallet, and drew out ten crisp $100 bills.

"These should help you get to Gaza and back." He called for the bill, then drove Hiram to the Denver airport. "Take the next flight to either Kennedy or Dulles airport, whatever connects with Tel Aviv. See me in two weeks in Washington. Be there."

There was no doubt in Hiram's mind he would. Nor in Peter's.

# 19

Major Lon Gavril of the Beersheba branch of the National Police Criminal Investigation Division repeatedly rang the bell of the small, single-story bungalow on Kadesh, then knocked on the door. Lights were on. Ravid's Taunus was parked in front, Rachel's Audi in the driveway. He could hear the air-conditioning, so he knocked a little harder, finally banged. No answer.

"Odd," Gavril told his younger partner, Lt. Dayan Stern. "She knew I was coming over."

Stern tried the door. Unlocked.

She apparently had left in a great hurry. Dirty dishes were heaped around the sink, and open cans sat on the counters, including a half-empty can of sardines. A half-eaten loaf of bread was on the floor, sardine juice staining the tiles and the dining-room tablecloth. Still moist. The water in the kettle on the stove was still warm.

The door from the main sitting room into the bedroom was open. Drawers had been yanked from the bureau. Bras, panty hose, jewelry, old concert programs lay scattered on the floor. The bed was stripped.

Lon Gavril was an orderly man, and it irritated him to see so many things out of place. The bedroom especially troubled him. Why were there no bedclothes? It was only Wednesday, and he knew Rachel, like most Israeli women, normally cleaned house and changed the linens on Friday, before the Sabbath.

"The American was supposed to be here, too," Gavril said. "I wanted to talk to him."

"It's odd he didn't call the police right away to report the shooting," Stern said.

"Very odd." Gavril walked out the front door. "I must call Bloom," he told his partner. "Check outside if anybody saw them."

Distinguished by a large shock of white hair, neatly trimmed, Lon Gavril was in his mid-sixties. He planned to retire soon after more than three decades as a Beersheba policeman.

Dayan Stern, with sandy hair, wire-rim glasses and a bouncy walk, was half Gavril's age. More and more Gavril found that he was working with much younger colleagues who could have been his children. Another reason for getting out.

From the police car radio, Gavril tracked Bloom at Ben Giton's ranch and informed him of Rachel's call, the preliminary results of the SWAT team, and now Rachel's apparent flight. Bloom was angry, angrier than Gavril had experienced in a while.

"You didn't find a body because there is no body . . ." Bloom spoke hotly in his native English, which he always used when riled up. ". . . Ravid is playing his bloody games, but he's gone too far this time, selling his country out to the Americans. His daughter is an accomplice, and now the whore of an American spy."

Gavril didn't pick up the thread until Bloom finally explained that Ravid and the American, a physicist named Landover from Stanford, had broken Dimona security impersonating Halakah Institute rabbis, all with Rachel's connivance.

Shin Bet was already alert to possible Dimona penetration. The Communications Security Service was already trying to analyze a pickup in telecommunications traffic between Dimona and Amman. But this was the first Gavril had heard of any American penetration.

Bloom told Gavril to put out the alarm for Rachel. "She's still asking questions about the new Russian physicist at Dimona. It's more than curiosity or sexual interest. As for this American—he's dangerous. May be armed."

Bloom was fifteen years younger than Gavril, but thanks to his friendship with Ben Giton, held one of the more senior positions in the security establishment. When Ben Giton became minister of natural resources, soon after Sherbatov started at Dimona, Ben Giton named Bloom the security chief. The job automatically made Bloom an assistant to the director of Shin Bet with responsibility for the Beersheba region.

Gavril didn't always agree with Bloom, but knew enough not to argue with him. Bloom was ruthless and vindictive. He crushed people. Never was there any discussion. You either did what he said or faced a vehement argument that he always won, if only because he could shout louder and always go to Ben Giton.

Gavril looked forward to his pension. Life had been hard. Soon he would need a prostate operation. Shura had already lost her left breast. He and Shura had their retirement apartment picked out by the sea in Haifa. He would do nothing to jeopardize that tranquil future and their few years left together.

But his balance had been shaken by this case. He faced a test of conflicting loyalties. He had once been close to both Ravid and Rachel. He had served with Ravid in the War of Independence. But in later years they had drifted apart. Mossad made Ravid too high and mighty, he thought. He was also too willing to condemn the SIBAT people and Ben Giton, whom Gavril had to work with.

Still, Gavril and his Shura, Ravid and his Lili, attended reunions every year with the other Haganah vets. Since Lili had passed away, Ravid didn't get out much. It had now been a couple of years since Gavril had seen Ravid.

Gavril watched Rachel grow up and rejoiced with her father at her decision to return to Israel after her expensive education in the States and England. Now that she was on the Kirya staff, he and Shura occasionally invited her to dinner in Beersheba. From an incident Rachel had told him about, he knew the roots of Bloom's fury. Though married, Bloom had made a play for Rachel, almost raping her. She rejected him and said he disgusted her.

Gavril was staring blankly at the windshield above the now silent police radio transmitter. He knew he'd have to pursue her. He hoped she was far away.

Stern returned from his tour of the neighborhood.

"Most places still empty. I met only one person who saw anything, an elderly man who noticed a van pulling away. He thought it was making a delivery or picking up something like laundry. He paid little attention."

"What kind of van?" Gavril asked automatically.

"He couldn't see it too well. Just a van, mud-colored, he said."

The two policemen went back into the house and spent a long time searching for clues. Where was the bedding? They looked in every corner, even outside in the backyard behind the shrubs, in the garbage can. The American must have rented the van. Did they put the bedding in the van? Why was Ravid's car out front? Was Ravid with them? Could they have gone camping in the desert? Nothing made sense. He reread the Shin Bet cable:

> Professor Hillsdale P. Landover Jr., married, childless, PhD in physics from MIT. Director, Stanford Linear Accelerator Center (SLAC). First trip to Israel. Immediately contacted by Embassy CIA upon arrival at the American Colony Hotel. CIA known to recruit college professors for contract assignments. Involved in two violent incidents since arrival in Israel: 1. death of an Israeli chauffeur for the American Embassy; 2. death of an Arab found in his room in the American Colony. Believed to be investigating Dimona. Working with Yosef and Rachel Ravid. Deception at Lod simulating departure from Israel. Entered Kirya complex as member of Halakha. Could be dangerous . . .

The phone rang. Gavril, at Rachel's desk, picked it up.

"Any leads?" It was the grating voice of Bloom.

"They apparently took all the bedding."

"What?"

"The bed has been stripped and we can't find any of the sheets or blankets."

"So they're in the desert fucking, you schmuck. Put out an all-points alarm."

"I was just going to do it."

"Do it now," shouted Bloom in English. "Dammit, this is a major security breach . . ." He paused for emphasis, choosing his words carefully ". . . Dead or alive, I want them caught."

Gavril didn't like the sound of that.

Bloom breathed heavily into the receiver. "I am in touch directly with General Ben Giton. We are counting on you."

# 20

THE ELECTRIC SMELTING furnace in the basement of General Rafe Ben Giton's *moshav* south of Beersheba could generate temperatures of up to 3,000 degrees centigrade, more than enough to melt gold at 1,063 degrees, enough even to bring gold to a boil at 2,966 degrees. The furnace, with its black cauldron, iron tilting rods, nest of portable slag dishes, and ten-ounce molds that looked like muffin tins had come from the Son of David Smelting Company, Ben-Zvi Road, Jaffa. Ben Giton told the company he was indulging an interest in metals since childhood when he used to pour molten lead into molds to make toy soldiers. The company cared little why the equipment was ordered but did insist on prompt payment. It received cash and installed everything in less than a week. Everyone was happy. The transaction took place two months after Dmitri Sherbatov went to work at Dimona.

To power both the furnace and the special cooling system for the smelting quarters, Ben Giton got the commander of the army base at Shivta to extend high-voltage cables from the military power station, about five miles from the ranch. The commander was happy to do this favor for an old buddy.

Ben Giton told curious friends he was enlarging and renovating his rec room. They said they were pleased that despite his heavy responsibilities in the Jerusalem cabinet, he would be taking time to relax and pursue hobbies. They noted how important such activities were for one's health and well-being. His wife Millie said she was delighted with the new rec room and looked forward to having her husband at home more.

169

Ben Giton and Bloom, both wearing safari jackets, walked down the stone staircase from the kitchen of the *moshav* into a dimly lit passageway that led to the smelter about twenty-five feet below ground. As they approached a heavy locked steel door, they could hear the hum of the electrical equipment.

"We've started the emergency melts," Ben Giton said. "By tomorrow we'll have at least 300 more ten-ounce pieces in Zurich."

Bloom did the calculations in his head. The 300 pieces would be worth about $1 million.

In his late forties, Colonel Simon Bloom was a squat man with thick powerful shoulders, beefy, hairy arms and a toothy, prognathous jaw. Dark-complexioned, he had permanent five o'clock shadow, which with sweat pouring from his body gave his face, even in the corridor's weak light, the sheen of a panther's skin.

In Flatbush, he had learned to fight with a knife and rumble with a Jewish street gang. At eighteen, he moved to Israel and joined the army, which gave him an education and a commission. He was in the '67 and '73 wars, commanding armored units under Ben Giton, and became an intelligence officer on the general's staff.

Like Ben Giton, who was a dozen years older, Bloom was a man of the right. He hated Arabs, wanted no peace except at the end of a gun, and believed it was Israel's divine right to dominate by God's will or force of arms most of the Middle East.

A few years after Ben Giton retired, Bloom, who had risen to lieutenant colonel, took early retirement and accepted a job with Ben Giton's foreign military sales company, Vanguard Enterprises of Tel Aviv. Bloom became the company's most aggressive and successful salesman. He sold Uzis and high-tech riot control vehicles to El Salvador, Honduras, Guatemala, Ecuador, Colombia, Panama, and Costa Rica and made money for himself and Ben Giton. When Ben Giton returned to the government to oversee the Dimona gold operation, Bloom was a logical choice as security deputy.

As they stood before the door, Ben Giton suddenly put a possessive arm around the younger man and peered around into his face. *"Ma schlomech* (how are you)?" he asked. Without waiting for a reply, he went on in English, smiling faintly: "We've earmarked something extra for your account—but you must get those fucking lovebirds."

"We'll apprehend them, General," Bloom said. "They can't get far. I'll prod Gavril."

"Prod? Hell. Give him a kick in the ass." Ben Giton squeezed Bloom's shoulders. "Gavril hasn't done a constructive thing in twenty years."

The general dwarfed the security chief. He was like one of the tanks he used to command: big, loud, lumbering, almost impossible to stop. His head was bald and smooth as gun metal; his eyes were as cold. His leathery leonine face, pitted by childhood smallpox and scarred by Israel's wars, resembled a topographical map: you could get lost in its tumuluses, ridges, and craters. He had considered cosmetic surgery in California, but never until recently had the time or money.

He loosened his hold on Bloom and slipped a coded plastic slash card into a Chubb slot below the door handle to activate the unlocking mechanism. At the green prick of light, he pushed open the door to a neon-lit chamber.

Two burly men wearing heavy gloves, soot-covered aprons, and helmets with visors were working around a black cauldron surrounded by steel tubing. At the bottom of the cauldron was a spigot controlled by iron rods. Through the spigot molten metal poured into ten-ounce molds.

On a cart along the chamber wall were a dozen gold bricks that looked like loaves of bread, but weighed thirty-five pounds each. Accumulated from "surpluses" at Dimona, the bricks were worth more than $2 million.

The two workers, Ari Shapiro and Bernie Herzberg, like Bloom, Brooklyn-born, had long served as the general's personal bodyguards and ran the smelters both at Machon 3 and the ranch. They were in the select group sharing the Dimona bonanza. Army retirees mainly associated with Vanguard, they were being rewarded for years of fierce loyalty shown the general. "My partisans," he called them, after the wartime followers of his hero, Josip Broz of Yugoslavia.

Ben Giton's "partisans" liked both their man and his vision of the world. He was no hot pink-and-neon reformer, no fag motherfucking peacenik. He accepted the world as it was, not as it should be. To him, might went far to making things right.

They liked his ideas of a Greater Israel incorporating the lands of Samaria and Judea. The '67 victory was the work of God reuniting the two halves of Israel. To yield even an inch of land would be a rejection of God's mandate. The gold from Machon 3 was a sign of divine providence, like the Red Sea separating or Moses smiting the rock in the desert for water. If Palestinians wanted a state, they could damn well talk to Jordan.

"Jordan *is* Palestine," Ben Giton said. Within Greater Israel, a Palestinian state was wrong and out of the question.

American Jews and The *New York Times,* he said, were usually unhappy with such positions. Too bad. Americans gave financial support to salve their conscience. That hardly entitled them to run the country. Instead of pressing buttons from distant shores they should live in Israel. Then they would be entitled to a say. Otherwise, they should keep their goddamned mouths shut. And people like Yosef Ravid, who were always taking their cue from the Americans, should get the hell out of Israel and go find a bungalow in Rockville.

The prime minister, needing support from the right for his coalition, had brought Ben Giton back into the government. The wily P.M., known as the Old Fox, gave him a lower profile, but still influential portfolio, natural resources, which was just fine for everyone. It put the general in charge of Dimona and made him the main government contact for the newly arrived Russian physicist Dmitri Sherbatov.

A gambler all his life, Ben Giton decided to bet the farm on Sherbatov's ability to make gold. He gave Sherbatov a blank check—"within reason"—to make his vision materialize.

As he had in war, now in peace, Ben Giton showed he could get things done. Army engineering units, whose commanders he knew, did all the work. They scooped out the tunnel for the superconducting magnets of the acceleration chamber and rebuilt Machon 3, installing bismuth bombardment vessels, palladium electrode tables, and a mass of other equipment to Sherbatov's exact specifications. Everyone thought it was part of efforts to improve Israel's military security. No one was disabused.

Within eighteen months the construction was completed, and within two years they had their first ingots.

Through Bloom he enforced security. Machon 3 became Manhattan Project II. Under penalty of heavy prison sentences, everything that occurred at the Kirya compound was already tightly held. Machon 3 became a secret within a secret, like one of those matryoshka dolls.

Security for Sherbatov was also elaborate. Ben Giton and Bloom both thought it appropriate that Lev Lermontov, who helped spirit Sherbatov out of Siberia, be put in charge. The talents of Lev's partner, Mordecai Simler, were put to use by attaching him to one of the more active police helicopter units.

Ben Giton had a formal relationship with Sherbatov but developed a good rapport with his brother, Misha Shifrin, who was the first to brief him on the exceptional gifts of Dmitri. Misha, who had a sharp political nose, had taken time from his musical career to serve on an advisory committee of the Absorption Ministry to integrate the new Russian immigrants. Ben Giton would have liked to have given Misha some of the gold "surpluses," but decided against it out of fear he would tell his brother.

Sherbatov obviously thought all the gold went to the central bank. Ben Giton figured the Russian probably would not be pleased with knowledge of private gain from his alchemy. No need for him to know anyway. He evidently wasn't interested in money. He had his new toys, was directly in charge of gold making, and had handsome living quarters. Sherbatov worried about a son in Russia, but in time that problem could be resolved.

The bulk of the production went to the Bank of Israel. Over the past year El Al 747s with Uzi-toting guards had carted at least 700 35-pound gold bricks worth $150 million to Zurich for sale through the Swiss Credit Bank for the Bank of Israel's account.

The gold bore the Stephanus Johannes Paulus Kruger stamp of the Reserve Bank of South Africa. The seal raised no questions. Israel had a longstanding arms trade with South Africa, and often took payment in gold, which it sold in Zurich. The only difference was that the quantities the Bank of Israel sold were a little larger, easily explainable by a pickup in military sales.

You could count on two hands those who knew of the operation: the governor of the Bank of Israel, the heads of Shin Bett and Mossad, the P.M., finance minister, foreign minister, a few top civil servants, men who could keep a secret, even with screws to their thumbs, fully realizing if markets knew, prices would plummet and the bonanza would end along with their careers.

Those aware of what was going on in the Ben Giton cellar were an even more restricted, more secretive group, including the two old bodyguards and several key Vanguard employees.

For now, a huge amount of Ben Giton's time went into the Dimona operation. He had taken a salary cut to come back into the government. He had no private fortune, and his expenses were huge. Upkeep of the ranch alone was more than most men made. Without his and Bloom's presence to drum up business, Vanguard was barely earning enough to pay its overhead. But it had discovered a fresh source of wealth from a

few extra bars periodically delivered from Dimona. As these were "surpluses" set aside from an infinite supply, it could hardly matter.

Ben Giton and the prime minister never discussed money, but the
P.M. well knew Ben Giton could not live on a ministerial salary. The
cabinet was not supposed to be a hardship. On the contrary. The P.M.
didn't mind what his ministers did on the side so long as they did it
discreetly and made sure not only that he didn't know but that the press
remained out of the loop. The P.M. and Ben Giton went back together
for more than forty years. They were political rivals, but never enemies.
Each had respect for the other.

The first Kruger brick the general filched from Machon 3 went into his
attaché case on an exploratory trip to Zurich. He had to learn the me-
chanics of private sales. He went to the Bankverein office on the
Bahnhofstrasse and was shown into a gold agent's office, paneled in oak
with pictures of sailboats and birds, soft carpets, and a cozy fireplace.
When the official saw the ingot with the Kruger stamp, he became deferential. They went together into a smaller, uncarpeted office where several clerks worked around a high-tech scale, what looked like an x-ray
machine and a lot of fancy computers.

The bar was weighed and put through the other tests. One of the
clerks made a calculation. The gold was of extraordinary purity—999.999
parts of pure gold per 1,000 parts. Ben Giton wondered how any impuri-
ties had entered at all.

"You can offer the gold for sale in the spot market," the banker told
him, "or if you want to speculate on a higher price, you can go into a
futures or options contract."

Ben Giton decided to sell in the spot market.

All easy. The only problem was that Ben Giton wanted his cash right
away. The official was sympathetic but noted a little red tape.

A buyer had to be found for the ingot and it would take at least three
days for the transaction to clear. The bank was simply a facilitator. The
gold would have to be stored and insured until it was physically transferred. Along with commissions from the sale, these were costs the seller
had to absorb. He could have the proceeds minus charges credited to his
account within a week.

If Ben Giton wanted cash immediately, however, he could take out a
loan against the gold collateral, which would automatically wipe itself out
once the sale was consummated. But it would take forty-eight hours for

the loan agreement to be drawn up and the money to be ready. And, of course, a little interest would have to be charged.

"If you had one-ounce, five-ounce, or ten-ounce pieces," the banker volunteered, "you would have no problem because such pieces are so much more fungible."

Ben Giton stayed two nights at the Baur en Ville and returned to Israel with 250,000 Swiss francs. He loved the beautiful Swiss money almost as much as his gold. The notes were such a pleasure to look at and feel, the substantial texture of the linen-weave paper, the subtlety of the colors, the solidarity of the value. One Swiss franc was now worth about a dollar. Not that many years ago it had been worth fifty cents.

He also loved how the size of the notes increased with the denomination. Not like the U.S. dollar, with its egalitarian pretensions. The Swiss had too much respect for money. How could you ever lose or mistake a 1,000 SF note that looked less like money than a fine serviette?

The experience at the bank was instructive. He decided that to avoid clogging the works for Kruger ingots that would soon be sold by the Bank of Israel, he had to produce the gold himself in the smaller denominations. He used most of the 250,000 francs to restructure his basement, buy the furnace and other equipment. The furnace now melted down each ingot into fifty-six ten-ounce bars.

Still, care had to be taken even about the smaller-denomination bars. It would be foolhardy to dump them all in Zurich. Vanguard now came alive as a gold merchant: the ideal mission for a military sales organization with global contacts.

Ben Giton sent trusted representatives on periodic gold-selling expeditions not only to Zurich, but to London, Paris, Amsterdam, Vienna, New York, Chicago, San Francisco, Honolulu, Tokyo, Beijing, Singapore, Bangkok, Delhi, Calcutta, Bahrain, Abu Dhabi, Riyadh. Even after transportation and other expenses, Vanguard's anemic bank balances, mainly at Rothschild in Paris and the Swiss Bankcorporation in Zurich, were becoming robust.

Ben Giton was in sole charge of the full operation. Only he knew the actual production numbers. He created two sets of books, one for himself, which included the "surpluses," and one for the Bank of Israel, which did not. There were no audits, no controls. He would never tolerate any surveillance or regulation.

The prime minister raised the idea of audits once, but when Ben Giton said he might have to resign, the subject was dropped. The P.M. was happy his slight majority was preserved.

For Ben Giton, everything had been working smoothly until that unfortunate mishap when his Peugeot, too heavily laden, provoked the curiosity of Corporal Klein at the guard post. Klein must have talked to Ravid's daughter before his accident. She had already been asking questions, and must have talked to her father, who, damn him, brought in the American.

"IT'S LIKE BAKING muffins," said Shapiro, as he and Hertzberg ever so delicately tilted the molten bullion into the molds.

"But even sweeter," said Ben Giton. Turning to Bloom, he added, "I love to watch the pour."

Bloom smiled. He liked it, too. Here was wealth creation at its most basic. They stood there for a few minutes, observing as some of the gold in the molds was already cooling and solidifying, fascinated by the way the men were able to control the operation. The noisy air conditioner was working overtime so the heat was bearable. Bloom looked at his watch. 10:33 P.M. He still had a few more minutes before he had to leave. From the ranch to the Beersheba police station was only thirty minutes, about the same time as it would take Gavril to reach the station from Rachel's house in Dimona.

Bloom had been thinking a lot about that woman. A bad egg. A traitor. Meddling in what didn't concern her and then turning herself into a whore for the American spy. He didn't care whose daughter she was. She deserved what she would get. And to think he was once interested in her. Lucky for him she had the rag on. Still, he did have fun wrestling her down . . .

As for Ravid, Bloom used to admire the man, his daring work in rescuing hostages at the Entebbe Airport, his brilliant penetrations of Hezbollah and Hamas. Ravid was tough, courageous, smart, apparently incorruptible. Still, he was too pro-American, liberal, fuzzy-headed about Israel's security, prepared to settle with the Arabs. How could somebody so smart be so dumb?

Ravid, Bloom knew, had always had it in for Ben Giton as well. Having learned from his daughter about the gold making at Machon 3, and moreover that it was run by the general, Ravid seemed determined to undermine the operation even though it was yielding vast returns for the

Bank of Israel. Bloom knew through Ben Giton that Ravid had gone to the P.M. But the P.M. was not about to kill the golden goose and upset the political balance. Ravid must have crossed the line and gone to the Americans. He could destroy everything Bloom and Ben Giton had built. Ravid was traitorous. And Bloom didn't believe Ravid was dead. No, he was up to his old tricks.

"So where do you think Ravid is?" Bloom asked Ben Giton.

The pouring had stopped. Shapiro and Herzberg were tossing the ten-gram pieces on the dirt floor and dowsing them with water. The small rectangles hissed under clouds of steam.

Ben Giton had been watching the show with interest. Suddenly, eyes darkening, he gave his protégé full attention.

"Ravid is dead."

"But Gavril couldn't find the body. There were no signs of any Arab terrorists in the area."

"*Rak rega* (hold on a minute). Do you think they leave business cards? Ask Gavril whether his men searched the cave for spent cartridges. If they did, it was probably cursory with flashlights. Get another team up there headed by someone else besides Gavril. My guess is you'll find cartridges, chipped rocks, and other signs of gunfire in the cave, and that the terrorists carted off the body or bodies to confuse us. Ravid is a trophy. They're probably showing off his scalp."

Bloom nodded in agreement, as if he were thinking the same thought. He made no effort to defend the position he'd taken with Gavril. "I'll send Weiss. He's younger. A good man. We'll definitely get to the bottom of this."

"What about the American?" Bloom asked. "He came back to Rachel's house. I spoke with him there on the phone."

Ben Giton was staring at his boots. There was nothing wrong with his boots, but the general often stared at them when he was thinking. He gave a coarse laugh.

"You had the hots for her once, didn't you?"

Bloom didn't answer.

"You think the American was getting some of the action?"

"*Is,*" Bloom said. "They dragged the bedding out in the desert. As we speak they're fucking away in some wadi. At least Gavril gave me that much information."

The general again put a hand on the smaller man's shoulder. "Simon, consider this scenario. If Ravid has been killed, and I think he has, then the American must feel he's got to tell her. If he goes to the police, he's asking for trouble. So he goes to her place, and she calls Gavril because she feels the police should be doing something. I don't think in those circumstances even an American would be bedding her."

"Why did they take off that way without waiting for Gavril?"

"You scared the shit out of her." The general squeezed Bloom's shoulder. "You found out about her little charade and told her on the telephone, right?" Bloom nodded. "And she knew damn well she could go to prison. The American knew it wasn't too healthy for him or his mission, either."

Bloom looked crestfallen. The general didn't often criticize him. "I suppose I shouldn't have called her. We should have just picked her up."

"I think that's right."

Bloom was relieved that the general spoke without anger. "It didn't occur to me she would try to escape."

*"Eehiyeh beseder* (it'll be okay). They can't get far. But take charge now. Don't screw up again. And don't forget to boot Gavril."

A FEW MINUTES after Bloom left, the telephone rang. Ben Giton picked it up. An operator's voice said: "Please hold for the prime minister."

Usually when they spoke there was good-natured ribbing, as befitted old comrades and competitors. This time the P.M.'s voice was tired, squeaky, and petulant as it bounced between the encoded and recoded scrambler signals between Jerusalem and Shivta. They jumped between Yiddish and Hebrew.

"What's this I hear about a security breach at Dimona?" the prime minister asked.

The general explained the day's events as well as he could. When he mentioned Ravid, the prime minister interjected, "He was well-meaning but a meddlesome fool. I agree with you he must be dead because he is not a traitor. I am disappointed in his daughter, though."

The P.M. was particularly interested in the American. "Our friends in Washington say the American . . . I have something on him some place . . . ah, yes, Professor Hillsdale P. Landover, Junior, of Stanford University, was sent here by the President himself."

Ben Giton's heart was sinking as he envisioned the price of gold plummeting. "The Bank of Israel will lose billions of dollars."

"Not necessarily. The Americans picked up something through Ravid and the CIA, but they don't know whether to believe it. Now, through Ravid's daughter this Landover probably knows something. He got to Machon Three, I suppose."

"Yes."

"So the question is what to do now?"

"We're strengthening security. We've got an all-points alarm out for the two."

"Do what you must to preserve security," the P.M. said. "I was thinking more about strategy."

Ben Giton said nothing, wondering what the Old Fox had up his sleeve now.

The P.M. went on: "You know that before any of this, Ravid came to see me. He asked me about Machon Three and I told him nothing. He said if what he'd heard was true, we were making a big mistake by acting independently and not sharing our knowledge with the Americans. I gave him short shrift. He sent a courier-delivered letter to me. I am now reading from it:

"Mr. Prime Minister, I believe we would improve the economic relationship and thus deepen political and military cooperation with the United States, which should be the main goals of our foreign policy. How could the Americans quibble about granting us military assistance when we were delivering something so valuable to them? We would propose joint gold-making, creating an ever-growing pool of capital for all sorts of projects that Congress need know nothing about. We would then propose that at least some of that money go into joint development of new weapons systems, such as new missile defense systems, antitank weapons, or aircraft with all sorts of new capabilities. Imagine the joy in the Pentagon at not having to answer to Congressional committees, or worry about cost overruns or the economic justification of any system.

"Mr. Prime Minister, the survival of Israel and the well-being of our people depend not on any temporary windfall that may develop from secret sales of synthetic gold but from the strength of our relationship with the United States. We must never lose sight of that.

"A final point. Imagine the recriminations when word finally reaches the markets, as it inevitably will, about our abilities to synthesize gold cheaply. Gold prices will collapse overnight, followed by economic uncertainties. Anti-Semites of the world will blame us. Our standing in the U.S. will fall dramatically. Should this occur, Israel would be in a state of grave danger.

"I remain your obedient servant et cetera. Yosef Ravid."

The P.M. paused after reading to give Ben Giton a chance to comment. The general could hardly contain himself.

"I think the analysis flawed for at least two reasons. Number one, if we tell the Americans today, tomorrow the news will be in the *Washington Post, New York Times,* and on CNN. And that will be that. We will be out billions of dollars. There are flies on every government wall in Washington. The Americans don't know how to keep a secret.

"My second point is that I just don't believe we face the kind of calamity that Ravid talks about. If gold prices fall, it will hurt us, and other holders of gold. But why should that lead to a global depression? Most gold simply sits in central banks. It's not used in world commerce. It no longer even backs currencies. Gold is a commodity—"

The prime minister interrupted. "But his main point, that we need to strengthen strategic cooperation with the United States?"

"I don't think that's the way to do it," Ben Giton said. "If we share our knowledge, it will leak to the world, and good-bye bonanza. They'll still sell F-16s and AWACs to the Saudis and probably cozy up again with Saddam Hussein. Strategically, their interests are with the Arabs. Where we have most resonance in America anyway is not in the White House but Congress."

"All right, my dear friend, you make interesting points, but I'm not sure we can put this genie back in the bottle so easily. The President knows something. He's got his man under cover, the physicist, now a fugitive, but even if he and Ravid's daughter should be put out of commission, there will be further inquiries, perhaps even official ones. Then we will have to say something. I can resist, but not for long. And yes, there could be anti-Israeli recriminations, as Ravid says, if we haven't told them . . ." He paused. Ben Giton said nothing.

". . . No, my thinking now is to do as Ravid wanted. A kind of preemptive strike that will serve also as a tribute to his memory. I will call the President and tell him, for his ears only, what we have done. Then, I will offer to share the technology, provided he can guarantee the security. I will even send the Russian over. You can escort him yourself. He can work with their physicists at Oak Ridge. Sure, we take a chance about leaks, but they'll owe us big if they leak it. By making the Americans our accomplices, we not only build up our bona fides in Washington but get time to pour a lot more gold."

Ben Giton again argued that the Americans could not keep the secret, but he could now see the cunning of the plan. Israel would still have weeks, if not months, before it had to do anything. Negotiations could easily be drawn out on those secrecy guarantees.

"So we help the Americans balance their budget," said Ben Giton. "They should be eternally grateful."

"Something like that," said the P.M. *"Lehitraot*-bye."

# 21

THEODOR HERZL, THE nineteenth-century Austrian journalist and play-wright who founded the Zionist movement, dreamed of Palestine as a place of refuge for the last Jewish tribe in bondage, the Jews of Russia. But it wasn't until the dying years of the Soviet Union, some four decades after Israel's founding, that Russian Jews were able to emigrate in large numbers.

The *Olim Hadashim,* as the immigrants were called, came from Moscow and Leningrad, Odessa, Vilna, Kovna, Gomel, Minsk, Pinsk. About Israel and the Jewish faith, they knew little more than that matzos are baked in the spring and penises of baby boys are trimmed. Few of the male immigrants had been circumcised. Surgeons who could perform adult circumcision, which involved a local anesthetic and stitches, were in high demand.

The *Olim* lived in cramped Jerusalem satellite towns like Gilo and Ramot just inside the West Bank. Life was rigorous. Some found their circumstances even harder than in Russia and soon wondered whether they had done the right thing.

Like everyone else, the Shmucklers appeared pale and uncertain. They wore plastic shoes and dyed blue jeans and carried six cheap suitcases. The trip from Moscow, which involved a twenty-hour transit wait in the airport at Budapest, had exhausted them. What distinguished them from many of the others was that they seemed really to want to live in Israel and not use their stay as a staging point for Brighton Beach.

After completing the lengthy immigration procedures, which included presentation of a birth certificate and internal identity papers stating their nationality as Jewish, they were entitled to an immigrant identity card. They received the equivalent of $500 from the Absorption Ministry to rent a hotel room and cover initial expenses and another $650 for immediate household needs. A little later they got their *teudat zehut,* permanent ID, entitling them to monthly stipends of $700 until they were able to find jobs and get settled.

Avram Shmuckler said he was an engineer, Tamar an economist. Neither Avram nor Tamar was a practicing Jew. They had never tasted the unleavened bread of Passover or even lit a candle in the window for Hanukkah.

But Tamar's papers luckily established she had a Jewish mother, which under the Law of Return gave both her and her husband citizenship. Otherwise, they would have needed two witnesses already emigrated from their Russian hometown, or a rabbi to sign an affidavit. Those unable to prove their Jewishness could not exchange their temporary immigrant ID for the permanent ID of Israeli citizens and were denied some benefits of the state.

They waited for and finally moved into a small apartment in Gilo, not much bigger, they said, than where they lived in Moscow but far better equipped: a bathtub, a new stove, and a small fridge. Neither Avram nor Tamar could find work; yet they seemed to have plenty of money.

One early spring day a few months after their arrival, they took a bus to Beersheba, at the southern limits of the old Judea. They saw the beautiful flowers of the desert—wild red poppies, lavender-and-white mustard plants, pink-and-mauve cyclamen, red buttercups, golden narcissus, and the dark green leaves of jujube trees—and fell in love with the area. They returned to tell their acquaintances in Gilo they intended to move to the south.

"But in Beersheba," people warned, "daytime temperatures are over 45 degrees Celsius!"

Yet nights were cool, and Avram and Tamar Shmuckler found solace in the landscape.

For years Beersheba, one of the ancient cities of Judah, served as little more than a trading post and jumping off point for the desert. But in more recent times it had grown and prospered, as a home for artists, writers, musicians, scientists, engineers, and a large, well-off retired community. There were pubs and restaurants, discos and bars, art galleries and a symphony orchestra. It even boasted the Ben-Gurion University of the Negev, where much advanced work was done to make the desert bloom.

Back in Gilo, Avram got a telegram that his nephew, a young entrepreneur in Geneva, had been hit by a bus on his way to work, and died in the hospital. Avram showed the cable to his neighbor, who offered condolences. He flew to the funeral. When he returned a week later he announced he had inherited a little money from his nephew's estate, enough to buy a new car and keep him and Tamar modestly. Avram bought a gray Audi. He and Tamar needed a strong car for the desert roads.

Soon the Shmucklers were comfortably installed at the Bet Sadot Valev guest house on HaAtzmaut Street, waiting for completion of a new apartment on Smilansky Street. A number of other immigrants had also made the choice of Beersheba, and the Shmucklers made new friends. They went to each other's homes at night to talk about politics. Many of them joined small right-wing parties that advocated expelling Arabs from Israeli-occupied lands.

Avram's best friend was Yuri Kartashkin, a lithe, powerfully built man who used to do some boxing in the Transcaucasian republics. Every day Avram and Yuri went for a long walk in the Lon Grove, a pleasant park out Tuviyahu Boulevard in the western outskirts of the city, near the country club and the Desert Inn. While Avram plodded along the paths like a tired water buffalo, Kartashkin had the gait of a tiger.

Tamar Shmuckler was a handsome, bosomy woman with beguiling eyes and wheat-colored hair gradually turning blond in the strong desert sun. She began spending a lot of time at the Rubin Music Conservatory where she now took piano lessons. Avram bought her a small upright.

"Never too late to learn music," she told her new friends.

She was much more popular than her husband. She seemed to have a warmer personality, fit in better. Her new friends said they loved her beautiful name, which meant date palm in Hebrew.

Together every evening the Shmucklers along with Yuri Kartashkin and his wife Lena and other new Russian immigrants dutifully went for mandatory Hebrew lessons at one of the *ulpanim*, government-run language schools, but they continued to speak Russian among themselves. How many times did they repeat the joke: "What will be the second language of Israel in ten years? Hebrew—because Russian will be the first language."

But the Shmucklers were among the quickest learners in the class and were already making small talk in Hebrew. Their teacher, Dr. Zakai, chided the others: "Why can't you pick up the vocabulary and grammar the way the Shmucklers do?"

Some of the Russian immigrants managed to get visas to Canada and the U.S., but the Shmucklers insisted they wanted to be part of the Israeli experience. No matter how much better life was supposed to be in North America, they were happily committed to life here. Tamar Shmuckler said they would be buried here, another thing that endeared her to her new friends.

During a period when Israelis seemed to be turned against each other, it was especially heartwarming and inspiring that Israel receive such unsolicited tribute from its newest citizens, said Dr. Zakai, one of the Shmucklers' admirers.

Sometimes after Hebrew class they walked to the concert hall for concerts that began promptly at 7:30 by the Beersheba Chamber Orchestra. They became patrons of the orchestra.

The evening when a critically acclaimed violinist, also a recent immigrant, made his Beersheba debut playing the Mendelssohn Concerto in G major, the Shmucklers left their Hebrew class a few minutes early. The violinist's name was Mikhail Shifrin. He had studied under Oistrakh, had been concert master of the Odessa Symphony Orchestra, and was now concert master of the Israel Camerata of Rehovot.

It was rumored he had a brother who lived at the country club and who worked at Dimona. The brother was also newly arrived, but no one had actually met him.

Because Mikhail was performing the popular Mendelssohn, there was competition for the tickets that night. To make sure they did not miss the concert, the Shmucklers bought their tickets the day the concert was announced.

After the concert, which was a great success, including the encore, the Chaconne from Bach's D Minor Partita, all the patrons of the symphony were invited to a reception backstage. Avram Shmuckler complained he was not feeling well and went home immediately after the concert. Tamar attended the reception.

The soloist's jaw dropped when Tamar leaned over to kiss him on the cheek. His grizzled, unruly hair seemed to spring out like the quills of a porcupine. In this befuddled state, he pumped her hand repeatedly, as if somehow that was the key to his enlightenment. She told him in Russian that from the way his concerto sounded, life must be treating him very well, and that Israel was lucky to have such great Russian musicians.

She drew an even sharper reaction from a taller, slimmer man with a mop of black hair and a geometrically lined face standing by himself in the corner between the bar and a table with hors d'oeuvres. He stared at her with brooding intensity as if she were Queen of the Night, but for the sake of convention managed to frame a tentative smile. He didn't speak, but his lips shaped the name *Tanya*.

She saw him out of the corner of her eye. Abandoning Misha, she walked over.

"Dima," she exclaimed in a whisper, trying not to attract undue attention from the two men apparently keeping an eye on him from an alcove. The room was crowded and animated, and no one appeared to pay them any attention. She steered him beyond a cluster of people, then turned to face him. She reached out and held his arms, rocking them gently. "You are alive. We thought you had drowned in a fishing accident. It is you, isn't it. You—and I've been watching you—without your tic."

Tension was building on his face, as if the tic were about to return. "Tanya, what are you doing here?"

"I might ask you the same question."

"Just as in Russia, I can't talk about my work. Now I shouldn't be talking to you at all." He looked into her eyes, and saw something of the young woman he had married so many years ago. In spite of everything, perhaps he still held some feelings of tenderness toward her.

"Kyril is not with you?"

"He is with Mama in Moscow. He will go into the conservatory next year."

"Oh! Splendid." Dmitri looked radiant for a moment, then added wistfully, "I miss him. . . ."

It was now three years since he had left. He tried to visualize the skinny, shy towhead with a violin almost too big for him, endlessly practicing scales and arpeggios. Amazingly, that old piece of wood must still be making beautiful sounds.

"He thinks you are dead," Tanya said.

He did not challenge her. He would always feel dreadful about abandoning Kyril. He thought of telling her how he had almost taken their son with him.

"Disappearing like that was a dirty trick," she continued, pressing her advantage.

"It could not be helped." He looked down at the floor, avoiding her gaze. Uncanny how she always knew exactly how to probe his weak spots. He looked up. His body quivered as he spoke.

"What about you? What are you doing here?" he asked. "This is a long way from Irkutsk."

She shifted her eyes to a far wall, rocking on her feet, speaking rapidly without emotion, as if the words had been memorized. "It is a small world, smaller than we often think." She frowned. "I remarried. We received permission to emigrate, and have just begun settling in."

"I didn't know you were so adventurous. Or Jewish."

"There are many things you don't know about me, Dmitri. You never really cared." Her face was flushed.

She was not exactly correct, he thought, but he had no inclination to argue. He had cared for her once. She had always been ill at ease with him in public because of his tic, and this made him feel even more like a pariah. He compensated by replacing what remained of their social life with work, and the gulf between them irrevocably widened.

"And your—husband?—where is he?"

"He was not feeling well tonight. But you will meet him."

"How do you know?" He was annoyed enough at her being here. Although he had not missed his ex-wife, now that she was here with another man, he felt the tug of jealousy. The last person he wanted to see was the husband.

"I hope you will meet him," she repeated. She suddenly pulled something out of her purse. It was a piece of paper that had been folded and refolded. She slipped it into his hand. Without saying another word, she turned her back on him and hastily left the room.

"Tanya," he called, but she pretended not to hear. He did not chase after her. He certainly wanted no scene. Thank God there were so many people in the room. Conversation was so animated the little drama went unnoticed.

Seeing Dmitri standing by himself, Misha detached himself away from a group of admirers and approached his brother.

"Strange seeing Tanya here."

"Yes."

"How did she get here? Was it just a coincidence?"

Misha posed the questions breathlessly, worry etched on his face. Dmitri's escape from Baikal had been his idea, and so far everything had gone well. To Israelis who mattered, Misha was a hero; Dima was a hero. Their lives in Israel seemed to be succeeding beyond his wildest dreams. Yet he knew the old saying: precisely when life seems the best, dangers are the greatest.

Dmitri tried to calm himself. With tremulous hands he poured himself a vodka from one of the bottles on the bar.

"She says she has remarried a man—he must be a Jew—and they have emigrated here."

The note was burning in his right hand. Should he tell his brother? No, better not, not now.

"Where is the husband?" persisted Misha.

"Here in Beersheba, but he was not with her tonight." He had to get away. He gently tapped his brother's arm. "Misha, please forgive me. I must excuse myself for a minute. I will be back."

He headed for the rest room and went into a stall. Sitting on the toilet, he slowly unfolded the white foolscap and read:

Dear Dmitri: For the sake of Kyril, I ask this one favor. You owe it to me and to him. Please meet Avram, my husband, tomorrow. He is extremely anxious to see you. He has some things to tell you that I know will be of interest. He will be taking a walk to Abraham's Well at 7:00 P.M. He will be by himself, and you also must be by yourself. It would be extremely unwise to talk about this letter, even to Misha. Think what you want of me, but think also of Kyril. I am not a completely free agent in this matter.

Dmitri refolded the note and stuffed it into his breast pocket. Flushing the toilet, he left the stall, slamming the door. He brushed past Lev and the other man who were always there for his security. He was furious, and helpless. Yes, she had become a KGB whore. No question about it. But to use their son as bait to hook him—that was beyond the pale. She knew he would never even risk a hair on the boy's head. Still, what if Avram, or whatever his real name was, told Dmitri that the boy was in danger if he did not go back to Russia? What a choice! Dmitri could not even think about it.

Dmitri returned to the reception, headed for the bar. People were starting to leave. Misha, still the center of attraction, planned to drive back to Jerusalem tonight. Maybe Dmitri could prevail on his brother to stay. He knew now he needed help.

Misha broke out of his circle. "Dima, you look terrible."

Dmitri poured himself another vodka, smiled wanly. "Former wives do that to you."

# 22

By THE RIVERBED at the southern end of Keren Kayemet Le-Israel Street at Derekh Hevron were two round stone wells, one open, the other covered by an arched stone roof. A wooden waterwheel perched nearby on a cobblestone courtyard surrounded by date palms.

Five thousand years ago Abraham led his sheep and oxen to this oasis. Chapter XXI of Genesis recounts settlement of a dispute over the water rights. *And Abraham reproved Ablimelech because of a well of water, which Abimelech's servants had violently taken away . . . thus they made a covenant at Beersheba.*

Although the wells were no longer in use, anyone who peered into them could still see pools of water, much as they must have looked in Abraham's day.

A few minutes before seven p.m. Dmitri turned from the Derekh Hevron intersection toward the courtyard. Traffic was light. Most people were at home eating dinner.

A man was standing by the waterwheel. Dmitri couldn't yet see the face, but there was something familiar about the shape and bearing. He drew closer.

The man at the waterwheel greeted Dmitri as if he were a long-lost brother, smiling broadly and extending his hand.

It was someone he had seen before. No, it couldn't be—the KGB man of Goryachinsk. Rostov.

Dmitri ignored the hand. "We already know each other."

"Ah, but we have never been formally introduced. What a great honor

190

to meet the great Dr. Sherbatov after so long." His voice was slippery. "We were neighbors, after all. At least we are able to meet here."

Dmitri did not answer.

"I am really delighted. They say that a man is never a hero in his own country, but believe me, you are a hero in yours, from Baikal to the Sea of Okhotsk."

Dmitri looked at him with loathing, and sudden dread. "Israel is my country now. You have no right to pursue me."

"You forget. Israel is my country, too. Tanya . . . Tamar, and I are very happy here. I only meant to say that you are a celebrity. Your adventures are well known."

"I don't know what you are talking about."

"You mean you have no recollection of flight by helicopter from the cold waters of the lake and no recollection of your work in"—he smiled—"in alchemy."

Rostov started walking toward a bench. "So tiring to stand after such a hot day. *All day those hordes of accursed flies like black thoughts*—You have not forgotten your Pushkin? *All night those hordes of black thoughts like flies*—Is that how it goes? I was never strong on poetry. . . . Why don't we sit in the cool of the evening and engage in a civilized conversation. I will not detain you long."

Rostov wiped his forehead with a soiled handkerchief, plopped himself down on the wood slats. Dmitri stood tensely and said nothing. Out of the corner of his eye he noticed a figure walking by the riverbed.

"Since there are so many connections between us, and since we both now live in the same town," Rostov was saying, "why can't we be friends. We must at least get to know each other better if only because your former wife is now my wife, and your delightful and supremely talented son Kyril is my stepson."

Dmitri was starting to feel sick.

Rostov took some photographs from his pocket and handed them to Dmitri.

"How long has it been? Three years since you last saw Kyril? You see how he has grown."

How Dmitri hated this man, but he devoured the pictures ravenously. The boy was unsmiling in all the poses. There seemed to be sadness in his face. At least, he looked healthy. Several pictures showed him in a dark school uniform and cap standing on a sidewalk. Another group of pictures showed him with his violin.

"Pity we could not bring him with us, but maybe he will be able to join us in a few years," Rostov said.

Dmitri couldn't help hoping. "You mean there is a possibility he could come out?" he stammered. He had not expected this.

"Of course, there is," Rostov said. "He should be with his mother— and his father."

Dmitri never took his eyes off Rostov. Rostov gazed at the ground. The sun was receding fast and the wind coming up.

"What is it," Dmitri asked slowly, "what is it you want from me?"

"Let me just say that what is done is done. No one wants you to put together a broken egg. Remember, this is an era of freedom. People leave Russia freely, and people return freely."

"You're asking me to go back?"

"No, Dmitri Leonidovich, you have freedom of choice. You can go back and see your son and be welcomed as the scientific hero that you are with your great genius and remarkable discoveries. That is a choice that you have always had."

Dmitri shook his head.

"Should you decide to stay here, Dmitri Leonidovich, there is a question of fairness. You were educated in Russia. Your research was conducted in Russia. But does your country benefit now? Does the Motherland get anything back from the resources it invested in your development? No. Others who invested nothing in you now get a golden windfall. That is not fair. Nor is it fair to your own son in Russia."

Damn them, they had Kyril, and would use the boy. And the blackmail would never stop. Even if they did nothing to the boy, the threat of some kind of harm was a form of pressure that he could not endure. How could Tanya have gone along with something like this? Why hadn't he brought the boy out with him . . . ?

Dmitri was getting tired of all the words, all the circumlocutions. He had to be strong, had to test the man . . .

"I don't know what you want. Until you tell me, we can have no dialogue."

Dmitri became aware of another presence, presumably the man by the riverbed. A baby-faced man, springy as a tiger, long arms loose at his sides, was now less than ten feet away. He was observing every move Dmitri made. Had he been able to overhear the whole conversation?

Rostov, shaking his head, waved the man off. "Please sit down, Dmitri

Leonidovich. I'm not going to keep you much longer, but hear me out."
His voice echoed with sadness, as if he were talking to a wayward child.

"I tried to explain that this is a situation in which Russia is the aggrieved party. Certain people in Moscow are terribly angry with you. You did the unforgivable by giving national secrets to a foreign power. They logically want you punished. But these are old-line people, conservatives who do not understand the modern era. Troglodytes. We can dismiss them.

"Others say that the celebrated Dr. Sherbatov should not be blamed, perhaps he was merely tricked by the Zionists. Memoranda were found in the files related to your efforts to develop gold fusion in the USSR. The documents show that you made proposals to do this work in the USSR. That is a mitigating circumstance. Of course, you could not suddenly stop your work and deny mankind the benefits of new knowledge and discovery. Had you not been faithful to your calling, you would not have been true to yourself. Yet these people still think you have obligations there. That is why I am here."

"How did you get linked up with Tanya?"

"You are jealous?" Rostov laughed.

"No, damn you!"

"Dmitri Leonidovich, please."

The tigerlike man started to approach the bench again.

In the lengthening shadows, another figure edged the park.

"This is very serious what I am telling you." Rostov's eyes were cold steel. "You must hear me out. Otherwise, it is not fair. You must, after all, think of Kyril."

"You keep talking about Kyril! Why don't you come out and say you're holding my boy hostage, that you're using him to get secrets from me? In the art of psychological intimidation you are as skilled as the bastards under Stalin and Brezhnev. I know your type. You are one of the thugs I was glad to leave behind."

"You say such terrible things, Dmitri Leonidovich. Can't you accept that I really prefer us to be friends? I like you. I admire you. One of the great scientists of the age. The thing is, we just have a little unfinished business together. It can be concluded in such an easy and amicable way, then when it's all over, maybe Kyril, our dear Kyril, will come out for a visit."

It was too much for Dmitri to bear, but he had to control himself. "Say what you want from me . . ."

The tigerlike man was now standing only a few feet away.

Beyond the stone walls, the fourth man moved stealthily behind a palm tree as if on patrol in the Hindu Kush. His arms were thick, his face thin and sharp.

Rostov shifted his weight on the bench. "It is simple, Dmitri Leonidovich. We want you to work for us." He paused to let the words sink in. "You can help us and we can help you. Tell our people about the process."

"The state now wants what it rejected," Dmitri said angrily.

"Not the state. Certain interests within the Motherland."

Anger turned to disgust. "The KGB wants to make some money?"

"You put it so crudely. We are all entrepreneurs now."

"You are all corrupt!" Dmitri shouted.

"Dmitri Leonidovich, why do we have to play these tiresome games? Russia is a new democratic country. The KGB no longer exists. But even new entrepreneurs collect old bills. Give us what you're giving the Israelis, and we will give you Kyril."

The wind was rising but could not dry the sweat on Dmitri's face.

Rostov drew up his shirt collar and readjusted himself on the bench. "Oh my. Desert nights can turn chilly . . ." He gave a shrug and looked up at Dmitri.

"Dear friend, I want to see Kyril here. You want to see Kyril here. Help our new entrepreneurs. Consider it a . . ." He seemed to search for the term. "A value-added tax—for the value Russia has added to your career. Within a year the boy could be here . . ." He thrust his fleshy jowls almost into Dmitri's face. Dmitri smelled vodka and garlic.

It was getting dark quickly. Clouds like bundles of soiled laundry trundled across the black sky below the bronze sickle moon. Shadows fluttered and danced around the date palms.

"If not, don't make me have to describe what can happen. But it will not be our fault. The blame will be one hundred percent on you. You will bear the guilt for the rest of what remains of your life. Now be reasonable—"

"You really are a bastard. I can't listen to you any longer." Dmitri turned and started to walk away, but the tigerlike man was quickly in front of him, grabbing hold of him.

"Yuri," Rostov ordered, "just bring him back to the bench. I have something more to tell him."

Dmitri, struggling to free himself, was no match for the former boxing champion. With his left arm twisting Dmitri's left arm back, Yuri's right grabbed Dmitri's neck in a choke hold, wrist bone against the side of Dmitri's Adam's apple.

Rostov leapt to his feet in front of Dmitri. "I have one more thing to tell you. I had hoped it would not come to this, but you have forced my hand. Now listen carefully because I will not repeat it. If you do not agree, I will immediately get on the phone to Moscow. Kyril will suddenly find himself in an unfortunate accident in which he will lose perhaps three or four fingers on his left hand. *Do you understand what I am saying?*"

Dmitri freed his right hand from the bulk of Yuri's body, reached up, twisted those thick thumbs away from his throat. But Yuri's fingers around his windpipe just tightened.

They did not see the fourth man who sprinted from the mottled shadows of the waterwheel. Almost in the same moment his silencer-affixed Walther PK .32 automatic fired two shots. Yuri's fingers loosened, and both he and Rostov fell to the ground.

# 23

**I**N THE DAYS immediately following Rostov's death, Dmitri remained in his rooms at the Lon Grove Country Club, too upset to work. While thankful for the presence of Lev, he saw chimeras everywhere. Would the KGB send someone else down? Would they harm Kyril? How to handle Tanya? He felt wretched and worried about the return of his tic. Life in Israel was imploding on him.

He was also troubled by the murder of a corporal in the Dimona security guard—Klein the name was. The bright young face haunted him. They had nodded to each other every evening as his car passed the gates. The slaying was officially called an act of terrorism, though no other reports had come of local terrorist acts, and no suspects had been detained. Dmitri was particularly disturbed by a snippet of conversation he had recently overheard that seemed to link Klein's death with the gold-making in Machon 3. How? Why? He would follow this up directly with Lev or Misha or even Ben Giton.

His living conditions, while certainly deluxe, suddenly depressed him. He wanted for no material thing—cable television, video movies, books, newspapers. The country club had tennis, but the sun was too hot, and he didn't know how to play anyway. There was a pool, but he hated swimming in chlorine. It hurt his eyes. Besides, children peed in the water.

Misha phoned from Tel Aviv. Misha, still the protector whom he would always remember attacking the schoolyard hooligans jeering at his tic. "Although it is always good to hear my older brother's voice, I am very upset. All this is not good for the soul. I should have stayed in Russia."

196

"Nonsense, Dimoushka. They would have destroyed you. You know that. You have done wonderful things here, and will do more. It has turned out better than expected. Thanks to you, the Bank of Israel is like Fort Knox."

"Rostov wanted to blackmail me. Misha, he threatened to cut off the fingers of Kyril's left hand . . ."

"Lev gave him and the other one what they deserved." Misha spoke with uncommon venom.

"I am more afraid for Kyril than ever."

"He is under protection, Dimoushka. No one will touch him, I promise. . . ."

"I can't help worrying . . ."

"It's all being looked after, believe me. This was a rogue operation. Rostov was a common criminal . . ." There was brief silence. ". . . I will drive down again to see you and we will discuss everything."

"Yes, please come down here . . ." He hesitated. "There is something else. Tanya wants to see me."

"And you probably don't want to see her?"

"I want nothing to do with her. Misha, please see what she wants."

"Certainly, if that is what you wish. Do not worry. If you don't mind my saying, Dima, what you really need is a holiday. A few days in Eilat does wonders for the soul."

"I am too sick," Dmitri said sourly. He was annoyed Misha thought his depression could be switched off so easily. But Misha was still the only person he could talk to. And Misha had friends in strategic places. He could pick up a phone, reach the right person almost immediately. As adviser to the Absorption Ministry and part of the leadership Sharansky's *Yisrael B'aliya,* he tried to promote understanding toward Russian immigrants, whom older-line Israelis considered gangsters and freeloaders. He made speeches and was becoming a real political personality.

THE NEXT DAY one of the security men let Misha into Dmitri's suite. The two men hugged. Dmitri was a head taller, still slender, with his wild dark hair shadowing his face. Misha was rounder, like a pumpkin, his hair gray and sparse.

"I have news for you." Misha sat down in an armchair, pausing to rub a handkerchief over the perspiration on his face. The outside midafternoon temperature was 43 degrees Celsius. "Good news . . ."

Dmitri's only reaction was a droop of the shoulders. He felt like the leaden skies over Golan, where they had taken him once for a supervised holiday. It would take more than a few words and smiles to shake off his melancholia.

"But first the bad news . . ." Misha looked proud of his discovery of the American cliché. "I have just seen Tanya. She is desperate and frightened. She explained to me how it all happened. Rostov threatened to have Kyril barred from the conservatory if she did not go along. She hated Rostov but wanted the best for Kyril, and for you. She sobbed continuously. To tell you the truth, Dimoushka, I feel very sorry for her."

"I believe she was a willing participant," Dmitri said. He sat opposite Misha on a faded plastic lawn chair, near the air conditioner, which was on full blast. He poured out Pellegrino into two glasses.

"It's your call," Misha said. "We can help or ignore her."

"What does she want?"

Misha arched his grizzled eyebrows. "She wants you back. That is clear. She has been in a difficult position. She is the mother of your son. Not unattractive . . ." Misha spoke cautiously, as if it were against his better judgment to probe his brother's broken marriage. "She regretted more than anything else leaving you . . ."

"Ignore ninety-nine percent of what she says. . . . She left me. She had no love for me. She was self-centered, an opportunist, never tried to make our marriage work. Believe me, I could never go back to her . . ." He slumped in his chair, eyeing the ceiling, voice softening. ". . . Even though, as you put it, she *is* the mother of Kyril." He sighed, the anger subsiding. "I don't know . . ." He shook his head repeatedly.

Neither spoke. Dmitri straightened up in his chair and gazed at his brother. "What I do know is, I want Kyril here. Do you think that could be done?"

"Complicated . . ."

"More complicated than getting me out of Russia?"

"I mean from his personal standpoint. He would miss his conservatory and his grandmother. He doesn't know you are alive."

"I think he may suspect. When I last saw him—we were fishing together on Baikal—I asked him to promise never to believe anyone who said I have drowned, and he did promise."

"You think he understood what you meant?"

"Children always understand more than we think."

"We can bring him here if that is what you want."

"I want it desperately. I'm so afraid Rostov's friends will penetrate his protection. . . ."

"Consider it done."

"I marvel, Misha, at what you are able to do."

"It all flows from the wonderful things you are doing at Machon Three." Misha finally pocketed his handkerchief. "Your well-being is one of the highest priorities. . . ."

"If that is true, Misha, why am I so miserable? This incident with Rostov seems to have burst the dam. I don't know where I am. I feel overwhelmed, unable to control my own destiny any more than I could in Russia. . . ."

He buried his face in his hands. Misha gripped him by the shoulders. "And what else is on your mind?"

Lifting his head, Dmitri said, "Don't you *see*, Misha? I am a virtual prisoner. My only companions are my guards. I wake up in the morning and am driven to Machon Three. At night I am returned. I can't meet people, normal people, except when I go to your concerts where I meet people I don't want to meet. I got out to see Rostov, but only because Lev was there. I have all the luxuries, escapist literature, any book I want to read, television, films, a lovely place to live.

"They even offer me raven-haired girls and unnatural blondes from Odessa and Smolensk via the clubs of Jaffa and Tel Aviv. They have throaty voices from smoking too much, use drugs. I can't bring myself to sleep with them and can hardly talk to them. They think high-energy physics has something to do with Jane Fonda's aerobics video."

Dmitri paused, felt himself sweating, turned the air-conditioning up a notch. "Misha, I love my work. There is so much more I want to do. I want to use particle physics in cancer medicine. Atoms eradicate malignancies more effectively than X rays or gamma rays. No side effects. I want to work on this, and I have other ideas. But I need some peace of mind."

"We want your happiness and security. What is it you object to most? Is it the lack of freedom?"

"I don't know . . ." Dmitri waved his hands, reluctant to be pinned down. "With more freedom, maybe I would not make more friends. I have always preferred being by myself. But I would like the option to walk by myself, meet whomever I might want. More and more I feel I have merely traded the old Soviet *apparatchiks*—bureaucrats—and their policemen for General Ben Giton and his police."

"That's not fair . . ." Misha looked offended. "You're not being held against your will." Furrows deepened in the cross-hatched V between his eyes. "They want the best for you, Dimoushka. But your security has to be paramount. Remember, you are bait for terrorists, a very important person, like the prime minister, or the President of the United States."

"More like a bar of gold."

Misha did not answer.

"At least," Dmitri went on, "the President of the United States goes places, summits, Camp David. I understand he often slips away to restaurants in Washington."

"You want to go out in Beersheba, in Tel Aviv? No problem. We can arrange cabarets, dinner parties. I didn't think you liked that sort of thing."

"I don't, Misha. But I do need a change. I don't mean just a little holiday in Eilat. I mean a change in lifestyle. I would like to go somewhere and perhaps meet other physicists . . ."

Misha smiled. "I said I had some news for you. I have held back only because I wanted to hear from you first. Very soon, perhaps within coming days, you will be going to the United States."

"No!"

"Yes. There is a new decision to release the gold-making information, on a highly restricted basis, to American government physicists at Oak Ridge, Tennessee. The prime minister wants to repay the United States for services it has done Israel over the years. You will accompany General Ben Giton and be received at the White House in a small private ceremony. You will be thanked by the President himself. Maybe he will invite you out to dinner in Georgetown or Camp David. Then you fly to Oak Ridge, where you will direct the technical work, under the code name of our gold mountain—Zolatoya Gora."

Dmitri's face brightened. He couldn't believe it.

"As for Kyril," Misha said, "when he gets here do you want him to stay with Rebecca and me or his mother?"

"With *you*, please . . ."

"But he will want to see his mother. He knows she is here."

"Well, he can see her then . . ." Dmitri threw up his hands.

"Dimoushka, it will all work out. You will see. Do not worry so much. Think about Eilat, or the States." Misha prepared to leave. He was grinning. "Next time you go to your laboratory, invent something more useful than gold. How about a thirty-hour day so I can find time to practice?"

"I will work on it. . . ."

Dmitri suddenly raised his hand like a policeman stopping traffic. "Misha, there's something else. Have you ever heard of a Corporal Klein?"

An instantaneous flash of recognition? Followed by blankness. "Not really."

"A Dimona guard. He was found in the desert, his throat cut."

"No, I have not heard the story. But it happens all the time, soldiers killed by terrorists, usually hitchhiking. Terrorists everywhere. Hamas makes our lives a living hell."

Dmitri went on cautiously. "One morning I overheard the security people talking about Corporal Klein. I had come early to the car and was waiting in the backseat as they approached. I only heard snippets, but I swear one of the men said Corporal Klein was killed for knowing too much about the gold . . ." Dmitri plumbed his brother's eyes. ". . . Misha, was one of our own soldiers executed by us for knowing too much about the gold? And if so, what was it he knew that cost his life?"

Misha looked uncomfortable. "I don't know anything about this, you must have misunderstood."

"I don't think so, Misha. Tell me, please. Something is happening here that I'm not aware of, and I must know."

"You are imagining things, Dimoushka. You will feel better once you have some travel . . ."

"You are not answering the question."

"I am answering to the best of my ability."

"I know that you know something. I can see it in your face. You know but won't tell. Why?"

Misha was silent, drank more water.

"We have always been honest with each other. Isn't that right, dear Misha? You have protected me, at times been a surrogate father. I told you about my work in the motherland. You told me about the plight of our people, you are responsible for my being here. Despite our age difference we have been closer than most brothers. . . ."

Misha nodded.

"Then why this secrecy now? What can be happening that you can't tell me? I want to know."

"This whole operation is secret. You know that. We are sworn to secrecy."

"Secret to the outside world, yes, but not to us."

Misha was silent.

"Answer me . . ." Dmitri raised his voice. Again he felt he was being swept over the dam. He had never been so angry at his brother.

"I need to make a phone call," Misha said.

"You can make a phone call in the next room."

"I need to make a secure phone call with a secure phone, scrambled signals."

"Well?"

"Well, I can't do that from here."

Dmitri said nothing.

"I will be back," Misha said.

"Go if you have to. I'm not stopping you."

Misha took a deep breath. "I know you are upset . . ."

"I want an answer about Corporal Klein."

"Dimoushka, please listen to me . . . I don't have an answer, but I can make inquiries and get back to you. It's the best I can do at this time."

Dmitri showed his brother to the door.

"I will have an answer in twenty-four hours, Dima," Misha promised.


MISHA RETURNED THE following afternoon. Dmitri showed him inside. The chairs were in the same configuration. But Misha refused to sit where he had before. He walked to the dining table and sat in a straight-back chair.

"If we place ourselves differently, maybe there will be more harmony," Misha said, smiling.

"I am truly sorry. I am not myself these days."

Dmitri sat at the table opposite his brother. He felt he was being totally unreasonable, holding his brother in any way responsible for what happened to Corporal Klein. Still, he couldn't wait to hear what Misha had to say.

"The facts are not pleasant, or neat and tidy," Misha began. "I didn't know any of this yesterday. The essence of what I got, which is to go no further than this room . . ."

"Who would I tell anything to anyway?" Dmitri said.

"All right, then. Ari Klein, parents are settlers, good people. A security guard, twenty-four, doing his military service at Dimona. Knew a little about physics, was clever and pieced together what you were doing for us at Machon Three.

"But he was a little boy with big ideas. He wanted us to give him some of your new gold. Since we fabricated it for practically nothing, he argued, why couldn't a little be given away? Who would notice that it all hadn't gone to the Bank of Israel? He threatened to leak the whole story to the press."

"Trying to blackmail us?"

"Exactly."

"He seemed like such a nice boy."

"Looks are deceiving."

Dmitri glared at his brother. "And so he was killed, and it was made to look as if the Arabs did it."

"That makes it sound worse than it was," Misha said.

"How would you put it?"

"A criminal act was dealt with summarily."

"Without trial, without proof?"

"I said 'summarily.' Remember, there was a threat to your project. Your project helps Israel fulfill its destiny. When you weigh the turmoil and cruelty in the Middle East, the feudal grip of the leaders here, Israel is the only democracy, the only place of liberal western traditions, the only state where dissent is tolerated, where you don't literally get your head cut off for having an independent thought."

"How does any of that justify cutting a throat. And what if the man were innocent?"

"They could not afford to take a chance." Misha drummed his fingers on the table as if practicing trills. He looked uncomfortable. "Simon Bloom acted on his own. He didn't even tell General Ben Giton. When the general heard about it he was furious. He told Bloom that Klein could have been put away for a long time, like Mordechai Vanunu, who revealed secrets of Dimona to the *London Sunday Times*. The general said summary executions had no place in Israel. Bloom has been chastized. The matter is closed. That sort of thing does not happen often. Believe me."

"Bloom is still the security chief."

"I told you it was not pleasant or tidy. Basically, General Ben Giton made his peace with Bloom. Bloom's dismissal would raise questions, details of this might be aired. Secrecy is critical. So they've buried the affair. It would have stayed buried were it not for your sharp ears." Misha offered a tentative smile.

"It's not amusing."

"Of course not."

"Look, I don't fault you, or General Ben Giton, but my gold project is indirectly responsible for the loss of someone's life. I don't like this."

"I agree with you. But focusing so much attention makes it worse. Better to ignore what we can't manage. An oil spill on the high seas often dissipates before reaching shore."

"Ari Klein doesn't come back to life."

"There is nothing we can do now."

"Remember, I left Russia because of the corruption there. Have we— you and I both—only left one system of corruption to join another?"

"I take your point, but I don't agree with it. Israel is light-years from the old Soviet Union, or even the new Russia."

"Not one life was ever taken at Goryachinsk," Dimitri said, shaking his head.

# 24

THE THREE MEN bound Landover's and Rachel's ankles and wrists, wrapped their victims in the sheets and blankets and, hauling them out the front door, dumped them into the rear of the van. Inside the bedding Landover could barely breathe. His wrists, secured behind him, were burning where the rope dug into his skin. Wiggling his head and neck, he managed to open an air hole. Rachel lay next to him, breathing heavily and obviously in at least as much distress.

The terrorists piled into the front seat. They turned the radio on, tuning to a station of incomprehensible Arabic jabber and static. The van started moving and its motor sounded depressingly good, Landover's sabotage attempt apparently a failure.

There were three men, giving credence to Landover's theory that perhaps the man in the cave had been badly injured or killed in the firefight. The redhead and second terrorist must have entered the cave, discovered the colleague, then Ravid's body. Landover now remembered Ravid had spoken about a letter from Rachel about the Dead Sea spas still in his pocket. Landover hadn't found it in his cursory search of Ravid's pockets. It would have had Rachel's address, which would explain how the terrorists could have reached the house so quickly.

After about a half hour, they seemed to have left the pavement and were traveling on the desert itself. No longer was there any traffic noise. It was a much bumpier ride. The van stopped. Landover tensed. He expected to be executed or left to die in the desert with wasps in his ears and ants feeding on his genitalia.

The terrorists jumped out of the cab, and a small light went on inside. Landover steeled himself. But the man who opened the rear doors ignored the human cargo. As he was lifting something out of the back, there was a clink like glass on metal, and Landover heard something roll. The man walked away.

Landover peeked through his air hole. In the dim light he saw the man carrying a small satellite dish, an antenna and a half-depleted six-pack of Cokes with one bottle lying where the equipment had been. The tall redhead and third terrorist were outside the van and he could hear them talking quietly and setting up equipment.

Landover focused on the Coke bottle. He maneuvered himself half out of the sheets and onto the bare metal floor toward the bottle. His bound hands felt the ridges. It had knocked around enough to have a jagged edge. He returned to his original position and concealed the bottle in the blankets.

After what sounded impossibly like a telephone conversation in Arabic, the Arabs returned the equipment, shone a flashlight on their enshrouded guests, laughed, slammed the rear door, and piled again into the front seat. As the engine came on, so did the radio. Soon they were back on pavement.

Landover rubbed the bottle against the rope. Like a rat's teeth, it gnawed through successive strands. At last his wrists were freed and he yanked off the masking tape covering his mouth and inched toward Rachel. Fingering her steaming face, he gently pulled the tape that sealed her mouth.

"Oh, thank God," she whispered.

He worked at the knots around her wrists until they were free. Then, shifting under the blankets, he freed her ankles and his own.

The men were talking animated Arabic against the backdrop of radio noise.

"Where are we?" Landover whispered under the blankets.

"South, into the Negev," she whispered back. "I heard references to Zofar, in the Arava Valley, maybe a couple of hours away. I think they've got some Bedouin friends. He talked to someone, maybe in Amman or Baghdad, about carting us over the border on the backs of camels."

"What about patrols?"

"Bedouins cross freely."

"So they won't kill us?"

"Not yet." She wiped her face and rubbed skin around her wrists.

"They're listening to an Israeli police radio frequency. An all-points alarm for us both. Breaching security, unauthorized entry, impersonation."

"Jesus," Landover said almost too loudly.

The van was slowing, and he cautiously raised his head from under the bedclothes. He couldn't see the road but now the upper walls of the van were a show of flickering headlights, red brake lights, and yellow flashes. Through the gap he saw a long line of orange markers that looked like gnomes' hats dividing a road construction zone from the flow of vehicles. Bulldozers, excavators, and other road-building equipment stood like an armored column along the shoulders. Landover flattened himself again. Truck headlights were bearing down on them from the rear. Brakes were grinding.

"Ready?" he whispered.

She squeezed his hand.

The van was going no more than ten miles an hour, then less than five. They heard the redhead curse.

"Now," Landover whispered. She squeezed his hand again and they bolted, tossing bedding over the figures in the front seat, hurling themselves against the rear doors. The handle gave and first Landover, then Rachel, tumbled onto the tarmac.

The redhead pivoted, throwing off the bedding. He was on the right side of the forward seat next to the door. In the seconds it took him to adjust his eyes to the rear headlights the two had disappeared. The redhead lunged over the seat, grabbing Rachel's right foot. As she fell on the tarmac, he was left holding her sandal.

The van stopped and the redhead opened the right-hand door, but the truck behind couldn't stop on a dime. Its headlights were flashing, brakes screeching, klaxon blasting. The redhead, still half inside the vehicle, shouted at his driver. The van suddenly accelerated and swerved inside the line of gnome hats onto freshly tarred pavement. The truck honked again, still braking. It was a twenty-six-wheel tractor trailer. The driver was cursing wildly in his cab. Now vehicles behind joined in the noise-making. In dead slow, the truck overtook the van and didn't stop.

The redhead jumped out. Ignoring the truck, he looked up and down the road, then into the chalky penumbra. No sign of his captives.

He was checking behind one of the bulldozers when a police cruiser, lights flashing, approached from the other direction. It stopped across the single lane south, blocking traffic. Powerful beams bathed the redhead's face.

Straightening his Dodgers jacket and making sure his kipa was in place, he smiled innocently at the two officers inside the cruiser. One of the officers got out, an Uzi slung under his arm.

"Sorry, Officer, the door of this rental van must not have been locked properly. It plumb blew wide open," the redhead said in an exaggerated western American drawl. "We were looking for stuff that might have fallen out. Sorry if we inconvenienced anyone." His face was smooth, open, a picture of innocence, St. Anthony before the temptations. His colleagues hunkered in the van, kipas in place, hands beside folds in their shirts.

The officer asked for identification and the redhead produced from his shirt pocket a U.S. passport, international driver's license, and car-rental papers.

The officer examined the documents.

"American, eh? Where from?" he asked in accented English.

"Durango, Colorado."

"I have a cousin in Philadelphia."

"You should visit Colorado, see the mountains. God's country."

"Someday." The policeman walked slowly around to the rear of the van and looked at the tossed bedding. Traffic was backed up. The other policeman jumped out and started directing vehicles around the cruiser.

"Enjoying the Negev?" the first policeman asked, handing the documents back.

"We sure are," Hiram said. "We've been camping out under the stars. On our way to the beaches of Eilat for a little snorkeling."

The officer stared at the sandal. "You can probably buy a new pair in Eilat."

The redhead quickly agreed, forcing a laugh, so distracted he had forgotten what he was holding.

"You have to be careful around here," the officer said. "There could be terrorists."

"Really?" Hiram said.

"You'll be all right in Eilat. Don't stop for anyone and get that door attended to."

"Sure will, Officer."

The policeman returned to the cruiser.

"Thanks for the advice," Hiram called after him. "See you in Colorado."

After the cruiser pulled away heading north the other two, who had sat tight during the interrogation, now joined the redhead on the gooey tarmac. One started checking around the road-building equipment, the other behind rocks and the mangy scrub growth.

After a few minutes of searching, Hiram called his crew back into the van. "Eilat," he ordered.

# 25

Barely dodging the massive front tires of the tractor trailer, Landover and Rachel had rolled onto the shoulder and hidden behind a bulldozer. Attention of the trucker and vehicles behind focused on the swerving van and the redhead who was half inside and half outside, then on the police cruiser. Landover and Rachel took advantage of the diversions to run deeper into the desert, merging into the filmy shadows of rocks and brush.

Breathless, they halted to take stock. They were equidistant between the police car and an old flatbed with a tattered canvas roof that was at the end of the line of vehicles, like a caboose of a freight train.

"Can you make it?"

Rachel was massaging her bare right foot. "Let's go."

Keeping to the shadows of the desert until the last moment, they overshot the truck to approach it from the rear. They could see the outlines of the trucker but it was too dark in the desert for him to see them. A headlight was closing in a half kilometer to the rear. They ran to the truck's backboard. Landover gave Rachel a boost, then scrambled aboard himself and they burrowed behind a load of watermelons.

Soon the column of vehicles was inching forward. As the truck drew up even with the police car, they peered out through holes in the canvas and saw her sandal in the redhead's hand as he was talking to the policeman. He seemed to be staring at them through the canvas.

Gears grinding, the truck passed the construction area and several cars overtook them. As they came to a crossroads, the truck slowed, turned left and after a few hundred meters pulled into a gas station. Flickering lights crept into the truck, forcing the stowaways deeper into its recesses. Like rodents, they felt secure only in tight, dark places.

They could hear the unscrewing of the cap and insertion of the nozzle of the gas pump. The driver was whistling what sounded to Landover like something from *Fiddler on the Roof.* After filling the tank, he went off to pay. They peeked through the slats. Pennants were flapping in the wind from a flagpole. In ghostly neon light they could see the driver, a dark, hirsute man in conversation with the cashier.

"Any idea where we are?" Landover whispered.

"Southwest of Dimona. A little place called Teroham. I've been here before."

"Should we get out and take our chances?"

"Definitely not."

"Okay. You call the shots." Landover gazed at the sere lunar landscape beyond the station. "I thought the desert blooms."

"It does. Not far away, at Sde Boker there are orchards and fields of vegetables—the kibbutz of Ben-Gurion. He said if we didn't conquer the desert it would conquer us. . . . Most of the country is desert . . . the Russian physicist would have done better inventing synthetic water."

The driver disappeared around back. Rachel's white shirt, face, and hands were smeared with fresh tar and grease, as if she were in camouflage before a commando raid. Still eyeing the office, she started rubbing her foot. From the dim light of the truck interior it didn't look as bad as she'd expected. Plenty of scratches but no blood.

"How is it?" he asked.

"Weals and welts doing fine."

"You run like a jackrabbit."

"Only when scared."

She stretched her feet and ran her fingers through her knotted hair. "That hand, it just sprang out and grabbed my foot. All hot and clammy."

"It was horrible," he said.

"I swear I've seen the face before. I just can't place it."

"What gives with the skullcaps?"

"They're passing as American Jewish tourists. Great cover."

"How soon before they figure out how we got away?"

She didn't answer. They heard footfalls and ducked behind the watermelons. The driver jumped into the cab and the old engine started right up. At the crossroads, the truck went south and they settled back.

"There's something comforting," Landover mumbled, "about the steady throb of an engine. Feeling better?"

"Like Lazarus's sister." She tried to laugh. "And you?"

"Like Lazarus."

As the truck picked up speed, wind whistled through the slats and spars. The canvas was like a luffing sail. They were on a highway undulating through luminous folds of desert. They seemed to have the road to themselves. On either side was a magical scape of dunes, hillocks, scrub growth, and bizarre rock formations. Occasionally they could make out the billowing jibs and mizzens of Bedouin tent camps guarded by spectral camels silhouetted against the crescent moon.

The desert air was chilly. They made a clearing in the rear of the truck, and side by side against the rear wall they shared each other's warmth. She sat cross-legged, still rubbing her foot. His hands and arms folded together like a praying mantis.

He had been left with his suit jacket. The tumble on the tarmac had smeared it with tar and torn a sleeve. The pockets, usually stuffed, were now empty. For warmth he turned the collar up. The truck bounced a lot. Like pregnant bellies, melons protruded from the wooden crates.

Headlights were coming up fast. They hid behind the crates like fleeing insects. Next time there would be no escape. The rush of thousands of amperes flooded the interior. They tried to disappear. Then the car whooshed past, and all was dark again and they could straighten up.

Happy to have survived so far, Landover couldn't help questioning why he, professor of physics at one of America's most prestigious universities and director of its world-renowned SLAC project, undertaking a mission for the President of the United States, was slinking behind watermelons in a dilapidated truck in the Negev.

He faced Rachel. "Maybe we should just turn ourselves in. The embassy will help us—"

"We wouldn't stand a chance."

"Why are you so sure?"

"I heard the charges on the police radio. Espionage. That's serious, *very* serious. They talked about extreme measures, which translates to shoot first."

"You're serious?"

"Very. Bloom is loyal to Ben Giton"—she punched out the names distastefully—"who must have gone ballistic when he heard I was showing people around Machon Three. He knows that Klein talked to me and probably suspects I know a lot. He also knows I'm a peacenik. I go to the meetings of Shalom Achshav, Netivot Shalom, and Oz v'Shalom. The right hates people like me."

"Like our antiwar movement during Vietnam?"

"Worse. . . . He'll deal with us the way he dealt with Klein."

"But you're the daughter of the deputy chief of Mossad, who was murdered by the enemies of his country."

She took a deep breath. Her big eyes seemed to melt. "They didn't like my father. He was too honest for them. He saw the corruption and didn't condone it the way others did, or rationalize it as a normal part of the market economy. He wanted what was good for Israel, all the people of Israel, not just an influential band of parasites."

Shivering, she hugged herself, blew into her hands.

"Can't your friend Gavril help?"

"Gavril's getting old. He's in the system and has to work with Ben Giton."

"But sooner or later either the redhead or Bloom will catch us. It's crazy what we're trying to do."

"Fighting for our lives is crazy?"

"Trying to escape is crazy. I'm not a damn fugitive."

"You are now."

"No."

"You still don't believe me about the police?"

"Sure, I believe you. I'm just looking at options. There are courts here, judges. We'll get legal counsel. I'll call the embassy. Shepherd could help. Israel is not some tinpot third-world dictatorship—"

"We know too much," she said firmly.

He still couldn't believe it. "They would create a diplomatic incident with the United States."

"Washington will write you off like a loan to Zaire."

"But the embassy, they have to help an American citizen. They can't just abandon—"

"You're here under cover, right?"

"Yes."

"Do you think they'll actually admit they sent somebody here to spy on Israel's most sacred and secret technology?"

"They want my report."

"Not if things go wrong, they don't. They'll run away from you faster than the speed of light. If they have to say anything at all, they'll tell the

Israelis you're a rogue operator, a loose cannon, an Ollie North conspiring with people of questionable loyalty to weaken an ally. You have nothing to prove you're on a White House mission, right?"

He shook his head.

"How can you possibly think you're worth an incident with Israel, especially in an election year?"

She pulled the neck of her shirt over her head like a monk's cowl and crossed her arms more tightly around her chest. "Look, I was born into this business. I know the way things work. Governments have no loyalties, only their own interests."

He stiffened. He was used to lecturing, not being lectured to. It was too much. He was tired of being pushed around. All the hostility and anger of the last thirty hours suddenly flooded over him.

"Maybe you know all about interests. Maybe you know about Israel. Maybe you know a lot of things I don't know. . . . What I do know is I'm just goddamn sick of this business, running like this, afraid of my own shadow, not being able to trust anyone. I'm tired of your Bloom, your Ben Giton, Arab terrorists who pretend to be Jews, Jews who—I'm supposed to make a report to the President."

In the moonlight, her face was set but her voice softened as she tried to reason with him.

"Think for a moment. Please. By now Ben Giton certainly knows who you are and what your mission is. He knows you're with me and that I know. You have a name in scientific circles, a reputation that carries weight. If you say the Israelis are synthesizing gold for a fraction of the market price, people will believe you, and the market price will drop. You think he wants that? Every day he keeps his little secret, hundreds of thousands more dollars flow into his pockets and his SIBAT followers. Remember, they named you, too, in that all-points alarm."

"Damnit, I'm on a presidential mission." He immediately hated the way it came out: defensive, pretentious, self-righteous, naive.

She looked at him, shaking her head, then looked away as if to give her full attention to the Negev night.

He sat there brooding. Self-pity engulfed him. He was bruised, cold, miserable. The truck rattled and bounced. His back ached. His head throbbed. He closed his eyes, pretended to be out of here. No good. He tried isometrics, pressing his hands close together, his feet hard against the floor. He let up and then started all over again.

Through the canvas that had gaping holes the night sky was magnificent, the stars like particles of rice spilled on velvet. Never before had he seen a better display, thousands, millions, billions of stars in those distant, hanging galaxies. He made out the North Star. He could at least confirm the truck was headed south.

He turned toward Rachel, who had pulled well away from him. She, too, had her eyes on the heavens.

How little he really knew about her. Did he want to know more? He had mixed feelings about what he already knew. She was strong-willed, opinionated. Sometimes she talked like God spoke only to her.

People had sometimes said that about him, he reminded himself. But it still wasn't that obvious to him why turning themselves into the police was a terrible idea, especially with the redhead in hot pursuit. That son of a bitch would never give them a second chance. The police might. Israel was a civilized country, a parliamentary democracy, an ally of the United States. In such places, the police looked after visitors, made them feel safe.

Yet police could also be trigger-happy. This was a nation at war for nearly a half century. Everyone was high-strung and nervous, carried a gun or a knife. And she was right, Ben Giton hardly wanted the Americans queering his money machine. If Rachel were right, he was endangering not only himself but her, too.

What a country she lived in, noble in purpose but so full of nightmarish contradictions.

He had to feel for her, admire her. Within less than twenty-four hours she had lost a father, been kidnapped by terrorists, and hunted by police, all because she and her father wanted to clean out some corruption in high places and she believed in peace. In America, such well-meaning whistle-blowers would go to the *Washington Post* or the *New York Times* and work with some reporter on articles that would stir up editors and reformers. In Israel, still under wartime censorship, it wasn't so easy.

Ravid had evidently been impressed by Washington's powers for good. Didn't he know that people in Washington could be as venal as any in Israel?

Landover had counted on discussing some of this with Ravid as they drove to the airport. . . . Poor Ravid. What a tragic loss. He would never forget that lifeless head on the cave floor slashed by a terrorist's bullet.

He glanced at Rachel, noticed strands of her hair were blowing across her forehead beneath the cowl of her white shirt. And he felt a sudden urge to touch her, feel her hair, smooth it out. She looked at him curiously, then turned away, making even more distance between them. He kept his hands to himself.

The road had widened. Instead of crinkled sand and parched hills, they were passing some kind of farm settlement with orchards and vegetable fields. A miracle of change. He ended the silence.

"Is this the Ben-Gurion place?"

"Sde Boker." She nodded.

"Couldn't we jump out here and join the friendly kibbutz?" He gave her a tentative smile.

She gave him a disdainful look, turning back to her own thoughts.

Shifting his body, he drew a little closer to her, but she pulled stiffly away. Dammit, did she think he was going to assault her?

As he adjusted his position on the truck floor, for the first time since their kidnapping he became aware of his money belt. In frisking him the terrorists had removed his watch, wallet, credit cards, notebook, Ravid's gun but had missed the wad of $100 bills stashed in light elastic webbing. So much had been packed into the last few hours that he had completely forgotten he was a walking treasury.

Rachel gave him another look as he unzipped his trousers and pulled out his shirttails to reach behind and under his shirt. He groped for a wad of bills and gave it to her.

"What's this?" Her apprehension turned to astonishment.

"What do you think?"

"They can't be real."

"Believe me. They gave me some cash before I left, and I bought a money belt. I forgot about it, and the redhead never found it."

She smiled faintly. "Who says God doesn't look after Americans." She was trying to count the bills.

Landover zipped his pants up.

"Do I see Ulysses S. Grant?"

"Yes."

"How many?"

"A lot."

She counted. "I count forty-nine."

"That could be right."

"What are you going to do with them?"

"I thought you might have some ideas."

"What do you mean?"

"Just what I said." He met her eyes. "We're in this together. You said so yourself."

"But I didn't think you believed me."

"I do now."

"You're not going to the police?"

He shook his head.

"Are you sure?"

"Yes," he said firmly.

She was still fingering the notes. Her eyes sparkled in a trapped beam of the moon. "We could buy this truck," she said, "or"—she pointed toward the cab—"rent the driver."

"Not a bad idea," he said.

She returned the bills to him. "Put them back," she said excitedly, "except for several that you can reach easily. I'll talk to the driver. I think we'll make his day."

"Tell him this is the land where miracles make new religions."

She rose and started banging hard on the truck wall, shouting to the driver in Hebrew. Landover heard a surprised response, and a conversation followed during which the truck began slowing.

"I told him we're tourists from California and that we jumped on the back of his truck on a bet that we could do it without his seeing us and that I won the bet. He was annoyed, said he never picked up hitchhikers. I said we meant him no harm and would even pay him for the ride. He's from a kibbutz near Dimona delivering melons to a couple of villages and a youth hostel down the road where he's planning to spend the night. I said if he took us to Eilat we'd give him one hundred dollars. He wants to see the money."

They were now past Sde Boker and back in the desert. The truck turned up a desert track. After several hundred yards of climbing they stopped on the perimeter of a deserted archaeological site. A sign hanging from an empty custodian's shack indicated in English as well as Hebrew that it was run by the national parks department. They had a commanding view of the vast starlit desert and beyond to the east the menacingly dark hills of Jordan. In their immediate vicinity the desert had been chewed up by excavations of crisscrossed trenches and mounds of earth.

"Looks like an old battlefield," Landover said.

"There are digs like this all over Israel," Rachel told him. "This is Avdat, home of a people called Nabateans who controlled caravan routes until they were conquered by the Romans . . . All Israelis are archaeologists."

They heard the truck door open and the driver jump from the high running board to the ground. The engine was still running, and the lights were on. Rachel yelled something in Hebrew, and she and Landover jumped from the rear to meet him.

What they saw was a swarthy man and a handgun swinging in a wide arc in front of his chest. After peering into the back to see if any other people were hidden there, he motioned them to walk toward the headlights.

He said something threatening in Hebrew, and Rachel replied in a friendly voice, smiling.

"He thinks we've damaged his watermelons and wants compensation. He wants one hundred dollars now. I said we didn't damage his melons but wanted to be fair and would give him what he asked."

Landover reached into the pocket of his jacket, but the driver shouted something, shaking his head and pointing menacingly with the gun.

"He wants me to get the money and you to keep your hands up." Under her breath she added, "Relax. It'll be all right. He's a kibbutznik."

She peeled off a note inside his pocket and held it up. The driver approached her still swinging the gun, grabbed the note, and examined it in the light of the headlights. He pocketed the note and spoke again in Hebrew to Rachel.

"For another one hundred dollars he'll let us ride in the cab."

"Tell him we'll talk more business when he puts his gun away."

After she relayed that, the driver, still pointing the gun, asked haltingly in English, "You California?"

"Yes. We also grow watermelons."

Rachel again said something in Hebrew and the man lowered the gun but still kept it in his right hand. "I told him I was Israeli and you were my friend and that I was showing you the real country and the good people."

"I get nervous when guns are pointed at me." Landover slowly lowered his hands and the man did not object.

"Too visible in the cab," said Landover. "But ask him whether he can make it a little more comfortable for us in the back of the truck. Tell him we're lovers." He was careful to say it casually.

She spoke to the man in Hebrew. Landover had no idea what she was saying but he made a little discovery about himself, that he not only was getting used to the sound of her voice but liked it. What he had considered as arrogance before now sounded more like quiet confidence.

This was a bloody land, but there was magic in it, too. In the glow of the headlights, gesturing fluidly as she spoke, her olive skin radiant, her chin uptilted, she could have been the reincarnation of her biblical namesake, even with her slacks billowing in the desert breeze, her T-shirt tight against the firmness of her breasts.

He recalled Ravid's words on the drive down from Lod. Yes, he and his dear departed Lili had named their only child after the younger of the two wives of Jacob, the mother of Joseph and Benjamin. She was "beautiful and well favored," the author of Genesis had said, "and Jacob had been much smitten."

Rachel had finished speaking and was apparently waiting for him to say something. Both knew it was time for them to get the hell out of Avdat.

"Tell him that if he drives us safely to a hotel in Eilat he'll get a hundred-dollar tip."

She relayed the proposal with approval. The man smiled even more broadly, showing a missing front tooth, and spoke in turn.

"He says it's three-and-a-half hours to Eilat and offers to take us there tonight in three-and-a-half hours if we give him the hundred-dollar tip and a hundred for a room."

She saw Landover's hesitation.

"Do it," she said. "I know these kibbutzniks. They are good at business but they do what they say. Besides, he has the gun."

Landover quickly peeled off the third and fourth $100 bills. A shakedown, but they were in no position to order a *sherut*.

This time the man took the notes directly from Landover. He even bowed slightly and in heavily accented English said, "Thank you very much." Then he said something more in Hebrew.

"He apologizes for the gun," said Rachel, "but says the roads are dangerous and truckers must be armed to defend themselves against terrorists. He says we are lucky to have jumped on his truck and not one belonging to Palestinians, that they take hitchhikers as hostages and slit their throats."

The driver walked back to the rear of the truck, and cut one of the melons into three pieces. He took one for himself and went to the cab. Then he returned with two blankets.

"No cost," the man said in English, giving Landover a friendly wink. This time there was no gun.

# 26

THE TRUCK WOUND south through the Negev, following saw-toothed mountain ridges and gorges hollowed out by prehistoric earthquakes—terrain not unlike Grand Canyon or Mars. The kibbutznik drove too fast, especially around the hairpins, for his passengers' taste, not to mention their sacroiliacs.

"He told me he's been driving trucks in the Negev for twenty years," Rachel said a little uncertainly, apparently trying to reassure herself as well as Landover.

"We can always jump," Landover said, trying for a lighter note.

They were behind the melon crates on one of the blankets, backs against the wall. They huddled inside a second blanket, again sharing each other's warmth. Now the truck slowed and Rachel saw a marker showing approaches to the small clay-mining town of Mitspe Ramon. In the deserted central square, a clock showed 10:30.

"Two hundred kilometers to Eilat," she announced. "Two to three hours more."

Almost immediately they were out of Mitspe Ramon and were back in open country. Landover picked up pieces of the cutup watermelon, offered her one, which she eagerly accepted. They slurped and threw pits out on the road like kids on a picnic.

The immediate danger of a hijacking by the terrorists seemed to have passed. A little food, a pool of money, at least the rudiments of a plan, and some of the world's most spectacular scenery buoyed their spirits.

"What do people call you?" Rachel asked. "Your friends, your close friends, your wife. You are married, aren't you?"

"Sort of."

"Like sort of pregnant?"

He laughed. "More like sort of grown apart. Our lives are different."

"What's her name?"

"Kate."

"Nice name."

"Shakespeare liked it. I'm more indifferent."

"What does she do?"

"Strategist for a software company in Silicon Valley. She's always on business trips. I think she's got someone on the side."

"How do you know that?"

"Telltale indications. Like when it's a man who answers the phone, hang up. Lots of wrong numbers."

"Do you have children?"

"No."

"So it's not so bad then."

"I can always pack a suitcase, true. What about you?"

"Friends, yes. Husbands, no. Children, unfortunately no." She adjusted herself on the blanket, not unhappy with the reconstruction of her life in seven words. "You still haven't told me, what does Kate call you? Certainly not Hillsdale."

He hesitated, then smiling sheepishly, "Hilly."

"Hilly?" she asked with mock disbelief. "You mean as in ups and downs?"

"Yes," he said, "and not so far off the mark, come to think of it."

"It's a wonderful name," she said. "I like it. Do you mind if I call you Hilly?"

He shrugged. "It's up to you."

"I've never met a Hilly before."

"There aren't many of us. As a matter of fact, I may be a singularity." She liked that show of humor, too. He threw his rind out the back and helped himself to another piece of melon and she did the same.

"The foxes and buzzards will thank us, Hilly. So will the Nubian ibexes and Persian onagers."

"Ibexes I know. What's an onager?"

"Wild ass, silly Hilly." She giggled. She felt light-headed, almost as if she'd drunk too much champagne.

"Hilly," she went on, still savoring it, "what are the chances of explaining all the particles of nature with a unified theory of the universe?"

He picked up a melon pit and formally presented it to her. "You mean like the Higgs particle?"

She held up the pit. "How do you do, Mr. Higgs." She made a muscle with her left arm. "Say hello to the Strong Force."

He obliged by squeezing. "I feel gluons." He turned to look at her. Framed by the whiteness of her shirt and the blackness of her hair, her face seemed to have a soft glow, and splinters of moonlight shimmered in her ball earrings.

For an instant their eyes met, and she smiled. She adjusted herself again, this time curling up on the blankets and laying her head flat so that her hair brushed his knee.

"Forgive me, but my unified theory is shutting down."

He pulled a piece of the blanket over her side, tucking her in, and soon, despite the rattle of the truck engine, he heard her soft, regular breathing. He tried not to move, staring out at wild gray shapes of the night that could easily have been ibexes and onagers.

Occasionally he looked down at a woman who less than seven hours ago had been a total stranger. He tried to gauge his feelings about her. Was he confusing something more romantic with the sympathy he felt for her over the loss of her father?

He was becoming sleepy himself but was afraid to fall asleep, afraid he'd wake up with the redhead leering over him. Still, despite his best efforts his eyes frequently closed and his head slid until he caught himself and straightened up again. It was the way it used to be at some eight a.m. classes at Princeton. As the truck plowed on through the night, the cycle repeated itself many times, until when he caught himself to straighten up, the sudden movement wakened her. She looked at him and smiled, rubbing her eyes lightly with the back of her hand, rising, stretching, combing her hair with her fingers.

"Sleep okay?"

"Not too badly. Yourself?"

"Dozed a little."

She looked out at the night. The land had now flattened and the truck seemed to be making exceptionally good time.

"I had a dream, about my father. He was on the beach, a different section from where I stood, and there were a lot of people in between, and he seemed to be trying to tell me something. He was shaking his head. I think it was a kind of warning. I could see his lips moving but couldn't get close enough to him to hear what he was saying. Every time I tried to approach him he would drift farther and farther away. But he still kept trying to tell me something."

Landover didn't believe in necromancy, but did know the inestimable sadness of losing a father. "I feel what you're going through . . . my father died four years ago. I was close to him and it was pretty devastating."

They rode on in silence. The terrain was changing. Along the roadside boulders seated atop sandstone pillars looked like giant mushrooms. A sign indicated the turnoff to Ouvda Airport. Rachel stood, banged on the back wall, and began new talks with the driver. Afterward she sat down again on her blankets.

"What was that all about?" Landover asked.

"I hope you like nightclubs," she said. "We're going to hit one of the raunchiest in Eilat. With the police after us, there's no way we can register in a hotel. But our friend can. The club is in the basement of the hotel he'll be staying at with your money."

They were now sailing through a colonnade of date palms, passing the first of a series of oases before Eilat. In the air was the salty tang of the Red Sea.

They reached North Beach, on the eastern shore of the harbor, near an elaborate marina system built into a horseshoe-shaped lagoon. Lights glimmered on the beach road. To the east the moon, still a golden scimitar, seemed to be slashing the shadowed hills of Jordan. The Dalia Hotel was next to the more elegant Galei Eilat. In the basement of the Dalia was the Copacabana.

The driver parked just down the street from the entrance, and Rachel told him they would meet him in the club after he had booked his room.

Rachel had cut a sprig of bougainvillea from one of the sidewalk bushes and tucked it into her hair. She had also removed her other sandal so that now with all her smudges she resembled a 1960s flower child. Landover still looked professorial and very American despite the wrinkles, smears, and tears of his jacket. As a couple of eccentric, free-spending Americans, they got a cordial reception at the club. People in Eilat were used to bizarre foreigners. The welcome turned warmer when Landover asked for change for a $100 bill.

They were shown to a table near the dance floor. About a dozen paying customers, mostly male, were watching a bored blonde do a striptease.

Several bar girls sat with customers watching the show and hustling drinks. Other girls sat together smoking and making small talk. Occasionally, one of them rose to make a tour of the tables, trying to drum up business.

The driver joined them then and seemed in high spirits. His name was Ibrahim Cohen, a Moroccan Jew, a fruit picker as well as truck driver for the kibbutz Noar Ha-Lootzi Lo'hem near Shivta. He had never had so much money in his life, and to show his generosity he offered to buy a round of drinks. Over the course of a floor show that included jugglers, acrobats, chanteuses, and more strippers, he got very drunk.

What conversation they had was mostly in Hebrew that even Rachel had trouble understanding fully. She served as interpreter as he told them all about his charming girlfriend Vera who helped run the Bet Noam Youth Hostel in Mitspe Ramon. The only reason he had agreed to their offer to drive to Eilat was that Vera was not in Mitspe Ramon. Her aunt had died in Tel Aviv and she had gone to the funeral. Otherwise, no amount of money would have kept him on the road tonight, he was that much in love.

After two Scotches Ibrahim invited one of the roving ladies named Rima to join them, and bought a bottle of what was loosely described as champagne, which he drank almost entirely himself. When the club finally closed he and Rima were a tangle of arms and legs, and she wanted to take a by now incoherent Cohen to his room. Rachel intervened, insisting she and her "husband" were responsible for their friend. When Rima persisted, Rachel finally told her, in Hebrew, to lay off or she'd call the police, and Rima indignantly left the table.

Rachel and Landover walked the wobbly Ibrahim precariously to the elevator. The room was on the second floor, twin-bedded with a small balcony looking out over a sward of grass bordered by poinsettia and bougainvillea. They found the key in his pocket. They chain-bolted the door and put him on one of the beds, where he began snoring immediately, jackhammer-like sounds that fairly shook shutters and windows.

Landover pocketed Ibrahim's pistol, an Uzi .9-millimeter semiautomatic. After taking turns washing, he and Rachel pulled the second bed as far away from Ibrahim as they could and lay down, curling up like two spoons. They immediately fell asleep.

At daybreak Landover was awakened by Rachel's short gasps. She was sobbing. He was about to say something but she put her finger on his lips, tilted her face upward and through her tears whispered, "I need a chance to cry. I will miss him so much."

Landover could smell the perfume of the gardens below as if in the waves of Rachel's hair. With his index finger he traced the slender ridge of her nose, the whorls of her ears, the lines of her strong and slightly jutting chin, the marblelike smoothness of her open neck. A cone of bright morning light filtered through the billowing gauze curtain, showing a sparkle of green in her wet eyes. Cohen was still asleep, the jackhammer now muffled. They lay there, close, without speaking. Words were not needed.

SOMEONE WAS UNLOCKING their door. It opened an inch, then was caught by the chain bolt. Whoever it was suddenly began banging and shouting in English and Hebrew: "Housekeeping maintenance—emergency repairs. Open quickly."

They were quickly up. Cohen hadn't budged. Landover moved toward the balcony, Rachel following.

"We've got to jump," he said. "Can you manage it?"

She was over the side before he was, falling into the soft grass no more than ten feet below. Breathless from the impact, he slowly picked himself up, looked for her. She was already on her feet. They made their way around a corner to the street in front of the hotel, hurried to a cab, and roused the sleeping driver.

"Take us to the Coral Sea," Landover said, recalling the name of Shepherd's hotel supplied by the embassy woman when he had called from Dimona.

The cab passed the now padlocked Copacabana entrance. Ibrahim's truck stood a few meters away, layered with sand and dust. All its tires were flat. Directly behind stood a dusty mustard-colored van.

At the Coral Sea, Landover paid the cab with shekels exchanged at the Copacabana. No one in the lobby took notice of them. One of the newest and best hotels in town, it was popular with eccentric foreigners. A clock in the lobby said 6:37. A single employee, who could have been Russian, sat behind the check-in desk. A yawning bellhop leaned against an empty luggage cart smoking a cigarette.

Landover picked up the house phone. "James Shepherd, please."

"The room does not answer."

"Could I have his number, please?"

"Sorry, we cannot give it out. Would you care to leave a message?"

"I'll call back."

"Did my husband leave me a message?" Rachel asked at the desk in her most pronounced American accent. Landover sat in an obscure corner of the lobby.

"And you are?" the clerk asked.

"I am Mrs. Shepherd. I just drove down from Tel Aviv." She smoothed her rumpled clothes. "I had a breakdown. Jim said he would leave the key for me if he wasn't in when I arrived. I desperately need to shower."

The clerk gave her a key, and Landover followed her discreetly into the elevator.

# 27

SHEPHERD'S ROOM WAS on the fourth floor. The bed had obviously been slept in. A big tan suitcase lay on a rack. Curtains and drapes were still drawn. Water dripped from a faucet in the bathroom. Yesterday's *Jerusalem Post* and the *International Herald Tribune* lay in pieces on the floor. Rachel hung a "Do Not Disturb" sign on the outside doorknob and turned on the radio. No news, but she did get Mendelssohn's Italian Symphony. She went into the bathroom and showered. Landover picked up the *Trib*.

After a few minutes Shepherd, in bathrobe and swimming trunks, lumbered in.

"Jesus." The startled CIA man saw Landover. "Where the hell did you come from?"

Landover smiled wanly. "We need help."

"Who's we?"

Rachel emerged just then from the bathroom. "I'm Yosef Ravid's daughter, Rachel Ravid."

They shook hands.

Shepherd now headed for the bathroom. "I'm all sticky. Give me a minute to wash this sea salt off."

Shepherd jumped in and out of the shower and called out from the bathroom, "Be warned I'm coming through." A towel around his midriff, he reentered the room and reached into his suitcase for briefs, a light shirt, and trousers and started dressing.

Landover told him about their escape from the redhead. "Everyone's after us—the redhead and his terrorists, and Ben Giton, Bloom, and all those people. You're our last hope."

Shepherd listened politely, asked a few questions. Nothing seemed to surprise him. "I knew you never took that plane, and were probably in some trouble," he said nodding to Rachel. "Your father made me believe the professor here had taken off for the States. Made something of a fool of me, but he also suggested I take a few days in Eilat. So . . . score's even."

"He's dead," Rachel said.

"Yes, I heard. I am very sorry."

"He was a good father, a good man, and he dearly loved his country," she said, almost in tears again.

"I was with him," Landover said. "That's when the terrorists first struck."

"Oh?"

"It happened in a cave in hills overlooking the Dead Sea. They almost got me, too."

"So you went to Rachel's house to tell her."

"You're well-informed."

"That's my business. Why didn't you go to the police?"

"Rachel informed the police after I called. I thought I should talk to her first. I brought some of Ravid's personal effects. Frankly, I also didn't think it wise to get involved in a police investigation."

"Maybe the delay helped them get away."

"It was only moments after he called that I told the police," Rachel put in.

"It doesn't matter." Shepherd seemed to lose interest. He looked at them. "I've been in touch with Langley." Sitting in an armchair near the bed, he crossed his legs and reached for a Marlboro in an open pack on the dresser.

"The prime minister called the President last night, told him that Israel has the capability to make synthetic gold at a fraction of the market price and in a spirit of cooperation offered the technology to the United States. . . ."

"Wow. That's a twist." Now it was Landover's turn to register surprise.

Shepherd lit his cigarette. "The President said Israel's willingness to share the information with the United States showed a true cooperative spirit that deeply impressed him. He offered U.S. government facilities for work with the Israelis in further advancing the technology."

"So we'll be making gold ourselves with their help?"

"Right on, old sport. And probably selling the stuff covertly, the way the Israelis are doing. You know the fiscal situation as well as I do. Uncle Sam's financially strapped. We say so every day. Programs are squeezed. Agencies are screaming. And suddenly this comes along. Too good to be true, a way to meet a lot of needs without having to justify it to Congress. Think of what *my* agency could do with a secret fund . . . And think of funding for the *sciences.* . . ."

"So that lets me off the hook," Landover said.

He was standing at the window next to Rachel. She had half parted the drapes and blue chintz curtains. The sun streamed inside. Outside was an idyllic scene: boats of all shapes, sizes, and functions tied up along the quays, gulls wheeling and cawing over the water, a lone jogger wending his way up the shore road.

"Not exactly," Shepherd said. "I hate to be the bringer of bad tidings. But remember, old sport, I'm just a messenger . . ."

Landover looked puzzled, Rachel leery.

". . . This is now a top-secret, government-to-government matter. Nongovernment people, even you, sport, can't be trusted. As you know, government people face stiff penalties for leaking secrets."

Shepherd leaned forward in his chair, adopting a concerned look. "It's all leading up to something that I must personally assure you I don't like. Our people shouldn't be doing things like this. It's not kosher."

Shepherd dragged at his cigarette. "They want me to break contact with you."

"What does that mean?"

"I said I didn't like it," Shepherd said. "I'm trying to help you. That's why I'm telling you this. I don't know shit about it, and am certainly not a party to it, but I can make some reasonable guesses what's happening."

Landover kept silent, waited.

"As I said, you're an outsider, an academic. You don't have a GS-15 bunker mentality."

The CIA man leaned back in his chair, thrust his feet with Gucci penny loafers on the bed, and blew smoke rings. He didn't seem exactly upset by the bind Landover was in.

". . . When it just seemed to be rumor, they called on you. You were useful to scope out the Israelis. No risks then. From the U.S. point of view, the chances of anything anyway were minuscule. Not much thought went into it. Now stakes are higher. Play is rougher."

Landover's face tightened. He felt himself flush with anger. "I have friends, fellow faculty at Stanford, the Association of Concerned Physicists, Andreas Vogl at *Positronics* . . ."

"Sure, but you have to be able to get to them. You're out of your element, Professor, a fish flapping in the desert sands." He seemed pleased with the metaphor, crushing his cigarette in a thick glass ashtray.

"I can't believe what you're telling me. The President asked me to come here. I was helping the President, my country, and now they want to—to eliminate me . . . ?"

Shepherd stared at him. "Another factor—just hear the messenger out, old sport—is the Israelis want you for penetrating Dimona, their most prized and secret installation, their family jewels . . . Unwittingly or not, you kicked them in the balls. They want you for making them look bad—that Halakha business, what a riot—and they want Rachel here for organizing it. At the same time the President is creaming for the gold formula. The Israelis have the chips and can make demands. Under such conditions, how much do you think anybody counts? Governments are different from you and me."

Landover was rocking on his feet. "So Rachel and I are being sacrificed so that the Halleck administration can get a little extra pocket money."

Shepherd smiled. His eyes skittering around the room, failed to meet Landover's. "I'm sorry, old sport, but it's only fair that you know the score. And like I said, I want to help you."

Landover remembered an incident years ago at home in Eugene involving his big tabby cat, Woolly, and a mouse. He had been reading in the study. He suddenly noticed the mouse in the middle of the room and the cat crouched next to it. The mouse seemed free to dash to safety. Yet for several long minutes neither the mouse nor Woolly moved. Finally the mouse made a desperate rush, only to be caught by powerful claws and returned to almost the same spot. Again neither animal moved. When the mouse made a new but far slower attempt to escape, Woolly again easily caught it. Then he seemed to tire of the game. Landover was about to rescue the mouse. But Woolly, perhaps sensing intervention, gripped the mouse with his claws and brought his jaws down on the tiny head. The crunch of tiny bone was clearly audible. The last thing to descend down the cat's maw was the stringy, quivering tail.

"Why are they playing with us?" Landover asked.

Shepherd gave a throaty laugh. "Welcome to the world of *real politik*, dear friends." He dragged on his cigarette. "Look, we're being too serious, too early in the morning. What do you say I order us a big breakfast. You guys must be starving. My mother always said never do anything important on an empty stomach."

Shepherd picked up the phone and ordered breakfast for three of scrambled eggs, sausages, croissants, orange juice, and coffee, explaining at length to room service that he had two guests and everyone was unusually hungry.

"Oh, I almost forgot," he said, laying down the receiver, "they're sending the Russian physicist to Washington to describe the process. He's going with General Ben Giton."

"Ben Giton!" Rachel's face was twisted in contempt.

Shepherd crushed his cigarette. "So you know him."

"Of course. Everyone does. He's a corrupt politician. He's accumulating gold for himself and his cronies, gold that should go to the state. He's responsible for the death of Corporal Ari Klein, who saw too much, and for the same reason he wants Dr. Landover and me out of the way. We could upset his little game. The whole point of this exercise, the reason why my father contacted you in the first place, was that he thought if Americans were involved, the corruption would end."

"Mmm," Shepherd said. "These are serious charges."

"It's true," she said angrily.

Mendelssohn had concluded and now the radio station began what sounded like the morning news roundup in Hebrew. A female reader in a breathless voice interrupted the male reader with a news flash.

Rachel interpreted simultaneously.

". . . A truck driver from a Negev kibbutz was shot dead by unknown assailants in his room in the Dalia Hotel in Eilat. His name was Ibrahim Cohen. He was from the kibbutz Noar Ha-Lootzi Lo'hem near Shivta. Police speculated on robbery as the motive. Cohen had no money on him when police found him. He had spent time in the hotel's nightclub last night with an American man and Israeli woman who are already wanted by the police. An informant said Cohen had several hundred dollars on his person while he was at the nightclub, and that the couple took him to his room and are believed to have been the last people to see him alive."

"The news reader," Rachel went on, "is giving physical descriptions that match ours. He says anyone seeing either one or both these persons should come forward to the police."

"Jesus," Shepherd said. "You guys have a way with the police."

"The terrorists must have shot Cohen. We saw their van outside the hotel. I know it sounds crazy, but they might have somehow remembered the watermelon truck and figured we would make for Eilat."

"It's an easily identifiable truck," Rachel added. "When we escaped from the van it was last in the queue. I saw the terrorist leader, a disgusting man with red hair, stare at it as we went by. He was talking to a policeman and it probably didn't dawn on him till later that we were inside. They must have figured we were headed for Eilat. Once they discovered the truck near the hotel, that's all they needed. In the hotel it wouldn't have been hard for them to find out which room the kibbutznik had, or even get a passkey."

"They sound like pretty smart terrorists," said Shepherd, skepticism in his voice. He turned off the radio.

"Dammit, it's what happened," Landover said.

"Of course," Shepherd said.

Landover stepped to the window. From a position just behind the drapes he looked wistfully at boats tethered in the harbor. If he could only just climb aboard one, sail away from all this.

"They unlocked the door," Rachel said, "but we had chain-bolted it, which gave us time to jump out the window. We were on the second floor, and there was a garden below. Ibrahim must have awakened, unbolted the door, and they killed him, hoping to throw suspicion on us. Yes, Mr. Shepherd, they are smart, apparently well-financed, and very creepy."

Rachel and Landover tensed up at the knock on the door. A woman announced room service. Shepherd told her to come in, and the three watched in silence as she pushed in a clanging cart heaped with metal warming dishes, salvers and cutlery, opened its leaves, and laid three place settings. In the center of the table stood a single white rose in a vase.

Shepherd signed the bill, fished for some coins as a tip. The woman, who looked like a Yemenite, thanked him and left.

Despite their serious new troubles, Landover and Rachel were ravenous. The coffee was hot and strong, the food good.

Shepherd ate a little, then rose and started sifting through clothes in his suitcase.

"Look, I do really want to help you guys," the CIA man said. "What I'm about to tell you now comes straight from spy school at Camp Peary. First, you've both got to change the way you look. Then you just evaporate." He threw Landover a Redskins T-shirt that said GO SKINS GO, and a pair of khakis. He tossed Rachel a white button-down oxford. "A little big for you but it's clean."

He asked Rachel what her shoe and hat sizes were. "I'll do some quick shopping for you on Hatmarim. New shoes, sunbonnet, hair dye, dark glasses. Stagecraft. You guys just finish your breakfast. I'll be right back."

Shepherd closed his suitcase, flicked the dials of the combination lock, picked up his room key, and headed for the door.

"Eat, clean up, take a nap. Use my shaving gear, old sport. We'll get you taken care of. It'll all work out. Trust me."

Shepherd adjusted the "Do Not Disturb" sign on the knob.

A warm sea breeze ruffled the drapes and curtains, and from the street below, the hum of morning traffic grew louder. Landover ducked into the bathroom for a quick shave and shower. Rachel, a grim look on her face, went for Shepherd's suitcase. Cowhide, big, deep, soft-sided, with all sorts of thongs and straps. Strings hung from the straps bearing the remains of ancient airline destination tags. His card, sealed in a plastic frame, was attached to the top—James L. Shepherd, U.S. Embassy, Tel Aviv. She played with the lock. It wouldn't open. She picked up a knife from the breakfast tray and started cutting at the sides to be able to pry open the top.

Landover could see her from the bathroom. "What the hell are you doing?"

"Trying to see what's inside this suitcase."

"Why?"

"Why don't you help me instead of asking foolish questions?"

He wiped shaving cream from his face.

"Get another knife, please."

He did and together they slashed and ripped around the soft edges until she was finally able to reach a hand inside.

"What do we tell him when he comes back?" Landover asked. He still had shaving cream behind the ears.

She pulled out the contents without answering, flinging shirts, trousers, briefs, socks, bathing suit on to the floor, then gave a sudden grunt of triumph, withdrawing what looked like a small loaf of bread. Her face was taut and white.

"Hilly, we've got to get out of here." There was new urgency in her voice. "I saw it catch the sun," she said, "when he was handing out the clothes. Feel it. You can't mistake gold."

He held it. It was heavier than lead, smooth and soft, almost oily to the feel. He started to comprehend. "Do you think—?"

"Why would he be carrying it around?" she interrupted. "The CIA doesn't pay its people in gold. Gold is not something you normally pack in a suitcase. One brick is worth thousands of dollars. You keep it in a safe place, a safe-deposit box. So someone had to give it to him, and pretty recently, too, on this trip. Who could have given him gold? Who has gold to give?"

"Ben Giton?"

"They must be working together. It's the only explanation. He knew everything about us, things that only Bloom would know. Now he's gone to contact Bloom, I'm sure of it. Please, Hilly. We've *got to get out of here.* They'll be coming for us in a few minutes . . ."

She took off her dirty shirt and put on not the white oxford Shepherd had tossed her but a faded yellow shirt she found in the suitcase. It was also too big but she made the loose folds into a stylish knot. Over it all she slipped on a white terry cloth robe from the bathroom, stuffing some of Shepherd's plastic jars of Excedrin, Vitamin B-12, and ibuprofen into the pockets, and handed Landover a tube of sunblock. She also took a big bath towel.

With no time for a shower, Landover changed his sweaty polo shirt, not for the Redskins T-shirt but a blue-striped oxford that he picked up off the floor. He slipped into Shepherd's khakis—too large at the waist even over his money belt but he managed to find a sporty canvas belt of Shepherd's to hold them up. He took one of Shepherd's jackets, a blue linen-and-polyester blazer with a Joseph Banks label. He made sure he transferred Cohen's gun. He folded one of Shepherd's bathing suits over his arm, and grabbed a towel. They looked to the world all set for a day at the beach.

Rachel cracked the door to the hallway. Another chambermaid was passing, and Rachel in American English, still barefoot, calmly asked where the best swimming was. Thanking the chambermaid, she walked calmly down the hall. Landover shut the door behind them. The "Do Not Disturb" sign luffed in the air currents.

He had no idea what they would do or where they would go. Instead of the elevator they headed for the red light at the end of the hall that said EXIT in English and Hebrew and walked the four flights down. They pushed the swinging doors into the lobby, full of tourists at the buffet breakfast in the dining room. No sign of Shepherd, or the police.

Rachel pulled him with her into the hotel gift shop. A pair of plastic beach sandals was hanging in a corner. They examined sunglasses and selected two pairs. Rachel was attracted by a broad-brimmed straw hat; Landover picked out a white golfer's cap. She took the sandals and a white silk scarf with a red-lettered logo: "EILAT Sun Capital of the World." They paid for everything with another $100 bill.

Rachel buckled on her new sandals, then tied the scarf rakishly around the hat so the sides came down. Landover put on the golfer's cap. They strolled into the hotel driveway behind a dozen French tourists in beach clothes and got into a taxi.

"Taba," Rachel said as Landover shut the door. The driver understood, even if Landover did not.

"You must pay my return," the driver said.

Rachel asked Landover for another of his $100 bills and handed it to the driver. "Will that take care of it?"

"Yes, madam," the driver said enthusiastically and gave her his card. "If you need someone to show you around, I'm at your service." The card said Ephraim Bernstein.

As the cab pulled out they saw a police car drive up. In the backseat was Shepherd. Next to him Rachel saw the sullen, pasty face of Bloom. Two police jeeps pulled alongside the hotel entrance.

"You Americans?" the driver asked.

"From California," Rachel said.

"I have a cousin in Bridgeport, Connecticut," the driver said.

"That's nice."

They took the black asphalt coast road south. Craggy granite and sandstone formations towered above them. In the early-morning light the colors were striking, not only the iron reds and copper greens that the sun teased from the descending phalanxes of stone, but the shimmering black of the asphalt, the sparkling emerald of the sea, the sapphire of the sky. The hills behind the Jordanian port of Aqaba were clearly visible. Farther south they could make out the tiny fishing village of Haqal in Saudi Arabia.

Eilat's beaches were still nearly empty except for a few well-oiled diehards soaking up the early-morning sun. Both sexes wore G-strings and some of the women, the foreigners from northern Europe, went topless.

Most of the pleasure boats were still neatly moored in their slips, the waters lapping at their sterns. Beyond in the gulf, feluccas with their lateen sails skimmed the water like shimmering dragonflies, dodging a constant traffic of oil tankers and ferries transporting workers between Egypt and Jordan.

As the sun climbed, the heat began to rise and the driver turned on the air-conditioning and shut the windows.

Twenty minutes later they approached road barriers and a series of shacks. They would have to run a gauntlet of sleepy-looking guards. The driver pulled up behind a luxury bus from Johnny Desert Tours of Eilat headed into the Sinai.

"I assume you know what to do," Landover whispered. Neither had passports nor papers.

Rachel straightened her bonnet, smoothed her slacks.

"Give me another bill and pretend to be a tourist."

The bus pulled away in a cloud of dust. They were next. The cab drew parallel to one of the huts and a middle-aged Egyptian guard, sporting a Saddam Hussein mustache and a stony expression, asked for their papers. The driver automatically showed his license. The guard gave it a cursory look, returned it, and then stepped up to the taxi's rear window.

Rachel began talking excitedly in Arabic. The guard said nothing and didn't change expression. She gesticulated, making sure he saw the greenback, often using the word "Inshallah," held up jars of ibuprofen and Excedrin and pointed to Landover. The guard looked Landover over, then suddenly smiled a friendly smile.

Landover had no idea what they were talking about but smiled back. That seemed to clinch it. Rachel shook hands with the guard, having taken care to make sure that the note in the palm of her right hand stayed in the palm of his right hand.

"Inshallah." The guard pocketed the note and waved them on.

As they drove off, the cab driver half turned around in his seat with a grin on his face: "They must have pretty good Arab classes in California."

"I grew up here." She wiped her forehead, waving away a big buzzing fly.

They passed Rafi Nelson's Beach Club now and pulled up farther along the spit of sand behind a bus at the wedding cake–like structure of the Hilton Hotel. A red, white, and black Egyptian flag rippled in the breeze above the entrance.

They walked purposefully into the lobby full of tourists, older, less boisterous and more fully clad than those at the Coral Sea. One group dressed in black and white, solemn Coptic pilgrims from Cairo, seemed to belong to the bus outside.

Rachel and Landover found an empty sofa surrounded by empty peacock chairs and sat down as inconspicuously as possible. A clock over the concierge's desk said 8:17. Landover ran his hands through his thick shock of graying brown hair. More of it, he was certain, had turned white in the last twenty-four hours.

"Okay, I give up. Now tell me how you did it."

She smiled proudly. "They like their *baksheesh*. They also like a good story. They don't care whether it's true or not so long as it's entertaining. Stamping passports all day is dull and boring work so I told him about your mother who we had brought to Taba from America and how she had become ill and how we had gone on a day trip to Eilat to get special medicine and that on the way back Israeli thieves had stolen our papers but failed to get our money, and that we had to get back to see your mother because she would be in a bad way if she didn't get her pills."

He shook his head. "You are incredible."

"This is the Middle East," she said.

# 28

THEY SAT SILENTLY for a few minutes, watching the never-ending parade in the lobby, mostly Egyptians dressed in flowing black or white, Westerners in brighter garb, porters struggling with suitcases. The terry cloth robe was bundled under Rachel's arm.

"What's next?" Landover asked. "You can't always make up stories about my mother."

Rachel adjusted the straps on her new Israeli sandals, made in Malaysia. "I used to come here sometimes with my father. He had a resident agent, a Bedouin from the Muezzeina tribe, an unusual man who had worked closely with our people in the Sinai. You know we were here for fifteen years and even discovered oil before we gave everything back to Egypt, including the oil that we could really use right now. . . .

"Hamid, I think his name was . . . Yes, Hamid el-Daub. He liked the improvements we made, paved roads, new hospitals, schools . . . We did a lot for his people, and he adopted some of our ways. Though a Bedouin, he said he couldn't stand the smell of goats and camels. He learned English, Hebrew, Italian, became an opera buff. He had the gift of an eye as well as an ear. He loved to draw, and the Israeli Military Government made him a professional engraver. Yes, we even had a printing and engraving bureau here, for documents, official papers . . . He was a terrific engraver. My father said he had the eye of an eagle.

"Anyway, Hamid set up a small photo business here after we left, and moonlighted for Mossad—as a forger. Not bank notes, only passports and IDs. His clients were our agents who needed a quick new cover. My

238

father sent him everywhere in Europe and the Middle East. All he ever carried was a little black case filled with one change of clothes and the paraphernalia of the forger's art—surgical cotton, a magnifying glass, toothpicks, and an ink pad. Now what I'd like to do is take a little walk toward where I remember the shop and see if he's still there."

She let Landover peek into the object wrapped in her rolled-up robe. "Later we'll see what we can get for this."

He saw the gold brick, and clicking his tongue, a wide grin on his face, he followed her out the door.

She put one arm around his waist. "Many newlyweds come here," she said airily. "Pretend we're among them."

The Copts, looking like a row of dominoes, had lined up to enter the bus. The new honeymoon couple walked past them, past a taxi stall, and toward the commercial district.

They found the photo shop down a side street just where Rachel remembered it, and, against all odds, Hamid was inside, working on some accounts, a cup of tea at hand, a photo of Begin and Sadat at Camp David on the wall behind an electric hot plate with a kettle on. The radio was tuned to an Eilat station.

Hamid looked like a bent string bean, long, slender face, sinewy arms, sparse white hair, perhaps in his midsixties. He was wearing an open-collared white short-sleeved shirt. Hanging on a hook was a snow-white *galabia.*

"Yosef Ravid's daughter!" he exclaimed as they walked into the shop and he got a look at Rachel. They embraced and placing a sign in the window that the shop was temporarily closed, he asked about her father.

Rachel did her best to describe Ravid's death at the hands of terrorists, then introduced Landover as an American physics professor, an old friend of Ravid visiting when the tragedy occurred and almost killed himself. She said she and Landover had been kidnapped by the same terrorists, then managed to escape, and now they both urgently needed passports. She did not say why they had not gone to the police, nor what they were doing in Taba. And Hamid did not ask.

"We can pay you," she said.

He shook his head. "I would not think of it," he said. "Your father was a very, very dear friend. I will do this gladly for his daughter, sadly in memoriam."

He made a gesture toward the kettle. "Can I offer you both a cup of tea?"

Rachel and Landover nodded.

"We drink it very sweet," Hamid told Landover, "but you do not have to have it that way."

"Thanks. I'd prefer it not so sweet," Landover admitted.

Hamid ran water into a kettle and put it on the electric coil, then directed a rueful glance at Rachel.

"It has been a while. My skills are rusty. Indeed, they have hardly been used since your father retired." He hesitated before continuing. "Yosef said he would speak to his successor about me, but no one has ever contacted me."

"I am sorry," she said.

"Not your fault. Not your father's fault. It's no one's fault. Times change, people change. New styles. New techniques. New relationships. I understand." He turned from his tea-making. "I have learned"—he gave her a wan smile—"never to ask too many questions."

She was silent.

"I miss your father more than you think. He was very kind. He said I was as good as Shalom Dani, high praise indeed."

Landover recalled the exhibit at Ravid's museum.

"The assignments Ravid gave me," Hamid went on, "were the high points of my life. I traveled all over Europe. I went to great cities . . . London, Paris, Rome, Vienna. Vienna was my favorite. I worked in someone's sewing room in a lovely apartment on the Hohenstaufengasse near the Schottenring Cafe, took the Eisenbahn, enjoyed *Marriage of Figaro* at the Stats Opera and dined on sauerbraten and Sacher torte at the Sacher."

While the water was still heating he walked over to a file cabinet. He was back on the old assignments, creating identities for anonymous people who had little in common except edginess.

He looked his two guests over now with a professional eye, then unlocked a drawer. "It has been so long I'm not even sure of my inventory." He rummaged through some folders and licked his lips. "Ah, we are in luck. A nice one from New Zealand, and another from Canada. Leftovers from old campaigns but perfectly good. Yes, I think I can help you."

He reexamined the two passports.

"The professor here could be from Toronto, certainly, and you, dear Rachel, how about a residence in Auckland. You could be of Ukrainian descent. I believe your mother was from Odessa, am I right?"

Rachel looked surprised. "What an amazing memory you have, Hamid."

He smiled. "We can give you a lovely name, Zvass, Ellen. There are Zvasses in New Zealand. Not many, but enough for people not to question. Born in Wellington. Now living at forty-five Dove Cottage Lane, Auckland, the largest city. Lemon trees. Harbor view. Does that suit?"

She nodded. "It's like getting fitted for a new skin."

He laughed. "I have always done well with my New Zealanders. Never a reject, as far as I know." He handed her a notebook and pencil. "Write down your date of birth. No need to invent. And, yes, you, too, Professor, date of birth. I have an impressive persona for you. Born in Winnipeg. But nobody stays in Winnipeg. Brrrh! They go to Toronto or Vancouver. I have fine addresses in Toronto. Eighty-seven Roxborough. Rosedale. Very nice. Upscale. Walled garden. A few minutes to Bay Street."

He thought for a moment. "Yes, I have it. Taylor, Robert. Bob, but only to close friends. Suave and dignified, yet firm when he has to be. Very romantic, like the actor. He fits you nicely, Professor. My Canadians are understated but dependable. They can be counted on, just like my New Zealanders."

There was excitement in his voice, enthusiasm, nostalgia. He was again enjoying jaunty promenades down the Kaerntnerstrasse with echoes of Mozart in the background and the ubiquitous scent of freshly cut flowers, whipped schlag, and chocolate cake.

He sat Rachel and Landover in turn before his studio camera and took their photos. "It will take just a little while to make the necessary adjustments . . . Let me throw in two international drivers' licenses. No charge. Part of the package."


FROM HAMID'S THEY walked to the *souk,* hunting for a shop that both sold and fabricated gold necklaces. There were several. They went into the one that looked most prosperous. Glass cases displayed hundreds of necklaces and bracelets of various thicknesses of gold.

They were greeted by the apparent owner or manager, a stocky man with a goatee who stood at the counter under a photo of President Hosni Mubarek. At a table in the rear a worker hovered over pieces of gold jewelry with a tiny, pointed pair of pliers and light hammer and did not look up.

"There is something I would like you to see," Rachel said in Arabic, and allowed the owner a peek into her towel.

He looked inside with interest. She withdrew the bar and handed it to him. He rubbed it, pressed it to his cheeks almost as if he and the gold were lovers, and finally took it to a scale at the other end of the counter where he weighed it. The scale said thirty ounces.

"If the price is right I would sell it," she said.

"I am not a bank."

"I thought you might have more need for it than a bank."

He laid the bar down. "I have all the gold I can use."

"Then I am sorry to have disturbed you." She picked the bar up and wrapped it again in the towel.

He put a restraining hand on her arm and smiled. "Three thousand dollars."

"Do you hear the camels of the desert? They are all screaming with laughter. They have never heard such a very funny joke." She again prepared to leave.

The proprietor lifted both arms in a pleading gesture, his white robes billowing in the updraft. He asked her to sit down.

"I prefer to stand." Now she also was smiling.

Landover, trying to follow the proceedings but not understanding a word, decided he, too, should smile.

The proprietor leaned against the counter, looked curiously at him, then back at Rachel. "I can do no better than fifty-five hundred dollars."

Her smile vanished. "The camels do not stop laughing. Now they are joined by the mountain goats."

The man's smile vanished also. "We are a poor country. I have workers to pay. I am a hardworking businessman."

"I am reassured," said Rachel. "I feared for a moment I had walked into a den of thieves." She didn't move. The man at the workbench began tapping a band of gold with a light hammer.

The proprietor said nothing but stared at the towel. Almost like a striptease artiste bearing a breast, Rachel pulled some of the folds back so that the treasure again showed.

The man reached out his hand, and she slowly withdrew the gold from the cloth and placed it in his palm. "The purest of pure gold," she said. "Thirty ounces. A value of twelve thousand dollars."

The man held it possessively, again weighed it, did some calculations on a piece of notepaper by the scale. "Seven thousand dollars. Absolute limit. Cash. No questions."

"It is worth twelve thousand dollars."

"Seventy-five hundred dollars. It is the highest I can go."

"I need eleven thousand dollars."

"Impossible."

"I am sorry." She reached again for the bar.

Without a word, the proprietor walked to the front of the shop, pulled down the shades, then returned to bend before the dials of a wall safe. He laboriously counted out $8,000 in $500 and $100 notes and laid the money on the counter. He moved his fingers toward the gold.

"You are taking bread from the mouths of children," Rachel protested.

"Allah will never let your children go hungry," he said, adding another $500.

She picked up the money. He picked up the gold.

"Allah protects you," he said.

"Allah is good." She stuffed the money inside her T-shirt.

"Inshallah," the proprietor said.

"Inshallah," Rachel said.

"Inshallah," Landover said.

They tried to merge into the crowds as they walked back to the Hilton lobby, but both could feel X-ray stares.

"Why don't we take a room, order a good dinner and wine, draw the curtains, and close out the world?" Landover suggested as they entered the hotel.

"If we only could," Rachel said. "They'll know where we are, if they don't already. Taba is a small town, teeming with informers who will easily remember us. We'd be in constant fear of every knock on the door."

They decided Hamid's shop would be safer than the Hilton.

Hamid tried to make them comfortable as he worked. He offered them more tea and sweet cakes, gave them year-old copies of *Time* and the *New Yorker* to read. When he finally provided the documents, they were still warm—four passports and two international drivers' licenses.

"Fallback identities are helpful. Especially appreciated when I was working for your father. Names are so easily checked these days. So I discovered that Ellen Zwass has a cousin in Wellington, Tamara Lewis, who looks an awful lot like her. And by coincidence, Robert Taylor is often confused with his cousin from Ottawa, Cedric Beaton. I was hoping

to give you a Visa card as well but unfortunately I have no more of these
in stock. . . ."

Rachel took both his hands. "Thank you, dear Hamid. Someday, I will
tell you how you have helped us. Then I hope to be able to thank you
properly."

"You must come again," Hamid said as they stepped outside the shop.
"You are always welcome. Always."


THE TOPOGRAPHICAL WALL map at the rental agency showed that paved
roads, gas stations, rest houses, civilization itself stopped a few miles from
the Sinai coast. Traversing the interior to reach the Gulf of Suez coast
meant pursuing camel tracks and dried riverbeds across a barren terrain
for at least 200 miles.

A brochure thumbtacked to the wall read:

> It is forbidden to drive in the interior. Land mines remain a danger years
> since the '67 war. Flash floods and eighty-mile-an-hour sandstorms may
> erupt with a sudden ferocity. Food, water, and fuel are not easily obtain-
> able. Because of the primitive and harsh conditions, the Sinai houses only
> 70,000 of Egypt's forty-five million people, including 2,500 Bedouins,
> whose contact with the outside is limited to occasional Egyptian army pa-
> trols, itinerant merchants from El Arish and Gaza, and rare journeys by
> camel to Port Suez or Cairo . . .

The matronly Egyptian woman office manager accepted their international drivers' licenses and asked for a credit card.

"I don't have a credit card," Landover said. "I . . . don't believe in
credit."

"We must have a security guarantee," the woman said. "How can you
be North American without a credit card?"

Landover bit his lip and started winging it. "I believe in cash. Our
Canadian economy is reeling from too much debt. We spend more on
interest on the debt now than even on national health. We've been living
beyond our means for years. Eventually someone must pay the piper.
That means—"

"We prefer cash," Rachel interrupted, knowing the woman sought a
lesson in more practical economics. Rachel pulled ten crisp $100 bills
from the front of her shirt. "Will this do for a security deposit?"

The woman looked at the bills for an instant, then extended her right hand. Rachel laid the money on her palm.

The woman smiled, showing dimples. "Irregular, but acceptable."

"I trust it's refundable," Rachel said.

"Of course," the woman said. She riffled through a folder. "I have an excellent car for you, our best, top of the line, specially outfitted for desert roads."

"We want the best," Landover said.

"When will you turn it in?" the woman asked.

"Tomorrow evening at Sharm Airport," Rachel said quickly. "We want to visit Saint Catherine's and Mount Sinai before taking our plane home."

"There is a $100 hazardous-road charge and another $100 charge for jerry cans of water and gasoline."

Rachel again reached inside her shirt.

The woman's face was all happiness and light as she accepted the new $100 bills. She said they would also need full insurance, which was $50 a day, minimum $100, also payable in advance.

As another $100 bill dropped, the woman gave Landover the rental agreement to initial in encircled areas and sign.

When they shook hands and Landover congratulated her on her faultless English, she proudly disclosed that she had worked some years ago as a secretary at the Egyptian Embassy in Washington and her sister still lived in Alexandria, Virginia. She also said she had cousins in Gaza. She had married the ambassador's chauffeur, and on return to Egypt he had invested in the rental-car business. Alas, she was a widow now, but over her mother-in-law's objections she ran the business herself.

The woman gave them a front-wheel drive tan Subaru. Landover checked under the hood. The oil, brake, and transmission fluid, windshield washer liquid, and radiator water seemed fine. But inside the passenger area, the dashboard ashtray was crammed with some earlier driver's butts.

The woman was apologetic, emptying the ashtray herself. "It is so hard to get decent help these days."

"No sweat," Landover said.

The woman urged them to buy bottles of drinking water there. "You can't trust what you might find at some roadside stand."

Rachel thrust a $10 bill at her for two bottles. "Don't bother with change. We must get going." Rachel was getting antsy.

The woman pointed them due south on the coastal highway to Nuweiba, built by the Israeli Military Command during its fifteen-year occupation of the Sinai. It was the first leg of the journey to Sharm el-Sheikh at the southern tip of the Sinai.

"A trip that once demanded several days now takes only several hours," the woman informed them pleasantly, and waved as they took off.

The day was predictably hot but the air-conditioning worked. The clock, however, was stuck at 4:12. Besides a full tank of gasoline they had a jerry can of gasoline and one of water in the trunk, all paid for under the rental agreement.

"My first time into the Sinai," Rachel said. "But my father was here in sixty-seven. He loved the colors, sense of space, the wealth beneath the surface. He said it had oil and minerals to last Israel for thousands of years and we were fools to give it up."

Several miles south of Taba they seemed to own the road. The Subaru handled well, smooth engine, sensitive steering, cushioned suspension. Thank God for the Japanese, thought Landover.

"Why don't you nap," Landover urged Rachel. She tried to oblige, closed her eyes briefly but couldn't sleep. "I just hope our luck holds. . . ."

"It will," and he was almost beginning to believe it. He still carried Ibrahim's gun.

To the right rose rugged beige cliffs of sandstone and granite, punctuated by stands of cypress. To the left were amazingly large and empty stretches of beach. Across the sun-dappled water were silver and golds of the coast of Saudi Arabia.

Landover felt exhilarated behind the wheel, somehow back in control, his senses sharpened, more acute than at any time since his arrival in Israel forty-eight hours earlier. He reached for Rachel's hand. She pressed his hand in hers, then moved up close to him on the seat. He put his right arm around her shoulders.

"I feel I'm back in Oregon headed for the drive-in."

"What's on tonight?"

"*Roman Holiday.* Audrey Hepburn and Gregory Peck."

"Not something with Robert Taylor?"

"Next week."

They both laughed. They drove along uneventfully until he felt her start to shiver and he turned off the air conditioner.

"Sorry. It's more nerves than cold," she said. She removed her sunglasses, wiping them on the tail of Shepherd's yellow shirt, then wedged herself away from him against the passenger door.

"Can we talk seriously for a moment?" she said.

"I thought we've already had some pretty serious talks," he said a little irritably.

"Hilly, Hilly . . . It's just that this has been, well, very emotional for us both. I like you very much. But I don't want you to feel sorry for me, or consider yourself obligated to look after me—"

When he started to answer she reached over and put a finger to his lips.

"Hear me out. Last night in the truck I was afraid you were going to leave me. I was hurt and angry. If you had gone to the police that would have been the end for both of us. You didn't, and by the skin of our teeth we are here.

"But remember, twenty-four hours ago we didn't even know each other. So many things have happened. My poor father's death, our kidnapping, the murder of Ibrahim—it seems like a lifetime ago. But count the hours. It was four p.m. yesterday when I came in the Cherokee to pick up you and my father. If life is a novel, our time together barely makes a complete sentence. . . ."

She threw back an errant tangle of hair from her forehead. "I guess all I'm trying to say, Hilly, is that we've been thrown together by circumstance, and it's way too early for either of us to be making emotional commitments. I mean, I am still in mourning. We don't know much about each other. Our backgrounds are so different, not professionally but culturally. As I said before, you're not even a Jew. . . ."

He had been about to pass a truck but now let the truck pull ahead. He cast a sideways glance at her. If before he had thought of her as a Modigliani, now with her dark hair framed against the window, he was reminded of a painting by Ghirlandajo at the National Gallery: a proud Florentine noblewoman, eyes ablaze, hair like thunder clouds, against a serene countryside.

"Do you think you're going to get rid of me so easily?" He reached for her hand, which was hot and limp. "Do you think that after what we've been through I could just abandon you? Even if there were no Shepherd I could never just go back to Palo Alto and resume a so-called normal life."

She sat in silence.

He took a deep breath. "Maybe you just want to get rid of me. Is that it?"

"No. I just don't want us to pretend anything. I want us to be honest. If it doesn't work, we must say so. Promise?"

"Promise."

"And if you suddenly have a chance to get out of here and something goes wrong with my passport or I break a leg, you must get out while you can. Don't worry about me. . . ."

"I don't promise that," he said.


NUWEIBA—AN OASIS on the beach where the Israelis had built a kibbutz-style guest house, now developed into the Nuweiba Hilton Coral Resort. Rachel and Landover made such good time they decided to stop for a Coke and parked at a place called Bedouin Bob's near tour buses taking pilgrims to Mount Sinai, where God talked to Moses.

A few Arabs in *galabias* that looked like pup tents sat on the beach. Stray mongrels, one with only three legs, snifffed the sand. No one was in the water. Rachel pointed to a sign that implored: IN RESPECT FOR OUR CULTURE, PLEASE AVOID NUDITY.

"When we ran the place," Rachel admitted under her breath, "it was pretty freewheeling . . . nude sunbathing, some hash."

In the small, seedy but air-conditioned reception area, they found a machine dispensing Cokes, but they lacked the right coins. They went to the desk, and Landover in English asked for change of a piaster note. A bald-headed Arab—perhaps he was Bob—was doing paperwork behind the counter. He peered at the newcomers. Obliging with the coins, he asked if they had just driven down from Eilat. When Landover nodded, the man politely asked him: "You're not Professor Landover, are you?" Landover started, felt sweat, then cold. "Why do you ask?"

The man looked at him in a friendly manner. "You have a message, sir. You are to call this number in Eilat and ask for a Mr. Shepherd. He has left messages for you up and down the coast, says it's urgent, an emergency. You can reverse the charges." He handed over a slip of paper with the number written on it. "There is a pay phone in the hallway."

Landover tried to regain his composure. "Thank you very much." He picked up his change. "You were kind to take the message."

"It was nothing." The man smiled. "We welcome Americans."

They walked over to the Coke machine and drew two bottles.

"Dammit," Landover said, uncapping his bottle. "It was a mistake to stop."

"You'd better call him," Rachel said, "since they'll know we've been here anyway. But do it quickly." They walked to the phone.

The Israeli occupation created good phone connections. With her Arabic, Rachel got him through on a collect call, and Shepherd picked up immediately.

Shepherd seemed to have been waiting for the call. Landover shared the receiver with Rachel.

"Thanks for getting back to me, Professor. I knew you would because you're a pretty smart guy. I wanted to help you, and you ran away. Imagine my surprise when I returned to the room."

"We didn't want to trouble you further."

"I didn't like the way my suitcase looked, but that's a small matter. . . ."

Landover was silent.

"Listen to me now, old sport. I have something very important to tell you. The higher-ups in Washington told me what I told you in the room was just totally wrong, that I had misunderstood, and boy, did I get my ears pasted. I'm in real deep doo-doo, Professor. You're a hero, the guy who came to his country's aid in time of need. The President wants to give you a medal. There was never any intention to do anything except honor you for your service to our country. The President wants you out of here now and in the Rose Garden. He will pin the medal on himself. Then you can go home to your good wife, resume your duties at SLAC, and pick up your normal life."

Landover said nothing.

"Don't believe him," Rachel whispered in his ear.

"The only condition," Shepherd continued, "is that you say nothing about what's happened and sign an oath of secrecy. That's it. Then you're out of it. Uncle Sam takes care of everything and I mean everything. Uncle Sam can be very generous. Your accelerator gets more juicy federal funding. Stanford wins more federal contracts. You get a chance to do more research, maybe win that Nobel. . . ."

Landover still kept silent. Rachel was shaking her head.

"Listen, old sport. It's better than wandering off into the wilds of the Sinai. That can be pretty dangerous. Believe me, there's nothing for you to run away from . . . You still there?"

"Yes."

"Look, we shouldn't be talking like this on the phone. Let's meet somewhere. Anywhere."

"And what about Rachel?" Landover could feel her eyes studying him.

"That's not my department. She's wanted by the Israelis. She should give herself up. That would make it much easier."

"She didn't do anything."

"She violated their laws. There's also an unsolved murder of a kibbutznik in Eilat."

"If it hadn't been for her the U.S. wouldn't know anything about the gold. We told you about that murder . . ."

Rachel was shaking her head. "Don't argue with him," she whispered. "Tell him anything . . . break it off."

"We can put in a good word for her," Shepherd went on. "I will do all I can, old sport. Uncle Sam will do all he can. Still, you should take this word of advice from a man of some experience: disentangle yourself, disengage. I'm serious. She's no good for you."

Landover squeezed Rachel's hand. She broke away gesticulating. "Break it off."

"So can we meet?" Shepherd asked.

"Sure, why not?" Landover said calmly into the receiver.

"Come back to Taba, old sport, the Hilton. It's neutral ground, perfectly safe. You can make it in ninety minutes. I'll talk to both of you and I'll talk to the Israelis. Maybe I can convince them to let her go. Then maybe you'll let me really put you on a plane back to Washington. Let bygones be bygones. I want us to be friends. Okay, Professor? Is it a deal?"

"We'll meet you in ninety minutes."

"Now you're showing how intelligent you really are. Time to stop all this foolishness. Remember, I just want to help."

Rachel ran ahead of him to the car, and Landover had to run to catch up.

She was in the driver's seat. They hadn't even locked the car. "That was too long. We must get out of here."

He handed her the keys. "You want to drive?"

"Please. You navigate. There could be roadblocks. Let's not let them win," she said resolutely.

He watched her start the car, adjust the mirror, and pull out. He was feeling angry, not at her, but at the whole damn situation that had so wrenched his life the past forty-eight hours.

"We need some kind of plan, some kind of strategy to hit back at them with," he said.

"What do you suggest?"

"Why don't we go ahead and leak the story and vicariously enjoy the plunge in the price of gold . . . Don't get mad. Get even."

"How do we do it?"

"Find a sympathetic journalist."

"Not many of those out here."

"I'm actually thinking of someone—name of Andreas Vogl—works in Zurich for a nuclear trade journal. Wrote me up once. A nice job. He's sympathetic, reliable . . . But you're right"—he looked around at the emptiness—"we're not out of the woods—the desert—yet."

"And a lot of people don't want us out," she said. "Hilly, it makes me dizzy, and sick, thinking of all the people after us—Bloom, Ben Giton, Shepherd, and the CIA and then that redhead with his team and phone calls to Baghdad. . . ."

She tapped her forehead lightly. "How stupid . . . I know now where I've seen him before. Believe it or not, I think he works in the canteen at KMG. There was a clean-up guy with carrot hair and a mop who seemed awfully interested in what we were saying. Just before we decided to change tables. . . ."

"Saddam has planted somebody at Dimona?" Landover sounded incredulous.

"You didn't notice him?"

"I was too busy listening to you."

"Arguing, you mean."

"There was a lot to absorb. But now that you mention it . . ."

She smiled. "Hilly, if I'm right, what an embarrassment for Bloom."

"We could leak that, too," he said. "Maybe the Israeli public should know about a security breach at Dimona."


SHE DROVE SMOOTHLY in the direction of Sharm el-Sheikh, passing the Bedouin village of Bir Zrir and following directions for St. Catherine's Monastery. The ribbon of black asphalt wound through the tawny landscape, away from the coast, and plunged into the mountainous interior. Every few miles they saw signs in English and French declaring: FOREIGNERS ARE FORBIDDEN TO LEAVE THE MAIN ROAD.

At their first police checkpoint Rachel slowed behind a tourist bus and they approached a barrier.

"Keep your fingers crossed," she said. "Egyptian police sometimes help out Israeli police. . . ."

When it was their turn, Rachel presented the car-rental papers and her Ellen Zvass passport to a listless, gap-toothed young man in khaki uniform wearing an armband that said Tourist Police. He handed back the documents and showed little interest in seeing Landover's papers. He did ask in barely understandable English where they were headed.

"Mount Sinai," Rachel said.

"Big buses, small roads," the soldier warned, gesturing with his hands.

"And the road to Sharm?" Rachel asked.

"Washouts. Not to go to Sharm today." He waved them on, smiling. "Have a nice day."

After they pulled away, Landover said, "That didn't sound good."

"They always exaggerate," Rachel said. "Anyway, we've got a good car and not much choice. And at least Egyptian police aren't looking for us, yet. . . ."

A few miles south, instead of turning right from the highway on the secondary road marked HAR SINAI and MONASTERY OF ST. KATHARINA, she took the coast road to Dahab and Sharm el-Sheikh.

"You know what Dahab means?" she asked Landover.

He shook his head.

"Gold," she said.

# 29

FROM A SUITE at the Taba Hilton Bloom telephoned the local police chief, Mohammed Druz, to inform him about the murder of the kibbutznik. The people he was after, Bloom warned, were armed, dangerous, and could kill again. He was hot on their trail but needed a police helicopter to track them along the coast road.

Mohammed thanked Bloom effusively. On anything unrelated to Arab-Israeli disputes, he was usually cooperative. "Even though our two governments may have some differences," Mohammed said, "there is no reason why we, as neighbors, cannot work together."

"We, two humble policemen, are setting the example," Bloom replied. They spoke in English, each trying to outdo the other in expressions of politeness.

Mohammed said he would create no obstacles to pursuit of the fugitives in Egypt. But the request for air support was more complicated. His small fleet of Bell 204s was grounded because of lack of spare parts.

"Is that something we could help you with, Mohammed?" asked Bloom. "We have the same aircraft and parts in Eilat."

"Oh, no," Mohammed said. "They must come from Cairo. We have our procedures. Still, I do want to help you. I know how important this matter is. I will check once again to see whether any spare parts have arrived."

"Thank you, Mohammed. I know you will do what you can."


A CARDINAL RULE of the Agency was never leave any bases uncovered. Despite the slimness of the odds that they would show, Shepherd kept

253

watch of comings and goings from one of the peacock chairs in the Hilton lobby. After all, these people were not accustomed to running from police. They might be desperate enough to want any way out of their situation.

But by now three hours had passed since his phone conversation with Landover, and realistically the chances of an appearance were zilch. He remembered other times he had been stood up. It gave him a perverse satisfaction to recall that each no-show had a pretty good excuse.

In Paris a disenchanted associate of the French president, who had promised information about drug running, was picked up belly distended in the Seine. Most recently, a man from Nablus who had kept him waiting all day was found with his throat cut.

Shepherd took one more look outside. Street hawkers, tourist buses, taxis and cars thronged the entrance drive. He was still confident they would be caught. They couldn't get far. Where could they go? They would stand out among the desert people. Just a question of time. Even though Mohammed Druz had refused a helicopter, Bloom had already dispatched a Shin Bet commando.

Shepherd had no scruples about not keeping promises. He would have told them anything. They could not be allowed to talk. Stakes were too high. Executions weren't exactly his specialty, but he would carry them out if necessary. Nothing personal. He was just neither squeamish nor sentimental.

But he was more than a little irritated. They had taken the $12,000 gold bar that Ben Giton had given him in down payment. He would gladly see them flapping on the sands.

His arrangement with Ben Giton aimed at finally resolving his financial worries forever. He'd worked hard for the U.S. government all his life. Now it was time to capitalize.

When Ravid sought him out and explained what was happening in Dimona under Ben Giton, Shepherd saw his window of opportunity. No sooner had he sent his message to Langley than he called on Ben Giton and laid a copy of the cable on the table as a token of what he could offer as a SIBAT consultant.

With Golan wine at the *moshav* they toasted their new relationship and eternal bilateral friendship. Playing his cards right, Shepherd figured he could make a lot of money, more than that dumb and dumber drunk, Aldrich Ames, who he'd seen around, and who had squeezed a lousy $2 million from the Russians.

Shepherd saw Ben Giton again about the President's decision to dispatch a physicist from Stanford to investigate. He and the general conceived the plan by which Shepherd paid one of his Hamas contacts to recruit the young knife-wielding *shebab,* who, unfortunately, despite the gold necklace and $500, didn't quite have what it took.

Ravid's decision to clam up and at least pretend to return Landover to Washington had brought the physicist another reprieve. But despite Landover's extraordinary luck, it was just a matter of time. Until the filching of his gold, Shepherd had nothing against Landover personally. The guy was one of those innocents in the wrong place at the wrong time.

When Shepherd told Ben Giton that Landover had returned to Washington empty-handed, the general seemed pleased and seconded Ravid's advice about taking a few days off in Eilat. "We'll need you fresh for the next round of consultancy." The general had what he wanted—delays in the presidential inquiry and more time for emergency melts.

Shepherd didn't learn the physicist was, in fact, still in Israel until a fuming Bloom phoned him at the Coral Sea the night before about the Dimona penetration. The general was mad as hell. Shepherd had been completely duped by Ravid. He should have suspected the tricky son of a bitch. Bloom's call disoriented Shepherd. Ravid had made a fool of him. Worse, his bonanza was in jeopardy. Bloom was flying down to Eilat because he suspected that's where the fugitives were.

Then Shepherd got the overnight encoded message from Cyrus L. Richards, the director of operations at Langley, about the prime minister's telephone call to the President. Things were moving fast. It was now even more urgent that Landover and the Ravid woman be taken out. Leaks from them could bring the operation down in both countries, and ruin his chances to, really, go golden.

Shepherd was trying to think how he could be useful in the hunt when the two had walked right into his Eilat hotel room. He couldn't believe his luck. The mice had dropped in on the cat. In the Eilat Shin Bet office, he told Bloom the mice were waiting in his room and only needed a pink ribbon. Then his complete and utter desolation when the little rodents vanished with $12,000 of his gold. On top of everything he had to endure Bloom's vituperation.

They were smart. He had to give them credit. It must be the Ravid woman, because the professor didn't know his ass from his elbow, an academic innocent. In pulling clothes from his suitcase he must have inadvertently exposed the gold. She'd watched him like a hawk, while Landover, the schmuck, looked at the pretty boats.

EVEN FROM HIS suite at the Taba Hilton, Bloom continued berating Shepherd for letting the mice slip through his fingers. And unfortunately right this minute, Bloom wanted to talk to him again and he'd have to admit his ploy had gone sour.

Shepherd took the elevator to Bloom's suite on the eighth floor. He knocked. Bloom interrupted a phone conversation in Hebrew to let him in, motioned him to take a chair, then took his time finishing the conversation while Shepherd stared at the wall.

"So they didn't show," Bloom finally said as he hung up. His voice was harsh, edgy. He was sitting at a desk covered with papers. Despite the air-conditioning, sweat glistened on his cheeks and forehead.

"I gave it my best shot," Shepherd said, sitting stiffly in an armchair. "Even did the presidential medal bit. But we suspected all along they wouldn't bite. You want me to get Washington to lean on the Egyptians for the 204s?"

"It would be counterproductive. Mohammed is a proud man and he's creating no obstacles for us on land."

"Israeli choppers?"

"They'd think we'd started another invasion."

"What about slipping just one across the border through the hills behind Taba. We just need one. They'd never know."

"Look, we don't want to risk an incident with Egypt," Bloom told him. "No government problems. Remember, this is more a private matter. It must *stay* that way."

"Okay, just a suggestion." Shepherd was ticked off. Regardless of the money, he was tiring of taking Bloom's shit.

Perhaps sensing he was reaching limits, Bloom gave him a smile. He had instructions to work with Shepherd, who could still be very useful.

"So we know they're south of Nuweiba. I've got a commando no more than a half hour behind them. They can't get far." His new tone was comradely, confidential—two policemen talking shop. "But they seem to have a lot of money. They were handing out hundred-dollar bills like mad at the rental agency."

Shepherd chewed his lips. He didn't want to admit they'd been able to make off with his gold.

"Oh, one thing, I almost forgot," Bloom said. "The rental agency told us someone who spoke like an American had been making similar inquiries. A young man with red hair. He was driving one of those hippie vans. Could that have been any of your people?"

"Not as far as I know." Shepherd was briefly lost in thought. ". . . The professor and the woman told me they'd been kidnapped by terrorists with a van, but managed to escape. They insisted that in trying to recapture them in the hotel, the terrorists killed the kibbutznik. I didn't believe them. . . ."

After a long silence, Bloom finally spoke. "Yes, I'm still here, Jim, just thinking. . . . That would explain how they got away so quickly without a trace . . ." Again there was a long silence. "Do you believe that now about the death of the kibbutznik?"

"I don't know," Shepherd hesitated, "but I don't think for one moment it should change our plans. . . ."

Bloom's dark eyes looked benevolently at Shepherd. "I'm glad you said that, Jim. This isn't a question of personal morality. It's a matter of enlightened national interest. The secret, the welfare of our two countries is not safe with those two on the loose."

"I could not agree more." Shepherd was relieved to be on more amiable terms with his nemesis. "If they go to the press, they have the power to destroy what your people have created and what you are now generously willing to share with us."

"It becomes a question of sacrificing for the common good."

"Exactly," Shepherd said. "The ancients understood this. They offered human sacrifices for a good harvest. This will be our real good harvest, Simon."

"We agree perfectly, Jim," Bloom nodded.

# 30

Dayan Stern and Lev Lermontov, in a black Toyota Cressida, were speeding south from Taba on the road to Sharm el-Sheikh. Dayan was driving. A thin young man with sandy hair and wire-rim glasses, he searched on the radio and settled for something in Hebrew belted out by Haim Moshe.

This was the first time Dayan and Lev had worked together. But the highly educated Israeli and big Russian immigrant, an Afghan war vet, had already established a good rapport. Dayan's intellectuality complemented Lev's strength and courage. Both were familiar with the case. Dayan had explored Rachel's house with Maj. Lon Gavril of the Beersheba detachment. Lev headed the security team for the Russian physicist.

Dayan held master's degrees from Hebrew University, Jerusalem, in Arabic literature and clinical psychology. Not only had he mastered Arabic in school, he had learned English from an American grandmother in Passaic, New Jersey. She was especially pleased that he was named after the famous Israeli general who had flirted with her years ago.

Dayan, who had worked with Major Lon Gavril in Beersheba, was now a rising young star in Shin Bet. He'd been recruited after military service in an intelligence unit near Chebaa inside Israel-controlled southern Lebanon, where he helped build a network of informers who alerted the army to cross-border raids by Hezbollah and the Amal militia.

Dayan was glad to have Lev beside him. The Russian seemed depend-

258

able, fearless, and skilled in the arts of war. After three years in Israel, he spoke passable Hebrew.

Lev told Dayan he initially had no strong thoughts about the Palestinian issue and wondered why everyone was so agitated. But the longer he lived in Israel, the more partisan he became. He opposed any concessions for a Palestinian homeland. "The Arabs are always knifing women, shooting rabbis, blowing up children in buses. Next we will have Katushas at Lod."

Dayan did not disagree but said he hoped that some day conditions would exist for peace.

THE WIND ROSE. A gritty haze turned the sun into a tarnished silver disk. Sheets of sand began flying at close to the horizontal, picking up brush and striking the Cressida with percussive sibilations.

Peering through the windshield, Dayan slowed but didn't stop. He passed a truck and another automobile. A motor biker hunched under a poncho. On the other side of the road more cars and trucks were pulled over. Dayan had experienced other sandstorms, he could maneuver through this one. He respected nature but refused to let it dominate him.

Lev said he had no desire to stop. "We have a job to do."

Orders from Colonel Bloom were to find a tan Suburu some place within hundreds of miles of the southeastern Sinai and arrest two suspects in the brutal murder of a kibbutznik. One of the suspects was an American physics professor and the other, his Israeli girlfriend. A dark-colored Dodge Ram van was also apparently interested in the Suburu. One of the passengers was a redhead who seemed to be American. But he could be half-Palestinian and dangerous. Bloom speculated the van might lead them to the Subaru but they were to be careful in approaching either vehicle.

They had left Taba no more than thirty minutes after the Subaru. Unlikely many such vehicles were on the coast road, but they still had miles of territory to cover. Dayan wondered why no helicopter was deployed.

The storm died as suddenly as it erupted. The desert looked freshly scrubbed, the sky radiant blue. The silence was the stillness of a cathedral. Dayan stepped on the gas. The car shot past a file of Bedouins busily shaking off the sand from their burnooses. Saddled on the swaying backs of tawny camels, they were also headed south.

Dayan was puzzled by the mission. "How does a distinguished physics professor get tangled up in something like the murder of a kibbutznik?" he asked Lev.

"Through the woman, the daughter of Yosef Ravid." Lev was cracking his knuckles, looking absently out the window. "She worked at Kirya. I have seen her, a physicist but also a tasty dish. It is said that Colonel Bloom once had an interest. They say she had some kind of grievance, and her father's disappearance has affected her mental stability."

"Disappearance?"

"Terrorists supposedly killed him in a cave above the Dead Sea, but no one has found his body."

"She doesn't sound like a murderer," Dayan said. "Neither does the professor."

"They were the last people to see the kibbutznik alive," Lev said. "They refused to go to the police. Fleeing the scene must mean they had something to hide."

"What was her grievance?"

Lev shrugged his shoulders. "I have no idea. I do not know her."

Dayan dropped the subject. He had his orders and would carry them out. In a promising career at Shin Bet, he had learned early to respect established authority. He pushed the car faster. Just before the road turned off to St. Catherine's Monastery, he passed a mud-colored Dodge Ram.

"You saw that?" he asked Lev excitedly.

"Yes, and I also saw there were three men, one dressed like an American with red hair under a baseball cap . . ." Lev was barely able to contain his own excitement. Bandits in the Hindu Kush. The thrill of the hunt.

Dayan increased the gap between the two vehicles, then pulled to the side of the road, stopped, opened the hood of the Cressida, and pretended to be working on the engine as the van passed them.

Dayan reentered the car and pulled away. This time he stayed behind the van, following it into Dizahov. It stayed on the main road, but then suddenly stopped and started backing up. Dayan knew it would be too obvious if he stopped as well. So he continued, again passing the van, observing it through the rearview mirror.

The van veered down a sandy track. Dayan stopped, looked at Lev who nodded his agreement, made a U-turn and followed the van toward a small beach settlement, including a cluster of concrete blockhouses, squat cabins, shacks of plywood, corrugated tin, and orange crates. A torn metal fence surrounded the settlement. A half-dozen old vehicles, including a big cement truck, were parked helter-skelter. Bedouin children played in the sand. Dayan pulled up several hundred yards away behind a dune where he could still have a clear view.

The van stopped in front of one of the cabins. The men got out of the front seat and sauntered toward the door. Two of them shook out what looked like head scarves.

Handy in that sandstorm, Dayan thought, rubbing his own gritty hair. Through his binoculars he noticed all three wore pagers clipped to their belts. Taller than the others, the redhead shot a glance toward the dune before entering the cabin.

They stayed inside less than five minutes, then the three emerged with a fourth person. The redhead and this new man piled into the van. The two others, still with their headgear, jumped into the cement truck.

The two vehicles moved off quickly, the truck in the lead, ovoid mixer swaying. Both headed south along the beach toward the Gnai el-Rein oasis. Then the truck swerved inland to join the main coastal road, while the van continued south along a narrow track.

Dayan stuck with the van, following it for two kilometers. It stopped between two hillsides still within sight of the sea. The redhead got out, opened the rear of the van, pulled out what looked like a roll of canvas and pegs. Dayan could not believe it. The man started erecting a tent.

Dayan stopped several hundred yards behind and watched. The setting was a swath of paradise. Behind the western mountains the sun was a fiery cuprous disk. Sprigs of pink oleander poked out of chaparrals of mesquite. From one of the hills trickled a spring that could have slaked the thirst of Adam and Eve.

"What about paying them a visit?" Lev said. He pocketed two grenades and checked the spring-loading mechanism of his P.K. Walther automatic inside his belt. He reached down to feel the knife inside his boot.

"Roger," said Dayan, checking his own Walther.

As they approached, the redhead was giving a half turn to the rope around one of the tent pegs he'd just hammered into the ground. He straightened up, waved, and greeted them with a big, toothsome smile.

"Sure is a beautiful spot here," he said in American English. "Ideal for watching the daily journey of the sun. Babbling brook, knockout scenery.

Everything except dancing girls." The redhead rocked on his feet. Dayan could see he was in prime fitness.

"Just checking it out ourselves," Dayan responded in almost as good American English. "You get awfully thirsty out here, and we saw this brook."

"Help yourselves. I won't even charge you. God's bounty. Tastes great, if you boil it first and avoid the camel dung." He laughed. "Where you guys from?"

"Israel." Dayan bent over the brook and cupped his hands to wash his face. Lev had stayed back on higher ground and stood motionless behind a boulder. "We're on a holiday," Dayan said. "Just wandering down the coast. I gather you're not from around here."

"Aw, shucks, how'dja guess?" The redhead exaggerated his western American accent. "Durango, Colorado. Biblical research for a thesis, Colorado State."

"Impressive." Dayan tried to stay friendly and loose. "You done Ein Khudra yet?"

The redhead looked puzzled. Dayan left him on the hook for a few seconds before adding "Where they danced around the golden calf waiting for Moses' descent from Mount Sinai."

"Sure have." The redhead flashed a smile. "Resting up now from all that study and research."

Dayan's eyes searched for the second man, who must have been just behind the back door of the van. "What a coincidence, a few hours ago we ran into another American, some professor from Stanford. . . ."

The redhead looked up, sudden interest on his face, then quickly cracked a twisted smile. "No way to keep us Americans down on the farm." Staring at Dayan: "Just where'dja'll meet up?"

"Up the road at Nuweiba. He was at a rest house. Don't tell me you know him?"

"He's supposed to join us here. Sure is a small world."

"An old friend?"

"My physics professor before I turned to biblical studies."

"You studied at Stanford, too?"

"I wanted to be a physicist but then decided to devote myself to a life of study of the greatest physicist of all."

Dayan gave him what he hoped looked like an understanding smile, listening hard all the time for the second man.

The redhead gestured toward Lev, still standing at the boulder. "Why don't you invite your friend up there to join us? We can boil some tea."

"He doesn't drink tea," Dayan said, backing away slowly. "Sorry, we really must be on our way. We've troubled you enough. Awfully nice meeting you."

Dayan saw the redhead's eyes shift to the van and heard scraping metal. He continued walking backward, smiling, his eye on the opaque window of the door, trying to keep the redhead between himself and the window. When he reached Lev's boulder, waving at his new buddy, Dayan said under his breath, "Phony as they come."

The redhead yelled something and rolled into a gully to the left. The rear door was kicked open, followed by an automatic weapon burst. But Lev and Dayan had expected it, and ducked safely behind the rock.

Lev threw one of his grenades. It hit the roof of the van and bounced a few feet to the right. They heard the redhead shout something, saw the second man jump from the van and flatten himself in a gully as the grenade exploded.

Showers of sand, stones, and metal rained down. The left side of the van still looked untouched, but the right was a mass of shattered glass and twisted steel tilting downward over collapsed tires. Part of the tent canvas had blown against the rear bumper.

"Where the hell are they?" Dayan exclaimed.

Lev's eyes strained against the darkening sky as they searched for the glint of a weapon amid the dunes.

"Better return to the car. They may try to destroy it. At least they're disabled."

Dayan covered Lev as the Russian started a broken field run up the path toward the Cressida. After about twenty yards Lev dove and twisted in the sand with his Walther braced in two hands. Dayan zigzagged the last twenty yards as Lev covered him.

The first burst came from the right. Dayan hit the ground. A second much closer crackled from the left. Lev answered the fire. Dayan crawled toward a heap of brush, hurled his second grenade at the closer position on the left, and ran.

Both were about halfway to the car when they heard the second explosion.

Lev dropped and Dayan was about to get up when they heard a voice that seemed to echo between the hills. A powerful voice, a preacher's voice, it seemed to come out of a bullhorn. But no church ever heard such words.

"Kikes, don't think you can escape. We'll cut off your circumsized dicks and stuff them down your fuckin' Jewish throats."

Dayan rose to a crouch. He passed Lev, saw his grim face and clenched teeth, and gave him a thumbs-up. Lev reciprocated with another blast toward the general area of the voice.

This time Dayan kept running, head bent forward. The car was too close to stop. More fire pinging off the rocks.

"Palestinians . . . Remember the Palestinians," the voice resounded from the dunes. "We will torment you the way you have tormented us . . . Agony for you Israeli scum . . . No escape. . . ."

Breathless, Dayan jumped into the driver's seat. Hunching behind the dashboard, he jammed in the key, gunned the engine, and steered toward Lev on the ground about twenty-five feet away, still shooting at the hill, at the voice.

The car was now drawing fire. One bullet smashed the windshield. Dayan braked, opened the passenger door, then smashed a fist through the milky glass for visibility. Lev leapt in, still pumping his Walther toward the dunes. Dayan spun the car around. More automatic-rifle fire. Bullets whined. The engine roared. Wheels screeched. Sand flew.

The magnified voice pursued them.

"The Palestinians . . . The Palestinians . . ."

# 31

SMOKY, CLANGOROUS, MALEFIC, devoid of identification, the cement truck seemed to have roared up from the rings of hell. "Strange," Rachel said, slowing. "It sticks like a limpet, refuses to pass."

Landover craned around. The toothlike radiator grille loomed above them. The height of the grille and angle of the sun made it impossible to see inside the cab. He felt the weight of Ibrahim's 9mm automatic pistol bulge in his pocket.

"I'm going to pull away," Rachel said, accelerating on the straight, smooth, and empty stretch of black asphalt, pushing the speedometer to 150 kilometers an hour.

Landover watched the truck drop behind. "Two figures in the cab. Couldn't make out their faces."

"Probably a couple of kids on a joyride," Rachel said.

Although she dropped the speed down to a more modest 110, the car still seemed to be flying. The truck had vanished. She leaned back in her seat and adjusted her Ray • Bans.

Pale cypresses weaved against an arid backdrop of shimmering copper and limestone. Hues of red, green, bronze, and rust melted in the mountains beyond. Thick clouds of purple and black clung to the higher peaks.

"With their camels and goats Bedouins live a life that's changed little since Moses. Some leap into the twentieth century. They suddenly realize it no longer has to take eighteen days to reach Cairo. The young men get tangled up with cars, trucks, alcohol, and drugs and are apt to go a little wild. . . ."

Landover was barely listening. The whistle of the wind, the heat of the sun, the rush of the colors made him languorous. He closed his eyes and soon slipped into that warm, billowy state between sleep and wakefulness.

Rachel yawned, caught herself falling asleep, opened the window wide. She shot a glance at Landover, slumped in his seat with his head wedged between the window and headrest.

"If you fall asleep," she said, "how do you expect me to stay awake?"

He opened his eyes and smiled. "Just meditating."

"Why don't you meditate to me, Hilly. Tell me some nice things, like how we'll get away from here to some place beautiful and live happily ever after."

"Let me think about it." The eyes closed again.

She sipped her Coke and licked her dry lips and left him alone. Soon she'd have her turn.

A road sign: the first she'd seen since passing Dahab. She was thankful for anything to help keep her awake. SLOW. It dawned on her that not only was no one behind but there was no oncoming traffic.

She dropped to under eighty kilometers . . . then sixty . . . forty. She saw other signs in Arabic, English, and French, warning of deteriorating road conditions on the approach to Wadi Kid.

The old riverbed, Cretaceous or Eocene, followed a jagged course running from the 7,000-foot Gebel Sabbagh Mountain down to the Strait of Tiran. The main north-south highway bisected its path about fifteen miles north of Sharm el-Sheikh. Most of the year the wadi was dry, so neither Israel before, nor Egypt now, felt a need to spend money on an overpass.

Rachel braked, slowed to camel speed as the asphalt abruptly ended and the Subaru thumped along an ancient limestone track pitted with gravel and rocks. Instead of flying across the land, the car was being sucked into it.

The perspective changed dramatically. Everything was bigger. Red granite cliffs towered over them. Almost as if part of a decorator's grand design, tamarisk bushes filled in gaps in the stones, their slender branches and feathery flowers interlacing in the breeze. At improbable angles black goats grazed on sparse grasses carpeting gneisses and schists. Above, vultures wheeled slow figure eights.

Rachel kept at dead slow. The car had good suspension and took the ruts and stones well. The last thing one wanted here was a flat tire or any kind of breakdown.

Above the car noises she heard an animal ululation from somewhere close by. The cries were high-pitched, full of agony, followed by a fierce shuffle, a weaker scream. Then, silence. A hedgehog seized by a leopard's jaws?

A rivulet coursed through the middle of the wadi but looked shallow. She edged forward. The Subaru easily forded it. The ground rose again and asphalt resumed.

Landover dozed through the entire crossing, his sunglasses teetering at the end of his nose.

The car had not gone more than a dozen kilometers before a new series of signs warned of another wadi, Um Adawi.

She heard the water before she saw it. This time it was more of a muddy torrent and looked dangerous, dark. Occasional twigs and up-rooted bushes raced by. The water was probably not deep but no telling, and it was at least twenty meters to the other side.

She stopped well above the bank, letting the engine idle.

"No wonder I dreamt about mountain streams," Landover said, rubbing his eyes.

"I guess we just wait this one out before trying to ford it," she said. "I'll look around."

Outside it was a furnace. Rocks glinted in the sun like knife blades. He put on his new golfer's cap and walked toward the edge, eyes upstream in case the proverbial wall of water should suddenly descend. But this flash flood, rising from hills to the northwest, seemed on the wane. The water did not seem deep. Downstream it wound toward the sea a few kilometers to the east. He bent down. The water was cool. He doused his forehead and managed to clean his sunglasses—

He heard Rachel's scream and the blare of the Subaru's horn.

In whirling clouds of dust, the cement truck was bearing down on them. A mummy's head was leaning out the cab window yelling something.

Chest pounding, Landover bent low and sprinted back to the car.

"The gas," he yelled. "Give it the gas."

She gunned the car forward into the water. The engine coughed and sputtered.

Landover scrambled over his seat and dove into the back, pulling the pistol from his pocket.

As the car spun its wheels trying to get traction on the mud and slippery stones, he fired a single shot at the rear window. The safety glass instead of shattering became clouded and striated. With his pistol butt he punched through the pane. The hole gave him a clear field of fire.

The truck chewed up the bleached dust of the vehicle path like a charging Tyrannosaurus, 200 meters away, 190, 180 . . . the cement mixer swaying like a distended belly. From the passenger side of the cab, the mummy still hung over the big sideview mirror. He slid a finger across his throat. Landover saw why the face looked blank. It was shrouded by a white dust filter and red-and-white head scarf that fluttered like the tail of a kite.

Despite its front-wheel drive and high suspension, the Subaru was not making much headway. It kicked up mud, foam, and spray. Rachel turned the windshield wipers on "high," and they beat like the sound of her heart. Water seeped through the floorboards.

The truck was still closing the gap, seventy-five meters, now sixty-five.

"They're going to ram us," Rachel yelled, her eyes on the rearview mirror.

As the car lurched forward, Landover steadied himself, took off his sunglasses, wedged the pistol against the lower right corner of the window frame, and bent his head to aim it like a rifle. He tried to draw a bead, squeezed off three rounds at the truck's windshield. No hits. The car shook too much, the truck was still too far away but it was still coming on full throttle. Fifty meters . . . Forty . . . He saw the black pits that were eyes above the dust mask. The mummy was now leaning way out the window waving a pistol.

"Stop the car," Landover shouted.

"Are you crazy?"

"*Do* it."

She flipped the gear into neutral, still gunning the engine.

"It'll die on us—I hope you know what you're doing." Crouched in her seat, she watched him intently through the rearview mirror. She'd bitten her lips until they bled.

He lowered the barrel slightly, ignoring the cab. The fenders, the two oversized front tires, the toothy radiator grille, the entire onrushing vehicular mass grew larger and larger, spitting rocks and dust.

Landover concentrated on the left tire as if it were the very last object on earth. Easy. Relax. Don't panic. Squeeze. The car was now stable.

Remarkably, his arm was also steady. Slowly he squeezed, then again and again and again. The chamber was empty.

"Take off," he called.

Coughing and spitting, the car jerked forward through the rush of water, pivoting, spinning, thrashing. The wheels found something to grip and the car began to move.

Twenty-five, now twenty meters. The truck was still gaining. The mummy made an obscene gesture with his middle finger and again drew a finger across his throat.

Landover couldn't watch. He looked down at water rising above the floorboards. They would die with wet feet.

The truck roared on toward them, was almost on top of them . . .

The huge left front tire collapsed. In the implosion of writhing steel, the truck swerved as if desperately seeking new points of direction, then teetered on its left side. The mixer tore from its davits, twisted around, and rolled forward onto the cab, crushing it like an eggshell. Sparks and shards of glass and metal showered like fireworks. The guillotine of crashing metal sliced the mummy in two, the upper part fell still clutching the gun.

The truck heaved and turned onto its left side, wheels spinning, radiator grille spewing steam. The mixer rolled off the cab and bounced across the terrain like a mammoth football.

Rachel kept the Subaru moving. The water's depth receded as they reached the other bank.

They could smell the gasoline and she started to look back.

"Step on it," Landover said, "it's not over yet."

The car coughed and spit but responded. They were now on dry ground and climbing toward where the pavement resumed.

The rumble felt like something high on the Richter scale. A quaking came first, then the explosion. The sky turned into a crimson-and-yellow ball of flame sucking oxygen from their lungs. They felt the scorching blast of heat entering through the break in the rear window, smiting exposed parts of their heads and necks.

The blast pitched the car forward and almost lifted it away. Pieces of rock and metal showered the roof. Landover smelled a pungency, like the turkeys his mother singed before roasting. Was it the car's paint, or his own burned hairs?

Debris was still falling as they got back onto paved road. Soon the burning remains of the truck were barely visible but smoke formed a wispy mushroom above the site.

Still no oncoming vehicles. They rode in silence, afraid to do anything that might unleash a new horror. A road sign told them they were headed toward Sharm el-Sheikh.

# 32

ONE LOOKED LIKE a Giacometti statue, the other like Peter the Great. One knew China and Southeast Asia like the palm of his hand; the other had easy familiarity with the former Soviet Union's Confederation of Independent States. Neither suffered fools gladly. Both were fiercely ambitious Yalemen. Their sense of mission grew out of both a great university and family tradition. Both wanted to head the CIA.

Cyrus L. Richards lived in a Manichaean world rigidly divided by good and evil. Had he been born a few hundred years earlier he might have held high office in the Church, possibly Grand Inquisitor. Now as the CIA director of operations at one of its four main directorates, he enjoyed at least as much power as many an earlier bishop of the Church.

Round-backed, skeletal, stoop-shouldered as the CIA's legendary Jim Angleton, Richards, born into a military family, controlled thousands of undercover agents in hundreds of outposts throughout the world. His empire, run on a $1 billion annual budget, included scores of safe houses and communications hubs, two or three dozen covert programs from propaganda campaigns to guerrilla wars, and the Camp Peary paramilitary training camp near Williamsburg, Virginia, otherwise known as The Farm.

During the Vietnam War, China-born Richards, who spoke both Mandarin and Vietnamese, ran the Phoenix counterinsurgency program in Kien Hoa province. The Vietcong were murdering villagers suspected of loyalty to Saigon. Under Phoenix, anyone suspected of being a Commu-

271

nist agent was executed. Richards approved hundreds of executions. If innocents died, so be it.

Gregory C. Oberling, the national intelligence officer for Warning, had oversight of both the biweekly report on developing trouble spots prepared for the DCI and the President's daily intelligence digest. He liaised with other branches of the huge intelligence establishment, organized seminars, lectured to new recruits, wrote position papers, occasionally testified before the congressional intelligence committees. He operated a kind of clandestine Brookings Institute. The intrusion on others' turf made the job delicate. He had to be a diplomat as well as administrator. But Oberling could lay on the charm when he wanted to. He had worked in public relations at the United Nations headquarters in New York in the early 1960s and entertained frequently. He still threw great dinner parties. The job also fit neatly with his academic background—after Yale, a doctorate at the Johns Hopkins School of Advanced International Studies.

At six-foot-four, Oberling, who was of Russian aristocratic background, looked down on mere mortals from his grizzled heights much as Peter the Great might have when discussing the canals of St. Petersburg with his engineers. Oberling generally did most of the talking, unless he met someone he considered worth listening to. Then he knew how to listen, folding long knotty fingers together as if in prayer and beaming beatifically.

Many of his predictions were on the mark: the collapse of the Soviet empire, the civil war in Yugoslavia, the weakening of Japan from rampant corruption, the threat of Islamic fundamentalism. He was faulted for not anticipating Iraq's invasion of Kuwait. Because he usually tried to present both sides of a picture, some saw him as an apologist for Saddam.

But Richards's record had a more recent blemish: he failed to anticipate the importance of Dimona gold. Richards had been preoccupied with other problems—atomic proliferation, ethnoreligious strife, human rights in China—and paid little attention to Shepherd's initial cable about Israel's alleged production of synthetic gold.

"I thought it was a joke," he later told the admiral. After reaching Shepherd on the secure phone and discovering he was serious but knew little more than what was in the cable, Richards said it must be an Israeli-orchestrated blue-sky con game to wheedle money from Uncle Sam. No other explanation seemed to fit.

Richards was too sophisticated to think it might be true. Before kicking the cable upstairs, he wrote in the margin in his neat script: "Another Israeli con game? Or is this guy smoking something? May be time to part this Shepherd from his flock."

Oberling didn't think much of the cable, either. But Oberling had one great advantage over Richards. He wrote nothing down.

The admiral rather fancied Richards's observations, and passed them onto the President. The admiral enjoyed undercutting people, especially his own people—it built up good creative tension—and knew the President would find the comment on Israel amusing.

Forget its brave and tragic origins, Israel had become just "one big royal pain in the ass," as the President liked to say. Israel resisted peace initiatives, pushed its weight around with the powerful lobby of Jewish groups in America, was always angling for more money. The budget director often reminded the cabinet that Israel was already receiving from U.S. taxpayers $3 billion a year, or the equivalent of $1,000 for each Israeli citizen. What about America's poor?

So when the Israeli prime minister called the U.S. President from Jerusalem, confirming that Israel was actually producing artificial gold cheaply, and furthermore volunteered to make arrangements to share the bonanza with the United States, the admiral felt as if the wind had suddenly disappeared from the mainsail of his sloop off Solomon's Island.

He had to endure an embarrassing though gentle presidential rebuke. Years of loyal service to Orville Halleck forestalled harsher recriminations. Also not to be forgotten was the CIA's much better analysis on Angola and South Africa.

Still, the admiral was annoyed at not being ahead of the curve, then further peeved by the clever initiative of White House Chief of Staff Harry Spitz to recruit a top-flight physicist to do a little sleuthing for the President. That was the sort of thing CIA people were supposed to think of. His men were asleep at the switch.

The admiral was just piqued enough to enforce a little penalty. He insisted that his two top deputies, each wrestling with impossible dilemmas in global trouble spots, take time out to meet the Stanford physicist at National Airport and escort him to the White House.

For Richards he had a little more in mind.

Born in Shanghai, the son of a peripatetic U.S. Army engineer, Cyrus Richards passed the war years at Fort Belvoir, Virginia, where he picked up his slight Southern drawl. His father, then a colonel, was building bridges across the Salween River as part of the campaign to expel the Japanese from Burma.

In 1946, Colonel Richards brought the family to China, where he was assigned to an army reconstruction unit at Tsingtao, the port north of Shanghai. They stayed in Shanghai for two exciting years, living in an army dependents' residence off Marshall Joffre Street in the French quarter. A PFC chauffeured young Richards and his sister every day to the American Quaker School on Bubbling Well Road, where both learned Mandarin.

During those formative preteen years Cyrus developed his lifelong revulsion against communism. Daily he overheard his teachers, parents, their friends, shopkeepers, express fears of a communist takeover—hundreds of thousands of refugees were flooding the fertile Shanghai plain as they fled Mao's blitzkrieg in the north and west. "If communism is so great," his father said, "why do so many vote against it with their feet?"

Richards joined ROTC at Yale, quarterbacked intramural football, majored in Far Eastern history, then shipped out to Korea in the Signal Corps. It was early 1953, and the war was winding down. In the Punch Bowl, north of Chunchon, he worked in 45th (Thunderbird) Division G-2 interviewing Chinese prisoners. After the war he made the short hop into civilian intelligence. Richards had all the qualities the new CIA was looking for: brains, upper-middle-class family of a conservative bent, facility with languages, appetite for work, feelings for God and country, a sense of mission.

After indoctrination and training, he ended up in Indochina, where the French were losing to the Viet Minh. Thanks to his facility with Chinese, he learned basic Vietnamese. In Haiphong he met an ideological soul mate, Colonel Edward G. Lansdale, the intellectual behind the counterinsurgency when the United States entered the war a few years later.

Richards deepened his knowledge of the cultures and languages of Indochina. Two years of the 1960s were spent in Laos organizing arms shipments to Meo tribesmen fighting the communist Pathet Lao, then three in Vietnam, where he became part of the rural reconstruction efforts that Premier Nguyen Cao Ky ordered to pacify the countryside.

The Phoenix program, developed by one of Ky's lieutenants, Tran Ngoc Chau, chief of Vietcong–infested Kien Hoa province north of Saigon, was in full swing. To make a new Vietnam rise from the ashes of civil war, thousands of freshly trained cadres were reasserting government control. Organized into census-grievance teams, they converted insurgents into government supporters by addressing their specific complaints and providing unconditional amnesty. Those who refused to be converted were considered die-hard Vietcong to be terminated.

The counterinsurgency program created a system of verification to determine whether those who claimed to have been converted were not secretly working for the Vietcong. Anyone with information about double agents was invited to step forward. Richards, now speaking Vietnamese like a native, was in charge of one of the main verification bureaus, in Kien Hoa, established to check the accuracy of informers' accusations. Corroboration was difficult. No one could be believed.

The Vietcong were stepping up their own campaign of terror, murdering villagers suspected of being loyal to Saigon. After viewing too many bodies, Richards supported retaliation in kind. He weighed, then approved, hundreds of executions. If one or two innocents died, alas, so be it. Heresy must be wiped out.

In the late 1970s, after more language training at the Foreign Service Institute in Rosslyn, Virginia, and assignments in Hong Kong, Thailand, and the Philippines, Richards went to Teheran. The shah, trying to catapult Iran into the twentieth century, was under attack by Islamic fundamentalists.

Still, Richards wrote in his coded cables, the shah might have held on but for the cheap shots from the international press. Their constant attacks against the corruption (no worse than Chicago or Plains, Georgia) undermined American support for the shah as it had for Ngo Dien Diem, and Chiang Kai-shek before that. After the shah's fall, repression by the Ayatollah Khomeini followed as night follows day. The parallels with Vietnam, China, and Cuba were striking. In each case a liberal press undermined regimes friendly to the United States, and the new regimes turned the countries into concentration camps.

Richards made his thoughts known. Friends of like persuasion engineered his return to Langley in the late 1970s. His warnings about the imminent fall of Iran won him the CIA's highest award, the Distinguished Intelligence Medal. In a small ceremony attended by only a few inside men, he was commended for "nurturing the pride of the directorate while working together to further the concept that this is one agency: working together."

*      *      *

GREGORY OBERLING'S FATHER, a biochemist at George Washington University, died early; his Smith–educated mother had taught Russian literature in English, wrote poetry, and was descended from Russian aristocracy, a grandfather who was a czarist general. She had cousins in Paris, New York, and Washington, who were direct descendants of the Romanovs.

Young Oberling, raised by his mother, spoke Russian early, was an acolyte during the long vigils of Russian Orthodox Christmas and Easter, and by age six could recite the names of all czars since Ivan the Terrible. At Yale, he was tapped for Skull and Bones. He went on to earn a doctorate in Soviet studies at the Johns Hopkins School for Advanced International Studies, and seemed headed for an eventual chair in Russian studies at one of the major universities. Princeton was already eyeing him.

But his mother's contacts led him to the CIA. Thanks to her Russian, over the years since her husband's death she had done odd jobs for the agency, translated for FBIS, and served as escort-interpreter for visiting Soviet delegations, cultivating certain individuals who seemed anxious to talk with her beyond earshot of their vigilant comrades. She moved from the leafy street in Georgetown, where she had lived with her scientist husband and where her son grew up, to a leafier street in McLean. She remarried, the CIA director of program evaluation.

"I can't think of a better place to work in America," she told her son. "I love it when I go there. Parties are like a class reunion. I see all those Yale men I used to know."

"And date?" her son asked slyly. Mrs. Oberling smiled.

Gregory Oberling's first tour was Moscow as a "very able" junior officer. After a brief interlude in Zaire, he returned to Moscow and over the course of an extended tour rose to deputy station chief, paying his dues by living through two fires in the cramped and crumbling embassy on Tchaikovsky Street.

Under difficult and at times dangerous working conditions, he assessed new Soviet weapons systems and was part of the team that painstakingly pieced together information on the Krasnoyarsk antimissile system that the United States later charged was in violation of the antiballistic missile treaty.

Like his mother, Oberling quietly cultivated high-level Soviets. Although the 1917 revolution had crushed the nobility, Soviets were always secretly thrilled to meet those with links to the royal family. A few old aristocrats who survived abroad managed to become wealthy again, or at least carry on as if they still were, sometimes thanks to the generosity of their American spouses, friends, and benefactors. This only added to their celebrity status.

CIA string pullers decided that before his ascension, Oberling needed broadening beyond Soviet affairs. So after Moscow and suitable interludes at Langley, they assigned him short postings in odd but pivotal places—Benghazi, Baghdad, Amman—with briefer sojourns in Buenos Aires and Mexico City. In all these places he continued to find Soviet counterparts to cultivate, and was quietly instrumental in three more defections.

The aura of nobility and his imposing bearing made people deferential. His secretary called him "Dr. Oberling." He laced his conversation with such words as "ontological," "epistemological," and "ipsissima verba." If some in the agency, including the admiral, regarded his mannerisms as affected, so be it. Oberling was being Oberling. He did not believe in altering behavior to toady to superiors. He was never subservient. Nor did he hide his light under a bushel.

While American lawmakers proclaimed their egalitarianism, they, too, were struck by the presence of this descendant of imperial Russia with his urbane New England accent bordering on Oxford, and quietly cheered his ascent up the ladder of the CIA. Absorbing the czar's people showed democracy in action, lawmakers said. Besides, who could be more loyal to the United States than victims of foreign oppression?

THE RIVALRY OF Richards and Oberling came to a boil over Iran-Iraq policies. Although Richards had no love for the Khomeini regime, he sought to bolster Iran. "Iran counterbalances Iraq," Richards argued. "Arming Iran will facilitate a better relationship with the new people who will take over in the post-Khomeini era."

Oberling countered that a major danger to the world was Iran's propagation of Islamic fundamentalism well beyond its own borders. "Saddam isn't one of these wild clerics, he's a guy with whom you can sit down and talk. Megalomaniac, sure, but with practical commercial sense unclouded by religious beliefs."

Iraq also had far more oil than Iran, Oberling noted, and wanted to use its oil exports to finance intensive capital modernization, presenting op-

portunities for American business. Increased trade would slowly liber-
alize Iraq.

SOON AFTER THE prime minister's talk with the President, the admiral
invited Richards for lunch at Charlie's Place on Chain Bridge Road. With
almost an excess of bonhomie, the admiral told Richards, "Well, we can't
win 'em all, can we, Cyrus, but not to worry, all's well that ends well."

Richards didn't comment. He knew he hadn't been invited to lunch to
talk but to listen. The admiral immediately returned to the subject a little
more loquaciously, acknowledging that he was indeed saddened, not by
the way the case turned out, but by the process that "did not leave the
agency smelling like a rose."

"We were not at our best," he continued. "I don't mind losing. I don't
mind errors of judgment. But I do mind being embarrassed. I mind when
a chief of staff does something we should have done. I realize this is
Monday-morning quarterbacking, but, Cyrus, we should have named our
own academic expert to look into things. Better our expert than his. I
don't like that son of a bitch carving a role for himself in our business."

Hard to imagine two people more ideologically opposed than Harry
Spitz and the admiral, Richards mused. The one was a former labor
organizer and Vietnam draft dodger; the other, scion of a wealthy Buck-
head Atlanta family who fought in three wars. That they were in the same
political party was a measure of the breadth of Orville Halleck's appeal.

"Sorry about that." Richards broke his silence, using the term so popular in Vietnam. It was always used lightly, without any real sense of
regret, which was what Richards intended. *He* would never have proposed an outside expert, especially one from a liberal university, to do the
government's work. Amateurs were the bane of the agency, the bane of
American foreign policy.

"No big deal." The admiral smiled, again pouring on the bonhomie.
"You'd fault me, I know, if I didn't bring something like this to your
attention."

Gold didn't come up again until dessert. At the second bite of pumpkin cheesecake the admiral stared at his fork.

"Cyrus," he said, sighing. "Our métier is so imperfect. Intelligence,
indeed all knowledge, is imperfect. How can one know everything? We're
always guessing, judging, trying to make deductions based on certain
facts, a few givens. Yet sometimes, as with this gold enterprise, there is

something that we've missed, hadn't anticipated, and we're left looking like shit on a stick, and then we haven't served our President properly. . . .

"So I ask myself at times like this, how do we get better? Is there some dimension we can add to our expertise? Then I recall my days at the academy and the impression made on me a half-century ago—will you believe it, I feel it was only yesterday—by a little Chinese general and master strategist who advised Ho Lu, the King of Wu. . . . I wanted you to have this."

The admiral brightened as he pulled from his jacket pocket a small package wrapped in red-and-gold-striped paper and handed it across the table. Richards held the gold ribbon as if afraid the package might explode.

"Open it," the admiral ordered.

Richards pulled at the ends of the bow and tore off the paper. Inside was a volume: *The Art Of War* by Sun Tzu.

"Have you read it?"

"No."

"Well, read it." He sipped his coffee, and wiped his lips fastidiously with his napkin. "It's about using common sense in war. 'Avoid your enemy's strength and strike his emptiness,' he writes, 'and then, like water, none can oppose you.' His work has been around for about twenty-five centuries, so he's not telling us anything new. Just basic truths we sometimes forget. . . ."

The admiral's mouth hung over his dessert plate. A morsel of pumpkin cheesecake, speared by his fork, hung in the air like a fat insect, then disappeared through his lips almost faster than the eye could see.

". . . Yet sometimes we forget about common sense," the admiral continued. "We get so close to the trees that we miss the clear, pristine logic of the forest. . . ."

Another fat insect vanished. "Sun tells us if the enemy strikes where we have taken no precautions, then we should have anticipated that strike—and taken precautions. That is a contradiction, isn't it? If we don't expect it, how can we take precautions?" He gave a high-pitched giggle. "But in our business, we try to resolve contradictions . . ."

He paused and eyed his protégé sadly, like the father who has to discipline a beloved son. ". . . For when one is surprised, one does foolish, intemperate things. It usually means a crisis . . ." He sighed again. "Cyrus, our job is to anticipate crises. When we fuck up, the

President gets little more from us than from the *New York Times* or the *Washington Post.*"

No doubt now about the admiral's rage. Richards knew that like himself, the admiral had only contempt for the press, and took the greatest of pleasure every evening in laying both the *Times* and the *Post,* only sports pages read, in his cat box and then pouring on a layer of fresh kitty litter.

# 33

AT MOST MODERN airports the plane taxis directly to the terminal. At Dulles there is an intermediate step. The passenger enters a high-tech bus. The driver sits in a cockpit, surrounded by glowing panels, dials, and intercom equipment. He can move his craft backward and forward up and down, so the floor of the bus matches the level of the floor of the aircraft. But it's still a bus. Passengers are jostled, their feet stepped on. Their luggage slides around. They refuse to move to the back.

Jim Shepherd plunked himself onto the hard bench and between his calves squeezed his briefcase, carryall, and obligatory duty-free Sabra liqueur, the orangy-chocolaty stuff that he couldn't stomach but Admiral Jackman liked to serve to guests. After the long flight from Lod via Zurich, he was stiff, achy, and grimy. The discomforts on the bus on this his first trip to the States in a year didn't help. The bus hadn't irritated him so much on earlier visits. But now little things irritated—the interminable wait for the bus to start, the preteen near him blowing sweet spheroids of bubblegum that periodically popped.

He tried to think of sex. That usually cheered him up. He liked rough Arab sex where you beat up the woman, or the man. There was a big-boobed woman across from him he wouldn't have minded porking.

He had been called back for consultations on the eve of Sherbatov's arrival in the United States. Ben Giton, getting set for his own trip to the States as Sherbatov's escort, asked him to stop at the *moshav*.

No sooner had Shepherd walked in than the general began his tirade. "Letting them go like that!" Ben Giton raged. "And you a profes-

sional . . ." Hairs bristling on his brawny arms, he waved off all protests.
". . . Throughout my life I have always held to basics—loyalty, patrio-
tism, family, friends, work, no fuckups . . ." Shepherd felt like a schoolboy. Making it worse was the realization that Ben Giton was right.

The general, known for his wide mood swings, later calmed down,
becoming almost friendly. He revealed that Bloom had traced the fugitives to Zurich. Surely with his gold, Shepherd rued, they could have
chartered a 747.

"We thought we had adequate resources," Ben Giton said. "Obviously
we didn't. They slipped through to Cairo, and took Swiss Air. From
somewhere they got new passports and apparently have plenty of money.
They are now a real threat. We must get rid of them fast, and we need
help."

"I'm on my way to Washington," Shepherd remonstrated.

"Precisely. We need your help from Washington."

Shepherd looked puzzled. He felt that his mustache was still there,
and tugged it gently. "For what?"

"Activation of Force Majeure."

Puzzlement gave way to astonishment. "General, I don't have that kind
of power." How could Ben Giton know of this, the most secret unit of
the CIA? Israelis never ceased to amaze him.

"Use your influence, Jim. You brought them Dimona gold. You're
smelling like a rose. Explain the stakes to the admiral and Cyrus Richards. They'll understand. Force Majeure, and you redeem yourself,
and *your* road is paved with gold."

"What about Mossad?"

"Mossad wants no part of this. It's soft on the girl, part of the family
and all that. We can't convince them she's a traitor. I can't press the issue
in the cabinet. The P.M. mustn't get involved."

"And the Swiss?"

"They've given Bloom a courtesy desk in the central police station,
some help checking hotel registrations. But no real commitment. Doesn't
involve their citizens, or their banks."

On the stopover in Zurich, Bloom told Shepherd: "We have Mohammed and the car-rental agency to thank. The rental lady filed a complaint
about the missing car, lighting fires under Mohammed. He suddenly
discovered the spare parts for those 204s. An aerial surveillance team
found the car at the Cairo airport.

"The car, a Subaru, had been through the wars. Thousands of dollars of damage. The insurance company balked. So Mohammed asked for our cooperation. I had Rachel's ID photo and a routine Shin Bet airport shot of the physicist, which I happily gave him. After interviewing Cairo airport and flight personnel, his people matched the pix with an Ellen Zwass and a Robert Taylor on a Swiss Air flight to Zurich."

SHEPHERD KNEW THE Force Majeure Bureau operated at the complete discretion of the director. The President could know if he wanted to know, but almost always chose not to. He had to have plausible deniability. Nothing was ever committed to paper or disk. Those in the loop called it the "accident bureau" because victims leaned too far from high places, collided with buses, suffered sudden massive heart attacks, were prey to fatal muggings and carjackings, and other acts of random violence.

Shepherd was damn sure FMB terminated Allende, Lumumba, Count Bernadotte, Dag Hammarskjöld. It screwed up with Castro and Saddam Hussein, but may have gotten one of Saddam's cousins from Tikrit.

SHEPHERD CARRIED A little bottle of Underberg in his jacket pocket. Old Hubert's secret formula might help. The finest herbs of forty-three countries macerated 44 percent pure alcohol, matured in casks of Slovenian oak. "To feel bright and alert," he read on the tiny print label, and swallowed the bitter brew. Some people stared at him. To hell with them. This was precisely what he needed. He felt the liquid course through his veins, met the stares head-on.

On a distant runway a 747 gathered speed for its liftoff. Beyond were the gentle swellings of the Blue Ridge foothills ablaze with scarlet and gold. He looked again at the woman with the big tits. He regretted his heavy agenda because he felt so horny.

THE BUS STARTED UP. Thank God.

He wondered who the agency would send to meet him. That would be his first indication of the temperature of the welcome.

Would the red queen ask for his head? What wild croquet matches and mad tea parties were in store? And the mock turtle's dizzying refrain:

*Will you, won't you, will you, won't you, won't you join the dance?* Yes, he had definitely joined the dance—and with more than one partner.

Would they suspect the extent of his relationship with Ben Giton? But Israel was a close ally and free-trade partner. Shepherd was merely assuring truth and openness in the relationship. No offense in that. He recalled the biblical words etched in the Tennessee marble lobby of the building at Langley: *"And ye shall know the truth, and the truth shall make you free."*

He ran over his little speech. Though they loved to move chess pieces around, he'd insist he was needed in Israel to see the gold project through. He'd explain as much as he knew about the gold project. He felt the two 100-gram pieces in his pocket. He'd talk of the fugitives, the threat of leakage that would destroy the golden-egg-laying goose, and finally of Force Majeure.

Perhaps he was worrying too much. After all, the signs did point to a hero's welcome. They had approved his business-class travel, and after the President accepted the prime minister's offer, the admiral had even sent him a rare hero-gram.

Anyone could see the dividends. Here was a miraculous stream of secret money that would never dry up. Ideally, the CIA would manage the operation and use proprietaries to sell gold in London or Zurich. Proceeds could go anywhere. No congressional oversight. What President wouldn't be creaming in his pants?


"GOOD FLIGHT?"

It was the DDO himself. Cyrus Richards led him to a chauffeur-driven black Chevrolet. No queues. No Customs forms. Shepherd showed his diplomatic passport and sailed through the terminal like the President of France. Someone was even delegated to collect his suitcase and deliver it to the McLean Marriott where they had booked him but where he would not have a chance to shower and shave before the meeting with the admiral.

Richards didn't expect an answer to his question, didn't care. But Shepherd was dying to voice his complaints.

"Except for that dumb bus ride. Why don't planes taxi to the gate the way they do in other airports?"

Richards gave one of his noncommittal smiles. Amenities at airports, except as they might relate to arrival of a head of state or the surveillance of a notorious terrorist, were of no interest. From his ordered mind Richards discarded anything extraneous to immediate concerns: day-to-day operations of the CIA.

The chauffeur, a solid, dark-haired, grave-looking man in a gray business suit, was wired with an earpiece. A bulge in his jacket hinted at a snub-nose 38-caliber police special, or possibly the more powerful 40-caliber Glock semiautomatic with a 15-shot clip to which CIA security was changing over. He took Shepherd's case and carryall and tucked them into the trunk. The men climbed into the car, Shepherd to the left rear.

"Thanks for the executive-class ticket." Shepherd pulled his trouser legs to save what was left of a worn crease. "In tourist class I'd be one dead tourist."

"The admiral wanted you fresh for our meeting," Richards said, settling back into the contours of the vinyl seat.

"I thought we were due at the Marriott for cocktails," Shepherd said lightly. A little badinage was always in order.

Richards gave a short laugh. "The admiral demands an immediate report from his man in the playing fields of the Lord."

The Chevrolet drew out slowly into the traffic stream, in the wake of a black limo bus headed for the Capital Hilton, then picked up speed. The drive from Dulles to Langley took twenty-five minutes.

The late afternoon had a tangy smell of leaves and overripe apples and pears. A pleasant contrast to the sere, ochre dust of Israel. Overhead, clouds like a fleet of tall ships were buffeted across the nacreous sky. The sun was slipping behind the slate-blue hills to the west, but darkness had already seized the sky's eastern flanks.

"It *is* good to see you, Jim." Richards leaned back, his right hand cranking the window a trifle. It was too chilly for air-conditioning but stuffy without fresh air.

Shepherd tried not to stare at Richards's right index finger. He'd forgotten about the missing joint. A freak accident years ago when someone, not even a Soviet agent, slammed a car door on Richards's hand. The amputation proved only a minor inconvenience: the stump faultlessly picked out the keys of his computer, and so gently squeezed the trigger of his thirty-eight that in the monthly target practice in the subbasement range, his marksmanship actually improved.

"How long has it been since we've seen each other?" asked Richards.

The wind coming in from the window whistled in competition with his reedy voice. "A year at least. Too long."

Shepherd smiled. "Yes, I should get back more often. I do miss colleagues here." He was determined to play his part well. "Alas," he added with mock weariness, "there's just so much to do in the field."

"And you're doing it so well." Richards's arms pumped the air in rhythmic cadences. "Dammit, Jim, we are proud of you. Getting that kind of material from the Israelis. What a coup. It means a lot to us. More than you think. There's talk of putting you in for the DIM."

Shepherd looked confused. Richards was staring at him.

"Distinguished Intelligence Medal. You have been away a long time. People here know what it is. Some would kill for it."

"No, Cyrus, you're the one who deserves it." Shepherd tried to recover.

"I already have it," Richards said.

"Of course you do. How stupid." Shepherd put on his sincerest face. "You, Cyrus, are the glue holding us all together. Where would we be without you?"

Richards did not protest. Shepherd knew Richards loved to hear the praise, and had not one grain of doubt that the statement was true.

Shepherd pushed on, he needed the operations chief as an ally. "Cyrus," he said, "you've saved our ass over the years. Your one hundred and ten percent backup for us in the field, your willingness to give us the running room we need, take our flak, your gentle reminders when we fuck up. I always feel better knowing you're in charge."

Richards stiffened. His eyes narrowed.

"I just thought some things needed to be said," Shepherd muttered, worried now he may have gone too far with the flattery. Richards was, after all, no fool.

Richards looked at Shepherd, smiling icily. "I'm already on your side, Jim. We all are."

"The work is taxing in Israel," Shepherd said a bit too defensively.

"You do it so well," Richards reiterated.

"And the family?" Shepherd would do anything to ingratiate himself. Years ago he had been invited to dinner at Richards's house in a roomy McLean Cape Cod. He remembered a mousy, squeaky-voiced wife and an anorexic daughter.

"Fine, everyone is fine, just fine." Richards signaled he had no desire to talk about family, or anything else just now.

The chauffeur, his bull-like neck thrust forward, kept the car at a steady clip of seventy mph. In the late-afternoon penumbra, the phalanx of glass, granite, concrete, and brick corporate buildings cast shadows across part of the four-lane Dulles Access Road. Behind aisles of trees and swards of green, the buildings stood like a special honor guard, welcoming all visitors and setting the record straight about what was important in America: Boeing, AT&T, Sprint International, Sheraton, Prudential Insurance, Kaiser Permanente, Scope, Lucas, PRC, ICL, Dyncorp, and Nissan. One sprawling building of solid green glass had the audacity to stand without a visible corporate name.

Richards's eyes were shut. Muffled snorts emanated from his mouth. Over the years of caroming from one Langley situation room to another, he had developed an ability to catnap under almost any conditions. Dozing off, moreover, was his way of saying he had learned all he needed to know from whomever he was with.

Shepherd settled back. He wasn't any worse off, he thought, and might even have improved his position.

# 34

THE CHAUFFEUR PULLED into the CIA checkpoint off Chain Bridge Road just above the Great Falls bend in the Potomac. Cars were beginning to head out. The road curved from the guard post toward one of the familiar landmarks, a silver-domed conference hall likened to a Tastee-Freez emporium. Here the agency held its larger staff meetings and briefed senior officials from other branches of the U.S. government, and sometimes from friendly foreign governments, on China and Russia's economic reforms or Iraq's chemical weapons stockpile.

The central structure was a huge glass-walled and prestressed concrete rectangle built in the early 1980s for $100 million. It resembled the State Department building at Foggy Bottom, and like the State Department was seven stories tall. It was connected by a covered walkway to an older building to the rear. The entire complex employed about 3,000.

Sprouting from the roof of the central building was a forest of ultrahigh-powered telecommunications dishes and antennae. Outside the entrance stood the bronze statue of America's greatest and earliest spy, Nathan Hale, Yale Class of 1773, eyes tilted heavenward, arms tied behind him, the gallows rope dangling around his neck, ready to give his one and only life for his country. The statue warmed the heart of Richards and the multitude of other CIA Yalies. Its double stood in front of Connecticut Hall on the Old Campus, and was the first thing freshmen associated with Yale. Dartmouth-educated, Shepherd never felt the same shiver of nostalgia.

Inside the perimeter of high fences and armed guards, the place looked like a college campus with its grassy knolls and sylvan walks, dining halls and library, and people toting notebooks. But no torn Levi's, half-laced running shoes, or ponytails here. The atmosphere was more Citicorp or IBM. Men and women alike dressed in dark suits. A few risked tweedy jackets. Some women wore Liberty or Vera scarves neatly pinned by gold broaches. Their sensible pump heels matched their handbags.

The chauffeur dropped Richards and Shepherd at the entrance to the main building. They showed their passes at the reception desk and took the director's express elevator to the top floor.

Admiral Carlos Jackman was waiting at a round oak conference table in a corner of his rectangular office. Annapolis, Class of 1941, former intelligence chief at the Pentagon, personal friend of the President, Admiral Jackman had served as director of the CIA for the past eighteen months. He was a short, stiff-backed, tight-collared man with a mischievous twinkle in the eye.

He had just nuked fresh popcorn in the General Electric Sunbeam microwave, and the place smelled like a movie house. Shepherd presented him with the bottle of Sabra liqueur.

"That's real considerate of you," the admiral said, standing the bottle on his desk. He was wearing a Brooks Brothers maroon-striped shirt and rather bright blue tie. His bass voice resonated with the confidence of a man who always knew what he wanted and didn't hesitate to use other people to get it.

Above the microwave hung a painting of the sinking of the *Bismarck* by the British navy in the South Atlantic early in World War II. On a table next to photographs of the admiral's wife, children, and grandchildren, stood a scale model of the destroyer *Carrington*, his first and only command. Models of the *Monitor* and *Merrimack* were protected by a glass case. On the opposite wall hung a large reproduction of Johann Zoffany's *Colonel Mordunt's Cock Match* against the Nawab of Oudh. The admiral loved a good cockfight, and Colonel Mordunt's, about to start a couple of centuries ago in the Arabian Desert, would be a beaut.

He had grown up in Macon, Georgia, where roosters were as common as doghouses. How many Sunday mornings had he set off, supposedly to church, instead to wager on those big black birds stuffed with corn and oats, armed with razor-sharp gaffs and steel spurs, ready to do battle across an innocent line of chalk.

Pansies in the Humane Society were trying to get the sport banned.

Lily-livered, ignorant bastards. How much chance did Frank Perdue's chickens have? Cockfighting was part of a tradition that went back to the Romans. American Civil War units, both north and south, kept roosters as mascots. When the Third Tennessee Infantry Division's bird finally croaked, it received full military honors at Arlington.

The admiral's windows looked over the darkening treetops at daubs of light from the spacious houses across the Potomac in Maryland. On the window ledge where he had designed an elaborate bird-feeding station, the last hatchers and thatchers and threshers and thrashers were chirping, strutting, fluttering, and puttering through a new layer of leftover popcorn.

His fingers were tapping the table near a full silver pitcher of ice water and large crystal bowl from Tiffany's filled with fresh popcorn. He used to deploy a silver bowl, but since he ate his popcorn salted, Grace, his secretary, complained that the silver tarnished and he shouldn't be eating so much salt anyway.

Five chairs stood around the table. One would have been occupied by the agency's deputy director, Walter Goddard, one of the Admiral's classmates at Annapolis, who had just died of pneumonia at Sibley Hospital. Goddard had gone into shipbuilding in San Diego after the war and later diversified into electronics. After the admiral resigned from the Pentagon, Goddard invited him to join his core enterprise, Paradigm Systems Inc., as a senior vice-president. After the admiral became CIA director, he invited Goddard, just retired from Paradigm, as his deputy. The funeral at Arlington was tomorrow. The admiral, shaken by Goddard's death, told friends he was determined to retire soon "to tend my birds."

Whoever got Goddard's job could be in line to be the director. Past presidents had selected new CIA chiefs from inside the agency about half the time, political friends the other half. President Halleck, criticized for cronyism in the selection of the admiral, this time would likely choose a professional from inside the agency.

Richards, sixty, and Oberling, fifty-five, were the acknowledged front-runners, but no decision had been taken, and the admiral liked to keep people guessing. Richards was understated, had no academic pretensions, was plenty smart, but didn't always try to show it. Oberling had more polish and confidence. He added class to the agency, but was at times overbearing.

"It's amazing," Oberling observed as they sat down after the greetings and other formalities of Shepherd's arrival, "how basically simple the great discoveries are. Fire, the wheel, the steam engine, electricity, the opening of the Great Pyramid. The keys are in plain sight, but visible only to a certain type of mind, one willing to challenge accepted wisdom, look in new directions."

"Well put, Dr. Oberling," the admiral said. "And Mr. Shepherd here, our own Champollion, will tell us how he was able to decipher this golden Rosetta Stone."

"The challenge of accepted wisdom." Shepherd smiled suavely at Oberling. The Underberg and now this not unfriendly reception made him feel better, even though it was well past midnight Zurich time. He drew out the two gold pieces, laid them on the table, pushed them like poker chips toward the admiral.

"One comes from a mine in West Witwatersrand, the other from Dimona. Both weigh one hundred grams. Which one has the Toni?"

Chuckling, the admiral picked them up, eyed them. He rubbed them as a French peasant might a Louis d'or, bit them, licked them, rubbed them against his cheek, weighed them in his hands.

"Beats me," he said.

"I wouldn't have known, either," Shepherd said, "except for the serial numbers." He leaned forward to project a little more drama. "I think you'll find in the lab they'll both prove at least ninety-nine and forty-four one hundredth percent pure. Remember, the little mine in Dimona that makes this stuff is inexhaustible."

The admiral slid the gold pieces in front of Richards, folded his manicured fingers into a cradle, and gave a proud, almost paternal look at Shepherd. "Some people around here think you deserve special recognition, like the DIM, for bringing this to our attention. I can't say I disagree with them."

"I think he's forgotten what the DIM is," Richards cut in. "Good to see you back in these precincts, sir."

"Good to be back." Would Richards never give up trying to move pawns? Shepherd caught himself staring at the abbreviated finger wiggling around the shiny gold surfaces like a headless guppy, and quickly lifted his gaze toward the admiral. "I was lucky, sir. The game seemed to be going our way."

"You make your own luck, son," said the admiral.

"Thank you."

"And when you're ahead," the admiral said, eyes on Richards, "you don't change the players. Or as we used to say in Georgia, 'If it ain't broke, don't fix it.' "

"Continuity is damned important," Shepherd chimed in. He wondered why the admiral was being so amiable. Could the original cable have been considered so wild they were indeed planning his recall? He looked deferentially at the admiral.

"The work in Israel is intense, sir, the pressure high. There are personal dangers. But I love it, and my experience there," he smiled, "can only help our mission."

"We hope you honor us with occasional visits . . ." Richards pushed the gold pieces toward Oberling. ". . . so that at least you can keep up with our customs."

Richards was like a pit bull. Shepherd was glad his only sin was a little memory loss about a medal.

Oberling lifted the two pieces like a nobleman receiving the offerings of a vassal. He brushed his forefinger lighly over the edges. "What are these worth?"

"Maybe five hundred dollars each," Shepherd answered.

"Impressive." Oberling sighed. "The fulfillment of the alchemists' dream." He gazed at a galaxy of lights across the river. "They've talked about it since the days of early Christianity. Transubstantiation. Changing the balance of the elements with their beakers, cauldrons, and magic formulas. So, it seems that the alchemists were right, only their timing wrong. Just a few centuries premature."

Admiral Jackman straightened his thin, fluttering frame, and raised his hand like a conductor signaling change in the tempo of the symphony.

"Our Russian alchemist arrives within the week," the admiral said. "The President will welcome him personally. Thank God they're keeping it off the White House calendar. Then it's Oak Ridge. Do I have the facts right, Cyrus?"

"Yes, that's correct, Admiral. We've organized a small tightly vetted group of physicists from the national laboratories who will be working with Sherbatov. The base metal is bismuth, which we've got plenty of. General Ben Giton told me we could be manufacturing our own gold pieces within three months. . . ."

"And security?" asked the admiral.

"As tight as Dimona," Richards said. "Wartime security. Manhattan Project."

Shepherd saw his opening, but waited until abatement of the roar of a plane following the Potomac to National Airport.

"A complication, sir, involving security." He flipped the two gold pieces on his fingers as if preparing sleight of hand. As eyes bore down on him, he spoke with well-rehearsed gravity:

"Before the prime minister officially informed the President, our professor Landover had gained access to Dimona. This unexpected visit angered the security-conscious Israelis, and they took it out not so much on the professor as on the person who helped orchestrate the breach, a junior physicist at Dimona named Rachel Ravid, who is the daughter of my source, Yosef Ravid, the former deputy head of Mossad. She's the original informant. She told her father, he told us. Yosef is now missing. There is a report he was killed by Arab terrorists, but his body has not yet been found, so . . ."

"That is a terrible piece of news," Oberling interrupted. "I worked with the old man. I knew him as a friend of America . . ."

"Me, too," said Richards.

"Ditto," said the admiral. "A fine man."

Shepherd continued: "Shin Bet tried to arrest Rachel—"

"Why?" Oberling exclaimed. "She's a hero."

"Not to the Israelis," Shepherd said, wishing Oberling would shut the hell up. "I would have recommended we intervene with Israeli security to obtain her release, but matters have gone much further now. Shin Bet wants to talk to both Rachel and Landover about the murder of a kibbutznik in Eilat, and those two have fled and now threaten to expose the whole operation."

Shepherd looked around, saw traces of incredulity, knew he would have to proceed with ingenuity and care, keep everything simple and focused.

"I believe they now pose a major danger to us. Bottom line: If they were to take it into their heads to expose the process, gold prices will collapse, and we're left with diddly-squat."

The admiral did not seem too unhappy with Shepherd's news. "We met the professor at the White House. Seemed like a harmless enough Indian. Didn't say much. Supposed to be one of the great experts. But brought in by that son of a bitch Harry Spitz. No time to run a check on him. We took Spitz's word. So who knows? Spitz could have given us shit."

"That Indian is now way off the reservation," Shepherd said.

"You mean he's now a fugitive." The admiral pronounced the word "foojatave" and let the syllables play out euphoniously on his lips, his Adam's apple bouncing up and down like a Ping-Pong ball above his tight collar. He liked the sound, reveling in the idea that the man whom Spitz had proposed for a presidential mission was being sought by foreign police.

"Tell us about the murder, son," the admiral said. "That sounds like something we need to know a lot more about."

Shepherd was prepared. He straightened his back, tugged thoughtfully at his mustache, presented his most ingenuous visage.

"It all started with the woman. The French say *cherchez la femme.* I'm afraid our friend—I don't really think he was a killer, too naive—got himself entangled with this Rachel Ravid."

"Oh, my." The admiral smiled. "A seductress. A Delilah."

"What she really wanted was a piece of the action," Shepherd continued. "A tawdry tale, I fear. I'll tell it the way I understand it. The sources are unimpeachable. As they were in my original gold cable." He looked thoughtfully at the admiral.

"She got the job at Dimona through her father, but their relations were increasingly strained. She'd become an outspoken supporter of the left, protesting in peace marches and demonstrations, even converting fellow workers. She was a zealot. They say when she was in London she had a Palestinian boyfriend."

"No!" exclaimed the admiral.

"She needed money for her causes," Shepherd continued, "and perhaps for her boyfriend, or boyfriends." He paused, tried to show pain. "It is said she may have even plotted her father's execution." He gazed at the faces around the table, torn between revulsion and disbelief. But no one interrupted.

"She was smart," he continued. "She was able to piece together what was going on in Machon Three. So she shamelessly asked General Ben Giton for a cut, threatening to go to the press if Ben Giton refused." Shepherd tried to look as if the story saddened him more than anyone. He went on:

"Ben Giton said he would study her request, but as you know, betrayal of official secrets, or even the threat of betrayal, is a major offense in Israel. Because of the dangers, he had little choice but to inform judicial authorities and seek to have her put into preventive detention. She pulled strings to stay out of jail while the legal process went forward. She then met our friend, the professor, managed to smuggle him into the Dimona compound, seduced him, and apparently convinced him to join her in the blackmail-extortion conspiracy to make their fortune."

He looked around again. He had their rapt attention.

"Somehow she got a warning of her impending arrest, and they slipped out of Dimona together just ahead of the police, heading south to Eilat. In Eilat, they met a kibbutznik named Ibrahim, used his hotel room as a love nest and hideout, and when they had no more use for him, killed him. They used false passports to cross the border to Taba and the Sinai, which may mean they have organizational backing. We were hot on their trail, but our Egyptian friends—well, you know Egyptians—anyway, we didn't get access to Egyptian police helicopters, so we always just missed them. . . ."

Shepherd poured himself a glass of water. Ice rattled in the silver pitcher. No one spoke. A crow's wings flapped on the sill.

"Although they slipped out," he continued, "we knew where they were at all times. I left phone messages at all the hostels on the road south of Taba. The professor returned my call from Nuweiba, halfway to Sharm el-Sheikh.

"A bizarre conversation. The voice of the professor I'd met at the American Colony, but the words of a hardened criminal. Yes, Admiral, that Stanford physicist possibly moonlighted as a hit man. He admitted shooting the kibbutznik. I said, 'Wait a second, Professor, you're talking about murder.' He said, 'Cohen was a meddler.' He expressed no sense of guilt or remorse.

"I urged him to turn himself in before more people got hurt. I told him that he'd gotten mixed up with bad company, the woman is wanted by the Israeli police and is dangerous, but since he was on a government mission, the authorities would be lenient with him. I said if he turned himself in, we'd get him out of all this and back to the States and even back to Stanford, and it would all be just a bad dream.

"He laughed and said the reason he returned the call was to give us one last chance to buy their silence. They wanted ten million dollars. I played along. Anything to keep him talking. He said they would let us know in future calls the means of payment.

"I asked how we could trust them. They'd obviously planned intricately. He said they'd accept gold at current market prices so that they, too, would lose if the market collapsed.

"Then he broke off. We knew their location, but, as I said, the Egyptians wouldn't give us the choppers. We rushed in a Shin Bet team by car, but it wound up in a gunfight in the OK Corral with some Hamas types. Another reason why we think they're working together."

The admiral rose to shoo the crow from the window ledge. "Interesting, very interesting." He returned to the popcorn bowl and with a handful of popcorn made another trip to the window, hoping to entice more thatchers and thrashers. Shepherd noticed he wasn't much taller standing than sitting.

Oberling looked puzzled. He pulled at a gray forelock. "The daughter of a former deputy head of Mossad working for terrorists who have just killed her father? And she'd actually helped? It doesn't add up."

"As I said, Greg, father and daughter grew to despise each other . . ." Shepherd's voice was a trifle louder, more emphatic. "With all those Mossad operations against Palestinians, she felt he was responsible for the death of innocents. They had false passports and plenty of money, things you only get with an organization behind you. A van load of terrorists was their security. Those are the people, Greg, who engaged the Shin Bet team. It does add up."

Oberling's eyes narrowed and his muscles tensed. He hated people he hardly knew calling him Greg. He held his ground.

"I can't see the security-conscious Israelis using a junior physicist who moonlights for Hamas in their most sensitive and secretive operation. Could the Hamas types have been hunting our friends, too? Wouldn't that explain it?"

"Not as well." Shepherd frowned, pulled his chair forward, looked his most earnest. "Remember, Greg, this girl hates her father, thinks he has sold out the cause of humanity, and she's got knowledge that could be of use to Hamas."

"You are saying," said the admiral, returning to his chair, "that this young lady was an agent of Hamas?"

"Not me, sir, Shin Bet. I'm just telling you what they think is a possibility and giving you some of the reasoning. If you don't like the message, don't shoot the messenger." As soon as he said it, he knew he'd gone too far. He must keep his cool.

"No one is shooting anyone around this table," the admiral said with a touch of annoyance. But he was still smiling, obviously enjoying himself. "Dr. Oberling has a point that it's indeed unusual for Israelis to let something like that slip by them."

"But that was exactly my point, sir," said Shepherd, softening his voice, the heart of reasonableness, but still on the offensive. "Shin Bet was on to her. She hadn't covered her traces well enough. All sorts of ties between her and the Palestinians. That's why she had to flee."

No one spoke. Had he stretched credulity too far with the Hamas connection? It was a calculated risk he had to take.

"Hamas or not," Richards said, jabbing the air with his abbreviated finger, "that pair poses a major problem for us. Problems require solutions."

Thank you, Cyrus Richards, Shepherd thought. The pit bull smells blood.

The admiral peered intently at the men around the table. Richards's cheeks were flushed. His upper lip revealed a long incisor. Oberling's fleshier face was pale, showing distaste for the proceedings, but he said nothing.

Shepherd broke the silence. He had his indictment, but he still needed a conviction. "We've got evidence they're now in Zurich. They apparently caught a Swiss Air flight out of Cairo."

"Zurich?" the admiral asked. "Why Zurich?"

"Zurich is the gold trading center. It makes sense in light of their stated intentions. And if they catch the ear of the *Neue Zurcher Zeitung* or one of the economic newsletters and get someone to put something in print that shakes the gold market, we're blown out of the water."

"So they could do real damage," the admiral mused.

"Right on, sir," Shepherd said. "And if we do anything with Force Majeure, it has to be there."

"If *we* do anything? What's wrong with the Israelis doing something?"

"There was a bit of a flap," Shepherd said. "Mossad wants out. Ben Giton asked Mossad but they refused. They don't want to go after the daughter of a former deputy director. It creates internal political problems."

"What about us and *our* internal political problems?" the admiral asked.

"I believe, sir, the pair must be eliminated before they destroy everything," Shepherd urged. "Time is of the essence. Israel gives us the formula. Force Majeure is our part of the bargain."

"So we're on the hot seat," the admiral said. He walked over to a mini-refrigerator and threw some ice cubes into a bucket. Over a glass of ice he poured some Sabra liqueur. He offered a similar libation to the others. They politely declined.

"Jim," the admiral said, sipping the murky brown sweetness, "you'll have to dictate a memo—what you've told us about the woman and the professor. Emphasize the sexual links, the murder of the Israeli, and the professor's callousness. Grace is staying late and will take the story from you. I want it on Spitz's desk in the morning for the President. Let's rub Spitz's nose in his own shit."

He took another sip, smacking his lips. His eyes were catching fire and his cheeks glowing. "Now does anyone have any thoughts about what we should be doing?"

Richards tilted his chair back, rubbed his temples, looked up at the chandelier-lit ceiling.

"The professor's not on our team anymore. He had a fling and took a life. He represents a major threat not only to the financial security of Israel but to our own efforts to get a little fiscal order here in Washington. I say: move, and move quickly. FMB can work with Shepherd, and cleanly, too. The President has no need to know. After he reads Shepherd's memo, he won't want to know."

Oberling, ashen-faced, was frowning and scratching his head. He stared at the admiral's empty glass, then the painting of the trapped *Bismark* being pounded by the British destroyers.

"I may as well say right up front that I'm not sure I like this. Not at all."

"None of us do," the admiral assured him. "We're just doing the best we can for our government." He smiled broadly at Oberling. "We're all friends here. Go ahead, tell us what you think. Give it to us straight. No holds barred. That's why you're here."

Oberling recalled the story of the top adviser to Saddam Hussein. Saddam entreated him to disclose his doubts about a particular strategy. A few hours later he ended up stuffed in a burlap sack. Still, Oberling was committed. If it was burlap, so be it. He drew paper from his pocket, and put on his bifocals.

"This is a little curriculum vitae of our man in Zurich," he said. "I know you're all familiar with it, but I bring it up just to point out that Professor Landover is a very distinguished gentleman, head of SLAC, which operates programs with the Department of Energy. He is frequently called as an expert before congressional committees. He is the author of innumerable technical works, a member of scientific commissions. He is respected by colleagues, admired by students. Working where he does, he would have to have received top clearances. No hint of his having any kind of underworld connections."

"Does it say there," interrupted Richards, "that he's got a weakness for the flesh? I recall he's been married a couple of times and according to the lore of Palo Alto was pretty much of a Lothario with special interest in pretty graduate students seeking some of his high-energy particles."

Oberling glowered at Richards. The admiral loved it but said nothing. His eyes moved from Richards to Oberling to Richards as if he were watching a tennis match, or a cockfight.

Oberling stiffened, crossed his arms. "Whatever Professor Landover's private life, his professional life is above reproach. And he is well connected. Any 'accident' engineered by FMB, however subtly, is likely to draw attention, comment, or even an investigation."

"Not if it's done right," Richards countered. "And I can assure you it will be. FMB has done this kind of thing before. And no one except people in this room and a few outsiders have even heard of FMB. The risks are negligible, contrasted with what happens if this guy and his girlfriend get to the press."

"I just warn you," Oberling interjected, "that things may go wrong. His wife will want details. She's going to wonder what he's doing in Zurich. What about the people in the cabinet who knew about the mission?"

"The wife is shacking up with her boss in a Silicon Valley software firm." Richards's voice was robotic. "She doesn't give a rat's ass. Besides, people have accidents all the time." He stared at Oberling. "Hammarskjöld, 1961 . . ."

Oberling's face flushed. "None of us has clean hands."

"Skeletons back in your closets, gentlemen," the admiral said. "No more rattling old bones."

"Or old phoenixes," Oberling said.

The Red Queen's wild croquet matches, Shepherd thought. He'd played it about right.

Oberling bent forward, leaned his large arms against the table and looked directly at the admiral.

"What I'm afraid of, sir, is that we may be condemning an innocent man. We have no evidence whatsoever of any criminal past. He doesn't even have an outstanding parking ticket . . ." He reached into his pocket and produced a copy of the FBI security check, which he handed to the admiral.

"We can assume such a man acts in line with his character profile. He might be naive about some things, but this Stanford physicist would be completely out of character to throw himself at the first woman he sees in a strange country, then try to blackmail that country's government. It's insane. Everyone knows the Israelis never bow to blackmail. Practically Article One of their constitution. And if he likes the Ravid woman so much, he can just take her back to SLAC as a researcher."

"Not after the murder in Eilat," Richards said. "Remember, there's a murder here."

Shepherd laid his own piece of paper on the table before the admiral. "I forgot to bring this out earlier. A warrant by Israeli police. They have witnesses stating Landover and Rachel were the last to see the kibbutznik alive. And Landover himself confessed to me on the phone. Instead of coming forward to the police, as I urged, they escaped. Seems pretty airtight to me."

"But we haven't heard from *them*," Oberling persisted. "We are condemning people on circumstantial evidence."

"How could we hear from them?" Richards asked in his dull, metallic voice. "Do we go to Zurich and invite them to please come to the police station? We must make judgments."

"They have the power to blow the gold operation sky high," Shepherd added.

Oberling persisted. "What if that Hamas bunch were really after Professor Landover and Ravid's daughter? What if the Hamas bunch really killed the kibbutznik?"

"And if the moon is really green cheese?" Richards asked.

The admiral reached under the table to stop the tape machine, then pushed out his chair and rose, holding the two documents. "This has been a fascinating colloquy, just fascinating, gentlemen. I thank you one and all. I think we can call it a day well spent."

As the three headed for the door, the admiral called out cheerfully, "And Jim, remember, on the way out, please, that memo. Grace will help you prepare it."

He straightened the knot of his bright blue tie. It matched the blue stone of his Annapolis ring, which caught the light of the chandelier.

"Let's stick it to Spitz."

# 35

A RADIANT EARLY October sun bounced off canopies and columns of the Baur au Lac terrace. Boxed petunias, pink-and-white roses, and mottled shrubs bordered the lawn, which sloped like a golfer's green toward the Burkliplatz Pier and Zurichsee. Inside the hotel, a Sunday afternoon dance band was playing Strauss waltzes, German polkas, and selections from *Camelot*. But as Landover took in this harmonious scene, the distant peaks above Zurichsee loomed in their membranes of icy mist and cloud, grim reminders of death and the fragility of life.

Thirty-six hours earlier, he and Rachel had won their deliverance from the Sinai. Their Subaru, looking worse than it performed, merged well with the jumble of camels and donkeys and other conveyances on the Sinai west coast road to Suez. Across the isthmus, at Cairo's international airport, they abandoned the car. Exhausted, they used a bit of their cash to buy new outfits at airport shops, stuffing their old ones, including Rachel's bonnet from Eilat, into a trash bin. They also bought two tickets for the next flight anywhere, which happened to be Swiss Air to Zurich.

The Boeing 737 had circled Zurichsee before landing at Kloten. They were seated in the rear of the plane. Landover looked out the window at the black mass of the lake, surrounded by those jagged, unfriendly peaks capped with snow and ice. The earth seemed to be opening into gaping jaws. He felt Rachel's hand in his. His face became immersed in tumbling cascades of hair. His lips tasted the salt of her cheek.

The thud of the wheels and the reverse thrust of the engines broke their embrace, and they laughed, surprised they still could.

301

With their new passports and outfits, they passed easily through Swiss Customs and Immigration, just another couple in town to consult bankers and test the higher slopes of Gstad or St. Moritz. All year round, such visitors made the city hum. Everyone understood, even the jackbooted policemen in battle dress whose Uzi tommy guns seemed to dip in salute.

After changing money, at Rachel's suggestion they taxied along the eastern shore of the lake to Kusnacht-am-See, where her father once lived as head of Mossad's operations in central Europe. She remembered a small hotel with rooms on the lake. Across the street James Joyce had penned *Ulysses*.

The Hermitage was still there, secluded, quiet, elegant. The taxi let them off under the porte cochere. Landover hurried inside and lay down a freshly exchanged 500 Swiss francs as room deposit. The desk clerk looked them over. He was accustomed to slightly eccentric, well-heeled foreign couples, usually unmarried.

The clerk took note of their passports and gave them the key to an exquisite room overlooking the lake. They glanced around at the gleaming white walls and oak-beamed ceiling, prints of sailing ships and birds, a queen-size bed covered with gold-colored satin spread, a kilim rug, director's chairs, a small writing table, and a marble bathroom.

They bathed, fell into each other's arms, and slept. They did not make love. "Please don't make me," she whispered. "I am not over my father." He said he was happy just lying beside her. They had known each other barely three days.

After Cairo the weather was almost chilly. He wore his new Egyptian cotton sports shirt and a safari jacket, which he worried looked out of place in Switzerland but was the best the Cairo Airport shop could provide. He'd find something more suitable later.

Stepping out for the first time since their arrival, they were a few minutes early for their appointment at the Baur-au-Lac. Landover surveyed the garden and the other guests while Rachel stayed behind to catch the waiter's eye.

They had agreed on Chablis, bouillon, gravlax and, in memory of her father, *bruntnerfleish,* the paper-thin slices of smoked beef that had been Ravid's first choice when dining out years ago. He also loved the local *geschnetzeltes,* she said, but these were too common for the rarefied *carte* of the Baur-au-lac.

Landover sauntered past the modish Jacques Lipchitz bronzes on the lawn, toward the one thing that seemed out of place in the garden, a huge tree soaring well above the hotel like Gulliver among the pygmies, a sign of a rougher-hewn past. Nailed into the trunk was a brass marker denoting Sequoia Gigantea and the date 1844. Not a long time as Sequoias went—some in California shaded Conquistadors—but certainly antedating by years this hotel and its comely garden.

A gift from California, the tree was magnificent, straight and tall, in a brilliantly hued uniform of russet and golden leaves and arching branches like the broad armored shoulders of an ancient warrior. Pausing within its expansive shade, tapping its rough and gritty bark, reaching up to stroke its striated leaves, Landover felt an infusion of strength.

Would he ever return to California? What about Stanford? What about Kate? Did he even want to go back? It was hard to see beyond the present.

Returning to Rachel, he cast cautious glances at the other tables. The only woman was rather plump, of a certain age, with blond-rinsed hair, wearing a mauve wool suit, Dior shoes that matched her ermine stole, and rings that flashed in the sun.

The other guests were all men, also at the far edge of middle age. The blond woman's two companions were both stout and obviously European. One with arched eyebrows was eating a chocolate *torte schlag,* the other, who had a scar on his face, was sipping Courvoisier. At another table, a lone fat man whose feet barely reached the ground, wore thick eyeglasses over a small, wrinkled face that made him look like an old bullfrog, was poring over the *National Anzeiger* and smoking a Monte Cristo.

Landover concluded they were all just good burghers enjoying Sunday in town. None appeared to take the slightest interest in him. He returned to the table and sat across from Rachel. She looked ravishing in the long-sleeved white silk Chanel blouse and the blue-and-red swatch of cloth also acquired at the airport that she had turned into a svelte sarong. She had pulled her hair into a chignon, and had half hidden it in a paisley foulard.

He grinned. "Sleep obviously becomes you."

She frowned, shifted nervously in her chair and looked up at the terrace clock. "Your friend Vogl is late." She stared glumly at the table. "The Swiss are never late."

"Journalists always are," he tried to reassure her.

"Maybe in America, not here. The Swiss invented clocks. Punctuality is next to godliness."

"He's not even Swiss-born."

"Swiss or not, we took a chance calling him out of the blue like that." Her fingers tapped the table.

"I thought we agreed this was the way to proceed." He was becoming a bit edgy himself.

"Hilly . . . I'm starting to get funny feelings."

"But how could anyone know we're here?"

"They have their ways."

He shook his head, puzzled and concerned. She had been right before in Eilat . . . "Is there someone in particular who makes you jumpy?"

She looked around but said nothing, then whispered, "Are you sure this friend of yours, Vogl, can be trusted?"

Their waiter suddenly appeared, starched and stiff-backed in his tuxedo, pushing a food trolley. He braked his vehicle and went into his act. Landover was thankful for the diversion and didn't even try to answer the question.

With a flourish, the waiter snapped a large lemon tablecloth as if it were a flag on a blustery day and laid it on the table. He then produced three powder-blue linen napkins, almost as large as the tablecloth, two of which he presented with a gracious bow. He set three gold-rimmed plates and bowls along with a full complement of silver.

"Your guest late?" the waiter asked.

"We will start anyway," Rachel said.

The waiter fussed over the bouillon, pouring generous dollops of sherry into the globe-shaped metal container suspended in the center of the trolley and firing the kerosene burner below it. The broth gave off a pungent, slightly alcoholic aroma. He ceremoniously ladled it into the bowls, spilling not a drop.

The bruntnerfleish and gravlax laced with dill were spread out on silver trays along with copious portions of black bread. The waiter presented a bottle of Premier Cru Chablis 1988, Landover's choice, uncorked it, and poured a little in Landover's glass. Winning approval, he filled the two glasses, thrust the bottle into a cooler wrapped in its own white linen jacket, and bowed again before taking his leave. Landover almost applauded.

Then he saw Vogl walk into the garden. "There he is." Landover jumped from his chair, waved. He felt better . . . here was a link with the past. Like turning on the closet light and seeing not the bogeyman but familiar clothes smelling of mothballs, a friendly, worn pair of shoes.

In his navy blue blazer, gray flannels, and open-collared gray-striped shirt, Andreas Vogl, European editor of *Positronics Today,* who had interviewed Landover nine months earlier in Palo Alto, looked more the professor than the professor. He was an angular, bony man of medium build, probably in his fifties, a few years older than Landover. Thinning dark hair topped a half-moon face bent forward as if in eternal contemplation. He had a thick, almost pouting lower lip and a boxer's gnarled nose; his eyes were big and wide, like a precocious child's.

He walked over briskly. His eyes took in Rachel.

"So what brings you to Zurich, Professor?"

"Oh, just a visit, taking a little time off." Landover shook hands and in a quiet voice introduced Rachel as a physicist from Israel's Dimona nuclear establishment. Rachel smiled nervously. Vogl looked amused, as if signaling his acceptance that a distinguished physicist was entitled to a fling.

"We ordered," Landover said apologetically. "We were ravenous and couldn't wait. Help yourself."

Vogl shoveled bruntnerfleish on his plate and began eating. He made no apologies for being late.

Landover turned to Rachel: "This is the man who has restored my confidence in the press." To Vogl, he added, "You know that colleagues from all over the country called me on that interview. An excellent job and I want to commend you."

"I had fun doing the story, Professor. A lot of positive comment. My publisher, never easy to please, was content."

His accent was what the British call "redbrick," as distinct from "Oxbridge," more working class than upper class. But there were also slight hints in his meticulous pronunciation that English wasn't his native language.

Landover decided to get to the real point of the encounter. He owed it to Vogl for interrupting his Sunday. He leaned over and said in a low voice, "We've got some rather important information to share with you."

"You're not going to make me work on such a beautiful day," Vogl said lightly, pulling up his cushioned wicker chair and helping himself to the gravlax. "And such pleasant surroundings."

Rachel was again tapping her fingers on the table. They sounded like little hammers. "Not here," she said firmly.

The waiter approached to ask how everything was.

"Fine," Landover said.

"We must go somewhere else," Rachel said nervously. She hadn't touched the food.

Landover turned toward her. "You sure?"

"Please, Hilly."

"Where?" Landover asked.

There was silence. Vogl layered gravlax on black bread.

Rachel said firmly, "We can't stay here."

"What's the matter?" Vogl mumbled with his mouth full.

"Too complicated to explain," Landover said.

"I'm sorry," Rachel said. She got up. "We must go."

"There's always my place." Vogl thought it all a joke.

"Is it far?" Rachel asked, standing.

"You are serious?"

"Yes."

Vogl swallowed hard. He tried to remember how he'd left the flat. No doubt a mess. He hadn't been expecting visitors. "Western part of town. Other end of the lake. Maybe fifteen or twenty minutes by taxi."

"Why not." Landover raised his fingers in the air to reclaim the attention of the waiter, who was there instantly.

"*Zahlen, bitte.*" Landover had picked up the term from a long-ago holiday in Vienna. The Viennese said *Zahlen*; the Germans said *Rechnung.*

He placed 200 newly exchanged Swiss francs on the table, and they got up, leaving the wine untouched.

# 36

As they headed toward the lobby, the man with the frog face looked up from his *Anzeiger,* took a cell phone out of his pocket, and dialed a number. He let it ring three times, then hung up, dialed a second number and repeated the process. He closed the phone, slipped it back into his pocket, laid some francs on the table, and walked rapidly away.

In the hotel art shop, an effeminate-looking man with a Van Dyke beard, elegantly dressed in a soft Italian suit, turned from Seurat's *Woman with a Parasol.* His cordovans clicked on the statuario marble from Carrara as he hastened from the gallery. The two met in the corridor, gave each other almost imperceptible nods. They exited the hotel and walked a few hundred feet up the Bahnhofstrasse where a black PTT Telecom van was idling. A slash-jawed man wearing a repairman's uniform sat in the driver's seat. Frog face and Van Dyke jumped into the rear. As the vehicle pulled away, they also changed into repairmen's clothes.

Landover, Vogl, and Rachel piled into a taxi, Rachel between the two men. Vogl gave an address on Luchingerstrasse. The driver looked Turkish, or perhaps Rumanian. Sidewalks were filled with Sunday window shoppers. People seemed relaxed, enjoying the venerable city. Children rode in perambulators and strollers, some tugging balloons, others tugged by parents and grandparents.

The taxi proceeded beside the trolley tracks up the golden mile of the Bahnhofstrasse, past the Kredietanstalt and the Bankverein, the Globus, Jelmoli, and Vilan department stores, the Grieder and Gucci fashion boutiques with their elegant luggage and Bally footwear, the Beyer and Bucherer windows stuffed with music boxes, watches, clocks doing funny things.

"Prices are sky-high, but people still buy stuff," Vogl was saying.

Rachel had discouraged Vogl from asking any questions in the taxi. So with his eyes on the fancy shops, he offered a running tourist commentary.

". . . Some of it's pretty hokey. Girls swinging on swings, boys milking cows as the clocks strike the hour, music boxes with clangs and symbols . . ." He pointed to a shop selling chocolates. ". . . Valrhone, Cailler, Nestlé, Suchard, Lindt, take your pick—nuts, raisins, nougat, honey, fudge, whiskey, cognac, Chartreuse."

At Parade Platz, where the driver crossed the trolley tracks to make a left onto Boersen Strasse, Vogl pointed across the Limat at the twin towers of the Grossmunster Cathedral. "Foundations by Charlemagne, sermons by Zwingli . . ."

A PTT Telecom van also turned. Odd, Rachel thought, for the PTT to be working on Sunday.

After passing a complex of tall, antiseptic buildings and then a bridge over a canal where turquoise-headed mallards circled lazily, the cab picked up Dreikonig Strasse through a quiet suburban area of stately homes and gardens.

Few of the homes were private, Vogl said. The real estate was too valuable. He pointed to discreet plaques in posts and walls at the entrances. In soft, weathered gold plate, the inscribed names signified private banks. "These are 'bespoke tailors' of the banking industry," Vogl said, "the merchant bankers, the deal makers, the really big managers of money. . . ."

Rachel was afraid to turn her head. If the van were indeed following, she might raise the alarm. Yet any unusual behavior by the cab would let the enemy know they knew. Better to give nothing away. She leaned back. Could she be imagining? After all, telephones die on Sundays, as on other days, and the van could be answering a call in the western part of the city.

Vogl, a walking encyclopedia, droned on. She listened with half an ear. Her hands folded on her lap were clammy.

". . . The banking scene is overcrowded here and hotly competitive," Vogl continued. "Something like six hundred banks in a country of seven million, and hundreds of private banks. So you take business where you get it and if it turns out to be a little slimy, so be it. . . ."

They left Dreikonig and turned up Tunnel Strasse toward the Sihl bridge and Wiedikon. The cab picked up speed. Oh, for eyes in the back of the head. Vogl went on about banks.

". . . They shape so much of what the city is. I daresay most of the hundreds of thousands of visitors are here to see their bankers and check their accounts. A friend in one of the banks says some people take out gold in their safe-deposit boxes to touch it, taste it, fondle it, then put it back. Solitary pleasures. Can you imagine? Too much gold does that to you . . ."

The cab was on the other side of the Sihl headed south on Uetiburg Strasse and the hills of Friesenberg.

". . . The Swiss got their start in the money game by helping the wealthy in France avoid the tax collector. Then they branched out. They were never much worried about legalities. All that counted was getting the money. I think it was Voltaire who said that if you ever see a Swiss banker jump out the window, you can be sure there is money below. Their clients have included not only drug dealers and tax evaders, but Nazis, the KGB, and dictators of the third world.

"When the Swiss enforced banking secrecy in the 1930s, it was to help Jews keep money out of Nazis' hands. Then Switzerland became the Nazis' financial refuge. Martin Bormann after the war actually collected interest on his Swiss accounts. The Swiss keep their own money in gold. Their currency is the only one today actually backed by gold."

Landover couldn't resist asking a question even though he knew he would win no points with Rachel. "So what would happen if there were suddenly too much gold in the world and its value were to drop substantially?"

Rachel scowled. Vogl stifled a laugh. "A lot of glum faces in Switzerland, let me tell you."

The cab turned on to Luchingerstrasse, a cobblestoned, residential street, stopped before an old gray stone town house.

"It hasn't changed much since Zwingli's day," Vogl said. He got out as Landover paid the driver. Rachel glanced through the rear window. No sign of the van. No other moving vehicles. A quiet street. Perhaps her imagination was running overtime.

Vogl stood under the stone arch, fumbling for a key to unlock the heavy oak door. "I'm on the fourth floor."

The house was in a row of similar structures rising from concrete and stone foundations as solid as the local Protestant bourgeoisie. The clumpy architecture lacked the friezes, caryatids, and other embellishments of Roman Catholic Paris, Munich, Vienna. Only window pots of tawny, rust-colored autumnal flowers violated the principles of Calvinist self-denial.

As the taxi pulled away, Vogl unlocked the heavy door and opened it into a dimly lit foyer. Landover waited behind him on a grayish cast-iron manhole cover until Rachel got in the door, but before entering, she again glanced up the street. A vehicle turned the corner. The PTT van? Too far away to be sure.

She stepped inside the foyer. Landover followed. Vogl shut the door, relocked it, and led the way up the stone staircase. She hung back. A door under the staircase probably led out back. She tried it. It opened easily, and she stepped into a courtyard.

On a spotlessly clean concrete apron stood a dolly with two large, lidded garbage cans. A hose, wound into a neat coil, hung from the wall of the building. Beyond the concrete was a small garden of marigolds, chrysanthemums, and boxwood, demarcated by yellow bricks. A low wire fence cordoned off a section of lawn beyond the garden, denoting the limits of the lot. The other buildings had a similar backyard and were similarly spotless.

To the right, a covered passageway between Vogl's and the neighboring building led back to Hopfenstrasse. Rachel edged into the corridor, crouching behind a stone battlement. The sun beat down on her back and showered the empty street before her.

A wrought-iron gate barred access to the sidewalk. She tried the gate, found it locked. She pressed her cheek against the iron, but the angle of vision was too narrow. She listened. The street was remarkably quiet. From one of the apartments she heard faint strains of the slow movement of the Linz Symphony. In one of the windows to the rear, an old woman clutching a watering can was sprinkling her window box zinnias.

Footfalls. Rachel froze behind the blocks of stone. Steps grew louder. Two people came into sight. A man and a woman. A rolling sound behind them. Suddenly a boy, about twelve or thirteen, appeared on a skateboard. The man wore a tie and jacket, the woman a frilly dress and heels, probably on their way to a Sunday family dinner.

She didn't hear the van until it was practically in front of the gate. It moved like a ghost ship at dead slow, tires sliding noiselessly over time-smoothed cobblestones, its aerial spikey and quivering. The vehicle stopped almost exactly at the spot where the taxi had stood, sunlight bouncing from its epoxy roof.

For an instant nothing happened. The van sat there, engine idling. Suddenly a side door slid open. She pressed herself into the stone. A man emerged. He was wearing thick glasses and dressed like a telephone repair man. Despite the outfit, he looked familiar, like someone she had seen somewhere in completely different garb. He surveyed the sidewalk, then disappeared, presumably stepping toward the big oak door. She could hear him try the knob.

He reappeared, now directly in front of her, his dark bulging eyes peering behind his glasses through the gate. He squinted against the sun. The Baur-au-lac! Yes. That face could not be forgotten. Fearing he might see her, she tried to dissolve into the stone. She could not move, was afraid to look. He pulled at the handle of the gate, but it didn't open. He backed off, reentered the van.

She backed furtively out of the passageway into the courtyard, then rushed to the door. She had to get upstairs to warn the others. The door was closed. She cursed not having thought to prop it open. She pulled at the knob, already sensing it wouldn't budge. She tried to turn the knob first in one direction, then in another. Her fingers slid over the icy smoothness of the steel. Nothing moved. It was firmly locked.

She pounded her hands against the heavy metal door. The pounding hardly sounded. She mustn't panic. The Swiss hated scenes, would immediately call the police. She looked for a stone. Vogl's apartment was on the fourth floor, he'd said, and maybe she could attract someone's attention. But the concierge kept things so tidy that she saw not even a pebble. Anyway, she had no idea which window was Vogl's.

She tapped the ground-floor window, presumably the concierge's. No response. Concierges poked into everyone else's business, but were never around when needed. She stood there knocking, it seemed, for an eternity. She was the woman in Edvard Munch's *The Scream.* It was probably no more than a minute or two before the door opened.

"Hilly! Thank God!"

"If you're finished taking the air," he asked calmly, "maybe you'd like to join us?"

She threw her arms around his neck. She didn't want him to see her tears.

"Is it a nice backyard?" he asked, drawing her inside.

Without answering, she disengaged and led the way rapidly to the stairwell. Landover took the steps just behind her. "I've given him the basics," he said. "He seems game to help."

The door to the apartment was ajar. Rachel closed it and secured it with the drop bolt and security chain.

Vogl was relaxed on a reclining leather chair, a yellow legal pad on his lap. He had thrown his blazer on the chesterfield. He didn't rise but beamed at Rachel.

"I regret there's not much to see around here. No *vue panoramique.*" Vogl gave the term an exaggerated French pronunciation. He obviously enjoyed the language. His voice was amiable. Despite his earlier reticence, he now seemed genuinely pleased to have visitors.

The room was, indeed, cluttered, but bright in the daylight between the half-opened translucent marquisette curtains. It was furnished with a brown sofa, a leather wing-back, an imitation Empire desk on which sat an IBM-clone PC, a hand-embroidered Berber stool, and several other North African artifacts including a blue-and-white Tunisian birdcage without the bird. Books and newspapers lay scattered on a speckled amber rug, and on an end table sat a copper *jezvah* full of grounds and a demitasse cup where old coffee puddled the bottom.

A number of paintings, perhaps Spanish or Portuguese, covered the walls. Vogl apparently had a fondness for clowns: laughing, sad-faced, contemplative, they appeared in many guises, shapes, and positions, one standing on his head.

She approached the front window that gave onto the street. A lugubrious Pagliacci in peaked dunce cap and foolish, outsize buttons followed her with his eyes, as did Vogl.

"It's a nice quiet place," Vogl said. "The good solid burghers don't much like noise. It's a place where you can get some work done in peace, or get your gold pieces counted."

She stood behind the translucent curtains. "Is there another exit?"

Both men looked at her strangely.

"Come here," she said sharply. "Tell me what you see."

Landover moved across the room. Vogl put aside his notepad and approached as well. Across the street a lone pigeon was perched on the bulge of a black iron window grille. A brindled cat with a white throat rubbed its back against a lamppost. A woman in a green *lodenmantel* completely camouflaging the shape of her body was crossing the street with a black poodle.

Directly below the window, three figures, one short, wearing shades, one with a beard, and a tall burly one, all dressed in the work clothes of telephone repairmen, were getting equipment out of the truck. Each carried what looked like a tool kit and wore web belts hung low like western gun belts with holsters for their hammers, pliers, and screwdrivers. The frog man was facing the door to Vogl's building. He carried a roll of wire. His gaze lifted. He removed his glasses. His eyes seemed to be on the very curtain behind which all three were standing.

"Is it those men down there?" asked Vogl.

"They followed us," she said. "They, at least the short one, were at the Baur-au-Lac. And now they're coming here."

Her face was white as the curtain.

"You can't be serious," said Vogl. "That's Mrs. Schmidt, from the ground floor, crossing the street with her dog. She must have just gone out, and those are repairmen, called to fix someone's phone."

"What do you bet it's yours?" Rachel said.

"Really?" Vogl asked skeptically.

"She is serious," Landover said. "It's what I was telling you. I didn't explain it very well. There are some people around who seem to want us out of the way."

Rachel cut in. "They must have picked up our trail at Cairo airport, maybe through ticket people, somehow traced us to the Hermitage, bugged our calls. This is big high-tech organization. We got too confident, Hilly. A mistake. We should have left Zurich right away. They've hooked us, and now they want to reel us in."

She faced Vogl, twisting the long ends of the foulard around pieces of hair. "By this time, there probably isn't a thing they don't know about Andreas Vogl, either."

"I won't ask you how you know all this," Vogl said.

He seemed more annoyed than frightened, as if he were faced with some household mishap, the coffee grinder not working, the shower running lukewarm, the *Anzeiger* arriving late. After all, he was in his own home, in a city known for the reliability of its police. It was the middle of a Sunday afternoon: afternoon strollers, cars stopping by the park, neighbors and families gathered, reading newspapers, watching television, counting money, listening to Mozart.

"Outside is a hit squad," she said. "They have nothing against us personally. If we met them at a party, we might even like them. They probably have wives and kids, go to PTA meetings, attend church. This is a job. My guess is they are highly professional, the best money can buy."

"Open the window, and I'll pour molten lead," Vogl said airily. He still had trouble taking the matter seriously.

"My guess is that we're too late. Your Mrs. Schmidt obviously opened the door for them. They'll read the floor from the mailbox downstairs." She twisted the foulard so hard that it pulled her hair loose. She quickly retied the scarf to cover it. "Is there a fire escape?"

Vogl shook his head. "Unless you want to jump four stories."

From the window they saw frog face heading toward the entrance, followed by the other two men. All three disappeared.

Landover looked blankly at the wall. First Israel and the Sinai, now Zurich. Was there no relief? At least earlier they had been a step ahead of the pursuers. Now they were cornered by professional killers. He could protest he was an American and a distinguished professor at Stanford as they cut him down with their silenced Berettas. Were these clowns to be his last view of the world?

Rachel had disappeared somewhere in the rear of the apartment. Vogl walked nervously to the phone, but stumbling over the wires, accidentally knocked the cradle from its perch on a side table. The coffee cup teetered at the edge of the table and fell, spilling a blob of dark liquid on the amber rug.

Vogl disentangled himself, carefully picked up the cup and the phone, blotted the mess on the carpet with some Kleenex. "The police are efficient. They will be here in three minutes," he told Landover. He started to dial, tensed, shook the phone and tried again, checked to see whether he hadn't accidentally yanked the cord from the wall jack.

"The line is dead." His cheeks were ashen now, his sense of invulnerability suddenly pierced.

Rachel hurried back into the living room. She looked at Vogl. "There's something interesting in the bedroom—some kind of dome window or—"

"Skylight," Vogl said. "It's why I took the apartment. The owner had it built, to be able to see the sky from his bed. I liked that idea."

"Well?" she asked anxiously.

"Well, what?"

"Well, is it a way out?"

"No."

"How do you know? Have you ever tried?"

"Of course not. And it's screwed in place pretty securely. It's not *décapotable*."

Landover guessed what it meant, but the use of the foreign word, capping that frustrating exchange, made something snap inside. His mood swung from near-resignation to rage.

"So can't we unscrew it?" Landover punctuated each word, as if he were addressing a child.

"I can't do miracles, professor."

"Come on, we're on the same side," Rachel said impatiently. She looked at Vogl's hair that badly needed combing, his fretful eyes. With bigger buttons he could almost be one of those sad-faced clowns himself.

"I know we got you into this mess," Rachel said. "Forgive us. No one anticipated this. We're trying to expose something, and they'll kill to stop us. Our only hope is to work together."

Vogl nodded, hesitated, as if trying to remember something. Then he stepped over to the Empire desk and pulled open a drawer below the computer to withdraw something maroon and shiny. It was a Swiss army knife. Without comment he handed it to Landover, who pulled out the screwdriver blade.

The doorbell rang. "Goddamn," Landover whispered, "they even want us to open the door."

Vogl asked in Schweitzerdeutsch who was there.

"Telephone repair," came back a gravelly voice. "We're here to fix the telephone."

"Oh thank you," Vogl shouted from the living room, giving Rachel a look of respect. "My phone is fine."

"We had to cut all service to make repairs in the neighborhood. We must check everyone's connections."

"I must take a shower. Please do other flats first."

"They are already done. Open the door."

"Not now. No clothes. Five minutes."

"Open the door now." The voice was harsher.

"Five minutes, please."

"Now."

Vogl turned the shower on hard in the bathroom, shouting. "I will be quick."

Landover and knife were already in the bedroom.

Rachel moved to the front door, checked the security chain, wedged a straight-back chair under the knob and squinted through the peephole.

She could see frog face and two younger companions, one burly with a slash jaw and cold eyes, and the third who despite the repairman's uniform had an effeminate face above a neatly trimmed Van Dyke beard. Each clutched his toolbox. They obviously preferred not to have to break Vogl's door down. Their expertise, Rachel thought, was execution in tranquillity.

She rushed to the bedroom. Another clown painting hung on one wall. Wearing a yellow coxcomb and puffed-out pantaloons, the white-faced Pierrot was balanced on a narrow wall, arms outspread, eyes facing the viewer, playful and yet tinged with a touch of fear, as if he were suddenly questioning whether he could take the next step without stumbling.

The skylight was just over the bed. It had a Plexiglas dome about three feet in diameter that seemed to fuse into the ceiling. No sign of screws, bolts, or anything that could be worked loose. Still, if they could somehow cut the dome away, then boost themselves through the opening, it was a way out—better than jumping four stories or getting riddled by silencers and dumped into a crevasse on the Matterhorn.

"For God's sake hurry!" Rachel urged.

Landover stood on the unmade bed. The mattress was soft underfoot, making him unsteady. Trying to keep his balance, he stretched on tiptoes toward the ceiling. Shifting from the screwdriver to a knife blade, he cut into the plaster and wood to see where or how the Plexiglas was attached. No way to detach or even gouge out the hard plastic plates. He pressed with such force that the blade folded back cutting a finger.

Vogl entered as Landover was sucking the blood on his hand. Vogl carried a big kitchen knife, another screwdriver, a hammer, a five-foot-high stepladder, and a bolt-action assault rifle.

"I found the gun in the broom closet." He passed the stock to Landover, who almost lost his balance as he grabbed it. His hand was sticky. Rachel stood by the bed.

"It's what they give us in the army reserves," Vogl said. "The army hasn't fought a foreign war since the fifteen hundreds, but thousands of guns like this are in closets and cupboards from Ticino to Konstanz."

He pulled out a brass clip from his pocket. The cartridges were snug as sardines. "It can even fire." He took the gun back from Landover and loaded it.

Landover again eyed the dome. Could they shoot a hole through it? Vogl looked up as well with the same idea. Landover got off the bed, and they shoved it aside, opening the stepladder just beneath the dome.

"You've got to muffle the shots." Rachel was already pulling sheets, blankets, and a comforter off the bed.

"Wait until I turn on the radio," Vogl said. As a rock 'n' roll station blared, the doorbell rang again. Vogl shouted in German: "Moment, moment . . ." He gave the words their full Germanic weightiness. ". . . I am drying myself off . . ."

Landover and Rachel wrapped the gun with the bedding while his bloody finger remained inside hugging the trigger guard.

The first shot ripped through the Plexiglas. Landover moved the barrel and fired again, following a circular pattern until the clip was empty. Each shot sounded like the pop of a toy pistol. Filmy crinkles and ridgelines crisscrossed the tough resinous material with little nipples where the bullets passed through.

Landover climbed the stepladder and used the stock of the weapon as a battering ram against the weakened plates. He managed to break through in the area around the holes. Now an opening, but still too small for a person to slip through. The rest of the material stubbornly held.

Put a lever in the right place, said Archimedes, and it will move the world. The hot smoking barrel was the professor's lever. He still couldn't rip the resin as he tore at the plates.

Rachel noticed the blood for the first time. She tore off a strip of sheet to wrap around his finger.

Vogl reentered the bedroom with a second clip. "What we really need is a cannonball."

The doorbell rang again, this time accompanied by heavy, persistent knocking.

Vogl hurried into the hallway. "Moment . . . moment," he shouted, sounding more annoyed this time. "I am just putting on some underwear."

"In a moment, they'll blow a hole through the door or take it off its hinges," Rachel muttered to Landover. Heavy metal thumped on the radio. She turned it up.

Landover bashed again at the Plexiglas with the butt of the rifle. The material still refused to tear or crack. No way to widen the breach. His hand was throbbing and his arm ached.

From the wall Pierrot in his pantaloons and yellow coxcomb was staring at the bizarre scene.

# 37

Vogl REENTERED THE bedroom, on a kind of adrenaline high. He was looking for something. He went to a corner and picked up a portable electric heater. Landover watched as he attached an extension cord, turned the heater on full blast so that the coils blazed reddish orange, and approached the stepladder.

Landover backed away, still gripping the rifle. "What the hell are you doing?"

"Bringing a little heat to the subject." Vogl held the heater by its metal handle, climbed the ladder, and wedged the coil into the jagged crotch of the dome, holding the appliance in place with both hands.

Of course. Landover, the physicist, told himself he should have thought of this. Plexiglas was a thermoplastic resin. Apply enough heat and the damned stuff melted.

The banging on the door grew louder.

"Moment . . . moment," Vogl shouted from the bedroom.

He was still holding the heater with both hands. "Find another clip in my right pocket. Time to reload."

Landover found it, inserted the clip into the breach, then moved into the living room, dropped to the floor, and drew a bead on the door. He wondered whether they were wearing flak vests. By now he was distinctly unmoved by the prospect of killing one or more of them.

The banging stopped. During a pause in the music he listened hard. A lot of shuffling, then scratching, rolling, and rubbing sounds.

Rachel moved up to him. "He's getting it," she whispered. "He can

318

almost push the heater through. He wants you to shoot through the door before they blow it up, then come back and help him widen the hole."

Landover quickly fired off four rounds. He smelled the cordite. His ears were ringing. He went into the bedroom. Rachel shut the door behind him, again wedging a chair under the knob.

Vogl was still holding the heater through the aperture. Then his head was through. Landover banged at the Plexiglas with the rifle stock, and this time there was give. Vogl handed Landover the heater, rose to the top of the ladder, and thrust himself onto the roof. He looked down on them, kicking at what was left of the Plexiglas, which looked like cakes of broken ice. Shards fell to the floor. He was smiling.

They heard a muffled explosion, which seemed to come from the living room. "They're coming in," Rachel cried.

Landover told her to get up the ladder, gave her a boost as she clambered through the opening, his hand feeling bone under a soft buttock. Voices in the living room. Someone was running down the hallway, searching the bathroom, stopping in front of the bedroom door.

Landover dropped the heater and clutching the rifle, moved up the ladder.

As he reached the top step he heard a burst of fire, more like a flurry of pings, apparently from a silencer-capped tommy gun, riddling the wooden door. The ladder buckled. He dropped the rifle, grabbing with both hands for the skylight frame. His feet flailed the air. He felt himself slipping. Rachel clawed at his shirt, and Vogl's surprisingly strong hands found his armpits and hauled him topside. The fresh air on the roof was like a tonic. Rachel and Vogl yanked him to his feet, and all started running, not daring to look behind or down.

The buildings on Luchingerstrasse were contiguous and had similar roof configurations of eaves, gables, and arches. But after decades of repairs and adaptations to new lifestyles, the roofs had become a jungle of lightning rods, television aerials, central heating ducts, copper and lead pipes, brick chimneys, wires, cables, sumps and drains, all serving apartments below. Through this jungle they headed north on a tarpaper track trodden by concierges and a few heartier tenants. A long drop to the cobblestone Luchingerstrasse on the right or the patchwork quilt of backyards on the left.

Surely with all the gunfire, someone had called the police. But Landover heard no sirens, nothing to mar the quiet Sunday afternoon except the strains of . . . was it now Beethoven? Bent over like a primate, he shot a glance back. Nobody coming yet. Maybe they felt too exposed on the roof. Now that the quarry had been flushed out, the hunters could choose their moment for the kill. Did Vogl know a way down—a fire escape, a fat linden tree?

Landover saw figures through the windows along the parallel block of Luchingerstrasse. No one seemed to be paying attention to the three trekkers. In the distance were tennis courts and a sports field. The sun flamed above the hills of Friesenberg.

They reached the roof of yet another building, the fifth crossed since their escape from Vogl's room. Broader and flatter than the others, this roof had been converted into a sundeck. Inside a space enclosed by a three-foot-high brick wall were a chaise longue, garden chairs, and a table.

On the chaise longue lay an overly endowed bikini-clad blond woman with sunglasses, totally oblivious to any intrusions, reading *Stern.* To the right of the woman, a trapdoor was open to a flight of wooden steps. Rachel, halfway down the steps, motioned excitedly, and Landover followed her down. At the landing they encountered the main stone staircase, leading down to a ground-floor foyer similar to the one in Vogl's building. Vogl was waiting for them.

"I guess they're outside," Landover said breathlessly.

"Not yet," said Vogl.

"The others will probably be down these steps in short order," Rachel said.

"Just follow me," Vogl said. "Stay close behind this time."

Vogl was already out the back door into the alley.

"Come on, Hilly," Rachel whispered, "he seems to know what he's doing."

No way to conceal themselves. They ran in the space between the two rows of buildings, hopping fences, stepping around garbage cans, scattering cats and squirrels, arousing leashed watchdogs. Landover looked back. He could see one of the so-called telephone men at the rear of the building they had just left, looking in their direction, pointing. Then he disappeared.

"They've seen us," he called out, then realized it was dumb to attract any more attention.

"Just keep moving," Vogl urged.

They were now behind Luchingerstrasse, headed south toward

Frauental. Behind one building on Frauental, Vogl told them to stop. He walked into an archway and found what he was looking for. A crowbar.

Landover thought Vogl was off his rocker. Rachel apparently thought so, too. "What good will that do?"

They suddenly saw. Vogl was kneeling over a manhole cover. "Here, don't just stand there, help me," he ordered. Together they removed the cast-iron lid and peered into the inky depths.

"I see men going into this thing from my window," Vogl said. "They take rifles and shoot rats. They gave me a tour once."

Vogl led the way down a metal ladder. Rachel followed. Landover brought up the rear. The hand grips were cold and slimy. He didn't want to breathe. The Swiss had a fetish for cleanliness but their sewers were sewers, like anyone's.

Before he got all the way down the hole, he heard Vogl calling up, "Let's get that cover back on, Professor."

Landover reached out, put his arms around the heavy iron disc and dragged it partly over the hole. He dropped down to a lower rung of the ladder and with upstretched hands brought the cover more fully over the aperture and snugly pushed it into place. It was like being locked into a tomb.

He edged down the ladder rungs into a chamber, dark except for small shafts of daylight through the holes in the metal cover overhead. He could make out pipes and cables hanging out of the walls like tentacles. From the floor came a throbbing sound. Water being pumped. As he climbed down he could see darker shapes of pipes and valves. Through his shoes, the floor felt cold and damp. He thought of Rachel still in sandals.

Vogl lifted the latch of a heavy metal door, which opened into a darker tunnel. Landover pushed the door shut, heard the latch click. He felt a long vertical bar on the inside of the door that apparently dropped into a hole in the floor to secure the door.

"I'm getting my bearings," Vogl told them. "I think I can figure the way. Just stay close to me."

Wisps of street light from airholes filtered into the tunnel, and as their eyes got used to the penumbra they could see the small fetid black stream that ran under their feet. They tried to straddle it but their feet soon squished like sponges.

They tried not to touch the sodden brick walls. Sometimes they had to bend their heads, but for the most part the spaces were wide and tall.

They could hear only the trickle of water and the echoes of their own footsteps as they picked their way through the sludge. Above this circle of hades, people were crossing streets, cars braking for lights, trolleys clanging for their unchallengeable right of way.

Vogl led the party. Rachel was in the middle and Landover brought up the rear. Vogl seemed exuberant, as if still on special pep pills. He paused for a minute. Rachel was about five feet behind him. Landover, ten or fifteen feet to the rear, caught up with them. He touched Rachel, felt her hands stiff at the sides of her silk sarong. She was shivering.

"Any idea where we are?" she asked, misery in her voice.

"We should be near Bachtobel Strasse," Vogl said. "That was the direction we took when we entered the tunnel. Bachtobel is a main drag that leads to the Sportplatz, the Sihl, and back downtown. There's an exit there. Topside, there should be trolleys, buses, and taxis. Not too much farther."

"But what do we do then?" Rachel asked. "We're at their mercy. We can't return to the hotel. We have no place to go."

"What about the police?" asked Vogl.

"That would be signing our death warrant," she answered quickly. "Some governments want us dead."

In a shaft of light, a fat black Norwegian rat made its way along the bottom curvature of the sewer. It halted a few yards from them and seemed to be listening. A second rat approached from the other side, halted, too, then dashed between their legs. Rachel barely muffled a shriek.

"Remember, we're the intruders in their world," Vogl said.

"We can't stay here," Landover said.

"I'm trying to think," Vogl said. "A friend of mine has an apartment on Mullerstrasse. She's a banker away in New York. She hides a key outside in case she loses hers. I think I remember where she puts it. If we can get there we can stay there."

Vogl moved forward again, and Landover, still bringing up the rear, tried to stay closer this time. Periodically he slowed to turn his head and peer into the darkness behind. Once he saw a bobbing pinprick of light. It remained suspended in space for a few seconds like a firefly. Hoping it was only some chance reflection of street light, he said nothing about it but picked up his stride, looking back more often. When he next saw it, the pinprick had magnified into something that looked more like a high-beam flashlight. He caught up with Rachel and Vogl.

"I think we're going to have company."

They both looked around, saw nothing.

"They're using light only intermittently, but whoever it is seems to be getting closer," Landover whispered, aware of echoes.

"Let's move it," Rachel whispered back.

They started running, kicking up cascades of the foul water. They had gone a couple of hundred meters when Vogl stopped. He faced right, before a barely visible door with a latch similar to the one they had seen from the pump chamber.

Vogl lifted the latch and pulled, but the door wouldn't budge. Behind them the light flashed again, still bigger. How could they avoid being caught in its beam? Whether they spent a few more seconds here to open this blasted door, or fled again, their pursuers were almost certain to catch up. At any moment Landover expected a burst of shots. No one spoke.

Landover moved into Vogl's position. The door was identical to the other one, and so, he figured, the latch should work as the other had. Vogl must have been doing something wrong, perhaps not holding the handle down long enough. Landover pressed down and kept the handle in the lower position for several seconds. Nothing.

He recalled that the other door had contained a locking bar that dropped into the floor. Vogl had opened that door because the bar was not in locked position. On this door, the bar might still be set in the hole. Something lifted the bar. But what? Not the latch, but something else.

The light from their pursuers brightened, and suddenly Landover saw it. They had been looking at eye level or above. But now toward the floor he made out the lines of a panel in the door. The panel slid out to reveal what looked like a brace and bit stowed inside. He found an aperture that fit the bit. Turning it counterclockwise, he could hear a cranking sound. He turned faster, and the door creaked open. They rushed through.

The chamber had exactly the same configuration as the earlier one, pipes and pumps and iron rungs of a ladder that led up to another manhole cover. Landover secured the door by forcing the metal rod back into its hole. He kept the brace and bit with him. Vogl climbed the ladder to dislodge the manhole cover. Shoulders pressed against the iron disc, he managed to move it far enough to poke his head outside.

Dropping his head down into the chamber again, he whispered, "So far so good. We're on Schweighof Strasse, near Bachtobel. Nobody around. A few cars. Climb out nonchalantly. We'll take the tram, unless we're lucky enough to see a taxi."

He stuck his head out again. Pushing with his chest and arms, he moved the cover just far enough on the sidewalk to exit. Rachel was next. As Landover climbed, he heard sounds from the other side of the door. Someone pulled at the latch. Let them.

He emerged into the fading sunlight of late afternoon at a curb in front of a gray stone municipal office building near a No Parking sign. A tan BMW slowed at a stop sign at a corner about thirty yards away, then roared off. As Vogl and Landover slid the manhole cover back over the hole, Vogl said, "Thanks, Professor."

"Thanks yourself."

"Don't worry how we look. Or smell," Vogl said. "Zurichers are used to street people."

They tried to walk purposefully down the street. A wealthy-looking couple approached—though it was only September she wore a little fox draped around her shoulders—and Vogl thrust his hand out as if seeking alms. The couple turned quickly away.

# 38

By TRAM AND foot they made it to a three-story red brick building set on a tree-shaded lawn on Mullerstrasse. From a high linden branch a pot-bellied crow cawed crossly. Vogl led the way up the brick path, suddenly stopped, bent down, and with one hand picked up a loose brick. With the other he grabbed a key the brick formerly covered.

Afraid of the attention he might be drawing from behind rows of curtained windows, he hastily replaced the brick, walked up a small stoop, and unlocked the door into a neon-lit lobby. Vogl then unlocked the ground floor left flat, one of two apartments at each level of the building. Once all three were inside, he doubled-bolted the door.

In the entry hall they stood for a few seconds, breathing deeply, too wrought up to speak, listening to the ticking of an antique grandfather's clock in the entry hall, hands at 6:36. Had only three hours passed since the *bruntnerfleish*?

The apartment was large and airy with spongy beige wall-to-wall carpeting emitting a soft glow. Furnishings seemed expensive: a pearl-inlaid rosewood table near the clock; the clock itself with its embossed ornaments and gleaming brass pendulum; the cloisonne figurines on the mantel; ceramic and ivory bric-a-brac on an étagère in a corner. Bookshelves. The books even looked read. A German expressionistic oil of a nude with red hair hung above the mantel.

Vogl edged toward the two bay windows in the living room, the others following. The windows looked out across a garden of snapdragons, begonias, and roses. A six-foot-high iron fence separated the apartment grounds from a little neighborhood park.

Parallel to the fence, almost camouflaging it, was a row of rhododendrons bordered with ferns. Through the greenery, they could see an unleashed schnauzer sniffing around tree trunks and shrubbery. Its square-headed, crew-cut master was seated on the same bench as a stout, plainly dressed old woman, their backs to the fence and apartment house.

"That's Spuehler, the concierge," Vogl said. "I don't think he noticed us, which is for the best."

The apartment, Vogl explained, belonged to Maria Sheinman of the fixed-income derivative group of the Swiss Credit Bank. She was on a weeklong business trip to the States. "We see each other a lot. I almost went with her to New York."

"We're damn lucky you didn't," Landover said.

Rachel brushed her fingers over the pearl purfling of the table. "She has very good taste."

"She knows good from bad," Vogl agreed, "and has the money to pay for what she likes. She travels a lot. But we met at a company party right here in Zurich. Brown Boveri. Believe it or not, she's interested in nuclear-power generation."

The flat offered all anyone could possibly need for a short or long stay: freezer packed with frozen foods, liquor in the liquor cabinet, exercise bike, TV and VCR, washer-dryer, touch-tone phone, brand new Digital PC, fax machine, Vogl's change of clothes in one closet, Maria's designer dresses in another.

But there was only one bath, beyond a commodious dressing area in the bedroom. Each of the three felt a crushing need to scrub and scour away the filth and stench of the sewers.

"Women's rights," Rachel insisted as she rushed down the hall and locked the bathroom door from inside.

She let her filthy clothes spill into a heap by her feet and ran the shower, wishing she had time for a long hot tub soak with fragrant bubbles, smelling salts, and perfumed soaps and oils.

She knew she looked like hell and hardly needed verification. Yet she could not ignore the mirror over the lavender sink. She barely recognized herself: hair like steel wool, eyes sunken and bloodshot, limp body parts. Could she be worth even the few dollars medical schools paid for fresh cadavers?

She framed her head in the mirror and closed her eyes so that she could barely see. It was a game she had played as a little girl. Pretend to be dead and see yourself as mourners might. From the mirror-game cascaded delicious feelings of self-pity that allowed her to enjoy a pleasant cry. "Poor little Rachel," she'd imagined people saying, "to have died so young."

She tilted her head upward, and peered through the lashes at the bony face, trying to give it a death-mask stillness. No, she wasn't beautiful. Her nose was too long, more like Streisand's, her ears too narrow, her mouth too wide, her teeth unaligned. During its and her youth, her country had higher priorities than orthodontics.

The undertakers would make her prettier. They would powder her nose, rouge her cheeks, pencil her eyes, press her mouth shut, paint magenta on her lips, dye her hair coal black, dress her in a nice long floral gown.

The mirror was clouding over from shower steam. Through the vapors a blurry shape slowly appeared. The round head was bald. Familiar eyes were not quite looking at her from a worn, creased, unshaven face. Lips were pursed. She rubbed the glass to see more clearly. If she turned around she knew she would lose him. His expression didn't alter. More steam veiled the mirror. She rubbed in vain. The image became more blurry, then slowly disappeared. Tears came to her eyes. She so badly wanted to say good-bye.

She must get hold of herself. She tested the water. Now it was too hot and she mixed it with cold. But not too much. She stepped in and let the water ripple along her body. Better. Wonderful. She increased the heat. The water almost scalded her. She just stood there, the water, a complaisant *auto da fe,* penetrating and purging her body's every fissure and fold.

Using Maria's fine collection of shampoos and conditioners from a rack above the tub, she washed her hair and applied copious amounts of conditioner to soften it. She continued to let the water run. Hot water: more practical than artificial gold, one of the great inventions of civilization.

Cleansed and relaxed, she was feeling not only human again but like a woman. She rubbed her breasts together, pinging her nipples, patting and squeezing her belly and hips, taking long and short breaths, bending, twisting, turning, probing her vulva with a warm wet finger. Too bad, she thought, nothing inside that flat, scrawny, unfulfilled little belly.

The last time, the one and only time—how long had it been? Nearly fifteen years ago in London. She distinctly remembered the nausea. Then, the scraping away, and the cramps. Something you never forgot.

She hadn't wanted a baby then. Impregnation was an accident, an encounter in a moment of emotional weakness, physical fatigue, mental exhaustion. She had been nearing the end of exams, too busy to keep track of her twenty-eight-day rhythms. A casual encounter, a fellow student, as impecunious as she.

Thank God, it had been swift. In and out of that place on Welbek Street in minutes. She could have been having a cavity filled or buying a handbag. Although the procedure was simple—"a tiny snip-snip" was the way the tweedy, greedy Marylebone doctor had put it—the little operation caused lingering pain. Whoever said it didn't hurt. It hurt. And it haunted.

She never told the boy. None of his business. Even had she felt something for him, she wouldn't have had the baby. No way, not then, though she had often dreamed of what might have been.

Her father had wired her the money, never asking her why she needed it so urgently. But he had guessed, or so he told her when she finally confessed years later. Still, he never questioned her about it, or criticized her, and never told her mother. Her dear cancer-racked mother, who survived Auschwitz and so badly wanted grandchildren, would have been so distressed. She died soon afterward. Yosef Ravid knew how to keep a secret.

Still, it saddened Rachel that she hadn't reproduced. She'd been too busy and hadn't met the right man. But she didn't want to die barren. As Meryl Streep said in one film, if she could she'd impregnate herself.

She stepped out of the shower, dried herself, and rubbed generous amounts of Maria's Ginseng body lotion into all the folds of her skin. Again before the mirror, she puffed out her hair with the towel and made faces at the glass. Yes, somehow she would get out of this mess, and yes, someday, with someone, she would have her baby.

Although she hesitated about raiding Maria's wardrobe, Vogl insisted. "Maria is the most generous woman . . ." Rachel chose an open-necked, white chiffon blouse cross-stitched in the Hungarian style in red, and an elegant pair of cigarette-legged white slacks. White was impractical, of course, but after the filth of the sewers it was perfect. She wore no bra. She hated them. Maria's C cups were too large anyway.

After all three had showered and changed clothes they discovered ravenous hunger. Rachel insisted on taking charge of the meal. "I'm as liberated as they come." She laughed. "So I have no compunctions about performing traditional women's duties." The two men had no compunctions about letting her.

She inspected the freezer, selecting packages of corn and lima beans, Swedish meatballs, and Belgian strawberries, and thawing them under running water. She started a pot of coffee.

To celebrate their deliverance, they tried to make the occasion festive. She found a bright red cloth to cover the wooden kitchen table. She discovered cheddar and crackers. Vogl knew where to rummage for plates, glasses, silverware, and paper napkins in assorted drawers and cupboards. He laid three place settings, aligned a pair of long white candles in winged brass holders, and produced bottles of Aligote and Chivas Regal.

"Should we be drinking Maria's liquor?" Landover asked.

"Not to worry," Vogl said cheerfully, using a corkscrew on the Aligote. "They were my contribution to the household."

Rachel placed three wineglasses on the table. As she bent over, inadvertently revealing cleavage, she felt stares.

She immediately straightened up. "Sorry."

"For what?" said Landover.

"Maria's clothes are too big." She felt unaccountably embarrassed.

Vogl looked amused. "We're family."

Rachel adjusted the blouse higher on her shoulders and used tiny blood-red cords sewn into the material, which she hadn't bothered with earlier, to secure it. She tinkered around the stove and cabinets, digging into a lower cupboard for pots and pans, finding a bowl for the strawberries, checking the progress of her thawing operations, often stealing glances at the two men.

They ignored her. Vogl was asking questions about the gold-making process and taking notes on a yellow legal pad. Landover spoke of atomic numbers, gold/79, Au 197, atomic bombardments, energy cycles, cold fusion, and the Russian scientist in Dimona.

She savored Hilly's new expertise, recalling her frustrations at initially trying to explain the process to him. At Dimona he had seemed so closed-minded, superior. She'd hated him then, wanted to ditch him. Yet now he could teach the course. Good, she thought. Though Vogl appeared to have no idea she knew more than Landover, it didn't bother her. It didn't really matter. Landover had the professorial authority, and Vogl's understanding was critical.

She poured herself a shot of Chivas Regal. She needed something stronger than wine. On an empty stomach, it was like swallowing hundreds of tiny bonfires. But it calmed her down. Both men were still too preoccupied to even notice her.

She watched Vogl twisted over his notepad, occasionally uncoiling an arm to reach for a piece of cheese. His hair was slicked down after his shower. She had an almost irrepressible urge to ruffle it. Though they had been together for only a few hours, Rachel felt she already knew him well.

At first, Vogl hadn't much impressed her, and his slowness to react to the reality of their pursuit had driven her up the wall. But now she liked what she saw—his unflappability, unorthodoxy, eclectic knowledge, ingenuity. Never would she forget his marching up the ladder with that electric heater to melt the Plexiglas dome, or the sparkle in his eyes when the effort actually succeeded.

She liked both men: Landover, the WASP academic who had stuck by her when he could easily have saved his own neck: dependable, generous, a little naive, resourceful. Vogl, Jewish like herself, as catholic as she in tastes and interests, introspective, moody, with hidden strengths. To both men, she owed so much. And now she also mentally thanked Maria Sheinman for her serendipitous hospitality.

She wondered about Maria. What a great life she must have—an absorbing boyfriend, a luxurious apartment, a civilized city to live in, challenging job, travel, no hit men.

Glowing from the Chivas, Rachel fantasized she was joined to both Vogl and Landover in celestial union. In Sartre's *No Exit* the male character loved the lesbian who loved the other woman who loved the man. No love ever reciprocated. Eternal sufferers. A vision of hell. As she was making dinner, itself a sacred archetypal act, she thought of rewriting Sartre, converting the infernal to the divine. Her play had two men and a woman, and the two men would love the woman, and, she giggled to herself, the woman would love them back. Rapturous eternal bliss.

Vogl suddenly was on his feet, eyes ablaze, breaking her reverie.

"What you've told me is sensational, mind-boggling," he told Landover. "The end of a chapter of history."

Landover looked up curiously.

"Think of it, Professor," Vogl went on excitedly. "Gold, the most stable of metals, the most brilliant, the most enduring—oxidize it, polymerize it, it stays the same—so now it can be mass produced, like hot rolled steel or Hostess cupcakes."

"You think you can make a story out of it?" Landover asked.

"How can we miss?" Vogl speared some cheese, turning to Rachel. "You were at Dimona, weren't you?"

"Yes. I was working on a separate project at Machon Two. Soon after the arrival of the Russian Dmitri Sherbatov, workers at Machon Three were forbidden to discuss their work even with their colleagues. Most figured the extreme secrecy had something to do with making the bomb. Only a country away, Saddam was threatening to incinerate Israel, and it made sense for us to be ready to punish him, perhaps preemptively. There were extensive excavations. We thought it was just another tunnel. It turned out to be the acceleration chamber. . . ."

She went on, becoming more intense, anxious that Vogl understand everything. Her eyes shifted from Vogl to the stove where she was trying to make sure nothing burned. She told of her meeting with the Russian physicist, the rumors, and then Corporal Klein's story about the gold ingots in Ben Giton's car. She described Klein's death, her disclosures to her father, who informed Shepherd, who informed Washington.

She lifted her nearly empty glass and drank to her father and Klein.

"You're ahead of us," Vogl said. He poured shots for all three. Swishing the dusky liquid in his glass, he said, "I appreciate your giving *Positronics* the story, but I don't understand how my winning a Pulitzer saves you."

She bowed to Landover, still seated. "It was Hilly's idea, and a good one. Once markets know about artificial gold, the price drops, and the economic incentive for killing us disappears. Publicity helps in another way: we're suddenly too visible for them. These assassins operate in the cracks and shadows. Remember Salmon Rushdie fought his *fatwa* by getting invited to every conference and talk show in America and Europe."

"It seems to be our only chance," Landover said.

Rachel basted the meatballs, put plates in the oven to warm. "Dinner in two minutes."

Landover rose, asking Vogl, "Mind if I have a look at that new PC?"

"Be my guest."

As Landover disappeared into the living room, Vogl and Rachel clinked glasses.

"*Salud, amor y pesetas*," Vogl said.

She smiled and took only a tiny sip. She knew she'd had enough. "Tell me more about your *amor*. Wearing her clothes, I feel I almost know her."

Vogl seemed content to talk about Maria. "We've known each other about seven years. She's younger than I am, married before, no children, well liked at the bank and plenty of friends outside. More sociable, more athletic than I am. I think we could have a future but I don't know for sure."

"Seven years seems long enough to find out."

"You're probably right."

"Is she pretty?"

"Not exactly a beauty queen but she wouldn't do badly in a wet T-shirt contest."

"You men." Rachel shrugged. "Big boobs, that's all you think about."

"Not me." He laughed. "I get turned on by wrist bones. Big wrist bones and I'm in ecstasy."

She looked at her wrists. "Mine are small."

"I like small wrists, too."

"How about Maria's?"

"Exquisite," he said.

"Have you been married?"

"Not exactly. But I had a long-term relationship in London before moving to Zurich. My philosophy is, a suitcase is cheaper than a divorce."

Landover returned, poured himself another Scotch, and refilled the other glasses. "Quite a machine in there . . ."

"It'll even play Beethoven's Ninth," Vogl said.

"You think it can fax our story to *Positronics* tonight?"

"Why not? I've sent things from here before. Dudley—the editor— he'll have the story when he arrives at work tomorrow, just a few hours from now in Falls Church, Virginia. It should be in the weekend edition. With an AP pickup, gold will be in full retreat before the week is out."

"To *Positronics*." Landover lifted his glass.

"*Positronics*," Vogl said.

"*Positronics*, and dinner," Rachel said.

"And to keeping the jackals at bay," Landover added.

"I'VE BEEN HUNTED before," Vogl said, midway through the meal. "Also by experts. I was eleven when the Germans—and some Austrians—were rounding up Jews in Vienna. . . ."

He seemed to want to tell the story. Landover and Rachel were happy to listen.

"We lived in a flat on Porzellangasse in the *erste Bezirk,* a few blocks from where Freud practiced. At first the Nazis sent the SS into apartment blocks like ours. They banged on doors of each flat, told people they had to move out within twelve hours. Just for a trip to the country, bring only one bag of belongings. Plenty of time later to return for the rest.

"Fears and rumors spread. People became panicky and hard to control. The extermination process threatened to bog down. It wasn't efficient. The Nazis worried about an organized Jewish resistance, which would mean diversion of troops from the Russian front. They had to calm us, do something reassuring so we would move out quietly. So with diabolical cleverness they switched messengers. Instead of the SS, they used *Jewish* boys.

"I was selected for the privilege of that job, while the rest of my family were sent off 'to the country'—the Germans said the separation was only temporary. They told all other boys the same thing. We'd been chosen, they promised, for very important duties. In exchange, we enjoyed privileges, enough food, a bed to sleep in, and when we weren't on our rounds, soccer, or rugby, which German soldiers, some still in their teens, joined in. It was all made to be good fun. We wore little uniforms with smart bandannas. We didn't know what was going on but believed we were important messengers.

"We lived in a camp by the Danube canal. Every morning we would assemble in the camp yard, then pick up the boxes lined up with our names on them. They were the kind of boxes that some street vendors still use today, filled with drawers you can store things like shoelaces, polish, spools of thread, and sweets in. We called them belly boxes because we wore them strapped around our bellies like the drums of soldiers on parade.

"Each drawer represented a city block. The Germans were very methodical. On cards in each drawer we found addresses, names of everyone who lived in each building. Our instructions were to knock on doors and tell people to be in front of their apartment block at dawn the following day to go to the countryside. We must stress to people the move was for their own safety, for protection against air raids and that our own families had already made the move and were happy.

"People listened to us and even gave us candy and fruit. In the mornings they went quietly. We were free to go anywhere we wanted so long as we accomplished our task. We returned to the camp because that's where the food, shelter, and games were.

"Then one day another boy I'd befriended told me he had noticed that some of the older boys he'd made friends with disappeared on their twelfth birthday. I hadn't paid any attention to the disappearances because there was always such great activity in the camp, new faces all the time, plenty of sports, and everyone having fun.

"My friend and I—both ready to turn twelve—were also hearing that people weren't coming back from the country, something was wrong. We decided to make a break for it. We stowed some food, and on our rounds the next day dumped our belly boxes in the canal and kept walking. At night we slept in the woods. Two days later we found our way to Hungary.

"In Hungary the authorities didn't crack down on Jews until 1944. Some of the richer Hungarian Jews bribed their way into Switzerland. I stayed in Hungary, joined a resistance unit under Tibor Rosenbaum, a great leader, who later started his own bank in Geneva, and helped them fight until the war's end.

"After the war, in a DP camp, someone got me documents and passage to England. I had an uncle who had gone to live in Clapham Junction in 1937. The Red Cross helped me to locate him. He felt terribly guilty about not having been able to do more to help the family and invited me to live with him—he'd pay for my schooling, and I gratefully accepted.

"Later we were able to trace the train that took my father, mother, and sister and thousands of other Jews. It ended up in Minsk. Near the station, German soldiers had already made other prisoners dig pits. The occupants of the train were ordered to walk to the pits. There they were shot by the Germans, and buried by other Jews, who were later killed. . . ."

Rachel listened with tears in her eyes.

# 39

OSWALD SPUEHLER WAS a light sleeper. Like many old men, he got up three or four times during the night to relieve himself, and it would take a long time to doze off again. The sheets were cold when he returned, and he would think about his backaches, his urine retention, the ringing in his ears, the limp he'd had since Stalingrad. Volgograd, the Russians now called it. At moments like these he would turn to his sex magazines and Trash videos and fantasize about youthful adventures. If sleep still eluded him he might try eavesdropping, though he had to work harder at it, his hearing was no longer as acute.

His wife had passed away five years ago. His son was living some place near Hamburg, never wrote or visited. He had practically no friends outside of his wartime comrade Gustav Maertz, now high in the cantonal police office. His main comfort was Putzli, the thirteen-year-old Schnauzer that shared his apartment and increasingly since Heidi died, his bed.

He thought of marrying again but he didn't know anyone well enough to ask, except Frau Diendorf, the concierge across the street who taught piano, took in roomers, and watched over children in the park.

They engaged in gossip-mongering that had some of the intensity of lovemaking. They would talk for hours about the latest deaths, illnesses, infidelities, robberies, scandals, frauds, who was doing what to whom. Sometimes other concierges joined in. They discussed people they knew, people they didn't know.

Spuehler's apartment was in the basement of the garden apartment building on Mullerstrasse. He lived rent-free in return for keeping up the inside and outside of the apartment house. While Maria Sheinman's flat overhead on the *rez-de-chaussée* was sunny and fragrant with furniture oil, lavender water, and sometimes baking bread, his was dark and musty, smelling of boiled cabbage, old socks, old newspapers, urine, and dog.

His policeman friend, Gustav Maertz, entertained him over dinners of beer and sausages with stories of prostitutes, smugglers, and racketeers. Maertz said the world's crooks loved Zurich because of its bank secrecy and the ease with which they could launder money. Spuehler could sit for hours listening to Maertz, who seemed to have his finger on the city's pulse.

Maertz had passed the police exam after the war and risen slowly in the ranks to a senior post in operations. He was a prodigious worker much admired for attention to detail. His industriousness brought him into the loop of nearly every major investigation from Clifford Irving to Banco Ambrosiano. He was the institutional memory of the force, as well as the man delegated to cooperate with foreign enforcement agencies.

Maertz and Spuehler had shared the war together in the Waffen SS and remained like brothers. They had always done things for each other. Spuehler, who had crossed the border first during the chaotic days of 1945, got his comrade into Switzerland in 1946 and worked out a way for them to get new identities.

Spuehler married a Schweitzerdeutsch woman, who had some money, and the two settled quietly in the country near Appenzell, a short drive away along the north shore of Zurich Lake. Spuehler was good with his hands and made bird-feeding stations, hundreds of them, which he sold to local, then national distributors. Better to stay home than work in a factory or shop where coworkers, well-meaning or malicious, might ask questions.

Maertz, who had never married, was always in touch. When Spuehler's wife died, Maertz found him work in Zurich as a concierge. He said Spuehler could be his eyes and ears in that part of the city. Maertz, who had built up a network of other informers, was interested in anything unusual, especially related to sex or money. No detail was too unimportant.

Spuehler was more than pleased to help his old friend.

As concierge, he soon learned the little secrets of everyone in his building. The kitchen door of each apartment opened to a communal level on the back stairwell. He found many jobs to do in the stairwell and always had a ladder and dropcloth at the ready.

Signor Ribouffi lived alone, kept his curtains and shades drawn, and was usually very quiet. But occasionally a man visited. What they did together was hard to fathom, but their voices grew loud enough for Spuehler to overhear. It was unclear whom Ribouffi worked for, but he seemed to have close links with a Milan prosecuting judge. The word "Ambrosiano" recurred.

When Spuehler told Maertz about Ribouffi and Ambrosiano, Maertz grew excited and set up a phone tap. He wanted to know everything Ribouffi knew about Ambrosiano and the Swiss connection. The case involved the Vatican, the P-2 Masonic lodge, organized crime, and any number of leading business officials—Guiseppe Ciarrapico, Umberto Ortolani, Licio Gelli, and Carlo De Benedetti. Making it even more interesting was the ritual murder of the head of the Banco Ambrosiano, Roberto Calvi, found hanged from Blackfriars Bridge over the Thames.

Spuehler thought nothing of entering the apartment when Ribouffi was away. He copied documents on his desk and passed them on to Maertz. One day he found papers that provided details about relations between De Benedetti, the chief of Olivetti, and Swiss banks during the sixty-five-day period through January 22, 1982 that De Benedetti had been deputy chairman of Ambrosiano.

"Very good work, my friend." Maertz was clearly excited. He bought Spuehler a bottle of Dom Pérignon. Spuehler was proud.

Spuehler didn't have to eavesdrop to know that Maria Sheinman was a Jewess. He could tell by her name and by her long nose, big tits, heavy-lidded eyes. Like the women he'd fucked at Oświęcim in '44. As noncommissioned officers posted at the siding where the boxcars stopped, he and Maertz had the pick of any women they wanted. They had no love for Jews, of course, but some of the girls were good lays.

It had not been a bad life serving as camp guards—light duties, plenty of food, plenty of fucking, films, even good music, Haydn and Mozart quartets by the prisoners.

Then both Spuehler and Maertz got their orders for the eastern front. For months afterward, life was hell. Spuehler still had a piece of shrapnel in his calf that forced him to limp the rest of his life. Maertz had been captured by the Russians and by a fluke escaped just before he was to be shot. An artillery barrage killed his would-be executioners, and though stunned and wounded himself, he managed to crawl back to the German lines, where he found Spuehler and the remnants of his old brigade. A one in a million chance. Then they walked 1,500 kilometers out of Russia.

In hushed reminiscences over their beers, Spuehler and Maertz recalled the "good days" at Oświęcim, agreed that their attentions had actually helped the women. They'd passed on the best lays to senior Waffen officers and heard years later that some of the women, reassigned as courtesans, had actually survived. Still, they hoped they never would run into any of those women, who would be old hags now, or the Nazi hunters like Simon Wiesenthal, who just wouldn't leave the past alone.

"Never say anything," Maertz had cautioned him. "Not even to your wife. No one will understand."

The führer was right. As individuals, maybe Jews could be dealt with. But as a group, anyone could see they were dangerous. Maertz called them a threat to society because they refused to integrate, setting themselves apart as if superior to everyone else. Spuehler agreed they were also a threat because they accumulated wealth and gave none of it away, except sometimes to Israel. In Europe, even in his native Germany, Jews were getting stronger. In America, though numerically few, they were everywhere, in publishing, finance, Hollywood, newspapers, television. They controlled the big firms. And by supporting Israel, upsetting the balance in the Holy Land, they were a danger to world peace. Everyone knew the next world war would be sparked by the Jews in the Middle East.

Except for his talks with Maertz and with Frau Diendorf, Spuehler kept his feelings to himself.

Although Maertz didn't show much interest, Spuehler paid a lot of attention to his neighbor, Maria. When he couldn't hear anything at her kitchen door he would move his ladder and dropcloth outside and paint the frame around her bedroom window. He had seen her undress, and one afternoon had even watched her making love to her Jewish boyfriend, a man named Vogl with a *schwantz* like a horse. While they were in various positions, Spuehler rubbed himself against the ladder to make his own *schwantz* harder. Later in the privacy of his room, he tried to ejaculate. He tried and tried, but failed.

Maria threw many small parties. From behind curtains of his front room, Spuehler studied her friends and reported to Maertz. Practically all Jews, he could tell. Something sinuous, simpering, conspiratorial about them. He didn't like their beards and beady eyes, the designer yarmulkes they wore like scatter rugs on their heads. They were all well-to-do and didn't try to hide it. They parked Alfa Romeos and BMWs, wore Chanel dresses, Bulgari jewelry, and Gucci shoes. Spuehler imagined what these same people would have looked like coming out of the boxcars.

Maria went on many business trips. Usually she asked Spuehler to hold her mail and to water the geraniums, hibiscus, oregano, tarragon, and basil that grew in flower boxes outside her front window. He also checked inside, studying everything she didn't have under lock and key. He knew about her job (in the Bankverein's internal comptroller's office), her parents (father remarried in London, mother deceased), her salary (235,000 Swiss francs per annum). He knew her Jewish friend kept some clothes in her apartment, made love like a horse, and brought chocolates. If the box were already open, Spuehler would take one.

This week, after Maria had left for New York, Spuehler did one round of his usual explorations in her apartment. Everything normal. He settled down to a routine of dutifully watering her window boxes every couple of days.


ONE EVENING AFTER visiting with Frau Diendorf in the park, he made himself some cabbage soup with ham hocks—it would last him the week—then watched a little television and decided to go to bed early. He awoke in a couple of hours. After relieving himself, he couldn't get back to sleep. He turned on a sex video, but when he had to get up to urinate again his attention was further diverted from the interminable coupling by the sound of the flushing of the toilet above, the shower running a long time.

Maria wasn't due back yet, would have told him if she returned early. Something was happening. He turned off the television set, swiftly dressed, put on his slippers, locked Putzli in the bathroom, quietly opened the back door of his flat and walked past the trash bin to the darkened communal stairwell. He was right. He could see traces of light through the jamb of the kitchen door of Maria's apartment. He drew close to the door and listened. He heard muffled voices: at least three people. One sounded like the man with the *schwantz*. Another man, and a woman. Not Maria. They were speaking English.

Spuehler returned to his flat. He didn't want the Jew opening the kitchen door to put out the garbage and finding him there. Who knew what he might do, maybe kill him and stuff him in the gefilte fish.

Back in his own flat, Spuehler released Putzli, who climbed in his lap in the recliner by the darkened television, and tried to piece the puzzle together. The dog snuggled into the folds of his undershirt and licked his face. "Nice Putzli . . . Nice Putzli," he said distractedly. An old cuckoo clock on the mantel had started to strike eleven p.m. He checked his watch. It was in perfect sync. He liked precision and order. He didn't like surprises.

He recalled his last conversation with the Jewess. She had given no indication that in her absence her flat would be occupied. She would have told him. Yet the boyfriend probably had the key and maybe the right to come and go as he pleased. But to have a party there? What was that about? A bizarre turn of events, even suspicious. Spuehler didn't want to get blamed if any valuables were missing. Perhaps it was an orgy.

He was so filled with curiosity that he weighed fetching a dropcloth and ladder and puttering around one of the windows. He wanted to see them, maybe catch them red-handed stealing the silver. But he would be visible, and perhaps mistaken for a thief himself. No, unfortunately, better to wait till morning. First thing he would do then: water Maria's plants.

So much excitement had made it impossible for him to go back to sleep. He got up, took a Pilsen from the fridge, poured a little in a dish for Putzli, and returned to his chair. Having lost interest in his porno video, he turned on the TV news, listening with little interest to accounts of a transport workers strike in France, a vote on the European Union budget in the European Parliament, communal strife in Russia and the Balkans, babies with AIDS in Gambia. The usual.

The beer tasted good, warmed his belly and his loins. He leaned back in the recliner. Its footrest extended. He relaxed, and again tried to imagine what was happening. He thought graphically about the orgy. Were they doing it on the kitchen table? He'd seen that happen in the porno flicks. Putzli climbed up on his lap again, licked his face. Spuehler pushed his hand into the dog's mouth and rolled him around a little.

Local news now. The broadcaster was describing the hunt for a particularly vicious band of terrorists right here in Zurich. Spuehler turned up the volume. This was a gang, a spokesman for Interpol said, with blood on its hands, and which now had targeted Zurich's leading bankers. The terrorists were bent on disrupting the joint annual meeting of the International Monetary Fund and the World Bank, about to be held in Zurich.

On the screen, a TV reporter stood outside an apartment building on

Luchingerstrasse in Wiedikon. A small crowd was milling around behind police lines. The reporter was describing how the terrorists had almost been captured in a flat on the fourth story. The camera zoomed on a window with a drawn curtain. Zurich police were cooperating with Interpol and enforcement agencies in the United States and Israel to foil the plot. The terrorists' contact in Zurich was a mystery man who had lived in this flat for the past five years (another zoom at the window), a man named Andreas Vogl. The camera focused on a head shot presumably from the apartment.

Spuehler's eyes almost popped. He straightened up in the recliner. The boyfriend—and he was sure he'd heard Maria say Andreas—a terrorist. Yes, now it made sense. He always knew there was something shady about that man. That was why he cultivated Maria. To learn about the bankers. Could Maria be a coconspirator? How lucky he was to have found out. What if he hadn't turned on the news? What if he had gone into the flat as intended tomorrow? He dared not think of the consequences. Thank God for television. He would have to call Maertz immediately. But he couldn't take his eyes off the tube.

The TV reporter was now interviewing residents of the building. A plump, well-dressed, middle-aged woman was primping herself, smoothing her hair as the reporter asked her how she felt suddenly discovering she had been living all these years so close to a terrorist.

"Oh, I would never have suspected," she said. "He was always so polite. He sometimes carried my groceries up the stairs. To think that he was a terrorist." She shivered, and her jowls shook. "I thank God that I am alive."

Spuehler reached for the phone. He had Maertz's home and office numbers. Sometimes Maertz worked very late. No, he was not at police headquarters. Spuehler found him at home.

"I just saw the television news," Spuehler said breathlessly. "You will not believe this, but the terrorists they are looking for are right here in the apartment upstairs."

"I am very tired and it is too late for such jokes."

"I am not joking." Spuehler shouted out the words, then in almost a whisper added: "I cannot talk too loudly or too long. They may overhear. I heard them in the apartment of the Jewess. It is her boyfriend they are after. I saw his photo on the news. He is the man they call Vogl. It was at his flat on Luchingerstrasse where they were almost captured."

"You are serious then."

"I do not call you at this hour to make jokes."

Spuehler reminded him that Vogl frequently spent the night with Maria but that Maria was now in New York leaving her flat supposedly unoccupied.

"Moment," Maertz said. "Please stay on the line. I will use my cellular phone."

Spuehler was beside himself with pride. Something would definitely happen now. Police would come. He felt good, took another swig of his beer. He had done something for the peace and security of his adopted city. Maybe Gustav would recommend him for a civic medal. He would like that. He could hardly wait to talk to Frau Diendorf in the morning.

He could hear nothing at the other end of the line but knew his friend would not hang up. He must wait patiently. He was used to that. Suddenly, he was struck by cold fear. He remembered his doors. He hadn't chain-locked them. And the windows. Anyone could force entry. At this very instant the terrorists could be coming after him. If he only had a longer extension cord. He didn't know what to do. Maertz finally returned to the line. Thank God.

"It is the flat directly above yours, the flat that looks out over the park?"

"Yes."

"Moment." Spuehler could hear the sounds, but not the words, of Maertz on the other phone.

Dammit, why the wait? Spuehler was becoming more nervous. He wanted to pull his curtains, get the Mainlicher Swiss army rifle out of his closet. He listened for sounds and looked anxiously at his abbreviated basement windows. Only blackness outside. The wind was coming up and leaves were blowing against the panes.

Maertz was back on the line. "Oswald, you have done good work. They are still there, *nicht wehr*?"

"I have not heard them leave."

"Good. Say nothing to nobody."

"What will happen?"

"I cannot tell you now. Make sure you stay inside. Under no circumstances leave your flat."

"But I may have to take Putzli for a walk."

"*Bitte*, Oswald. Do as I say. We will talk later."

Spuehler pulled the shades, chain-locked the doors, and went to the fridge for another can of beer. The newscast was over. He had lost interest in his sex video. No question of trying to sleep. He would look for an old movie on the TV. He loved old movies, especially about the war. And in a way, he was at war again.

# 40

Aftrer dinner, Vogl sat at the keys of Maria's new computer. Rachel and Landover, as consultants, looked on from either side.

Vogl started writing:

Once again man has been able to replicate the greatest secrets of nature. Man-made rubber lessened dependence on the rain forests of southeast Asia and helped the Allies win World War II. In the 1950s, the General Electric Company synthesized diamonds, lessening dependence on natural supplies from South Africa and Russia.

Deep in the Negev Desert, where Israel constructs the atomic weapons it will only use to save itself from annihilation, scientists, using principles of nuclear bombardment in a particle accelerator, are secretly creating artificial gold at a fraction of the cost of mined gold.

Gold's 4,000-year reign as the driving force of world economics and politics officially ended a few months ago with the new production from Dimona's Machon 3 unit, according to Dr. Hillsdale P. Landover Jr., director of the Linear Accelerator Project at Stanford University, who recently toured the facility . . .

Vogl paused, glancing at Landover for approval. Landover nodded.

"Terrific so far," Rachel said. "I wish I could see their faces when they read this . . ."

Vogl went on composing:

Small quantities of the manufactured gold, indistinguishable from newly mined gold, have already been sold on international markets, creating a

344

bonanza for the manufacturers. Key to the development is the bombardment of target foils of bismuth, one of nature's most plentiful elements.
Bismuth is often found free in nature. It also occurs as the sulfide bis-
muthinite and the oxide bismite and is frequently associated with ores of
tin, lead or copper.

In the accelerator, high-speed projectiles of Argon-40 and Neon-20
knock four protons from the nucleus of bismuth to create an isotope of
gold. Tiny amounts of bismuth are bombarded at one time. But the process
takes place at almost the speed of light and can be repeated ad infinitum to
create commercial quantities. The only restraint is the energy needed to
stage the collisions. But a variation of cold fusion has resolved that problem.

The Israelis expose palladium rods to deuterium gas in a sealed flask,
then slowly raise the temperature. The introduction of the gas and the
temperature adjustments have now been found to create enormous quantities of heat, which is converted into the cheap electricity that propels the
particles into high-speed crashes.

The crystalline structure of the palladium becomes supersaturated with
deuterium ions. The ions are so densely packed that they begin to fuse,
releasing the heat, said an Israeli scientist who is familiar with the project,
Dr. Rachel Ravid—

Rachel interrupted. "I'm not a doctor. Never finished my Ph.D."

Vogl erased the Dr. He put the article together within ninety minutes.
It was 1,500 words, longer than most *Positronics* articles. He printed it
out, they gave it a final read before faxing it to the *Positronics* office in
Falls Church, Virginia. It was 4:40 P.M. there. He phoned Leo Dudley,
the editor-publisher, who was still in the office, and tried to describe the
development.

"Are you drunk or something?" Dudley interrupted sourly.

"Cold sober."

"Or maybe smoking something?"

"Please listen to me, Leo." Vogl made another stab at the explanation.
"Israel is making artificial gold in commercial quantities at their nuclear
research center in Dimona. I have the full story and have just faxed it to
you. It sounds like a major development. A new chapter of economic
history. We have the beat on it. I wanted to tell you personally before you
saw my fax."

"How in hell did you get the story?"

"From scientists who have followed it, were there, know all about it. They're quoted by name. It's not hearsay, Leo."

Dudley was silent.

"It's competitive," Vogl went on. "We don't want to lose it to *Nucleonics* or *The Wall Street Journal.*"

"I'll look at it." Dudley's voice remained skeptical. "But I already have the next issue laid out. We close in twenty-four hours."

"You'll remake it after you've read this. It's as big a story as either of us will ever get. We'll be quoted around the world."

Vogl did not mention the hit squad and the threat to their lives. That would only complicate matters. Dudley would be reluctant to publish anything influenced by personal considerations.

"How do we know somebody isn't just setting us up for a killing on puts in the gold market?" Dudley asked. "Who the hell are these scientists anyway?"

"Dr. Hillsdale P. Landover Junior, of the Stanford Linear Accelerator Center. Remember? We profiled him several months back. And an Israeli physicist friend of his, Rachel Ravid, who works at Dimona. Both have just come to Zurich from Israel. They were at the site . . ."

Hearing her name and Landover's on the telephone, Rachel suddenly went pale. She shook her head, pointing at the phone, gesturing to Vogl to hang up.

"I can't talk much longer, Leo . . ."

"Dammit, you made this call. Now I want to talk. Tell me more about this . . ."

Rachel was now signaling furiously.

"Forgive me, Leo. Something's happening here. I'll call you back. Later at home . . ." He hung up as Dudley was in midsentence.

"Gentlemen!" Rachel exclaimed. "Transatlantic calls are monitored. Our names trigger alarms. And the concierge—"

"Christ, I forgot all about Spuehler. I should have called him. He could suspect burglars and call the police." Vogl walked toward the phone.

"No," Rachel insisted. "No time. We must move out."

"And go where?" Landover didn't relish another emergency exodus.

"Anywhere. Out of the city. Out of the country. Come on, Hilly . . ."

Vogl was about to say something.

"No arguments, please, and no noise."

Landover started turning off lights. "No, keep them on," Rachel said. "Everything normal. Turn on the CD. Give them some music. Otherwise, they'll think we've fled and look for us on the street. There's a back way out through the kitchen, right?"

"Yes," Vogl said. "Where we put out the trash."

In Maria's room Rachel quickly grabbed one of Maria's wraps, a full-length black Aquascutum raincoat with a hood, and stuffed a lipstick and comb into the pocket. She thrust her bare feet into Maria's aerobic shoes. Vogl took a gray tweed jacket from his closet and handed a blue blazer and beret to Landover. They didn't speak. From the darkened living room Rachel peered through the curtains into the deserted park.

"Stay in the shadows," she whispered as they filed past the trash bin on the landing.

Out on the grass, they walked briskly between the apartment house and the shrubs along the border of the park, hopped the fence, and crossed the street headed east. So far, all clear. At the first cross street, Beethovenstrasse, they turned north away from Zurichsee in the general direction of the railroad station five kilometers away.

As Vogl rounded the corner, he glanced behind him. Two patrol cars from Tessiner-Platz, with lights flashing but no siren, had suddenly pulled up in front of the apartment. Another squad car was now coming down Beethovenstrasse toward them.

"Just keep walking normally," Vogl said. "I'll handle it if they stop."

The car pulled up at the curb. The driver and his partner looked curiously at them. Landover put his arm around Rachel and the two walked ahead. From the sidewalk, Vogl shouted in Schweitzerdeutsch:

"You haven't seen a black poodle, so high?" He raised his hands to his knees. "I was taking him for a walk for a sick friend and he ran off."

"We only look for two-legged dogs," the policeman said through the open window. His partner leaned over the passenger seat. "There are fines for walking dogs without a leash."

"Oh, I didn't know. I don't live here, Officer. I'm visiting my sick friend and doing him a favor by taking out his dog." Vogl spoke politely, humbly, full of respect.

"Ignorance is no excuse," said the officer behind the wheel. "Your friend should know the regulations. Where does he live?"

"Farther up on Beethovenstrasse, 1827."

"Where are you from?" the other officer asked.

"Winterthur." Vogl felt his position becoming precarious. "I work for an insurance company, the Guardian Reinsurance Group. You have no doubt heard of us. You may even need some extra insurance. I could help you." He smiled obsequiously.

"Do they allow you to walk dogs without a leash in Winterthur?" the other officer asked.

"I don't have a dog in Winterthur, but if I did I would of course pay attention to the regulations. I respect the law."

"You are lucky your friend's dog is lost," the second officer said. "If we saw that dog without a leash, we would have to give you a summons."

"I will return immediately and get the leash. My friend did not tell me."

"What is your friend's name?" the driver asked.

"Schultze, Karl Schultze. We went to hochschule together."

"Be sure to warn him."

"I am sure he already knows."

The car moved forward and made a left on Mullerstrasse.

There were no other moving cars on Beethovenstrasse. Vogl looked at his watch. Nearly eleven p.m. He caught up with the other two. "We need a council of war." They retreated into an alley.

"When they find the flat empty," Vogl whispered, "they'll come after us."

"We need a cab," Landover said.

"They don't cruise here."

"We need a car . . ." Rachel looked around at the silent buildings. "Unless you find us another manhole."

Landover asked for Vogl's Swiss army knife. Vogl handed it over, and Landover walked off.

"Where the hell are you going?" Rachel asked frantically.

"Just stay here, I'll be right back."

Cars were parked overnight on the east side of Beethovenstrasse. Landover walked nonchalantly up the street, hands clasped behind him. As he drew alongside each car, he backed against its door, tried the handle. He passed about a dozen cars this way, until one opened.

A Jaguar 5.2 liter engine, tan, almost new. The fragrance of leather swept over him as he swiftly slid into the driver's seat. With Vogl's knife he loosened the dashboard fastenings and separated the plate, revealing a mash of crossed wires.

Flashing blue-and-red lights rounded the corner and were coming up Beethovenstrasse toward Mullerstrasse. He flattened himself across the front passenger seats, his belly twisted over the armrests. The flashes grew brighter, then receded. He saw the police car turn left, like its predecessor, and disappear. Again the street was deserted.

Landover found the ignition wires, carefully joined them and the engine turned over immediately. A dulcet sound, like a cat's purr. He loved Jaguars, the best engineered, most finely honed of all cars. And this one not only sounded great but had a nearly full tank of gas. He made a U-turn and returned to the alley, astounding his two friends. Vogl got in back, Rachel in front.

"So they teach car theft at Stanford," Vogl said.

"My dad tinkered with cars. Taught me the rudiments. This one's child's play."

"Hilly, you're marvelous." Rachel kissed his cheek.

Sitting behind the wheel of a fine automobile went far toward restoring Landover's sense of well-being. "Care to check out events on Muller-strasse?" he asked.

"No games, please," Rachel said. "Get us as far away as possible from that block."

Directed by Vogl, Landover headed north toward the town center. Turning east on Bleicherweg, they could see a police helicopter, its spotlights like spiders' legs crawling across the night landscape. Now more cars. They joined a traffic stream.

"The fastest way out is through Basel to France," Vogl said. "We can be out of the country in less than two hours. If the Jag isn't reported stolen—no reason why it should before morning—we ought to have no trouble crossing the border."

"So let's go to Basel," said Rachel.

At the bahnhof they avoided a bustle of prostitutes and their johns and picked up signs for Baden, Brugg, and Basel.

"Whatever you do, don't speed," Rachel said. She switched on the radio. It was just after midnight. The news was in German.

"Turn it up," Vogl said. After the newscaster had gone on for a few minutes he howled, "Oh, no . . . listen to this . . ." He gave a simultaneous interpretation.

"Three terrorists are still at large. They are believed to be preparing to assassinate bankers at the coming IMF and World Bank annual meeting . . . My God, they mention my name as one of the ringleaders . . . They're giving descriptions of the three of us, calling us killers, international terrorists, asking anyone who sees us to report immediately to the police. This is crazy."

"We had a narrower escape than we thought," Landover said.

"They must be desperate," Rachel said. "They wanted to eliminate us quietly with no publicity. Now they're sounding the general alarm. It's not the way they like to work. It means questions from the press. . . ."

"I'd love to see the faces of those policemen who lectured me about walking a dog without a leash," Vogl said.

"I don't think you would. Thank God they don't listen to their own police reports," Rachel said.

As they settled into the soft leather upholstery, the Jag began the gradual ascent into the neatly sculpted mountains. It was picture-postcard country. The road was well-banked, four lanes. On the hillsides in the moonlight they could see freshly painted farmhouses, barns, and churches, and cows folded into sleep along the checkerboards of pastures. Railroad tracks ran parallel to the road for much of the way. They heard the whistle of a high-speed electrified train as it approached and overtook them. The world had returned to a semblance of normalcy.

They rolled into Basel at 12:50 A.M. and followed the road along the Rhine toward St. Louis and Mulhouse, past railroad sidings, storage depots, and chemical and pharmaceutical works illuminated by arcing yellow halogen street lamps. Behind chain-link fences and locked iron gates, the plants carried names like Hoffmann Laroche, Ciba Geigy, Rheinchimie. The streets were empty. The Jaguar pulled into a deserted side street and halted.

Vogl got out. "Okay, let's do it."

Landover used the floor lever to open the trunk and exited as well. Vogl crawled into the trunk space, trying to make his spare frame conform with the harshly ungiving contours. He adjusted himself so that his head faced outward.

"Lucky I don't have claustrophobia."

Landover closed the trunk gently. "Okay?"

"Okay," came the muffled reply.

Rachel lay on the rear floor. They had found a camel hair lap robe in the trunk, that Landover spread over her. From outside the car looked empty. A border guard would see only a lone male driving into France after hours for a good time.

Landover climbed back into the driver's seat and pulled out on the main road in the direction of the customs house.

"Remember to use your *second* Canadian passport," Rachel said from under the robe.

He fingered the two in the breast pocket of the blazer and drew out the one of Cedric Beaton from Winnipeg.

A taxi was ahead. He caught up to it. Two men in the backseat looked like they, too, were after a good time. In Basel, clubs closed at one a.m. but in St. Louis they stayed open as long as customers would spend money, usually till dawn.

Landover had no car papers, no ignition key. He hoped he didn't draw an overly observant border guard. He suddenly noticed some dashboard wires still sticking out around the steering column. He'd forgotten to put things back together. He pulled to the side of the road.

"Sorry," he called to his cargo, "last-minute adjustments." He stuffed the wires back into place and refitted the plate. Out onto the main road again, he trailed a second cab. Signs read: RALENTIR, LANGSAM, and DOUANE. Over a customs hut a single spotlight. The cab driver didn't even stop. Landover followed his lead.


THEY WERE OUT of Switzerland.

On the French side a bored-looking officer with a blue kepi waved the cab through. Landover slowed, adjusting his beret at a jaunty angle. The officer stopped him, and Landover rolled down his window, his Beaton passport in hand, his stomach clenched.

The officer riffled through it. *"Pour quelle raison vous visitez la France, M. Beaton?"*

Vogl had prepared him.

"I am sorry I do not speak French. I am visiting the Club des Artistes. I am told to look for Sabine."

The officer laughed, returning the passport. "Best to keep your wallet and your pecker in your pants," he said in accented English, waving Landover on.

They passed the Club des Artistes, a large roadside inn, well lighted, with several cars in front and a queue of waiting taxis. "Blow a kiss to Sabine," Rachel said from the backseat, throwing off the coverlet.

When Landover could no longer see the customs hut in the rearview mirror, he turned down another deserted street, and popped the trunk. Vogl emerged whistling the "Marseillaise."

Taking turns at the wheel and trying to sleep in between, they reached

Paris as dawn broke, entering from the Autoroute du Sud at the Porte d'Orleans.

Paris was already throbbing with life. The first rays of sun made the queen of cities resplendent as a diamond tiara. From wholesale markets at Rungis, *gros camions* had already begun deliveries of fresh fruits and vegetables and 375 different cheeses to the Rue Daguerre, Rue Monsieur Le Prince, Rue de l'Université, Boulevard Clichy, and scores of other markets. Open-slatted trucks were carting moaning livestock to the abattoirs at Rungis and the Porte de la Chapelle.

From side streets came the muted bellowing and clanging of garbage trucks and the mosquito-like buzz of the *facteurs* on motor velos bearing sacks of mail. Cafes were cranking up shutters. Men with long black aprons and white shirts were placing nested chairs around iron tables for a new day. Swarthy laborers from Abidjan, Algiers, and Tangiers, hugging tall brooms, opened hydrants and guided the night's flotsam and jetsam in rivulets along gutters toward the sewers. Kiosks and pigeons stirred. There was the ubiquitous perfume of baguettes, croissants, and pains-au-chocolat from thousands of *boulangeries*.

After the all-night drive, the newcomers were exhausted, but the sights and scents of Paris aroused such excitement that no one felt sleepy. Beneath a pink-and-cerulean sky, they drove slowly down the Avenue du General LeClerc to Denfert Rochereau and the great lion on his granite pedestal, celebrating some insignificant and rare victory over the Germans. They parked the Jaguar on a side street and took a table at the Cafe Splendid.

"The city of light," Rachel said. "I love it."

"No bad vibrations?" asked Landover.

"What I'm feeling is relief," she said. "Paris is bigger than Zurich. We'll melt in more easily."

"We'll have to get rid of the car," Vogl warned.

"Eventually," Landover said.

A *panier* of croissants arrived with three grand crèmes. Rachel stretched her legs lazily. The croissants were slightly crisp on the outside, still warm.

"For the time being I order us to relax," she said, and yawned.

Someone holding a pastis, he might have been up all night, too, was causing multicolored lights to flash with the arcing balls of a Thunderball pinball machine.

Vogl, carrying his *grand crème*, walked past the machine to a bank of telephones.

Rachel reached across the table to hold Landover's hand. "I am so happy to be alive."

# 41

**T**ELEPHONE WIRES WRITHED around Traudl Sommer like snakes of the Medusa. Clocks on the wall told the time in New York, Chicago, Singapore, Tokyo, Hong Kong, and Sydney, Australia. Not quite thirty, Traudl was the chief gold and currency trader at Bagge & Co. Now she awaited a call from Grubl that would trigger the short sale of 50,000 ounces of gold.

Besides consuming endless cups of coffee and knowing how to swear in German, French, English, Italian, and Luxembourgeois, Traudl made instant judgments on the spreads—the bid and asked prices—for gold and currencies for immediate delivery or up to one hundred days in the future. Bagge, which stood ready to buy or sell on her quotations, could lose a lot of money if she miscalculated. She rarely did.

The Rothschilds taught the world what one could do with foreknowledge when they cleaned up on the London Stock Exchange after their carrier pigeons brought them news of the victory at Waterloo. Traudl and two associates now had information they figured would allow them to clean up in the gold market.

Normal financial transactions looked forward to a rise in the price of an acquired security or commodity. Short sales anticipated a fall. Short-sellers sold what they didn't yet own, pledging to cover or buy in three to six months later at, they hoped, a lower price. They made the difference between the buy-in and earlier selling price. Should the price rise of whatever it was being sold short—gold, silver, or stocks and bonds—it was more expensive to cover, and the speculator lost money.

Risks existed in any market transaction, but surely in this case they were practically nonexistent. Rudy Pelli had dined with them the previous night on his return from the monthly central bank governors meeting in Basel. Pelli, retiring governor of the National Bank of Switzerland, wanted to do something for his old friend Franz Grubl, chief trader at the Corona Bank, and Grubl wanted to do something for his old friend Pelli. Both wanted to do something for Traudl Sommer.

Pelli told them what he had learned in Basel about *Positronics Today*. The Washington newsletter was planning to publish an article in the next few days about synthetic gold-making in Israel. It came up at Basel because the publication had sought comment from the Fed and Treasury. Fed people said the report was baseless, but as a courtesy informed fellow central bankers of the incident in Basel at the top-secret monthly meeting of governors of the Bank for International Settlements.

"Naturally, they *have* to deny it," Pelli said.

"Whether or not the information is true," Traudl piped up, "publication by *Positronics* will immediately impact the market."

All three smiled, and ordered another round of Courvoisiers.

Traudl and Grubl were old colleagues. She had worked with him at Corona before moving over to Bagge. He had taught her the basics of the trading world, which she took to rapidly and naturally.

Soon she was bringing lucrative ideas to Grubl. They shorted the Swedish crown and Canadian dollar ahead of everyone else. They anticipated the collapse of sterling in the European Monetary Union, the turn in German interest rates that hit the mark, and positioned themselves for the appreciation of the yen. When he promoted her from clerk to trader, he told her she'd go far. She was still only twenty-eight. Bagge promoted her to chief trader less than a year later.

After she moved, she and Grubl stayed in touch. It was important to have allies, even in competing institutions, people to tip you off to things, to exchange confidences with. She and Grubl talked several times a day, often lunched together.

Grubl might have been interested in more but never made a play. He wasn't married. Traudl suspected he was gay. Whatever, she would have gone to bed with him if he had asked. As a woman in a male-dominated profession, she played the system rather than fight it, using every asset God gave her.

The call came through at eight a.m., soon after she arrived at work. *"Guss Gott."*

"*Guss Gott.*"

Speaking in both English and German, Grubl excitedly said that last night he had reached the editor-publisher of *Positronics Today,* a man named Leopold Dudley. He had phoned the Falls Church, Virginia, office of *Positronics* identifying himself as Karl Schweitzer, a reporter he knew on the *Neue Zurcher Zeitung.*

Grubl related the conversation. "I told Dudley NZZ had heard *Positronics* was about to publish a report on synthetic gold. I asked him whether that was true. Dudley confirmed that such a report was in hand and planned for publication in the next issue coming out Monday. He declined to go into details but he did agree to fax the published article to Schweitzer at the NZZ on condition that *Positronics* be credited in any news story."

"*Grossartig,*" she exclaimed.

"It's worth the chance," Grubl said. "Pelli thinks so, too. And you?"

"Let's go for it." It would be her biggest coup.

"What's the Far East doing now?" Grubl asked. He was not at his desk.

They had almost forgotten. The big fear at dinner had been that the story would leak out before they could act and the market would nose-dive before their orders were in.

She pressed a few keys on her console and a price flashed on the screen. "Still strong—$395 at the opening in Hong Kong. We have time to lock in." She and Grubl now each had to line up 500 Comex August put contracts. It meant each would borrow nearly $750,000 in forty-eight-hour call loans.

Puts limited the risk. One put was an option to sell 100 ounces of gold at a specific price. A higher price would mean only loss of the cost of the put. At dinner they looked over tables from the Comex division of the New York Mercantile Exchange and found one contract to sell 100 ounces of gold in October at $393.70 cost $3,330. For 1,000 October puts, the cost was $1,665,000. Should the price drop by October to under $100, which they fully expected, they would make at least $15 million, split three ways.

Traudl had no difficulty contracting the puts. A gorgeous day, mottled by sunlight and shadow. She was thinking of a castle in Spain with her $5 million as she looked out at the yellow-green leaves of the big chestnut tree on the Bahnhofstrasse wagging in the autumn breeze like thousands of chattering tongues.

# 42

As WASHINGTON NEWSLETTERS went, Leopold Dudley's *Positronics To-day* was small-scale, circulation only 1,500, built up over the years painstakingly and single-handedly. His clients in a score of countries were government agencies, industry and universities, and some individuals with an interest in nuclear affairs. Dudley was proud of his elite subscription list, a who's who of the field: the Congressional Research Service of the Library of Congress; the Academy of Sciences in Moscow; Beijing University's Department of Physics; Mitsubishi Heavy Industries in Tokyo; the Institute of Scientific Research in Paris; Framatone, Paris; the Siemens Company, Munich; ASEA Brown Boveri, Stockholm and Zurich; General Electric, Stamford, Connecticut; Baltimore Gas and Electric; Ontario Hydro; Hydro Quebec. For $1,000 a year, subscribers received twelve ten-page issues on what the masthead said was "THE NUTS OF NUCLEAR KNOWLEDGE." Better, or more lively, he thought, than the *New York Times*'s: "All the news that's fit to print."

Dudley's actual readership was several times his paid circulation, and he frequently got feedback. Sometimes people wrote seeking more information. Others challenged or expanded points in the articles. He loved the dialogue. He replied to all letters, printed the better ones. He especially loved the steady flow of subscription renewal checks. He had few cancellations.

A spare, stringy man, Dudley was divorced and lived by himself in a two-bedroom condominium at the Palazzo on Columbia Pike near Leesburg Pike. His threadbare office next to a music store in a shopping center on Leesburg Pike was an easy fifteen-minute drive from his condo. He had two grown children and few friends. Nothing in his life rivaled the importance of *Positronics.*

The newsletter was named after the positively charged electron discovered in 1932 by Carl Anderson of Cal Tech, then only twenty-seven. Niels Bohr and Ernest Rutherford, two of the more senior physicists of the day, dismissed the discovery out of hand. Four years later Anderson won the Nobel prize. Like Anderson's positron, *Positronics* was meant to be provocative, mind-stretching, ahead of its time.

Although the material was copyrighted, Dudley knew that some clients reproduced articles and distributed them widely. He wrote at the bottom of page four: "Copyrighted Material: Reproduction illegal," but it was not easy to enforce copyright laws in Moscow and Beijing, let alone Tokyo or even Washington. He took no action. Better pirated than ignored.

Dudley had the field to himself. The nuclear power industry still employed hundreds of thousands of people worldwide, but it seemed to operate in a news vacuum. Because the industry was no longer politically correct, the general media ignored it, except for negative news like the dysfunctions at Chernobyl and Three Mile Island, the demonstrations against perfectly safe plants, and the disposal of nuclear waste. The bigger newsletter operators also ignored the industry; they needed ten times Dudley's circulation for overhead. Dudley exploited a niche.

He liked to think he ran a lean-and-mean operation. He maintained a small network of correspondents. While indulging in a few foreign trips chiefly to sell the newsletter, he kept his basic operating costs to bare bones. In earlier days he had an assistant, but as she did little but answer the phone he replaced her with an answering machine.

He preferred working by himself. He didn't have to invent tasks. Thanks to his economies and the steady growth of his subscribers, he was comfortably in the black.

What his promotional material called the *"Positronics* Global Information Network" consisted of three special correspondents: one for Europe in Zurich, for Asia in Tokyo, and one for Latin America in Buenos Aires. They did some traveling but mostly worked the phones in their regions and submitted material about important personnel shifts, technological changes, bigger contracts, trends in public policy and public opinion. Dudley himself covered North America and the Washington agencies.

From correspondents' reports and his own gleanings he put the journal together, often rewriting in the manner of senior editors on the news-magazines. An alumnus of United Press International and a former Washington editor of *Business Week*, he enjoyed distilling complex material, adding context, enlivening. *Positronics* was serious, but who said it had to be dull?

Liveliness also helped sell it, at least in America. He used puns in his headlines, like the one for a story about a new suction pump for cleaning out nuclear contaminants in a rotation chamber; the head read: THE SUCK STOPS HERE. He varied typefaces, indented for emphasis, made imaginative use of graphics, even commissioned illustrations. Correspondents sometimes grumbled about the compression, or the jazzing up. But he made it clear that he would always exercise his *droits du redacteur*. As he paid above scale, complaints never went too far.

To print, he felt no compunctions about using cheap Mexican labor, Federal-Expressing the disk from his word processor to a reliable little photo-offset firm in Guadalajara. Back came the 20,000 sheets, always within seventy-two hours. Later he was able to send his entire file by modem, which further reduced his costs and the time between closing and publication.

He aimed to get the newsletter out on the last day of every month and hired temporary workers to collate, stuff sheets into 1,500 envelopes, affix computerized address tabs, run the envelopes through his postage meter, and mail them.


DUDLEY GOT THE call from Vogl late Monday afternoon. He thought his special correspondent in Zurich was off his rocker. Something about Israel and gold. Vogl was insisting that Dudley publish whatever it was right away. Dudley was put off by the breathlessness of the tone, the bizarreness of the message, the rudeness of the cutoff.

He decided to get even by ignoring the fax. He wouldn't even check to see whether it came in. He had an early dinner date with one of his very few friends, Phyllis Warsaw, a divorced mother of two, and didn't want to be late. He still hadn't chosen the venue. He was torn between Ivy's Place or the Yenching Palace, both just down the hill from Phyllis's house on Newark Street in Washington's white ghetto of Cleveland Park. Nothing expensive or showy. Phyllis preferred Yenching, run by the son of an old Chinese war lord, where Henry Kissinger planned Richard Nixon's rapprochement with China. Phyllis, whose father had been a reporter in China, liked the feel of history in a restaurant.

Late in the meal Dudley started having second thoughts. It was dumb not to have at least read the fax. What if Vogl really were on to something? He apologetically told Phyllis he had something in the office that couldn't wait. Having grown up in a newsman's family, she knew enough not to ask. She, an instructor in French literature at American University, didn't understand a thing about *Positronics* except that it provided a good income to Dudley and gave them some neat foreign trips. He gave her issues to read, which promptly put her to sleep.

The little white note inside his fortune cookie the waiter brought made them both laugh: "The party is over."

Motor running, he kissed her absently as he dropped her in front of her big wooden frame house flanked by magnolias next to a D.C. Court of Appeals judge and a retired foreign service officer, and took the Rock Creek Parkway to the Theodore Roosevelt Bridge and Route 66 to Falls Church. He was back in his office by 8:30 P.M. less than a half hour later. In the machine's receiving tray the fax was waiting, along with overnight press releases from Electric Boat, Union Carbide, and Fermi Labs.

It was a sensational story. From nuclear bombardment under normal atomic-power generation, Vogl was reporting that the Israelis were creating atoms of gold from atoms of bismuth. Gold was being synthesized at a fraction of the cost of market gold. The story had a lot of facts. It quoted good people.

Still, Dudley had a million questions. Had anyone actually seen the artificial gold? He wanted more details about the process and the sources. Did Israel officially acknowledge the discovery? If Israel had really developed cold fusion, how come word hadn't seeped out in the scientific press? Wasn't that discovery even more important than artificial gold? What did Treasury, the Federal Reserve, and the White House have to say?

He decided to call Vogl back. It was the early hours of Thursday morning in Zurich, but so what. Correspondents knew they were on call all the time.

He couldn't reach Vogl. A man answered the phone at his apartment and in German-accented English took the message to call back. Then the man started asking Dudley questions—who was he? Why was he calling at this hour? How long had he known Vogl? How long had Vogl worked for *Positronics*? When was the last personal contact? The man refused to say why he was asking all the questions. Dudley hung up.

What about the woman Vogl occasionally spent time with? Maria something or other's apartment was the alternative number for reaching him. Dudley called the alternative number. Oddly, another strange man, with the same gruff mannerisms, the same German-accented English, and the same unwillingness to be informative, picked up the phone and took the message.

When Vogl finally telephoned back, Dudley was in his Columbia Pike apartment trying to piece things together. But Vogl himself was not very informative. He said he had no idea who the men were in his and Maria's flats but would check into it. He was calling from a pay phone on his way to Paris.

"Paris?"

"Just a little business."

"Anything the matter?"

"Meeting Maria there on the way back from New York. Also have some interviews at Rhône-Poulenc."

"But what about your Dimona sources? You just can't abandon them if we're going to do this gold story."

"They're with me."

"Traveling with you?"

"Yes."

"How'd you organize that?"

"They also have business in Paris and we decided to drive together. It was convenient for all of us. And it helps the story. Portable sources. No end of background material. I'm prepared for any questions at any time."

"Sounds odd. You're not in any trouble, are you, Andreas?"

"I hope not."

"If I were you, I'd want to find out who's answering my telephone."

"I intend to look into the matter."

Dudley was nonplussed and annoyed. He didn't like mysteries. *Positronics* had a good name, and he wanted to preserve it. He trusted his correspondents but they were far away and could easily have entanglements that might color their news judgment. In return for the high pay he expected complete honesty.

"How did you get this story anyway?"

"I tried to tell you earlier. Professor Landover called me. He was in

Zurich with his friend Rachel Ravid, who works at Dimona. We met at the Baur-au-lac. They filled me in."

"Why did they tell it to you?"

"They felt it was a major development that the world should know about, and I have to admit I agree with them. The professor had worked with me before and knew I was reliable."

"It could cause the price of gold to crash and rock the monetary system."

"Exactly. That's why it's a great story. We're ahead of the curve. We're ahead of everybody."

"How do we know we're ahead of the right curve? It may be so great a story that we're out there all by ourselves."

"These are responsible sources."

"Do we have documents, any independent verification?"

"Nothing that isn't top secret."

"Any chance of getting anything?"

"Not at this time."

"Have you actually seen the gold?"

"No."

"Have your sources?"

"I don't know. I'll ask them."

"Why aren't they in Dimona now?"

"They're on holiday together."

"Why are they telling us all this? Aren't they killing the golden goose?"

Vogl was silent for a few seconds. When he spoke again, it seemed as if he were weighing his words.

"Listen, Leo, the woman is a kind of whistle-blower. She says there's some corruption in Israel and that the wrong people are profiting from Dimona gold. The money from the sales goes to fund the right wing. She's afraid if the right gets too strong it'll hinder the peace process. There's a retired general named Ben Giton who runs the gold operation. He's also a leader of the right. She says he wants to take over the country and money from the gold is already helping him. But she believes he's bad news for peace."

"And the guy from Stanford? Where does he come in?"

"He was investigating. The CIA had heard of the discovery and sent him to find out. That's why I say it's competitive. The White House knows about it, key people in the cabinet, and you know how some of them blab. We could lose the story."

"I'm not going to get boxed into anything because of imagined competition. This thing has to sell on its merits."

"Don't you *see* the merits of this story, Leo?"

Dudley was silent.

"Why be so negative and suspicious?" Vogl went on. "I thought you'd be enthusiastic."

"I'm just trying to get answers."

"I'm answering as best I can. You can never reveal—or know—one hundred percent of a story. But we know enough in this one instance to easily justify publication."

"It's my publication, I have to take the responsibility for what's published."

"I've given you an excellent story that other publications or CNN and the networks would kill for."

"Are you offering it to CNN?"

"No, dammit, I'm just trying to make a point."

"Point *made.*"

Both men's voices had been rising. Neither spoke now.

Finally Dudley resumed the conversation, probing on a new front, his voice softer.

"Andreas, if the Israelis really have cold fusion, isn't that more important than artificial gold? Do we have the right lead? Unless you're a gnome of Zurich, who cares about gold anyway these days? Cheap energy will revolutionize the world. Shouldn't we be writing that?"

"I wrote what Israel is doing. It's making cheap gold secretly. It seemed to me that was pretty sexy. You can write a story any which way you want. I wrote it the way I saw it." Vogl's voice now clearly expressed exasperation.

"An editor has the right to shape a story?"

"Of course—"

"What about comment? Have we called the White House and the Israelis to get their formal reaction?"

"Leo, be reasonable." Vogl's voice rose again. "I haven't been in a position to do that. I've been working all out—and taking considerable risks—to get the basic story to you. Isn't that something better done in Washington anyway?"

"Andreas, I wish you wouldn't keep telling me my business."

"Leo, I'm sorry, but you've got the contacts. The Washington people would never call me back."

Dudley was silent again. He had become angry and was trying to figure out why. After all, Vogl was just doing his job.

But Dudley hated people telling him what to do. He had worked long and hard to achieve his success. He cherished his professional independence. Furthermore, he'd been counting on a quiet early closing and taking off for some rest and recuperation with Phyllis at her waterfront cottage on the Patuxent. Now if he decided to run with Dimona gold, he would have to work hard over the next few days shaping the story and remaking the issue.

"You are going to use it?" Vogl finally asked.

"I don't know," Dudley said. "Call me back later."

Dudley already knew he would run the story—his journalistic instincts left him no choice—but he didn't want to give Vogl the satisfaction. Yet of all the stories he'd worked on in his life, this one was making him the most uncomfortable. He didn't like the way Vogl had dropped it on him, without warning. He didn't like having to accept so much on faith. It was as if there were an ulterior design; he felt he was somehow being used.

And the story had negative implications. *Positronics* stories were positive, focused on problem-solving to get the nuclear industry to work better, more efficiently, to build up public confidence. The intent was wealth-creation through the spread of knowledge to increase efficiency and productivity. Vogl's story was not about wealth creation but its destruction. Once markets reacted, government and personal assets would be depressed by billions, if not trillions, of dollars. The story would trigger a financial implosion, perhaps even an economic depression. Although *Positronics* might gain some renown and resulting wealth, he could be hurting millions whose savings were in what was supposed to be the world's safest investment.

LATE THURSDAY AFTERNOON officials started returning the calls he had placed earlier that day for reaction to Vogl's story.

Phillip Lamont, the undersecretary of the Treasury for International Monetary Affairs, asked Dudley what he was smoking. Dudley explained it was from his Zurich correspondent who had it from unimpeachable sources.

"I'm afraid I can't help you," said the undersecretary. "I think you'd better look under the tablecloth and see if somebody's pulling your leg."

Harold Funk, the spokesman for the Federal Reserve Board, called the report "baloney," added "you can quote me on that," and hung up.

Chaim Herzog, the Israeli financial attaché, laughed. "In my country we believe in neither alchemy nor the tooth fairy. We have enough real problems—we don't need made-up ones."

Jim Eager, the White House press secretary, said in a flat, disinterested voice: "The United States knows of no commercial gold-making operation in Israel. Period."

Wilson Bright, the State Department spokesman, gave a similar statement.

The CIA spokesman listened, then asked: "Can I tell you something in strictest confidence?"

"Of course." Could this finally be some hint of confirmation?

The spokesman had a plummy voice. His name was Benjamin Franklin Coates. Recently, in line with policies of greater openness, CIA spokesmen had started giving their names. Spokesmen were obviously so low on the totem pole it made no difference. Dudley figured the name was made up anyway. Coates paused for effect. "If you publish that report, your publication will become the laughingstock of the Beltway."

Dudley had been around Washington long enough to appreciate full well that denials of big or embarrassing stories had to be expected. From his days at UPI and McGraw-Hill, he knew denials often signaled the opposite, and the stronger the denial, the greater the likelihood of concealment of the truth.

Denials were part of Washington folklore, telling their own story of the city's masquerades, charades, and chicanery. The Nixon White House ridiculed the Watergate allegations. The Reagan White House for weeks denied Iran-Contra. The Bush White House denied helping Iraq arm before the Gulf War, even as Export Import Bank, Commerce Department, and other government records subpoenaed by Congress related the opposite.

Still, the denials didn't make the Dimona gold story any easier to publish. Dudley looked at his options. Not to publish, he rejected. As someone—was it Hearst or McCormick—once said, "Publish and be damned." He could turn the story around to lead with the cold-fusion process. If fusion had really been developed, this had more far-reaching applications than cheap gold. The world would no longer need fossil fuels, or even nuclear energy. He'd have to start a new publication. Call it *Fusionomics*. But the fusion details were skimpy, and Vogl would not be very cooperative. Impossible to redo in time for this issue. He could always make fusion the subject of the follow-up.

He considered turning the story into a box on the front page. He even thought of a headline: DIMONA—THERE'S GOLD IN THEM THAR HILLS. It could be treated lightly, accorded full denials. Such a box would be well read. Xerox machines would work overtime. True or not, it would be entertaining. He might base a whole subscription campaign on it.

Or he could just reshape Vogl's story. He looked at the fax again. Actually, it read pretty well, though there were places he could liven it up and Vogl took too long to get to the point.

After talking some more with Vogl, who called twice from Paris, Dudley went to bed with a head full of ideas. Just before going to sleep he was roused by a phone call. The caller was also from Zurich, but far more personable than those who had picked up Vogl's phone, and apologized for calling so late.

"I hope I have not awakened you."

"That's all right." Dudley looked at the clock on his dresser. It was 12:05 A.M.

"My name is Rudy Schweitzer. I am a reporter with the *Neue Zurcher Zeitung*. We have a report that we want to check out. We have heard that *Positronics* has information about artificial gold being made in Israel and that it plans to publish the story in its next issue. . . ."

Dudley was flabbergasted. "Where did you hear this?"

"A source from one of the banks."

Dudley decided he couldn't lie, especially to another journalist.

"Yes. It will come out Monday."

"Oh, that is very interesting. Would you be so kind as to fax the story to me when it comes out? *Positronics* would be fully credited in anything the NZZ publishes."

Dudley took the NZZ fax number. He was fully committed. Let the chips fall where they may.

THE BLACK CHEVROLET turned off the beltway onto Leesburg Pike, heading east into Falls Church and the heavy traffic of shoppers and commuters early Friday evening. The Pike, otherwise known as Route 7, was a long strip of fast-food emporiums, Mexican and Chinese restaurants, supermarkets, gas stations, drive-in banks, real estate offices, and traffic lights.

Although it was stop-go, the car made relatively good time, aggressively switching lanes to take advantage of opportunities to advance, otherwise tailgating to prevent anyone from pulling in front. Two burly men were inside, both crew cut, both in dark business suits. They looked straight ahead and did not speak. The driver had lighter hair and a thicker neck and was tapping the steering wheel to the beat of the music from the car radio. It was switched on to a DC station, WGAY, and someone named Clarence Carter was singing something about stroking. "You stroke it to the east and you stroke it to the west, and all the time you stroke it just the way she loves the best . . ."

The car pulled into a shopping center and parked near the Safeway. Both men emerged. The driver carried an expensive-looking attaché case. He could have been an executive making a business presentation. The other man went into the trunk and lifted out something bulky wrapped in a black plastic trash bag.

They did not enter the supermarket but headed for one of the shops at the far end of the mall where there were fewer people. They stopped in front of a music store that had closed at six p.m. But their attention was on the shop next door, with a sign in its window saying THE NUTS OF NUCLEAR KNOWLEDGE.

They stood in front of the music shop, studying its window display of jazz and rock 'n' roll CD's and posters for country-music stars. Then, reassured they had not attracted attention, both put on rubber gloves, and quietly stepped inside the shop next door. The man in the back of the store leaning over a word processor looked up annoyed. The driver swiftly approached the desk, saying as if he were a courier:

"We've come for the fax from Zurich."

His companion placed the heavy trash bag on the floor, immediately locked the door and pulled down the Venetian blinds over the front windows.

"Who the hell are you?" the man at the desk asked. "This is a private office. Get out of here before I call the police." He picked up his desk phone and started dialing, but had only managed the nine and the one when the driver yanked its wire from the wall jack.

The driver opened his briefcase, took out a crowbar. He came around with the instrument outstretched and put it against Dudley's neck.

"The fax please," the driver said as Dudley struggled against the man's grip and the cold iron.

"Jesus . . ." Dudley shouted. The driver tightened the vise.

"He's not Jesus." The dark-haired man laughed. "He's Sergeant Friday, you dumb fuck. Just give him the fax please."

Now the dark-haired man was at the desk, searching through papers scattered near the computer. He picked up a piece of flimsy onion-skinlike paper and started reading:

" 'Once again man has been able to replicate the greatest secrets of nature . . .' That doesn't sound . . ." He read further. ". . . Yes, maybe we have it."

"Is that the fax?" the driver asked Dudley, who was in such pain he could not speak. He tried to nod but in that grip could barely twitch his chin.

"Thanks for being so cooperative. You're a real doll." The driver removed the crowbar.

Dudley tried to catch his breath. "Who are you?" He was coughing. His eyes were swollen. Tears flooded his cheeks. He was the color of a boiled lobster.

The driver smiled. "Friends of friends."

"Not friends of my friends. What do you want?"

"We have it now. Thank you very much."

"You can't come in here like that . . ."

Dudley backed toward his cell phone on another desk, tried to keep it out of their line of sight as he pushed the TALK button. Keeping an eye on the one with the crowbar, relieved when he put it down, and on the dark-haired man who was reading the fax, Dudley again started dialing 911.

Both men turned on him. Like a hunter snaring a rabbit, one slipped the plastic trash bag over both Dudley's head and the receiver and pulled hard at both ends. Again Dudley struggled and tried to claw the plastic open, but the other man bent his arms firmly behind him. The bag muffled Dudley's screams. He thrashed around like a headless chicken until he lost consciousness and crumpled to the floor.

The driver then sat at the computer and began reading the screen.

"For hundreds of years man has sought to change baser metals into gold and discover the elixir of youth. Now, if the story told to one of our correspondents can be believed, it seems that an émigré Russian physicist in Israel, working at the Negev Desert nuclear site of Dimona, has done the former. Although Israel and the United States officially deny there is any such development, our correspondent has interviewed certain individuals who insist that the breakthrough has been achieved at a fraction of the gold-market price and that Israel has already produced several hundred grams of the metal . . ."

"Okay, let's do it," the driver said. He pocketed the disk and took two bottles of Four Roses from his briefcase, filled a glass, left it on a table, lit up a cigarette, and left it burning on the table edge, inserting the pack in Dudley's jacket pocket. He sprayed the room with what remained of the whiskey in the one bottle and then opened the other and dumped even more whiskey around.

His partner unscrewed the cap of the gasoline can and began to unwind a role of primer cord. He pulled off the plastic bag, stuffing it half into his trouser pocket. He soaked Dudley's clothes, the desk, and all the papers and books in the area.

Within thirty seconds the can was empty. He wrapped it inside the plastic bag. Both men walked to the rear door, unrolling the primer cord.

"Ready?" the driver asked his partner.

"Ready."

He lit the cord with his lighter and they casually stepped outside, shutting the door behind them.

They came out into the back alley among the black Dumpsters and strolled around the corner. They were several storefronts away when they heard a muffled explosion. As they got into their car, they could see flames leaping from the store front.

Driving west on Leesburg Pike, they passed the fire trucks sirening east.

# 43

SKYSCRAPERS SPARKLED SOUTH and west of Central Park. From the window of her room on the twenty-third floor of the Sherry Netherland, Maria Sheinman stared at the myriad shapes that seemed to be dancing with the stars. Directly below, the gilded equestrian statue of William Tecumseh Sherman caught the headlights from Fifth Avenue. Maria loved that statue, especially the way Saint-Gaudens designed the figure of Victory to sally forth with her arm raised in a karate *teisho* to repel any attack.

The pulse of traffic signaled that people were still dashing off to bars, pubs and clubs, movies, meals, assignations. Taxis sliced through the rippled folds of the park and along Fifth Avenue from the Battery and the new in places in TriBeCa, SoHo, and the East Village to uptown hotels, clubs, and duplexes above the clouds at the edge of civilization around 96th Street.

Maria had been coming to New York for years and knew what to avoid—the park on foot at night, the subway anytime, eye contact on the street. She walked fast, locked taxi doors, waited for doormen, kept an aerosol container of Oleoresin Capiscum in her purse along with an expendable $50 bill. It used to be $20.

If she sensed New York's dangers, she also knew its pleasures—Lincoln Center, the Russian Tea Room, Blue Note, Village Vanguard, Tramps, the Guggenheim, the Whitney. Tonight she would have loved to have heard John Scofield at the Blue Note or sipped a piña colada under the old tin ceiling at Tramps.

She was on the Credit Suisse team that had prepared new interest-only strips and structured notes, and as one of the presenters, was still immersed in leverage and spreads, caps and floors, equity-index swaps, and compound options. She had just finished a working dinner in a private suite.

Her team had devised a product based on the spread between the interest rates on short-term taxable and tax-exempt instruments. Higher taxes would reduce yields on the tax exempts, increasing the spread. Lower interest rates would narrow the spread by cutting taxable yields. She went on at length about the need for sophisticated hedging strategies to protect sound investments. With her portfolio of visuals—charts, graphs, and slides—she felt she had done pretty well explaining the new notes. The response seemed good. She would make follow-up calls over the next few days. Salomon's and Banker's Trust seemed particularly interested. Lunch with Salomon's tomorrow.

But tonight, as pressures eased, she would have enjoyed more than the inside of this hotel, where she'd been cooped up for most of the past three days. Cipriani's, the Sherry bar, would have been nice. Yet after dinner everyone had drifted off for trains to Scarsdale, Chappaqua, and Massapequa.

She was the only woman at the meetings. She considered, and quickly rejected, inviting one of her colleagues for a drink. Unfortunately, gender equality hardly eliminated double standards. She hated sitting at a bar alone, and it was too late to call friends. All she wanted was a little camaraderie; yet she well knew any man would take a late-night invitation, no matter how innocently meant, as a proposition. The last thing she wanted was some drunken mutual-fund manager jumping into her bed.

She was tired of meetings that went on too long and she missed fresh air and exercise. But the health club was closed. In-room calisthenics might have relieved her tensions but she had to consider guests in the room below.

A few years ago it was fun being a bachelor career woman. Now, trips like this were getting tougher. However elegant the hotels and generous the expense account, the glamour was wearing thin. The work was hard, the hours long, the mental and physical strains increasingly challenging. Hotel rooms were lonelier. She missed her routines at home, her walks on very safe streets, her aerobics classes performed to classical music where one belted out the "Alleluia Chorus," her talks with her mother and girlfriends, her afternoon sails on the lake with Andreas, her evenings in the cafe with Andreas, the weekends in the mountains with Andreas, and most of all, she missed Andreas.

Strange, moody, melancholy, insecure, brilliant Andreas Vogl, with his deep passionate eyes, tousled hair, stooped shoulders, gnarled nose, gentle fingers. They had known each other a long time. Already seven years. He was thirteen years older, but she liked older men. Andreas had experienced so much of life, knew so much. He had seen the war.

She didn't know the war. Her parents had made it from Hungary to Switzerland just in time, and she'd been born in Zurich. Yet from the time she could remember, the war was all they talked about. The war was part of her childhood, too. But Andreas was truly a war child. His parents had been murdered by the SS. He escaped the Gestapo, fought as an adolescent in the Jewish resistance in Hungary, survived by his wits.

If the child is father of the man, she saw the child in Andreas with his sense of insecurity, insatiable curiosity, constant yearning. His need for comfort and reassurance at times cried out. Yet when she responded, he always retreated, put up the walls, grew guarded and reserved.

Andreas had been married once while living in London. He told Maria he had been much in love, then one morning without any warning, his younger wife, an aspiring actress, left him a good-bye note in their Islington kitchen and never returned. She had run off with some producer from the BBC. Andreas left London because he never wanted to see her again and was afraid of bumping into her in some West End eatery or on the tube.

Maria met him at a Brown Boveri Christmas party. She was then part of the Credit Suisse *equipe* that served the company. He was starting as a correspondent for *Positronics*. He got a little drunk that night, told her about his life. She listened sympathetically. He was not crude and vulgar like so many German types she knew. Andreas Vogl had stature and substance. She loved his cosmopolitanism, his tales about the weirdest things, his sense of humor.

Soon he changed his ways for her, gave up drinking and smoking, stopped chasing other women. The only thing she had against him was his reluctance to make a commitment.

She had asked Andreas to join her on this New York trip.

"Oh . . . it is tempting," he had said, but in the end he really couldn't take the time.

She turned from the window, sat on the bed, kicked off her black suede platform heels, listened to them plop on the floor. Of course, he had the time. *Positronics* still owed him holiday time from last year.

Over these seven years she had eroded some of the barriers. He needed her. She knew it. She wanted him to move bag and baggage into her flat. It would save him money. He would find it more convenient to live downtown. She would make room for his clowns. But no. He wanted no change. A few days in, a few days out. A suitcase was cheaper than a divorce, he said tiresomely. Someday she would tell him the present arrangement might be all right for him but wasn't for her. Still, she wanted no confrontation. She feared losing him.

She removed her Barrera pearl necklace and started pulling off her ribbed turtleneck. At least she could get comfortable. Her nail file was on the bedside table, and she absently began smoothing her nails. Maybe there was something on the television.

The phone rang. She reached for the receiver, assuming it was Andreas. "Hello!"

"Ms. Sheinman?" The voice was coarse, grainy, with some kind of mid-Atlantic accent.

"Yes."

"My name is Shepherd. I'm from the U.S. government. I need to talk to you."

"At this hour? You must be joking."

"I know it's late. But it's urgent."

"It can't wait till morning?"

"No, sorry."

"What's it about?" She laid the file next to the phone.

"Can you meet me at Cipriani's? Or if you prefer, I can come up to your room."

"I don't invite strange men to my room."

"Downstairs then."

"How do I know you're legitimate?" She said it lightly, her tone suggesting interest. It was better than the infernal triad of O'Brien-Letterman-Leno.

"I have ID."

"It could be fake."

"Some things you have to trust."

"So you think I should trust you?"

"Yes."

"I was ready to go to sleep. It's been a hard day."

"It's to your benefit to see me."

"Is it taxes?"

"I'm not IRS."

"I know what it is," she said saucily. "You've heard of our sophisticated hedging strategy and want our interest-only strips or structured notes."

"None of the above."

"Well, *what* then?" Her voice was less genial.

"Not over the phone."

"Look, sir. I don't normally meet strangers in hotels. Be more specific or good night." Although she had welcomed the diversion, she had the right to know what it was all about. After all, this was New York.

"It concerns your relationship with Andreas Vogl."

"What?"

He repeated the sentence slowly, emphasizing the name.

"Andreas? How do you know Andreas? What about Andreas?"

"Downstairs."

"Is he all right?" She suddenly felt cold.

"Downstairs."

"No, you tell me *now* or I'll call the police."

"I am the police."

"I don't believe it. Police don't play these games . . ."

"I'm not playing games, Ms. Sheinman."

"Well, then tell me whether he's all right."

"Yes. He's all right. For the moment. But you must explain your relationship to this man."

"Mr. Vogl is a friend of mine."

"We know. He was in your apartment in Zurich."

"How did you know that?" She was suddenly very frightened.

"It's my business."

"He comes to my apartment anytime he wants. But I don't see why I have to tell you all this."

"It's all important, Ms. Sheinman."

"Mr. Shepherd, or whatever your name is, what is the police interest in Andreas?"

"He's a fugitive, a terrorist. He's involved with some pretty disreputable people—"

"That's absurd."

"We think he's linked with Sheik Omar Abdel Rahman, the guy who blew up the World Trade Center, who plotted to blow up tunnels and bridges. . . ."

"What? This is nonsense."

"Police raided his apartment in Zurich, found a cache of guns and explosives. And printed matter. There was abundant evidence he and a couple of others were planning to blow up the World Bank/Fund meeting in Zurich. Who knows how many innocent people would have been killed? They escaped from his flat, then used your flat for a few hours. That's how we know about you."

"This is the craziest thing I ever heard. He's one of the gentlest men in the world. I've known him for years."

"I can assure you, madam, this is not crazy. Maybe you didn't know *all* about him. People have their darker sides."

"He's a Jew. Jews don't work with Islamic revolutionaries."

"They worked with the Nazis."

"I don't want to talk to you," she practically screamed.

"Police found the arms, explosives, and literature. He and his coconspirators have now fled to Paris. One of the coconspirators, you should know, is a woman, who seems rather liberal with her favors. . . ."

Maria said nothing.

"Now please come downstairs right away. We need to know everything you know about Andreas. You can help him by talking to us. We can help him. Maybe he was taken in. He may not realize the seriousness . . ."

She felt drained. There seemed to be no getting away. "Give me a minute," she said weakly. As she hung up, she saw she was shaking. Her face was burning. She was short of breath. She searched for a Kleenex in her carryall.

The phone immediately rang again. It was the hotel operator.

"Ms. Sheinman, can you take a call from Paris? The caller's been waiting on the line."

"Yes." She could barely speak.

"Maria?"

"Andreas." She was crying. "What's happening? I just had this horrible call. They're saying terrible things about you."

"That's why I'm calling. Maria, listen, please. Please . . . are you there?"

"Yes."

He spoke excitedly in Schweitzerdeutsch. "Whatever they're saying, it's totally wrong. A pack of lies. Disinformation. Listen, there is a giant conspiracy, involving governments and big money, big policy interests, and I've been caught in the middle and am very expendable. They think we know too much. I've been trying to reach Dudley, *Positronics* was going to publish an article about artificial gold that I had just written. They want to suppress the information to keep gold prices from falling and make money, millions of dollars . . ."

It was hard for her to absorb all this. But she had a question. "They say you have friends, a woman . . ."

"You remember earlier this year when I flew on short notice to California on several stories because Dudley came down with shingles? That's when I interviewed that professor at Stanford, Hillsdale Landover, about Chernobyl. Well, he and a woman friend of his from Israel, another physicist, contacted me in Zurich and told me this fantastic story about a secret gold project in the Negev developed by a Russian-Israeli named Sherbatov—alchemy in which gold is made from cheaper metals after atomic bombardment. Then just as they told me the story some people tried to kill all three of us and we've been on the run ever since. I'm scared, Maria. I feel I'm back in the goddamn war . . . Tell me how did you find out about any of this?"

"I just put the phone down with a man who told me. He called himself Shepherd. He invited me for a drink."

"Oh my God."

"Andreas, just tell me what's going on—"

"He's a big cog in the conspiracy. CIA. I don't know him but they say he's a real scumbag, and dangerous. . . ."

"He told me you're dangerous . . ."

"I trust you know better."

"He also told me . . . that this woman you were with was, I think his words were 'liberal with her favors.' "

"Look, this Shepherd is an expert in disinformation, and wants to turn you against me. Rachel is in love with Landover and Landover with her. I'm here only because I was around when they needed help and Landover remembered me. I let myself get involved. My God, I love you. You must realize that by this time—"

"You haven't exactly given me much occasion to realize it. We never really talk about you and me. You run from it. You're so preoccupied, so distant. If you would only have come to New York with me none of this would have happened." She started crying again.

"You're right, Maria. God knows I wish I had."

"It's just that . . . all this comes as such a terrible shock. I do, of course, want to help you. What do I do?"

"Tell me exactly what Shepherd said."

"I'm supposed to meet him now." Her hand gripped the phone so tightly her knuckles were a bloodless white.

"Can't you say you have a headache or something?"

"No. He says he will come to the room if I don't go down to the hotel bar. I believe him. I should call hotel security . . ."

"Call the police."

"He says he is the police."

"Yeah, you'd probably have trouble if you called them. And if you tried to get away you'd be a fugitive. Dammit. I'm so sorry I got you into this. I should never have gone to your apartment . . . I'm afraid the only choice is to cooperate. Be friendly. Don't protest too much."

"I've already told him I thought his story was rubbish."

"Good, and thank you. But now let him think he's planting doubts in your mind about my innocence. Be friendly. Tell him you agree I should turn myself in and get a good lawyer, that I can't be a fugitive forever."

"I hope that last is true."

"I want this nightmare to end."

"It has to."

"He's the key, this Shepherd. He can call off the hounds . . . But be careful. And remember, I love you. I obviously haven't conveyed that clearly enough but I do. I'll ring you up at one a.m. your time and you tell me what happened."

He hung up then.

She sat on the bed, the phone still pressed to her ear. She couldn't move. Slowly, she put the receiver into the cradle, stood, looked out the windows again. Searchlights scythed squares of the night into glittering checkerboards. Somewhere an ambulance wailed.

She slipped the turtleneck back on and was about to slide into slacks but decided on her businesslike black faille suit. She reached for the necklace, which lay coiled on the bedspread, ran a comb through her hair, and put on fresh lipstick.

The procedures were routine, like a pilot's checklist before takeoff. She was dressing not for anyone in particular, certainly not for that man downstairs. Years of European womanhood kept her from going anywhere in public without full confidence in her *maquillage*. Dabs of Spell-bound by Estée Lauder under her earlobes and she was ready. She took up her handbag, made sure she had her coded-card plastic room key, and opened the door.

# 44

THE FOOT SPRANG out of nowhere.

She looked up at a bull-like man with a bushy mustache and plaid, polyester sports jacket hovering in the doorway. The face was oleaginous.

"Hello, Ms. Sheinman. . . ."

From her throat a frightened wheeze.

"The bar was crowded. I thought I'd save you the trip."

"I prefer the bar." She caught her breath and took a step into the hall. Had she put the pepper spray in her purse?

"Not just yet." He pushed her back into the room. He chain-locked the door.

"What is this?" She was now more angry than scared. She stood clutching her purse.

"Sit down."

She remained standing. To sit would give him an advantage.

He shoved her onto the bed. As he pulled up an armchair she reached for the phone and dialed the operator. The first ring wasn't complete before he yanked the receiver from her. He placed the chair in front of her and sat on the edge, his legs apart and enclosing hers.

"Tell me about Andreas Vogl."

She just stared at him.

"Do you hear me?"

"I'd like to see your ID," she said.

"You may see something else."

"I don't believe you work for the U.S. government."

"I don't give a fuck what you believe. Now, unless you want me to hurt you, *tell me about Vogl.*"

"What do you want me to say?"

"We need to know everything there is to know about him. Don't hold anything back. Every detail is important for the pursuit of our inquiries." In resorting to bureaucratese, he sounded almost friendly.

She had no idea what to say. She had to think, somehow get more control of the situation.

"Talk, goddammit. That shouldn't be so hard. He's your lover, isn't he?"

"Andreas is a good man. He survived the Holocaust. His whole family was killed. He's no terrorist."

"How did you meet him?"

"Years ago . . . at a party, a Christmas party."

"Whose party? What happened?"

She felt his knees tighten against hers and the heat of his crotch. His legs were like logs. He drew his chair still closer, pinioning her. His eyes seemed to be undressing her.

"It was at a company party."

"What company?"

"Brown Boveri . . ." She had to go along with him. She hoped she'd think of something. ". . . I was invited because we had been discussing an underwriting. He looked uncomfortable standing by the canapés. We got to talking, found we had a lot in common, including an allergy to shellfish."

"Did you go to bed with him that night?"

"We had a lot in common . . . one thing led to the other."

"Did you sleep with him?" His voice was harsher.

"Yes."

"Tell me about it."

"How can the U.S. government be interested in that?"

"You sleep with a terrorist, you catch his fleas."

"For God's sake, we are not terrorists!"

"Did you stroke his cock?"

"*What?*"

"You heard what I said. Did you stroke his cock?"

"I don't know . . ."

"You must know. Did he have a big cock? A big juicy cock. Did you suck it?"

She couldn't bring herself to speak. She looked away again. The useless telephone caught her eye.

"*Look* at me," he commanded.

She could see the spittle on his chin.

"Well, lady, if you can't say it, then show me. Show me what you did." He inched closer, widened his legs.

"For God's sake, no!" She leaned back a little on the bed. If she could only get some space she could knee him in the groin and make a try for the door.

He grabbed her hands and forced them between his legs. "Now show me, goddammit. Unzip me and give me a demonstration."

She felt his mustache against her nose. He unzipped himself and forced her hand onto his bulging penis. No more. She brought her knees up hard, which only seemed to irritate him.

"I love the rough stuff," he said and slapped her face. Her nose began to bleed. He groped at her breasts.

"Now *do* it." He squeezed her nipples.

"My nose is bleeding, you don't want my blood . . . all over it." She turned, sniffling. "I have Kleenex in my bag."

He eased up a little and she stretched for her purse on the bed. Her hand found the Kleenex but also the pepper spray. Before he knew what was happening she had aimed the aerosol spout at his face and squeezed the activator.

He howled, about to hit her more viciously this time, but rubbed his eyes instead, then covered them as if that somehow could stop the burning. She snatched up her nail file on the bedside table and stabbed him in the crotch. He howled louder, hands flaying wildly and this time managing to clutch her hand and pull her on top of him. They struggled on the chair until it overturned.

"I'll kill you," he shouted, "you goddamn bitch."

She felt his hands tighten around her neck. Her nose was bleeding over his shirt. Her hands touched something on the floor. It was the base of the phone knocked off the bedside table when they fell to the floor. She managed to grip it and raising it above his head, brought it crashing downward once, then a dozen times—long after his hands had loosened around her neck.

When she stopped, his face was a mess of fractured bone, cracked teeth, and pink-and-rose-colored pieces of flesh. Somewhere underneath, his eyes were closed. Her own nose was dripping on the corpse, but a stream of his blood trickled through his mustache, staining his lips and chin. His big hands lay lifeless on the floor.

Unbelievably the base of the phone was still intact, though splattered with his blood. She heard the dial tone, saw the receiver a few feet away, and returned it to its cradle.

All was silent except for her stentorian breathing. She slid away from him and lay on her back, trying to get her nosebleed under control.

A few minutes later she was able to put the ashtray back on the bedside table and slide the chair from under his back and put it in position.

She bent over the corpse. She could see where her nail file had penetrated the skin around the pubic hairs. She forced herself to stuff his still warm, flaccid penis back inside his underwear, rezipped the fly.

Surely he had not only sex but murder on his mind. She must have seemed expendable. After humiliating her sexually, he would have killed her, telling his superiors that she was a terrorist who almost got the upper hand on him. Or she could have become just another unsolved rape-murder in the Big Apple.

The silence was intimidating. She switched on the television set. Better for there to be voices in the room in case neighbors had heard the thumping and screaming. The movie channel was showing Mel Gibson and Danny Glover in one of the wild police chases in *Lethal Weapon II*. She turned up the volume.

She plugged in the phone on the bedside table and was about to call the police when she realized they might arrest her, at least hold her for questioning. She had killed a member of the U.S. government. Police would identify with the victim, never believe she had cause, never believe what he made her do. What proof did she have? They would see her as part of the gang in Zurich. She would have to find a lawyer, spend time in jail. A trial. Months, years, trying to defend herself. Even if she were acquitted her career would be a shambles, her life ruined.

She had to get rid of the body, eliminate all evidence it was ever there.

In his jacket she found a wallet with a Virginia driver's license and U.S. government ID. Also a U.S. diplomatic passport. Yes, he really was who he said he was, though the government card did not identify a specific agency or department. The face in the photos looked younger, almost handsome, in sharp contrast to the puffy, bloody, pulverized mash on the floor.

She went through his credit cards held together by a rubber band. Some carried the name James Smith. In an inner side pocket was an

unusually large wad of money. She counted out fifty-two $100 bills and
two 100-gram gold pieces. He obviously didn't want to get caught short.

She also found a small black address book. The writing was cramped,
barely legible. The names meant nothing to her. Also in his pockets were
a soiled handkerchief, an old American Airlines boarding pass, a folded-
up paper napkin, and a clipping from a Knoxville newspaper. The clipping was about a Russian-Israeli physicist, Professor Dmitri Sherbatov,
who had just joined the scientific community at Oak Ridge.

She threw his IDs and money into her briefcase among her documents
on derivative products, put the clipping, address book, credit cards into
her purse, along with the coded key-card to get back in her room again.

She took a deep breath and opened the door into the hall. It was
empty. The service elevator was at the other end of the floor. She walked
rapidly, pressed the button, rode the elevator to the basement. In a dim
hallway, a lineup of canvas laundry carts waited for the chambermaids'
morning call. She chose one that still had dirty sheets and towels,
wheeled it to the elevator and back up to her floor and room.

To move 225-plus pounds into the basket was going to take ingenuity.
There was no easy way. She turned the cart on its side. With all her might
she slid, heaved, and pulled the body, finally edging it partly inside the
canvas liner, then gradually lifted the cart, hoping the canvas would not
tear. Once she got it to ankle height, the rump slid deeper into the
basket, drawing shoulders and head with it and giving her greater pur-
chase. Using all her strength she got the cart upright and Shepherd's
back fell to the bottom, legs protruding. She bent the knees partly but
could not push them all the way in. She covered the body, including the
legs, with the soiled linen.

She wheeled the cart to the service elevator and brought it back to its
original position in the subbasement. Back in her room, she straightened
the chair and with horror saw the size of the bloodstains, hers as well as
his.

Cold water for blood. She spent the next sixty minutes with a wash-
cloth and soap. In her suitcase she had some spot remover which she
used up. The rug looked a little better.

She would have liked to check out immediately, go somewhere else
fast. But the room clock showed 11:55. One hour to wait before Andreas's call. She would not shower because she might not hear the phone
if he called earlier. She drew water for a bath instead and exhausted, lay
down on the bed. She hadn't thought it possible but she fell asleep.

* * *

THE PHONE RANG a little after 1:15. She picked up the receiver. "Hello," she said groggily.

"How did it go?"

It was hard to answer. There was no apparent sign of disorder. Could it have been just a nightmare?

"How did it go?" he repeated.

She suddenly saw with horror she had forgotten to wipe the red stains from the ivory phone. "Oh God . . . it was terrible . . ."

"Tell me."

"Too awful to talk about now."

They spoke Schweitzerdeutsch so rapidly, every word slurred. Just as well. Transatlantic calls were likely to be tapped.

"I'm scared, Andreas." Her voice broke. "I wish you were here."

"I wish I were there, too."

She stared at the phone.

"I must check out, get out of this place. Call me on my cell phone in an hour."

She wiped the phone clean and anything else she'd forgotten the first time around—the doorknob? the wooden part of the armchair? the sink? She packed quickly, left a $25 tip for the chambermaid with a little note about how sorry she was about the accident but her period had come unexpectedly.

Downstairs she explained to the night clerk she just had news of her mother's stroke in Zurich and had to fly home right away. She tipped a sleepy porter, who, full of commiseration, helped her with her bags into a waiting taxi.

"Grand Central, please," she instructed the driver once the cab door was closed. At the station, she stuffed her bags into a locker, pocketed the key, took another cab for 45 West 21st Street.

The Tramps doorman looked her over—a single woman at this hour? Occupying a whole table?

"My friend is on his way." She gave him $5, flashed her business card and a confected smile. She asked to sit at the rear where the music was not so loud.

She was ushered to a table next to one of the muraled pillars below the beautifully restored old tin roof. A waiter brought her a piña colada.

She tried to relax listening to the creamy-smooth Mary Coughlin band, but the horror of the night persisted. How could the power of the U.S.

government be so appallingly abused. What could make a supposedly well-educated government servant attach so little value to another human being?

She studied Shepherd's address book. Who was this General Ben Giton and why were his name and phone numbers underlined? Dmitri Sherbatov's name, with one phone number crossed out, another in Oak Ridge penciled in. She connected the name with the clipping in her purse. She also saw a notation that looked like an appointment. "Admiral—9:30 Oct. 6 504 OEOB."

The call came at 2:16.

"Oh, thank God!"

Andreas sounded as if he were next door.

"I love you," he rattled in Schweitzerdeutsch. "I never realized how much."

Tears came. It was the first time he'd ever said that. "I love you, too . . ."

"Can you tell me what happened?"

"He came to my room. Did terrible things . . . Andreas, he's dead."

The line was silent. Vogl was apparently trying to absorb it. "They will come after you. You must leave the country right away."

"I can fly to Paris tonight."

"Too dangerous. They're closing in on us here. We can't stay in Europe."

"I'm ready to go anywhere."

"You have cash?"

"A lot, including his."

"Pick a place."

"Where we will be together?"

"Yes. I will join you within twenty-four hours."

"South America? People are always going to South America."

"Yes. Brazil . . . I have a cousin outside of Rio. Retired from Volkswagen. We exchange greetings every New Year's. Once I visited him while I was on a trip for *Positronics*. He's part owner of the Hotel Sans Souci in Teresópolis. Do you know Brazil?"

"No."

"Everyone goes to Rio, which is hot and crowded, and the streets are dangerous. But behind are the mountains, cool and fresh and beautiful, like the Alps. Teresópolis is like Zermatt without the snow. There are farms, fruit trees, vineyards, and mountains with names like Finger of God, Finger of our Lady, Priest's Nose, Devil's Needle . . ."

She was speechless.

"Fly to Rio tonight. Take a bus to Teresópolis. The ride takes about two hours. Stay at the Sans Souci on Avenue Presidente Roosevelt and wait there for me."

"I will be there."

"My cousin will help us. He has contacts in São Paulo."

She took out Shepherd's address book from her purse. "I almost forgot to tell you . . . I've got his address book. There are many names and telephone numbers. I also have a clipping about a Dr. Sherbatov in Oak Ridge. Isn't he the Russian Israeli you mentioned?"

"Yes."

"There is a phone number for him in the address book with what could be a Knoxville area code. Maybe useful?"

"You have it there in front of you?"

"Yes, 615-483-3555. Something else. Appointment/ Admiral/ 9:30 A.M. Thursday 504 OEOB . . . Whatever that means."

"Maria, you are wonderful. . . . I feel so guilty putting you in such danger."

"We are in this together now."

"In twenty-four hours the Finger of God."

# 45

Unlike most of the other great churches of Paris, St. Sulpice does not merge easily into the urban landscape. Its two unmatched towers are alarming apparitions in the narrow cobblestone streets of the Latin Quarter. The burnished bronze belfries are too fat, like the puffed-up breasts of the pigeons cooing around the splashing fountain in the plaza. The tiers of columns on the portico look like something imported from a Moslem holy place.

But like Robespierre, who made St. Sulpice his Temple of Victory, and Napoleon Bonaparte, who used it for his inauguration gala of 1799, Robert Pyle loved this old pile of stones. During lunch hour he often took the Metro from Franklin D. Roosevelt Avenue near the offices of the *Washington Post* to Mabillion and walked the three blocks, a welcome breather from the phones, faxes, querulous messages, press conferences, interviews, the pressures of daily foreign correspondence.

Paris was the choicest of all foreign assignments. It had fantastic restaurants, splendid vistas, the most beautiful bridges in the world, women who even when not born beautiful looked chic. Many abodes, even small ones, could be superb. Whether overlooking the Seine or tucked in little cul-de-sacs, none was far from an open-air market, cafe, or boulangerie. Robert's pad on the Rue Eugene Labiche lay between the Bois de Boulogne and the street market on Rue de la Pompe.

Yet the City of Light was not an easy place to live or work. Hours were long. With a six-hour gap between Paris and Washington, editors continued calling well past midnight even though the day began at least by ten

387

a.m. After three years the *Post*'s foreign desk piled on assignments as if convinced its Paris correspondent did little but play pinball, eat three-star meals, and ogle the sirens of Pigalle.

Robert didn't mind. He loved and lived his work. Everything he did, even Aline, the mistress he took after Sophie left, was for the greater glory of the *Washington Post*. Aline wrote for *Le Canard Enchaine* and fed him factoids, salacious gossip, and an occasional scoop.

Why had Sophie moved out? She hated not only the French but the *Washington Post* foreign desk. Rarely did she see her husband. He had to travel at least half the month and when home he lived on the phone. He was on call even during vacations. Once they parachuted him into Gaza from a holiday retreat with the two kids at a *mas* south of Grasse. Finally, she had enough. Refusing to compete, she took herself and the kids back to her family's farm near Fairlie, Vermont. He missed the kids.

Sometime after their departure Robert discovered St. Sulpice. He bumped into it almost by accident one day walking down from St. Germain-des-Prés. Standing as if transfixed in the square with the pigeons, he marveled at its architectural eccentricities. Despite its mixed origins as a medieval church completed along classic lines in the 1600s, he saw the structure as a grand and harmonious whole.

Bach reverberated through the stones. Robert walked in and from a pew in the rear heard the full blast of the pipe organ—6,688 pipes, his guidebook noted. When the organ stopped, the silence was as awesome as the music. He felt himself transported out of the city, out of the country, out of the century.

He strolled through the church. In the side chapel, right of the main door, hung a Delacroix mural of Jacob's struggle with an angel of God. Its primal energy blazed through the dimness.

A bronze meridian line ran from a plaque in the floor of the south transept to a marble obelisk in the north transept. From a window in the transept sunlight struck the line at different points every day, marking progress toward equinoxes and solstices. San Sulpice was the earth's fulcrum.

So Robert learned to swap his computers, telephones, fax machines, complaining colleagues—for an hour or so with his gray stones, meridian lines, Bach, and Delacroix. For one pressured journalist, a heavenly trade.

When Landover phoned Robert at the office, identified himself as a physicist and said he had a major story for the *Post* so sensitive he didn't dare speak its name, St. Sulpice was where they met. Robert specified the Lady Chapel at the east end because it was always empty.

"I'm six feet tall with a bit of scruffiness on the face," Landover had said, and taking stock of both his whiskers and a recently acquired outfit in the cafe mirror, added, "I'll be wearing a boatman's cap and a leather jacket."

Landover, Rachel, and Vogl were renting a small furnished flat on Rue Lavoisier near the Madeleine. Vogl had tried repeatedly but unsuccessfully to get through to Dudley in Arlington. Then one morning in the *International Herald Tribune,* he discovered the headline: NEWSLETTER PUBLISHER DIES IN FIRE

> Leopold Dudley, a former senior Washington correspondent of *Business Week* who founded *Positronics Today,* a newsletter on the nuclear industry, died yesterday in a fire in his office in Falls Church. The three-alarm fire destroyed four stores at the Crestwood mall before it was brought under control. Damage was estimated at $1.5 million.
>
> Dudley, the only victim, died of cardiac arrest before the fire broke out in the premises he used as his publishing office. Arlington County hook and ladder chief Harold Hutchins said the conflagration was probably started by one of Dudley's cigarettes. Firefighters found a whiskey bottle clutched in his hand amid the charred wreckage. . . .

"He doesn't even smoke," Vogl exclaimed, getting up to show the others the article. "Or drink whiskey."

The *Washington Post* could not be destroyed so easily. Moreover, from the Watergate scandal, which led to the ouster of a President, it had a reputation for intrepidness. Landover told Robert Pyle the story they had was "even bigger."

Only Landover and Rachel attended the meeting at St. Sulpice. Vogl said his presence would be counterproductive, the reporter would only want direct sources.

Robert Pyle sat in a pew below a Virgin and Child floating above a cascade of plaster clouds. Shadows from candles flitted on the wall. He asked questions, taping onto his Sony recorder. They showed him a printout of Vogl's article, then the clipping about the mysterious fire in Falls Church.

"These people play very rough," Rachel said.

Robert said, "They won't monkey with the *Washington Post.*"

The session lasted nearly two hours. As they piled detail upon detail, Robert enthused, "This does sound big." When they finished, Robert asked where he could call with questions.

"No phone yet in our flat," Landover said quickly. "We'll call you."

"At noon every day then, until we get the story in the paper."

The following noon Robert had a few additional questions. Within forty-eight hours he had filed 2,500 words, describing not only the gold-making process and breakthrough in fusion, but also a CIA- and SIBAT-inspired conspiracy to silence those who had initially tried to inform the public.

Although Landover continued phoning every day, Robert had no news about the story's disposition. "This often happens," Robert said. "It *is* annoying. But it does no damn good to query the editor. It's like querying God."


GRACE SOMETIMES ACCOMPANIED Admiral Jackman to Room 504 of the Old Executive Office Building, the CIA director's office in town. The second office was handy for running the political side of the director's job, mainly jawboning politicians, and made it more convenient for him to attend White House meetings. Today Grace came along and from her cubicle in the anteroom entered his inner sanctum with a muffled step. The admiral's eyes were closed and she did not want to disturb him. She laid some papers on his desk and departed.

The admiral heard her enter but roused himself too late to catch her. He saw that among the papers she had left was a card listing his appointments for the week, including one in two days with Jim Shepherd, who was stopping in just before his departure for Paris to bolster the Force Majeure unit.

The desk was neat, the way he liked it. Messy desks, messy minds. Cyrus Richards was a clean desk man. Greg Oberling's desk was a disaster area. The admiral still wasn't sure whom to recommend, or whether he even wanted to retire. He now felt like hanging on as long as possible. For after this job came the big Nada. Better to die with your boots on.

Pens and pencils stood in a little white alabaster boat on the admiral's desk. A stapler and magnifying glass lay next to the boat. Between two bookends were Webster's New World Dictionary, *The Art of War,* by Sun Tzu, and two field guides to North American birds. He had just found *The Birds of Cyprus* in a secondhand store, but it was too tall and heavy to fit with the others, symmetry would be off. He left it on the coffee table at the other end of the room in front of the sofa.

The admiral glanced at his window ledge. Although he had laid food out for the cardinals, chickadees, and mockingbirds, even for the pigeons, the crows had put them all to flight with their fearsome flapping of wings. Too many crows on 17th Street, the admiral thought.

With a manicured right index finger the admiral straightened the papers in the in-basket, including the memo from Benjamin Franklin Coates, the CIA's communications director. He saw that Grace had also slipped some new papers into the bright red jacket of the DIMONA GOLD file, labeled EYES ONLY, that was directly in front of him on the desk.

The agency was following events in scores of countries that could have any bearing on America's position in the world, but DIMONA GOLD now preoccupied the director because it now preoccupied the President. The director reread the memo at the top of the file, a summary that President Halleck had dictated of a conversation with the Israeli prime minister.

A call came from the prime minister of Israel, which I took in the Oval Office at 11:20 A.M. After the usual formalities, he said he wanted to tell me of an extraordinary development in his country. I expressed the deep gratitude of the United States that Israel chose to share the information with its closest ally.

He described a process for making gold cheaply by the nuclear bombardment of cheaper metals. He said Israeli scientists had already produced commercial quantities of artificial gold at their nuclear research site in the Negev, and he offered to send a delegation to the United States to instruct us in the process. He assumed the United States would take extreme measures to protect the information.

I said the United States would be delighted to receive such a delegation and was anxious to work with Israel. I said I would have to ask the secretary of the Treasury about the broader implications of synthetic gold, but agreed that for the time being until we completed our assessment, extreme measures were needed to protect the information. I mentioned the Los Alamos project during World War Two. The comparison seemed to please him . . .

The prime minister said eventually markets would learn of the process. In the interim, he confided, Israel was making discreet sales of the artificial gold in Zurich. These offerings had been successful and had already yielded the Bank of Israel more than $10 million. The prime minister said his experts thought gold was in a long-term upward price trend, and that sales were welcome to prevent prices from rising too quickly. He said nothing prevented the United States from making similar forays in the market . . .

A smile on the admiral's lips.

He now read a clipping from the *Washington Post* about a fire at a small newsletter operation in Falls Church and the death of the proprietor. Unfortunate, the admiral thought. But no omelets without breaking eggs.

Another clipping, this from the *San Francisco Examiner*:

Disappearance of Hillsdale P. Landover, Jr., director of the Stanford Linear Accelerator Center (SLAC), is attributed to possible psychiatric disturbances. Dr. Milton Gross, a psychiatrist associated with Stanford University, said Professor Landover suffered from a schizophrenic bipolar imbalance, and that severe stress symptoms caused by overwork can be especially debilitating when combined with the cultural shock of sudden relocation abroad.

"This could cause such an individual to become vulnerable to the seductive call of violent political movements and cult groups and to be less able to distinguish between right and wrong," Dr. Gross said.

"Professor Landover had a brilliant mind that just cracked," Dr. Gross concluded.

Professor Landover was last known to be in Paris. He arrived there via Israel, the Sinai, and Zurich. A spokesman for Interpol, who declined to give his name, said he believed Dr. Landover "is in league with international terrorists, possibly radical Palestinians seeking to disrupt the annual meeting of the International Monetary Fund and World Bank."

Professor Landover left suddenly for Israel in mid-September, giving no explanation to Stanford colleagues or his wife Kate Standish. She told the *Examiner* that although her husband was undoubtedly a brilliant man, she had "occasionally noted a tendency toward erratic behavior" in him.

And this clipping from the *Jerusalem Times*:

Doctors at the Mount Sinai Hospital said today that Rachel Ravid, daughter of Yosef Ravid, the former deputy director of Mossad who was killed last week by Arab terrorists, suffers from functional psychosis.

Soon after her father's death Ms. Ravid began to exhibit "symptoms of mental instability, in which her personality was seriously disorganized and contact with reality impaired," according to Dr. Myron Cohen of the Mount Sinai Hospital staff.

In mid-September Ms. Ravid walked off her job as a technician at Kirya-le-Mehekar. According to security officials at the Dimona research center, she may have joined a radical Palestinian group seeking to disrupt the annual meeting of the World Bank and International Monetary Fund in Zurich.

"This is a double tragedy for a distinguished Israeli family," said Simon Bloom, director of KMG security.

And now the admiral studied the memo from Coates.

The *Washington Post* called us for our comment about a story they contemplate running by Robert Pyle. (Paris correspondent. Rated 39.2 on Media Performance Monitor, possible score 100. Considered "rising star" but unstable personal life: lives with mistress who works for the *Canard,* excessive reliance on gossip, unfriendly to USG.)

Pyle interviewed an American physicist from Stanford and an Israeli scientist who used to work at Dimona. All three were acting like Salman Rushdies. They claim assassins are being directed not by Iranian religious fanatics but the CIA.

Pyle has filed some cock-and-bull story based on interviews with the two individuals, who claim the Israelis can synthesize gold cheaply and their process is now being shared with the United States . . .

The admiral read on. The memo was detailed. Obviously large chunks of the *Post* story had been read aloud to Coates, who unfortunately didn't have an ability to summarize. He had ended the memo with a note in his neat parochial-school penmanship:

*What do we tell them?*

A few minutes later the admiral had Richards on the line.

"The *Post* is calling us?"

"Expected."

"Recommendation?"

"Blow up Fifteenth and L?"

The admiral chuckled. "That would make too many people happy."

"Second best: Denigrate sources. Disinform. Make the Postmen think twice."

"Excellent."

"Send him a CARE package with some selected clippings on the professor and the Ravid woman?"

"Bingo again."

"Call Gaylord personally. Tell him the whole thing is absurd, that if he prints that story, the *Post* becomes the laughingstock of the Beltway."

"Cy, you are reading your Sun Tzu."

The admiral buzzed Grace to get Richie Gaylord, executive editor of the *Washington Post,* on the line. Mr. Gaylord was in a meeting but would return the call when the meeting broke up.

Within fifteen minutes Gaylord was on the line. "About that story from Paris," the admiral said. "It's junk, unadulterated cow shit. Whoever your correspondent is, he's been hitting the cognac, the hemp, or maybe just been away too long. Call him back before he gets you, your paper, and the United States government into some real trouble."

"There's nothing to the story?" Gaylord asked weakly.

"Absolutely nothing. Imagine people trying to manufacture gold. So in Siberia they found Merlin the Magician. My grandson is screaming for a Power Morph. When I was a kid, I wanted the tooth fairy. I wanted the Lone Ranger's white stallion so I could yell Heigh-ho Silver. It's not the real world, Richie."

"What about the scientists who are the sources?"

"I'll fax you some stuff on those two. They're a couple of crazies suffering delusions. Clinical paranoia."

"That's a little hard to believe. Admiral, Landover was an internationally known professor of physics at Stanford."

"*Was* is the operative word. Marital problems, extramarital love affair, work stress. It all set off something—bipolar. He's off his rocker. Possibly some effect of the radiation that physicists are subject to. Sad but true. It's all in the clips . . . Hey, don't take my word for it. Look at the material."

"It's a pretty strong denial."

"Talk to any nuclear physicist and he'll tell you it's a joke. Such characters will also sell you the Brooklyn Bridge and then bottled water from the fountain of youth. Don't make the *Post* a laughingstock. Too many people depend on it. My favorite paper."

"All noted, Admiral."

# 46

THE EXECUTIVE EDITOR himself placed the call to Paris. After abbreviated civilities, Richie Gaylord came to the point.

"I know you've worked very hard on the gold story, Robert. It is an interesting tale. One that challenges the imagination. And you've told it well. There are nice touches, the allusions to alchemy, the description of the security system at Dimona, the explanations of particle acceleration and bombardment . . .

"But without substantive evidence, the article makes charges about international conspiracies. We can't publish something like this on the basis of statements from one or two people. Frankly, Robert, there's not enough proof the gold is actually being manufactured. Everyone we've talked to here denies it."

"But—" Robert fell silent. It was futile to challenge the collective judgment of the *Post*'s roundtable.

"So I'm afraid we've decided we can't run it, at least not now."

Robert was still biting his tongue.

"Let me say," Gaylord went on, "that we did not know until we received the yarn that you were even working on it. You should keep us better informed about what you're doing. It avoids later misunderstandings."

"I was trying to get the piece out as quickly as possible," Robert said. "It's impossible to capture the importance of such developments in a memo. The story was so strong I thought it would stand on its own."

"Okay, it's just a small procedural matter," Gaylord said dismissively.

"The basic thing, Robert, is we can't get the story *confirmed*. You haven't given us a smoking gun."

Robert was silent.

"And I must tell you," Gaylord continued, "we also have indications your sources may have some delusional problems . . ."

"A Stanford physicist and a section chief at Dimona are suddenly considered unreliable? Who says that?" Caution to the wind, Robert let his voice rise.

"Other scientists, doctors . . . I don't want to argue, Robert." Irritation crept into Gaylord's voice. "We've also spoken to people in a position to know . . ."

Robert didn't ask who. He assumed the CIA. "It's a cover-up—"

"We can't *say* that without more evidence. More reliable sources. I'm sorry. I suggest you put the matter on the shelf. It can always be revisited later. Look, there's a great deal of interest here in Muslim fundamentalism. Maybe it's time to visit Algiers again. How about an updater on the European far right, an assessment of the new President of France, something about the Europeans' move toward a shorter work week . . ."

Robert mostly tuned out. He had been genuinely impressed by both Landover and Rachel. But he was a soldier. If the boss wanted him to go to Algiers, he'd go to Algiers. He hoped his files on Le Pen and the German neo-Nazis were current.


WHEN LANDOVER PHONED from the cafe at noon the following day, Robert fixed another meeting at St. Sulpice.

"No need for more than one to go," Landover said when he stopped back in the flat to tell the others he was on his way. He was thankful for something to do. The waiting was unbearable. He was not used to sitting around, doing little more than reading the papers and watching his beard grow. Rachel was wonderful, but the tension was eroding romance.

Rachel said she ought to accompany him but was already late for the coiffeur to punk cut her hair and retouch its unaccustomed blondness. Vogl had been up all night phoning New York and was organizing his trip to Brazil. He had passed along the data from Shepherd's notebook read to him by Maria, including the phone number for Sherbatov at Oak Ridge and the notation about a meeting with the admiral. Somewhere between calls Vogl had picked up croissants for breakfast.

Although they felt sorry for Maria, now a full member of the fugitives' club, and were depressed by the news of Dudley, Shepherd's death seemed a turning point in their ordeal. Shepherd had to be pivotal in the conspiracy against them. Perhaps now the clouds would finally lift.

As ROBERT EMERGED from his building on the Rue de Berri to make his appointment with Landover, in the cafe next door a diminutive man who looked like a frog, dressed in plaid shirt, gray corduroy trousers, and a navy blue beret stood up without asking for *l'addition* and laid a bill on the table. Tucking his *Liberation* under his arm, the man, who couldn't have been more than four-and-a-half feet tall, followed Robert down the Rue de Berri to the Champs-Élysées, then down the Champs to the Franklin D. Roosevelt subway station. The man's feet were spinning to keep up with Robert's stride.

In the Metro, Robert changed at Concorde and took Montparnasse-Bienvenue to Sevres-Babylone. Emerging from the station with its pervasive odor of stale Gauloise smoke, Robert rose into the fresh air and merged with the midday crowds. The little man's feet spun again. Robert walked briskly along Rue de Sevres to Rue du Vieux Colombier and followed it three blocks to the portico of St. Sulpice. Struggling to keep up, the little man managed to enter the church a few minutes after Robert.

Stuffing his beret in his pocket and dutifully crossing himself, the little man moved prayerfully along the apse toward one of the giant shells that served as holy-water stoups. He spotted Robert in the Lady Chapel. Then, with a twinge of excitement, he recognized Landover behind the facial hair.

It was a short meeting. Landover and Robert, both grim-faced, rose to leave. They shook hands and parted outside the church. Robert headed east toward Odeon, where he was to have a coffee with a former Algerian minister in exile.

Adjusting his Baltic sailor's cap, Landover went west on Rue du Vieux Colombier toward Rue de Sevres and the Sevres-Babylone metro, on a direct line to the Madeleine. The short man, beret pulled rather far down over his ears for such a warm autumnal day, kept about thirty paces behind Landover, who walked slowly, head slightly bowed, preoccupied.

Traffic was heavy. Buses and taxis were rushing down special lanes on the Rue de Sevres. The man drew closer. Landover stood with a crowd waiting for a light to change on the Rue du Cherche Midi. They were now within an arm's length. A bus was running the light. Landover paused at the curb ready to cross Cherche Midi.

He felt eyes on him and turned. The squat figure behind looked familiar. Landover faced the street again, racking his brain over where he might have seen this odd chap before. The bus was ten or fifteen yards away, speeding along the inner lane.

Suddenly it came back. The Baur-au-lac terrace. The telephone repairman at Vogl's place. Landover spun around just as the little man arched forward, palms outward, primed for the lethal shove. Landover pivoted to the left, turning so rapidly the man was still bent forward when Landover's right elbow smashed into his left shoulder. Losing his balance, the man flailed, trying unsuccessfully to grab Landover's jacket, and tilted sideways in front of the thundering bus.

Brakes screeched. Klaxons blared. Screams. A woman fainted. The swerving bus dragged the body at least a dozen meters under the axle of its front right wheel. Leaves and trash piled in front. Blood smeared the street. As pandemonium erupted, Landover eased his way from the crowd, crossed the street, and disappeared down the steps of the Sevres-Babylone metro station.


BACK AT RUE LAVOISIER, Landover described what happened.

"No time to lose," Rachel exclaimed. "We've all got to get out of here—right away."

Landover asked Vogl to write down, as if making a court deposition, precisely what Maria told him about Shepherd's last moments. Vogl presented two neatly handwritten sheets of foolscap, which Landover pocketed. Landover also made note of Shepherd's appointment within twenty-four hours in the Old Executive Office Building. Rachel jotted down Sherbatov's phone number in Oak Ridge.

They taxied to the Gare du Nord and waited for the TEE to Brussels. "Too risky via Charles de Gaulle," Rachel said.

The Jaguar remained in an underground parking space below the Arc de Triomphe. Landover was unhappy at abandoning that beautiful, dulcet-running, life-giving machine, but they couldn't risk driving it across a frontier. No time to write a thank-you note to the owner, but at least they had left a full tank of gas.

They waited in the Brasserie du Nord. The lively eatery was festooned outside with stalls of coquillages behind which old men with frayed leather gloves deftly pried open clams, oysters, and sea urchins. Inside, an enormous music box played the brash, bouncy rhythms of the Belle Epoque.

A drunken German old enough to have been in the war was singing along. His Commerzbank visa card lay on the table in front of him. As they hurried for their train he bumped into the German's table, profusely apologized, spilling some beer from a glass and palming the card.

Vogl worried that the card would be useful only for charging, until he noticed the pin number neatly written on the back.

In the station a compliant money machine yielded $5,000. A little war reparation. He half grinned.

At Zaventem Airport they paid cash for their tickets and split what remained of their assets three ways. Inside the cavernous waiting room, Vogl gave them the name and phone number of his uncle's hotel in Teresópolis and tried to convince them to join him.

"Later perhaps," Rachel said. "Hilly and I must first face our dragons."

# 47

THE TOWN OF Oak Ridge, straddling Black Oak Ridge in the mountains of east Tennessee, has managed to survive its traumatic birth. After wartime Washington chose it as the fabrication site for the atomic bombs dropped on Hiroshima and Nagasaki, the town stood for years as a symbol of the awesome destructive powers of science. But as Rachel read in the tourist literature at McGhee Tyson Airport while waiting for her rental car, Oak Ridge is now "one of the more inviting small communities of America and a great place to raise a family."

The plants where uranium was separated and enriched were now part of the Oak Ridge National Laboratory, the most important of a score of federal scientific research centers. But Oak Ridge, Rachel learned, also consists of: a symphony orchestra; a playhouse; three schools of performing dance; three museums; six parks; nine playgrounds; three recreational centers; an arboretum; twenty-six lighted tennis courts; thirty-two soccer fields, and a public school system that averages more than twenty National Merit finalists annually. Population of 30,000 is half the wartime level. Average summer temperature: 75 degrees F; winter: 35 degrees F.

She dialed the number Vogl, via Maria, had given for Dmitri Sherbatov. "Alexander Inn," a woman answered in a southern drawl. Rachel booked a room and asked for the address.

"It's 210 East Madison Road, Oak Ridge. Fifteen minutes west of Knoxville," the woman said. "Now you have a very nice day."

Rachel set off in the rented Cavalier. Although this was her first trip to the American south, she had no difficulty getting her bearings. First her father, then the Israeli army, had taught her to read maps. They had also taught her to shoot guns. Her plan was wild, but no wilder than Hilly's. Hilly was right. They had to stop running.

At a light she checked her face in the car mirror. Lipstick red, hair blond, eyes mascaraed. Still the Streisand nose but now a resemblance also to Madonna. Good. Yet despite her punk cut, and the sagging black cotton jersey sack dress picked up in a Paris thrift shop, she had no assurance she wouldn't be recognized by her nose, her expression, her walk. Passing a bus on the inside lane, she felt the stares of the riders from their portholes but self-consciously kept her eyes on the road.

She turned into a small shopping mall. Bruce's Hunting and Fishing smelled of tobacco, oil, leather, and metal. The lone salesman, perhaps Bruce himself, fat, with a loud checkered double-knit jacket and tie clip like a dollar sign, was busy with an equally fat customer but gave her a smarmy smile.

"Just look aroun', ma'am. Be right with you." When he spoke, he didn't bother to remove the matchstick from his lips.

Beside the shiny leather jackets, a rack of belts caught her eye. Big buckles, shiny metal tabs, made for Hell's Angels with macho beer bellies. She chose the shortest one and ambled along racks of fishing rods and reels, exercise machines, baseball gloves, footballs, golf clubs, and tennis rackets until she found what she was looking for.

They were all laid out in the big glass display case: black and silver, dull and shimmering, names like Davis, Raven, Braun Multipractic, Smith & Wesson, Taurus, Sturm/Ruger, Intratec, SWD, Jennings/Bryco, Beretta, and Glock. If you needed a little more firepower you had the sleek Ruger Mini-14 semiautomatic with fiberglass folding stock, spidery black AT-22 semiautomatic, stubby Mac-10 submachine gun, a trim AK-47. By the AK-47 a sign said: "forty rounds a minute—especially handy for a forest of possum, squirrel, and deer."

When Bruce sauntered over asking how she was doing today, she gave him her warmest smile and said she was looking for something a little more modest.

"Your best buy would be the Raven," he said brightly. "It's a compact twenty-five caliber. We call it the world's most affordable handgun—only $127. A steal."

He jingled keys from his pocket, unlocked the case from the rear, drew out the silver gray weapon, and laid it affectionately on top of the glass.

"A very good choice," the man said smoothly. "Small, handy, reliable, inexpensive. We move a lot of these. What every lady needs these days for self-protection."

Like a toy, small, smooth, remarkably light, the Raven folded nicely into her hand, could be concealed in her palm. Seven strips like notches stood out below the hammer.

"What's it made of?" she asked.

"A good reliable zinc alloy," the salesman said. "The best you can get for the money. Never heard any complaints."

"Made in USA" read an inscription. She would be helping American workers.

Rachel drew a sight line down the barrel. Something especially menacing about handguns. Like a fat pit viper that suddenly appears in a crack in the floor. In the army, rifles had seemed more—honest.

"I read about those poor tourists in Florida who got themselves killed and figured a woman traveling alone needed some protection."

The salesman gave her an understanding nod. "You never know. A lot of bad eggs out there. The wife keeps a Beretta in the kitchen drawer. I'm never without protection myself. Can't be too careful these days." As he spoke, the dollar-sign tie clip rocked and rolled over a hunk of stomach.

Rachel laid two $100 bills on top of the case.

"Cartridges?" he asked, eyeing the money.

"Yes, of course. I nearly forgot." She smiled shyly, put another bill on the table. "And this belt as well." She fastened it around the waist of her baggy dress. Now it showed much more leg, and went better with her punk hairdo.

The man sauntered to a locked cabinet, pulled out his keys again, and drew two boxes of shells from a drawer. She slipped the gun and shells into her purse.

He made change for the purchases and gave her a receipt, never asking for identification or even her name. No mention of registration. She could have been buying a loaf of bread, or a can of baked beans.


IT WAS ABOUT teatime when she found the Alexander Inn opposite a park of black oaks, magnolias, boxwood hedges, and syringa bushes. She parked in the lot and walked into the lobby with her single brown canvas suitcase bought at the Galleries Lafayette in Paris. The place seemed cheerful and welcoming. A girl in a lemon dress was at the tourist information desk arranging a bus tour for a group of students. Laughter erupted from a small party in the bar. A few other people were milling around. No one looked like security.

She registered as Tamara Lewis from Auckland, New Zealand. The clerk, in a dark blue business suit and white shirt with a name tag that said BOB, couldn't have been more delighted to see her and welcome her to America. He gave her a key for room 416. Ms. Lewis should not hesitate to ask for anything that would make her stay more enjoyable.

"Need the bellhop to carry your luggage?"

"No, I can manage. Thanks."

She would have liked a cup of tea but picked up her suitcase instead.

The room looked over the park. She tossed the bag on the luggage rack and opened a desk drawer. A Gideon Bible and some stationery. She wrote Dmitri's name on an envelope, put a blank sheet of paper inside, sealed it and retraced her path to the front desk. She asked friendly BOB if he would leave the message for Dr. Sherbatov. BOB slipped it into the cubicle for room 403.

Rachel returned to her room, loaded a clip into the Raven, slipped it back into her purse, and knocked on 403. No answer. She went back downstairs and told the desk she had stupidly left her key in her room. When a bellhop went up with her this time, she tipped him $10, saying her room number was 403 instead of 416.

"Now you have a nice day," he said, unlocking 403.

Rachel shut the door. The room looked well lived in. Towels and clothes strewn over the backs of chairs. An open suitcase on a luggage rack. She riffled through it. Underwear, T-shirts, socks, jeans, nothing of interest, not even a gold ingot. She peered into the bathroom. Familiar Israeli toothpaste, a package of plastic razors, a jar of one-a-day multiple vitamins, a hairbrush full of hairs. Dirty socks and shirts thrown into a corner next to the bathtub. Very Russian.

She walked to the spindly desk. Sections of yesterday's *New York Times* lay next to a well-thumbed Russian-English dictionary. Some longer words in an article were underlined. A letter had been started in longhand. She deciphered the Cyrillic script to make out something like "Dear Misha . . . very nice town . . . good scientists . . . I like pancakes and eggs . . ."

She sat in an armchair facing the door and waited, the Raven in her lap.

The room was dark when she heard the bolt click and the door swing open. He entered, closed the door behind him, flicked the light. The bulb was dim. The chair was in shadow, and he did not immediately see her.

"Stay where you are and don't do anything foolish," she commanded, uncoiling in her chair.

He started, stared at the uplifted hand with the gun, and raised his hands. "I don't have any money," he said. His English was better than she remembered.

"I don't want your money." She stared at him, stiff, tense. "I have some things to tell you. I want to make sure you listen."

He stood by the wall, lips tight and slightly quivering, he looked grimly at her darkened form and did not move.

Rachel noticed that he had on an open-collared shirt and rumpled trousers. The same kind of outfit that Hilly had worn through much of their flight from Israel. They seemed to have almost the same build, the same way of rocking on their feet, the same narrow cheekbones, tousled hair, sweeping eyes. But this man's hair was wilder and he seemed a little taller. Again as at their meeting in the Dimona canteen, she had that sense of altitude, a lofty peak high above the clouds.

She must not let her earlier sympathies for the man interrupt what she had to do.

"You never expected to see me alive, did you?"

"I do not know you, madame."

"Look at me, Dmitri Sherbatov." She stepped forward, moved her head out of the shadows. "I know my hair is different." She ruffled her punk hairdo. "But the head is the same and will never forget. You and I had a talk once. You told me things about yourself in Russia, your *babushka*. Your brother is a concert violinist. You had a son at Moscow Conservatory. You had a remarkable escape from Lake Baikal . . ."

A flicker of recognition on his face. "No. It cannot be . . . the woman from Machon Two?"

"*Shalom.*" Her eyes bore in on him. It was uncanny, the resemblance to Hilly.

"Yes, yes. I remember very well. You asked me about Sakharov. We talked about knowledge. You said you did not want to know too much. Perhaps you were right. Why are you here in Tennessee, in my room, with a gun?"

She leaned forward. "We have been through hell because of you."

"I do not know what you are talking about. Please put the gun down."

She kept it pointed at him. "You were making gold for Israel, and now you're making gold for the United States. I'm not supposed to know that, am I?"

"Very few people know." His voice was calm.

"And because I know, people have been murdered by your people . . ."

"My people? I know nothing about any of this . . ." His hands were slowly dropping.

"Keep your hands up and stay where you are." She waved the pistol at him. "I know how to use this."

The hands went up again. The face drooped like a hound dog's.

"I have been doing," he began, ". . . a technical job for Israel and now for the U.S. . . . They call it 'technology transfer.' I do not know of these other developments you speak of."

"Then let me tell you about these other developments."

He looked at her uncomprehendingly.

"Some gold you made at Dimona went into the private hands of General Ben Giton . . ."

He shook his head. "The gold went to the Bank of Israel to make Israel a stronger nation . . ."

"Some of your gold, I repeat, was diverted by Ben Giton, for the political groups he supports, including SIBAT, Women in Green, orthodox religious parties, extremist settlers' groups, anyone else against the peace process. He funneled gold into his personal accounts to pay off his friends."

"I do not believe that."

"You should ask him. He is here, isn't he?"

"The general returned to Israel for new elections. We were invited to the White House, then he introduced me to American scientists here. A good team, learning quickly . . . But how do you know anything about this?"

"How do I *know?*" It was as if a dam burst. She immediately lowered her voice. People in the next room might hear. "I have been living a nightmare because of you and your technology. That's why I am here. I am at the end of my rope."

He looked puzzled, rattled.

Rachel's words rushed out in a torrent. She couldn't keep anything back. She wanted this man to understand what he had put her through.

She told him about Klein's discovery and mysterious death by alleged Arab terrorists, her disclosures to her father about something smelly going on, his efforts to inform the prime minister, the alerting of the Americans via Shepherd, Landover's visit to Dimona, her father's untimely death, the chase by Israeli security, the escape from Arab terrorists, the flights to Zurich and Paris, the timely assistance of Vogl, the aborted efforts to work with *Positronics* and the *Washington Post,* the abuse of Maria, Shepherd's double-dealings and death and the finding of his notebook, the attempted execution of Landover.

"It was all so terribly unfair and unjust," she said. "All we wanted was to make Israel a better country."

She looked closely at Dmitri as she spoke. He stood still, hands raised halfway. He had a pained expression.

"What a terrible story." His eyes showed his distress. "I, too, wanted to help Israel. I knew nothing of any of this. Please believe me . . ." He thought for a moment. "Except for the death of the corporal. I did make an inquiry about that . . ."

"You made an *inquiry*?"

"Yes, I accidentally heard about the death of Corporal Klein. They finally admitted to me he was executed but said he was a blackmailer. He had learned about the gold-making operation and wanted to be paid off to remain silent. . . ."

"And you believed that?"

"I believed the person who told me that."

"And who was that, pray tell?"

"My brother, Misha."

"The violinist?"

"Yes. But he is well connected beyond the musical world. He knows General Ben Giton better than I do. I told him I was unhappy that someone's life was lost because of my gold process."

"Unhappy? And what about Corporal Klein's unhappiness, and the unhappiness of those who loved him?"

"I believed my brother when he said Corporal Klein threatened to compromise the entire project. He also said later that the authorities regretted the summary action and that nothing like this would ever happen again." His eyes implored her to believe him.

"You are either very naive, Dmitri Sherbatov, or a very clever actor."

"I am not acting."

She glared at him. "Ben Giton was both enriching himself with your gold and financing his political causes."

"I am a scientist, not a policeman. They allow me to manufacture gold, to make the dream of alchemy come true. This is my dream, too. They give me equipment, everything I need to work. I need few personal material goods . . . I believe I am helping people, at least Israeli people. . . ."

"And what are you doing here?"

"I told you, this is technology transfer, a way Israel pays debts to the American people."

"But in Israel Ben Giton takes a cut for himself. Who knows who takes the cuts in America?"

"I make gold and hope it will do some good. They would not let me make gold in Russia. They wanted me to make weapons. I refused. Eventually they would have arrested me, killed me. I try to make Israel a better place, but I cannot make a perfect world."

She looked at him backed up against the wall, supplication in his face, hands up as if he were being crucified. Could it be that he had just let himself be used and honestly was ignorant of what was happening?

She looked at her weapon, heavy, grotesque, bending limply. She could never pull the trigger. She looked at the man again, then tossed the gun on the bed.

She watched him lower his hands, walk to the bed, pick up the weapon gingerly as if it were the tail of a dead rat. He placed it in the bedside table drawer, closed it.

He begged her to sit down in her chair. "What can I do?"

"What can you do?" She laughed, resuming her seat. Then suddenly the tears came and rushed down her cheeks. She didn't even try to wipe them. Here she thought she had been all cried out, now she cried as never before, as if this could somehow exorcise the demons. Her father seemed to be in the room and she tried to reach out to him.

Dmitri sat silent. At one point his right hand flicked forward but pulled back in midair. Then when her hands reached out, he took them.

"We can be friends," he said.

She couldn't believe it. She was holding hands with the man she thought she had come to kill. A few minutes ago she was prepared to die. Now she wanted very much to live. She pulled her hands back and started swabbing her cheeks with her fingers. "I must look a mess. I am not by nature an hysterical woman."

"You have been through a lot." He rose to get her some tissues.

"You can help me and a couple of others clear our names, get the withdrawal of the murder squads, give us back our lives. Are you willing to do that?"

He returned with a batch of tissues. "I will do what I can, if you allow me to take you to dinner."

She straightened her dowdy dress and ran a hand through her too-short hair. "Let's go."


THEY WENT TO the restaurant downstairs. As they entered, Rachel nervously looked around, her antennae up. The place was starting to fill up, men in slacks and sports coats, women in pantsuits and baubles. Conversations were animated. Security people always stood out. She sensed none.

The hostess in a starched maroon uniform showed them to a quiet table in the corner and wished them a pleasant evening. "Your waitress tonight is Cindy."

Dmitri had eaten there before. He said the catfish reminded him of the *omul* of Lake Baikal and added he had taken a liking to pecan-pumpkin pie.

This time, no one to pull them apart, they talked until the restaurant closed, then continued over coffee and cognac in the nearby empty cocktail lounge.

Rachel went into further details about the horrors of the last two weeks. She also talked about Landover—his intelligence, his Americanness, her affection for both him and Vogl. Dmitri occasionally asked questions or interjected such comments as "terrible," or "I can't believe it," or "how could they do that?" He agreed to sign a statement detailing how she and her friends were put through hell by the venality of Shepherd and Ben Giton.

Dmitri told her about Rostov and Tanya, his hopes of getting Kyril out of Russia, the emptiness of his life in Beersheba.

"Take Tanya back," Rachel advised. "She obviously had little choice. What can a single woman do against the KGB? I am sure she is right that had she not agreed, Kyril would have lost his position in the conservatory and she would have been stuck in Irkutsk forever, perhaps jobless. Perhaps in Perm Twenty-two. You must not be too hard on her. By taking her back you will make her happy, Kyril happy, and eventually yourself happy."

"Why do you presume that humans have a right to happiness?"

"You sound so Russian."

Dmitri shrugged.

# 48

LANDOVER WALKED FROM the Tabard Inn on N Street to a pay phone on Connecticut Avenue. He wore a new lightweight suit, white shirt, cinched-up necktie, and a growth of gray-black beard. He dialed the White House and asked for Harry Spitz.

"Office of the chief of staff," a secretary answered.

"I would like to speak to Harry Spitz," Landover said.

"Who is calling, please?"

"Professor Landover of Stanford University."

"I'm sorry, who?"

"Landover, Stanford University."

"L-a-n-d-o-v-e-r?"

"Yes."

"I will see if Mr. Spitz is in, sir."

Landover played with the coils of the phone as he leaned against the window of the booth and stared at the morning pedestrians. Most were well-scrubbed yuppies with degrees in law, business, or international affairs, leather attaché cases surely crammed with papers, backpacks bulging with work-out clothes and bottles of designer water.

It was taking a long time. Too long. He was about to hang up when the secretary returned. "Mr. Spitz is tied up right now."

"Did you tell him who was calling?"

"Yes, I did."

"And he refused to come to the phone?"

"He's in a meeting, sir. Any message?"

Landover took a deep breath. "Yes, I do have a message. Ask if he doesn't want a still sharper knife to stick in my back."

"Pardon me . . . What?"

"I think you heard me . . . Ask him about treachery, disloyalty, breaking of faith, betrayal. Ask him if he knows what happened to Judas Iscariot."

Silence at the other end. With frigid formality, the secretary's voice came back: "Do you wish to leave a number, Professor Landover?"

It had been foolish to try to count on Harry Spitz. Spitz would have needed not only courage but loyalty to come to the phone. As they said, you need a friend in Washington—get a dog. He could hear beeps at the other end. They were obviously recording the call, and already trying to trace it. He hung up. Yet he took satisfaction at being able to vent his anger, even at an anonymous secretary.

On to Plan B.

He walked down the east side of Connecticut, past the park with the Longfellow statue where homeless men sat with pigeons, pigeon droppings, bottles in paper bags, and an unending flow of fast-food trash. He continued south to Connecticut and K, the hub of the city, where every third person was either a lobbyist or worked for one. Or else homeless. By the escalator at the Farragut North Metro entrance a black man of uncertain age in torn jersey, baggy trousers, and Rastafarian braids was struggling with something that sounded like Bach. Landover found a $5 bill next to the little bottle in his pocket and tossed it into the open violin case.

He crossed K Street and walked down 17th Street along the western edge of Admiral David Glasgow Farragut's park, past the high mansard roof and brick-and-sandstone facade of the Renwick Gallery. He crossed Pennsylvania Avenue.

The Second Empire wedding-cake edifice stood next to the White House. With its decorative columns, skylit domes, elegant fretting, and 553 rooms, the Old Executive Office Building was like no other building in Washington, or the world. It was completed in the late nineteenth century when government was much leaner, and served for a while as home for the combined State, War, and Navy departments. Eventually State moved to Foggy Bottom, and the War and Navy departments folded into the Pentagon. White House agencies moved in to fill the void. The OEOB became an extension of the West Wing of the White House, absorbing the Council of Economic Advisers, National Security Council and even a few ultrasecret in-town offices of the CIA.

Like most buildings in Washington, the OEOB accommodated tourists' desire to see inside the government. Landover had a place on the 9:15 A.M. tour. A few minutes early, he descended the stone steps from 17th Street, pushed open a heavy wooden door, and walked into a shadowy basement corridor toward the security desk.

About twenty people in shorts, jeans, and T-shirts, presumably other members of the tour, were milling around behind the desk. The tour guide, a young, chubby-cheeked man in a dark suit, greeted Landover, checked his name off a list, and asked him to produce some ID for the uniformed security officer. Landover showed his somewhat beaten-up Cedric Beaton Canadian passport to the officer perched on a stool like an airline ticket clerk. The officer glanced at the passport, made Landover walk through a metal detector, then handed him a temporary pass to clip to his lapel.

"Take a seat. Tour leaves in a few minutes," the chubby-cheeked man said. Landover sat on a hard wooden bench and looked at the *Washington Post*.

The group set off at 9:20, most taking the slow, clanking elevator behind the guard post. Landover and a few others walked two flights of stairs to the starting point of the tour, the old War Department library, a three-story atrium below a stained-glass vaulted ceiling. Thousands of books sat in alcoves behind lacy iron railings and balustrades. Landover stood at the rear of the group as it assembled in the library. The guide was talking about the building's creator, Alfred E. Mullet.

". . . A government architect with an eye for things Parisian, Mullet chose the style of the Second Empire, seeing in it the flourishes that would help capture the enthusiasm of postcentennial America. Although Mullet was a gifted architect, he suffered from severe depressions. An argument over his commission apparently led him to take his own life soon after the building opened. . . ."

Landover backed out of the library doorway, telling no one in particular he needed to find the men's room. He remembered one by the stairwell and walked swiftly toward it. The place smelled of fresh disinfectant. It was empty. He entered, flushed a urinal, then gingerly reopened the door and looked into the hallway. Empty. To put himself well out of range of the group, he started mounting stairs again.

Poor suicidal Mullet. Landover didn't feel suicidal, but Plan B could be. After his run-in with the assassin in Paris, the murder of Dudley, the *Washington Post* fiasco, and even now with Sherbatov's promised cooperation, his chances for survival seemed close to nil.

Rachel had begged him to drop his "wild" plan. She'd urged immediate flight to Brazil to join Vogl and Maria. "Sherbatov will put the heat on, but it will take time. In Brazil we can be safe. Why push our luck."

But Landover refused. "I will not spend the rest of my days jumping in fear of my own shadow deep in the Amazonian rain forest." He left her in their room at the Tabard Inn.

For him, he told her, there was no other way. He was outraged at a treacherous, ungrateful government. He felt angrier here than in Paris or Zurich, where it was more impersonal. The assassins were simply doing their job. Here, he was in his own capital, back from the war, like a Vietnam vet, only to find his country wanted no part of him. Walking the same city where two weeks ago the President himself had courted him, promised him the moon, now he felt defiled, violated.

He was armed with Maria's account of Shepherd's death, as told to Vogl, and the statement Rachel had Sherbatov write for the director of the CIA. Rachel would mail out copies to all major media outlets if he didn't come back.

Along a cross corridor on the fourth floor he smiled when he spotted a man with a ladder, evidently a janitor or electrician, making repairs in the ceiling. He was wearing gray overalls, a cap, and a heavy cloth shirt. His custodial staff pass hung on a chain around his neck.

"I need your help, or better still, your supply closet," Landover told the man. "We've just burned out a lamp in 504 and the admiral is about to have a meeting . . ." He tried to assume a senior intelligence official's air of unchallengeable authority and hoped he'd remembered the room number correctly from Shepherd's notebook.

The man grumbled something, stepping down from his ladder.

"Too many budget cuts," Landover said apologetically. "Not enough people to do the work. I know. It affects us all. I'll take care of it if you just get me the bulb, a regular one-hundred-watt if you can spare it."

The man said nothing but led Landover down the hall, turned right, and stopped in front of a nearly invisible wooden door. He extracted a key from the ring on his belt and opened it. He yanked a string and a low-wattage bulb lit up a treasure house of fittings, power tools, neon tubes and bulbs of all kinds. The closet was barely big enough for two people.

As the man reached up for a bulb on a high shelf, Landover picked up a Black & Decker drill on a lower shelf, weighed it casually, then brought the blunt handle down on the janitor's head. The man slumped to the floor. Landover took out of his pocket the small bottle of chloroform, soaked his handkerchief, and covered the man's nose and mouth. Shutting the door from the inside, he stepped out of his own clothes and into the man's janitorial garb. He tore his own shirttails into strips that he used to tie and gag the janitor. He then gave him a second stronger whiff of the chloroform. He wasn't sure from bug-hunting days in the Boy Scouts how well the stuff actually worked on people.

He gathered up an assortment of lightbulbs in their paperboard boxes, slowly reopened the door. Two women were conversing at the far end of the hall. With the janitor's key he locked the door from the outside and returned to the ladder, which was in the other direction from the two women. He put the bulbs in the janitor's tool kit with its wrenches, pliers, and hammers, picked up the kit and the ladder as if he had carried such equipment for years, and ascended the stairs again, heading purposefully to Room 504.

The door was unlocked. The first high-ceilinged room was an empty outer office that looked out on the freshly cleaned Winder Building, where Lincoln used to read Civil War cables, across 17th Street. The secretary was apparently on her morning break. The door to the inner office was shut. Landover held his breath and opened it.

A far larger room. A working desk at one end and two easy chairs and sofa around a fireplace at the other. A skinny man was seated on the sofa looking at a thick picture book. The pictures were of birds, and even upside down Landover could make out the title, *Birds of Cyprus*. The man himself had an ornithic bearing, tight collar accentuating the beaklike face. His legs were spindly above spit-shined, pointed black shoes.

Landover set the ladder down, and as the little man slowly lifted his head, Landover sat down next to him on the sofa. He placed the toolbox on the floor by his feet. He had told himself he would kill him if he had to. He hoped it wouldn't be necessary. . . . But, like Rachel earlier, he felt at the end of his rope . . .

"What the hell are you doing?" asked the man, now alarmed at the intrusion. "You're not the regular janitor . . ."

"Nor am I Jim Shepherd, whom you were expecting. Correct, Admiral Jackman?"

"How the hell did you know . . ." The admiral didn't try to move.

"Shepherd is dead," Landover said, pushing his beard in the admiral's face. "Killed in self-defense by a woman trying to protect herself from rape and murder."

"I don't know what you're talking about." The admiral drew his head back to get a better look at the intruder. A flash of recognition. "Say, you're that nutty Stanford professor, aren't you?"

"Not so nutty you won't want to listen to me . . ." Landover thrust an arm over the little man's shoulder.

"I have things to say that should be of interest."

The admiral folded his bird book. A smile suddenly wrinkled his lower jaw and his voice was smooth again. "You're good, Professor Landover. Real good. The unexpected. You come up all the time with the unexpected. Brilliant. Obviously you've read the classic by Sun Tzu, *The Art of War.*" It sounded foolish even to the admiral.

Landover pulled from his pocket Vogl's account from Maria of Shepherd's last moments. "Read this, Admiral . . ." He put the paper in the admiral's unsteady hands. Intimidated by Landover's arm, the admiral dutifully read, then handed the pages back.

"Why should I or anyone believe this? What proof do you have that Jim Shepherd is dead?" His voice had recovered some of its confidence.

"His corpse is a John Doe in the New York City morgue. Your people will find it now that they know where to look. Maria took his ID and notebook, told us what was in the notebook. How do you think I knew you'd be here waiting for him to show up?"

"How should I know? What do you want anyway?"

Landover clenched his teeth, clamped a grip on the admiral's left shoulder. "Give me and my friends back our lives."

"I'm afraid I don't catch your drift. . . ."

"I think you do. It's not all that complicated. Surely you've heard of the murder in Falls Church and the little accident with a bus around Saint Sulpice in Paris . . ."

The admiral's face tensed at the mention of Falls Church. He quickly recovered. "Your statement accuses Shepherd of attempted rape, says the woman killed him in self-defense. If Shepherd is dead, the woman could have seduced him and murdered him. Happens all the time in New York."

"Not that kind of woman. She was in the city on business, running international banker seminars. It doesn't fit, Admiral, and you know it doesn't."

"Does she have witnesses?"

"How could she?"

"Is she prepared to testify?"

"Of course she'd testify, if her safety could be guaranteed. She's afraid for her life, thanks to your assassins."

The admiral shifted position on the sofa, but didn't try to get up. Landover's arm, his grip looser, still hung over the shoulders. The admiral looked up at Landover, his jaws rising and falling like a gamecock sniffing grubs on the lawn.

"Your Maria kills an agent of the Central Intelligence Agency. You and the Ravid woman kill a kibbutznik in Eilat and some Bedouins in the Sinai. Seems to me like a lot of international terrorists now trying to save their skins. . . ."

"That stuff about international terrorists is a lot of crap. You know that. All invented by Shepherd and Ben Giton's people. They know we know about their ripoff of the gold—"

"You're ahead of me . . ."

Landover reached into his pocket and handed over the second envelope. "I think you know, or at least have heard of, the man who made this statement—the Russian physicist Dmitri Sherbatov, the man you and President Halleck wanted me to find. Well, he is found. Read what he says."

The admiral unfolded the sheets and read slowly. The pages dropped, like fluttering leaves, onto the cover of his bird book.

"Is this genuine?"

"Of course. You think I'd risk my life coming here to see you if it weren't? Call Oak Ridge, talk to the man himself. His phone number is there. You know him, surely, since he passed through Washington a little while ago to meet the President."

"More of the unexpected, Professor. Again I congratulate you." The admiral fidgeted. "How the hell did you reach Sherbatov anyway?"

"Rachel Ravid contacted Sherbatov in Oak Ridge, also through the magic of Shepherd's notebook. She suspected Sherbatov was part of the conspiracy. He is not. He's a pure scientist, research-driven, has no interest in money, is certainly no conspirator. Sherbatov was giving his alchemy to the state of Israel. He thought all the gold he made went automatically to the Bank of Israel. Little did he know that every second ounce went into Ben Giton's pocket. And some into Jim Shepherd's."

"Quite a story, Professor, if it checks out."

"You know damn well it will. General Ben Giton not only enriched himself but used a lot of the money to fund the Israeli right. The U.S., which is pushing hard for peace in the Middle East, should want to put a stop to his shenanigans."

"Will you let me get up to make that phone call?"

"Remember, should anything happen to me, Admiral, every newspaper, radio, and TV station will know."

"I am going to make that phone call, Professor."

The admiral stood and walked stiffly over to his desk. Landover followed him. He knew better than to trust the man too far but he also knew he really couldn't kill him.

After conversing with Sherbatov, the admiral called out to Landover, smiling broadly: "Uncle Sam owes you one, son."

He picked up the phone again. This time he spoke to a man called Cyrus. "Close the book on Force Majeure before they do some real damage." The admiral spoke into the receiver loudly enough for Landover to hear. "Also check out the New York City morgue. Shepherd missed an appointment with me. I think he may have gotten himself into big trouble in the Big Apple."

As the admiral put the phone down, Landover walked over to him. "Is Force Majeure what I think it is?"

"Don't ask me anything about that, Professor. What you overheard is to assure you that your troubles are over. But no details. What I can say is we, your government, are victims of grave misunderstandings."

"How can I believe that?"

"My word, the word of Uncle Sam. Isn't it still worth something?"

"What about your word when you sent me to Israel? Several people's lives have become a living hell. Innocents have died."

"I can't undo what's been done. But I can try to make amends. . . ." The admiral leaned back in his chair, folded his hands behind his head. "Professor, I want to be fair. Here's an offer . . ." He hesitated, considered for a moment. "To make you a part of our . . . well . . . our extended family." He smiled. "That entails loyalty, not letting out family secrets—you understand why we must insist on this. But you and your friends then live to be rich and old."

Landover looked at the crinkled brow, hookish nose, eyes never at rest. Here was the keeper of skeletons in America's closet. "Before, you wanted to silence us by . . . how do you people put it? . . . terminating us. Now, you will bribe us for that same silence?"

"Simplistically put  . . .  But yes, essentially that is correct, Professor."

"How can we trust you?"

"I am not a dishonorable man, Professor." His eyes met Landover's. "But someone has to do—whatever needs to be done to protect this country. You say you want your life back. I am giving it to you. We have made a mistake. An accident of war. You have strayed accidentally into where our shadows fall, and as I said, we are sorry and will make amends."

"And if we refuse to be silent?"

"First, no one will listen to you. The story is too far-fetched for any reputable newspaper to print without confirmation, and it will never be confirmed. But why make an issue of it?" The admiral smiled. "Many things in life are far better left unsaid. You are unfaithful to your wife. Will you tell her?"

"Maybe if I want to separate from her."

"Better to take a mistress, keep your wife, and have the best of both worlds."

"But if one sees an injustice, shouldn't one blow the whistle so that innocents aren't hurt next time?"

"A noble ambition. But, Professor, we are part of the national security apparatus of the United States. We fight wars by other means. In all wars some innocents die. To protect the larger good they become expendable."

Landover could hear some movement in the outer office, perhaps the secretary returning from her coffee break in the White House mess. He hoped the admiral hadn't pushed some button under his desk to summon the Secret Service.

"Cleaning dirty linen in public neither protects innocents nor helps the United States," the admiral continued. "Oversight is invented by Congress to curry favor with the media. So that the blow-dried-hair bunch can get their pictures in the *Post* and appear on *Good Morning America*."


WHEN HE FINALLY stepped out into the maze of corridors, dressed as the janitor, Landover still could not be sure the admiral hadn't already made another call and ordered up a little mishap in front of a bus on Connecticut Avenue.

He made it back to the Tabard Inn without incident.

Later, in describing the day to Rachel, Landover said what he regretted most was the injury to the janitor. The admiral had promised to fix everything. The janitor would pledge never to breathe a word of his "accident" and would receive $25,000 in cash and a month's extra vacation.

"The admiral," Landover said, "wants to buy our silence, too, for a lot more than twenty-five thousand dollars."

"Let him." Rachel smiled wanly. "It's better than wars we can never win."

AT 40,000 FEET on the way to Rio, they were holding hands. There would be plenty of time to talk about the future.

VOGL AND MARIA met their plane in Rio with a bottle of Marcus James blanc de blanc. Maria and Rachel embraced like old friends. That evening while they were walking along the beach together watching Brazilians light up candles to the goddess Iemanja at the edge of the water, Rachel whispered to Maria, "I think I am pregnant."

IRONICALLY, EVEN AS more and more synthetic gold was being quietly produced by both Israel and the United States, world prices of gold moved steadily higher. Analysts attributed the activity to fears of new inflation, which boosted demand for basic commodities. They also pointed to increased purchases by the thousands of newly affluent investors in China, India, and the former Soviet republics that were using gold as a form of savings and a hedge against bad times.